Acclaim for The Song of a Manchild

"*The Song of a Manchild* is an intriguing modern fable about one man's utterly new take on self-invention. This book is a welcome addition to the LGBT literary canon."

—Marshall Moore
Author, *The Concrete Sky* and *Black Shapes in a Darkened Room*

"Owens gives us a tender and wildly imaginative tale of a man struggling to achieve a sense of belonging in our increasingly complex world. As this whimsical and sensitive novel unfolds, Kel's friends and family come to terms with the unexpected, and Kel finds help where he least expects it. Owens has written an inspired fantasy of a gay man who could achieve the seemingly impossible while creating a new life for himself and his loving family. *The Song of a Manchild* is a must-read."

—David M. Pierce
Author, *Elf Child*

"Owens provides a riveting and emotional tale of love in his search for male motherhood that blurs the line between fantasy and reality, creating the perfect fiction novel."

—David Alston
Journalist/Photographer,
Upscale Magazine
Exclusive Magazine

The Song of a Manchild

HARRINGTON PARK PRESS
Southern Tier Editions
Gay Men's Fiction
Jay Quinn, Executive Editor

This Thing Called Courage: South Boston Stories by J. G. Hayes

Trio Sonata by Juliet Sarkessian

Bear Like Me by Jonathan Cohen

Ambidextrous: The Secret Lives of Children by Felice Picano

Men Who Loved Me by Felice Picano

A House on the Ocean, A House on the Bay by Felice Picano

Goneaway Road by Dale Edgerton

Death Trick: A Murder Mystery by Richard Stevenson

The Concrete Sky by Marshall Moore

Edge by Jeff Mann

Through It Came Bright Colors by Trebor Healey

Elf Child by David M. Pierce

Huddle by Dan Boyle

The Man Pilot by James W. Ridout IV

Shadows of the Night: Queer Tales of the Uncanny and Unusual edited by Greg Herren

Van Allen's Ecstasy by Jim Tushinski

Beyond the Wind by Rob N. Hood

The Handsomest Man in the World by David Leddick

The Song of a Manchild by Durrell Owens

The Ice Sculptures: A Novel of Hollywood by Michael D. Craig

Between the Palms: A Collection of Gay Travel Erotica edited by Michael T. Luongo

Aura by Gary Glickman

Love Under Foot: An Erotic Celebration of Feet edited by Greg Wharton and M. Christian

The Tenth Man by E. William Podojil

Upon a Midnight Clear: Queer Christmas Tales edited by Greg Herren

Dryland's End by Felice Picano

Whose Eye Is on Which Sparrow? by Robert Taylor

The Song of a Manchild

Durrell Owens

Southern Tier Editions
Harrington Park Press®
An Imprint of The Haworth Press, Inc.
New York • London • Oxford

Published by

Southern Tier Editions, Harrington Park Press®, an imprint of The Haworth Press, Inc., 10 Alice Street, Binghamton, NY 13904-1580.

PUBLISHER'S NOTE
This is a work of fiction. Names, characters, places, and incidents either are the products of the author's imagination or are used fictitiously, and any resemblance to actual persons, living or dead, business establishments, events, or locales is entirely coincidental.

Cover design by Jennifer M. Gaska.

Library of Congress Cataloging-in-Publication Data

Owens, Durrell.
    The song of a manchild / Durrell Owens.
        p. cm.
    ISBN 1-56023-480-6 (soft : alk. paper)
    1. Gay men—Fiction. 2. Pregnancy—Fiction. 3. Coccidioidomycosis—Patients—Fiction.
4. African American gays—Fiction. 5. California—Fiction. I. Title.
    PS3615.W45S66 2004
    813'.6—dc21
                                                                            2003009797

For Jerry

Acknowledgments

I would like to first thank God almighty, my savior, as my ancestors like to say, "for bringing me from a mighty long ways." I want to give special thanks to my brother, Gary, and his wife, Brenda, for being there when I needed a helping hand.

I also want to give a special thanks to my sister-friend, Antoinette Clark. I owe a debt of gratitude to my friends Keith Sarden, Steven Fields, Julius R. Perkins, Joan Muira, James Devereaux, Alex Vanhorne, Ana Baker, Ed Smallfield, Marshall Moore, Stacey Vickers, Victor Riabo, Carlos Gonsalves, Dino Henderson, and Walter Kelley. I'd also like to thank David Alston, Christine Shields, Leon B. Toles III, David Amador, Lewis Buzzbee, Angie Stuart, Wayne B. Daniels, Dr. Lawrence Mirels, Dr. David Stevens, Judy Jones, Karlo Chamarro, Heberth and Kelley Barragan, Charlene and William Bradford, Eduardo Santana, David Marino, and Richard Perry. And a special thank you also goes out to Ed Wolf, who dared me to take the next step toward publication of my work.

Thanks to those who put forth effort to read my work when I needed the support and to those who reminded me constantly that my work was not being done in vain.

Thanks for believing!

Chapter 1

The beginning of the second year of the new millennium found me standing in line ahead of two other men at the Vulcan, a bathhouse in Oakland. I arrived there after going to see the film *Before Night Falls,* an epic tale about the life of the gay Cuban writer Reinaldo Arenas, who fled Cuba after suffering political persecution and sexual repression at the hands of the Castro regime.

While waiting for check-in at the Vulcan, I stood on the top rung of a short concrete staircase and watched, on the television monitor, an actor I'd seen in *Caligula,* a movie on the rise and fall of the Roman Empire. Caligula was sprawled out in a chair, and a machine was stretching his eyelids wide open as a hand placed drops in his eyes. I hadn't planned on going to the baths after seeing *Before Night Falls.* I was diverted. Had I gone to the movie with my boyfriend, Chad, or with my friend Scott, fate would not have propelled me to this hothouse of men, frolicked in around the clock, twenty-four/seven sex. But here I was. Something in a minute square corner of my mind told me it wasn't too late to turn around, walk back down the stairs, get in my car, and go home. Yet an irresistible force, considerably stronger, kept me glued in line. It was dark and cold outside, and I had no plans for late evening. I'd gone to my office that afternoon and worked a couple of hours poring over thousands of photographs in an attempt to identify the usual suspects. I'd found who I was looking for. Why had I gone to the baths instead of my warm suburban home in Richmond, where I could devour leftover holiday food, watch a video, drink some champagne, and nod off to sleep during the slow scenes in the low-budget video about teenage suicides in a Detroit suburb during the 1970s?

To be honest, I longed to be touched, held, stroked, and even admired. Sex was secondary. It didn't take long for me to, as some would say, ply my trade. Within moments I had chilled, got undressed,

1

wrapped a soft white towel around my waist, and was cruising through the narrow hallways of the bathhouse, past tiny rooms. Some closed doors were locked. Other doors to other rooms were ajar as men lay upon thin mattresses under dim lights stroking themselves on their stomachs, prone and indiscriminate, waiting with the need for fulfill-ment. I wondered if deep inside, beneath the surface of their skins, they had felt like I did, lost and vulnerable. The intoxicating smell of sweat comingled with testosterone quickened my senses and made my eyes water. My penis grew hard and three times the size of its flac-cid state.

I didn't have to go to the baths. I wasn't forced to go. I'd made a conscious decision. It was my own free will that drove me there. I didn't stay long. Within two hours I had sex with three men and had two orgasms. I'd long ago dropped any guilt complex when I lost my virginity. I'm always safe. So I thought. Like nicotine or gambling, sex clubs can be extremely addictive. I go less frequently these days. It's not because my libido has waned or because I feel an incredible sense of being jaded. No. I've made up my mind to go cold turkey. Two of the past three times I came home from the sex club, I went to pee and found blood in my urine. I thought I'd passed a kidney stone. The first time I found blood in my urine, my reaction was as casual as if I'd found a gray strand of hair in my eyebrow. I was interested.

I flopped down on my sofa and told Chad, my boyfriend of five years. He calls me Head but my real name is Kelvin Maxwell Warren. Most people know me as Kel. I was born on the West Coast and Chad's from the Southwest.

Chad was watching cable television. His face was caked with Nox-zema. The fragrance stung my nostrils. Chad's favorite TV network, *Entertainment!* or "E!" was on. E! was showcasing the lavish estates of rich and famous Tinseltown celebrities. Once popular, now fallen, slightly vulgar 1980s soul singer Nathan Laws was in the spotlight.

"Oh, Head! Don't start with that crap again," he blurted out, his square goateed face twisted in disgust.

"It's probably a kidney stone. That's all. But it was so thick and red. About the size of an M&M. It didn't even hurt coming out. Made me think I had a tiny miscarriage."

"Didn't it come out of your dick and not your ass?" Chad said, ready to challenge me.

"Yes."

"Then why would you think you had a miscarriage? You'd have to shit the baby out."

"Through my bowels?"

"Rectum. It's the biggest hole in a man."

"The blood clot came out of my dick, Chad. I figure the first man to give birth to a child will have to be bigger than the trunk of an elephant. Some babies can weigh up to eleven, twelve pounds, even more. A real top would never recover. It would probably kill him," I said.

"How many men the size of an elephant's trunk do you know? Even a premature baby wouldn't make it through. The poor baby's head alone would get stuck."

"Well, there was this one guy I dated everybody called King Kong. He had what looked like a third leg."

"I thought you told me he couldn't fit all the way inside of you."

"I did. He couldn't. I introduced him to my best friend, George."

"Has King Kong given birth to a baby out of his dick? I don't think so. The first man to have a baby will need a caesarean. They'll have to cut the baby out." He brought his hand down like a hatchet for emphasis.

I conceded that it would not be possible, biologically, to conceive a child. It would take a miracle to deliver a baby through a man's urethra. It sure enough was not made for that. The urethral canal is too small. Was a man's stomach big enough, though, to carry a child? I pondered.

"You remember a year ago when they misdiagnosed you with valley fever?" Chad went on to answer his own question. "You started pissing blood after they put you on fluconazole, that dick-of-death medicine for valley fever. I don't see why after you stopped taking the medicine a year ago for something you didn't have it would crop back up all of a sudden."

I couldn't tell Chad that I'd been to the baths that evening. Couldn't tell him I had engaged in some rather vigorous sexual escapades. I swallowed. I leaned over and rested my head on Chad's shoulder.

"Don't even think about it. Get off of me. All you going to do is fall asleep. Stop it, Honeydew Head. Stay up tonight. Keep me company." He nudged me away like I was a puppy getting too frisky at the wrong place and time.

"I'm not going to fall asleep. I want to feel you, Chad."

"See, that's what I mean. Then you will be out like a light. I might as well go home and watch television by myself. You are too sensitive. Old big-headed thing."

I sat straight up on the sofa. My back was stiff. My eyelids were heavy.

What if it was like Chad said and not only that it was from lingering side effects of the fluconazole, the antifungal medication I was put on when the doctors thought I had valley fever? After all, I took ten tiny pink pills a day. Five, every twelve hours, like clockwork. I've never had bloody urine after sex before I was misdiagnosed with valley fever. The doctors never told me what I had been ailing from. Is this the connection? Is this a precursor or harbinger of things to come? Or was it my first miscarriage?

If they think they can get away with it, doctors are known to withhold life-threatening information from patients. Sometimes, it can be the end results and harmful consequences of prescription medication they've prescribed. Like most of the professional world, they are afraid of lawsuits. Some of them arrogantly believe they are God's gift. Still, I wondered if Chad was right. With every passing minute, I was growing more apprehensive about Chad wanting to make love to me that night. After I'd done my bump and grind thing at the baths, I hardly had any stamina left.

Chad didn't come on to me sexually after I told him about the bleeding that night. He reminded me of his own bouts with blood in his urine when he was deeply depressed.

I was off the hook. I took a deep breath. Exhaled.

Quiet as it's kept, since my mysterious illness, Chad's sexual prowess has waned. I felt relieved that Chad shared his related blood-in-urine confessions with me. That still didn't mean that I was totally convinced that something else, perhaps even more ominous than a mysterious illness, hadn't made a beachhead and lurked somewhere deep inside of me. I was beginning to think that if I wasn't a hypochondriac at this moment, then I was sure on my way.

I wonder if medical science will one day develop a medication to control sexual addiction. I would have a big problem if it costs 3,000 dollars a month the way fluconazole does. Would I have to make the decision to dish out beaucoup moola, to be treated for sexual addiction? A self-inflicted condition created only by me. What would a reasonable man do? Pack it in, convert to abstinence, disappear into the make-believe world of monogamy, get castrated, become a monk, or seek professional help and moral support. I decided to do the latter.

Last night, I went online looking for support groups for the sexually addicted. Of course, there were millions of Web sites. I found a site that had a support group and chat room for sexually addicted nonmonogamous pre-middle-aged black gays. Bingo. I was delighted with what I found until I scrolled down to the middle of the Web page and noticed that they wanted a picture of me. They didn't just want any kind of a picture, but one where I've got an uncontrollably gigantic erection that will-not-go-down. They wanted a man with a hard-on for life! The bigger the better is what they preferred. Half, semihard, or limp erections were not welcome into this support group or chat room entry denied. Was this a sex club or a support group? I went back and reread the Home page. It was printed right there in words as clear as the King's English. The Web site was called "Support Group for Sexually Addicted Nonmonogamous Pre-Middle-Aged Black Gay Males." In my blind excitement at having discovered a potential cure for my ailment, I'd glossed over and hadn't read the fine print. A warning was posted. No law enforcement types need apply. Well, excuse the hell out of me! I wasn't trying to join to spy or launch a Web site investigation. I was seeking moral support from a group with similar concerns about sexual addiction. Gay black private investigators can be sexually addicted too. Are gay black private investigators, peace officers of the law, seen as brothers and sisters from another planet? Are we seen as enemies of the black community? Are we too blue to be black, too black to be white, too straight to be gay? Sometimes, I kind of feel like when 1950s crooner Little Anthony wrote the song, "I'm on the Outside Looking In," he wrote it about me. I clicked the exit box in the upper right-hand corner and logged off. Sent the Web site into cyberspace. Damn!

On New Year's Day, I rolled out of bed, went to the bathroom, and peed. Like a self-fulfilling prophecy, during the middle of my stream, a clump of blood fell to the bottom of the commode. Shaped like a tadpole and as dark as cranberry juice, it hit the water like a tiny pebble.

I found an old toothbrush that belonged to my ex-boyfriend, Hank, in a shelf underneath the sink and fished out the clump of blood. It was as slippery as a jellyfish. I had quite a time holding it steady on the edge of the toothbrush.

It wiggled, reminding me of the fat red worms I once baited my fishing pole with when I was a little boy.

If I'd been a professional scientist or an infectious disease specialist, at a lab or clinic, I'd have the means to take a specimen, place it on a slide, microscope it, and make a self-diagnosis. By design, I'm a private investigator, trained to investigate crime and help put the convicted away for all eternity. I leave textbook scientific research tools in the hands of those charged with upholding what the great Greek physician Hippocrates decreed, in 437 B.C.: "Cure the sick; do no harm."

The telephone rang. It was Chad.

"Hey, Juicy Head. Happy New Year."

"Same to you. How was the party last night?"

"I've got a hangover that's off the hook."

"You got drunk. Who drove you home?"

"I didn't get drunk. I only had three glasses of white zin."

"For real. Then why the hangover?"

"Empty stomach. I drank on an empty stomach."

"Why'd you do that for?"

"You know I've gained twenty pounds in the last two months. All this holiday food."

"It's a new year, Chad. You can always make a resolution to go back to the gym."

"All right already. Quit jacking me, Balloon Head."

"Are we still going to Sears to scavenger hunt for DVD players?"

"I forgot. Look, pick me up about three o'clock."

I showered, got dressed, and drove to Barnes & Noble at Hilltop Mall in Richmond to find a book on sexual addiction. I found the health care section. Sure enough, books about sexual addiction. At first, nothing I picked up off the shelf appealed to me until I came across a book titled *Sexual Addiction: A Black Gay Man's Guide to Sexual Health,* by Roger Wilson, PhD. I looked at the dedication section. The book was dedicated to Chad Smith. It read, "For Chad Smith, my first love, whose legendary sexual addiction cured my own."

I was curious. Was this the same self-confessed every-great-once-in-a-while asexual Chad Smith I'd slept with less than five times in five years? I flipped through the book, and in the middle section I looked at photographs of Chad and his love, Roger, sitting on a ledge at Ocean Beach in San Francisco, drinking beer. They both wore faded blue jeans and identical white muscle tank tops. Chad had a silver nose ring. A thin silver ring was stuck in his right eyebrow. His face was cleanly shaved. Roger had a salt-and-pepper spiked haircut and bright blue eyes that seemed to sparkle. A blinding hypnotic smile.

I paid for the book and left the store.

I got back home and finished the book. Had I found a cure? What I found was hope and a sense of quiet vindication. What would the world have to gain if I were to let it repress my sexuality, persecute and pass judgment on me for living a life with no holds barred? Chad had been the kind of man I wanted to become. If not a sexual outlaw then an expatriate, who sometimes drifts in and out of the country of promiscuity. I didn't need to look any further. Had I not been smitten with Chad, a documented survivor of sexual addiction? I put *Sexual Addiction: A Black Gay Man's Guide to Sexual Health* on my bookshelf in the study next to *Keeping the Spark Alive in Long Relationships,* by

Bernie Zilbergeld, PhD. If Chad could recover from sexual addiction and I could recover from a near-death experience, nothing could stop me from breathing and living the life I wanted to live. I got in my car and went to pick up Chad, the man who once had a legendary sexual addiction. I'd like to show him a few tricks of my own humble trade.

Chapter 2

I picked up Chad at his apartment and we went to Sears off of Macdonald Avenue in Richmond. As soon as I parked, Chad quickly opened his door and left me to lock up the car. We went our separate ways. I watched him disappear through the entrance of Sears with the vigor of a rookie cop executing a search warrant on a crack house. I shook my head.

By instinct, I found my way to the Infants and Toddlers Department. Everything was half off. I marveled over blue and pink receiving blankets, Scooby Doo pajamas, booties, undershirts, caps, Pampers, socks, baby bottles, baby bags, cradles, cribs, basket nets, Q-Tips, cotton balls, pacifiers, jackets, sweaters, knit and wool gloves, baby oil, powder, hair shampoo, combs, singing books with nursery rhymes, and bubble bath. I picked up a tiny hairbrush and rubbed it up against my cheek. I imagined combing the soft black strands of hair on a baby's head. My eyes misted. I bumped into a short big-boned woman looking at baby rattles. She had olive skin and long black ringlets that fell halfway down to her shoulders. Her eyes were coal black. She picked a rattle up and began to shake it rhythmically. It wouldn't be long until the moment would come when she'd just break out and dance the cucamonga, I thought. She looked at me, read my mind, and smiled. I smiled back.

"My husband won't go to Lamaze classes with me. You go with your wife?"

She spoke in broken English.

I twisted the silver ring on my right hand. I was in a quandary. How could I reply without exposing my own dilemma? There are similarities and obvious differences. Chad wasn't wifely. Neither was I. Chad and I weren't married, except in the spiritual, soul mate sense. The social mores of our country are probably, to some degree, as repressive as those of whatever country this woman fled from in Latin

America. Had Chad taken on some of these mores? He didn't even want me to have a baby. How could I tiptoe around this woman's question without letting the cat out of the bag?

"Some men get gun-shy about things having to do with babies. Changing diapers, wiping up puke, bottle feeding, and disciplining. That can be a drag for some of us." I left out the part about me wanting to have a baby without any kind of support from Chad. Who knows? She'd probably be against it too. God knows the entire planet would be against it. I'd become a man at odds with the world. At least her husband wasn't against her pregnancy. For that, I envied her and resented Chad.

"What's your name?" I said and extended my hand. She shook it.

"Maria Alvarez. And you?"

"Kelvin Warren. Everybody calls me Kel. Maria, do you guys want a boy or girl?" I asked.

"Healthy baby. Don't care what it is," she beamed.

"Me too. I don't even want to have a sonogram."

"Huh?"

The cat nearly fell out of the bag but I managed to push it back in and recover.

"You know. I don't want to know if the baby is a boy or a girl."

"Oh, right. My husband wants to know right away. I tell him no. Wait. Already he has plans to put the baby to work at El Portal, the restaurant we own on San Pablo Avenue." She laughed.

"We've had dinner there. Hope he plans to cook as well as the chef who's there now. I mean he can burn! Those tacos, especially the tamales, are off the hook." I laughed.

A burly Latino male who looked like Antonio Banderas walked up and put his hands around Maria's waist. He nodded at me.

"Honey, this is . . . what you say your name is?"

"Kel," I said, extending my hand to him. He shook it hard.

"Yes, Kel. My husband, Lorenzo Alvarez."

"What's up?"

"How's it going?"

"Good. Nice to meet you but we've got to get along," he said, taking his wife's hand as she turned around and waved good-bye.

"Bye, Kel, and good luck with the baby."

"You too."

By the time I found Chad in electronics, my shopping cart was stuffed with a complete wardrobe of tiny Scooby Doo wear for the baby. I'd taken a crib and bassinet outside and tossed them into the back of the jeep. I pick up some but not all of the basic things I would need as an expectant father.

"Look, this shit is crazy off the hook! Dope! It plays six DVDs and CDs too. Four hundred watts! Damn! Check it," he said and twisted the volume knob to full pitch. Chad was so busy turning and switching knobs he didn't notice my shopping cart stuffed with baby stuff.

Chad was crouched over a row of DVD and CD players. He had the gleam in his eyes of a little boy on Christmas Day. He'd fallen in love with a Panasonic DVD player. I was savoring the fresh smell of baby powder I'd sprinkled on the back of my hand.

"What's that smell?"

"Oh, you like it. It's baby powder," I chortled.

"Baby powder? Did you take a bath in it?" He sneezed.

"Of course not. I couldn't resist pouring a little of it in the palm of my hands and rubbing it on. This is great stuff." I stuck the back of my hand out for him to smell.

"Oh, Head. What you go and do that for? I bet people were looking at you like, what is this guy doing in here?"

"I found the cutest little Scooby Doo ensembles. I know what I want to put on my baby the day I leave the hospital with little Chad Junior," I announced, and a warm feeling washed over me.

Chad stood up and put his forefinger to his lips the way librarians do when you talk too loud in the library.

"Shhh! Before somebody I know hear you talking rubbish. Man, people kill me. When they hear about a going-out-of-business sale, leaving carts full of crap in aisles so that someone could trip, fall, and break their neck," he said and shoved my cart out of the way. I watched the cart roll into a stack of VCRs, nearly causing a small avalanche.

"Chad, don't."

"What you mean?"

"That's my shopping cart. These things are for my unborn," I said and hastily jogged down the aisle to retrieve the cart.

Couldn't he see that I had lost interest in what I'd originally come to Sears to find? I'd found a whole new world. I put the back of my hand up to my nose and took a long whiff as if the fragrance of baby powder would give me protection against what I sensed was Chad's fear.

Chad fingered the knobs on the DVD player. He stuck in a CD by Grover Washington Jr. and twisted the volume up to an obscene level. I thought the DVD player had more watts than I'd ever listen to unless I was seriously interested in going deaf.

Chad was doing a better job coaxing me into buying the DVD player than the salesman, who had the look on his face of a young man with two years to go before he finished high school and who hoped he didn't end up in customer service for all eternity. I no longer had the slightest interest in buying electronic equipment, but I bought it as a compromise with Chad. I hoped buying the DVD player would make him think that he had good taste (not to say that he didn't). I thought he'd also take it as a compliment to his keen eye in knowing how to spot a good bargain when he saw one. Then he'd realize that I had not come into Sears and taken leave of my senses just because I preferred to hang out in the baby nursery department rather than in the fascinating yet sometimes wacky manmade world of electronic devices. Had I begun to lose my grip on reality? Fallen off a cliff into the world of make-believe, fantasy, or science fiction? "Oh, this is really too far-fetched to believe." I cringed at the stereophonic world yelling at my back.

Standing in line to pay for a DVD player seemed awkward compared to the splendor of things to bring a new life into the world. Chad told me he'd be waiting at the car.

When I got outside, the temperature had fallen twenty degrees and the skies were streaked a dark blueberry. Orange porch and street-lights winked in the East Bay hills.

"How did this get in here?" Chad had popped open the hatch of the Jeep and found two long boxes that contained the crib and bassinet I'd bought.

"I bought them when you were looking at the DVD players. You won't believe how cheap they were."

"Head, I'm telling you! Stop it! You got money coming out of your ass and you just wasting it! You know there are no refunds! No re-funds!" he repeated.

"I don't plan on taking anything back, Chad. I bought this stuff for keeps."

I opened the passenger door on the driver's side and piled my bags stuffed with the baby clothes in the backseat. I shut the door and climbed behind the wheel of the Jeep. Through the rearview mirror I watched Chad set the box with the DVD player in the back of the Jeep next to the other boxes. He climbed in the car and slammed the door hard. I leaned over a little to look at his window to see if it was cracked. I drove off.

On the way back home, we listened to Avant's new song, "My First Love." As the song ended, I clicked the garage door opener and rolled in.

When we were unloading the goods I told Chad about my plans.

"I want a baby, Chad," I said, opening the door to the backseat, taking my bags out.

"You want what?"

"A baby. I want to have a baby. I'm not playing. I've made up my mind. Come hell or high water. I'm going to conceive a child. And I don't mean adopting one either. My baby is going to have to come out of me," I said as I stood in front of the garage door watching him make his way around to the back of the Jeep.

Chad opened the back door of the Jeep. He took the Panasonic DVD player out of the trunk. I watched as I stood in front of the ga-rage door. He seemed to be big-time pissed. Chad left it up to me to take the bassinet and crib out of the Jeep. I trudged the beds upstairs and dropped them in what would be my baby's nursery.

When I got back downstairs, Chad had already begun to take the old Sony stereo CD player apart to take it upstairs to the guest room. I sat down on the sofa and watched him. I knew that he'd heard me when I told him that I wanted to have a baby. He seemed to be pretending to be too busy to talk. That's when I clicked on cable and flipped the station to the baby channel. I watched a mother caring for her newborn. The show seemed to grab Chad's attention the way I had been unable to. He stopped putting the DVD player together, came over, and sat down next to me. And he began to watch the show. It was the first time I'd ever seen him watch anything other than E! with so much interest.

"Ah, she is so cute. Isn't she a darling?" I said, looking at a little baby girl with a Tootsie Roll skin that seemed to be as smooth as silk. She had dimples, tiny black ringlets, and a red bow atop her head. A tiny version of a beautiful woman, I thought.

"Head. Listen to me. Don't let this hurt your feelings. I'm taking you back to your doctor tomorrow."

"Why?"

"I wonder if that medicine you took when they thought you had valley fever gave you brain damage? Now you think that you can get pregnant. Oh, Head."

"Chad, I can do it. All I need is to do the math. How many men have had a baby?" I said, rubbing my hand across my flat stomach. "I heard about this one Asian guy in New York in the Village."

"What?" Chad laughed. "Head, that's a myth and science fiction. You tell me how many? Other than movie stars like Arnold Schwarzenegger and what's that other guy's name, Dustin Hoffman. And they are movie stars. Look at me; I don't have any children. Nowhere."

"See, that's what I'm saying. Don't you want a child, Chad, to come from your own blood? Anyway, Dustin Hoffman played a drag queen in *Tootsie*."

"Head, I want a baby, but not like this. I thought we agreed to use a surrogate."

"Oh. I'm not good enough to carry your child. Is that it? Why do men think a woman should be the only one to suffer through pregnancy and childbirth? That's so pigheaded, selfish, so twentieth century. We are two years into the new millennium. What's wrong with new ideas?"

"You know good and well I don't think you are not good enough. Oh, big-headed thing. How you going to look walking around? A tall bald-headed muscular guy wearing gold earrings, pink slippers, a moustache, and a maternity dress? On Halloween in the Castro you can work it, but for nine months out of a year? You must be out of your freaking mind. You think our life is one big science fiction project? Poor Head. Get a life."

He got up from the sofa and went into the kitchen. I could hear him rummage through cabinet drawers. He came and sat back down. Chad was holding a tiny piece of paper. From the corner of my eye, it looked like one of the slips of paper a pharmacy gives to patients warning them about the possible harmful side effects of prescription drugs. I watched the young mother smile and suckle her baby on television. I grabbed my chest and fondled my nipple. It was hard. I was remembering when I was fourteen and a thin milky substance would come out of my nipples. That is when I discovered that I wasn't like other teenage boys. It went on like that all summer long and didn't let up until I returned to school in the fall. I'd begun my freshman year at Kennedy High in Richmond. That was the summer my girlfriend, Cookie, aborted my would-be firstborn. No sooner had I discovered my manhood when Cookie got pregnant. I turned around and lost it when she had the abortion.

Chad interrupted my half daydream.

"Head. Look at this," he said, dangling the tiny piece of paper in front of my face like it was a winning lottery ticket.

Chad went on, "I don't see anywhere on this paper about the medicine you took where it says that it causes permanent hallucinations. Stop it, Head. I'm really starting to worry about you. Even if you could have a baby, it might turn out to be a Mongoloid. That's the one thing a woman thirty and over fears the most. Head, you'll be thirty soon. You'd be too old, Head."

"That's not fair, Chad."

I was crushed the way you get when you find that someone you've really wanted to be friends with really hates your guts. I wasn't about to concede. I didn't let up.

"I can do it, Chad. Why you so worried about what people may think when they see a pregnant man? Once I break the ice, then everybody is going to want to jump on the bandwagon. Besides, when I get pregnant, I'd finally start to look like all the other thirty-year-old men with premature beer bellies. Don't you want me to look my age?" I said cheerfully and slapped him on the knee. I didn't tell Chad that deep down inside I was worried that childbirth would kill me.

"Head. Look at me." He took his hand and turned my face around so that our eyes met. He continued, "I don't care what the world thinks about us. I do care about what that medicine you took after being misdiagnosed with valley fever has done to your mind. The next thing I know you'll be telling me that a Negro can fly."

"We can fly, Chad. Didn't you know it was a black man who created the first idea of the airplane at the turn of the last century? He called it an airship. Who knows? Maybe he was gay and wanted to be the first man to have a baby too."

"Oh, brother, here we go again with men in books. Look, I'm going to finish putting your DVD player together. Then I'll let you take me home. You need to rest. You got way too much going on in that big head of yours," he said, looking at me sorrowfully.

By the time Chad put the DVD player together, I'd learned a few things on television about postnatal care. I got even more interested. What I learned made me want to gain further information. Having a baby is serious business. You think I'm lying? I decided to get some books on prenatal care. Talk to my mother? She might trip, so I decided not to tell her about my decision to have a baby until I got to my third trimester.

Over dinner, Chad seemed distracted. His dark face had softened under the glow of the candlelight. I picked at the gumbo; separated the crab from the shrimp, the sausages from the chicken, and the okra from the tomatoes. I set all the various pieces on a plate. It was early in the evening and yet I was imagining how it would be to wake up with morning sickness.

"Head. What are you doing? Sister Woman went through a lot of trouble making that gumbo for us. You making a mockery of it," he chastised me. Chad called my mother, Ester, Sister Woman.

"All I'm doing is making a family tree. Here is the mother, the crab. The daddy is the sausage. The shrimp are the babies and the chicken and tomatoes nieces, nephews, and cousins." I pointed to each family member with my fork. I smiled.

Chad joined in.

"And where, pray tell, are the grandparents?"

"Dead. All my grandparents are dead, Chad," I said, sullen.

"Well, my grandparents are still alive."

Chad spooned brown gravy, a soggy cracker, and a grain of rice out of his bowl and set it down at the top of the plate. He then went to the cabinet, took out a corn tortilla, rolled it up very neatly, and put it on the plate.

"Now there," he said like a man who had finished cooking dinner after standing on his tired feet in the kitchen all day long.

"Who are they?"

"My grandparents. The brown gravy is my grandfather and the cracker is my grandmother. She's white," he said, laughing.

"What's up with the grain of rice and corn tortilla?"

"Well, the rice is the Chinese guy who does my laundry every week."

"The corn tortilla?"

"My dead ex-boyfriend from Mexico."

"See, we already got a mixed family. Why don't you want me to have a baby? I know it's not my right to bear a child. It wasn't our right to vote but Congress passed the Voting Rights Act in the 1960s. Now look at us, a black congressman from every state in the union."

"That was an act of Congress, Head. Having a baby is an act of God. Wait! So let me get this straight. You're telling me that some mad scientist is going to artificially inseminate you with a fertilized egg and you'll get pregnant, right?" He looked at me, his face wrinkled. He seemed to be curious. I hoped he was coming around to my point of view. If he wasn't then I hoped that he'd opened the door to explore the options and further discussion.

"Before that happens I'll probably have to undergo an implant of an artificial uterus. Otherwise, I won't have the tools connected inside of me to support and protect me and the baby." I didn't let up. I felt my confidence mounting.

"Head, this is gross."

"It's only gross if you think it is."

"Why don't you follow in your eccentric ex-boyfriend's shoes and do drag? Get it out of your system. And call it a day."

"Chad, I don't want to be a drag queen. Not any kind of queen and I don't want to be a woman. If having a baby means getting my loins sliced in half like a pickle shoved into my pelvis to create a uterus, all bets are off. I'm backing off."

"Who is going to come up with the implant idea and whose eggs are you gonna use and put inside of you?"

"Naomi. She's still cow-pasture fertile. My way of keeping it real. Naomi, she my friend."

"Oh, Head, you telling me that you are going to become the groom of Frankenstein? Have you talked to Naomi about this yet?"

"I plan to."

"You know her boyfriend, Shorty. He's going to blow his top."

"That's it. He's her boyfriend, not her husband. He doesn't own the copyrights to her eggs or vagina."

"Oh, Lord. Here we go with the vagina monologues. All right, you mark my word. You going to start some shit you won't be able to stop. I'm not letting you use my sperm to do it. You know what? You're on your own," he warned me with a wiggle of his finger in my face.

I could feel my grip on any sense that Chad was coming around to see what possibilities lay ahead for us slip through my hands like water. Was I losing my mind? Had I gone crazy? Was I ever going to turn his mind sentiment around? We were done with dinner. I cleared the table, rinsed the dishes off, and put them in the dishwasher. Put the leftover scrapings of the family tree Chad helped me make into a plastic bag, took it outside, and put it in the garbage. He finished putting together the stereo and led me by the hand upstairs to my bedroom. Chad began to kiss and undress me. It was unexpected. We made love for the first time in the second year of the new millennium. I had a strong urge to record the encounter. It was like a rare falling star. Chad held me afterward so close until I could feel his heart thumping in his hairy chest. Oh how I longed to be able to bear the fruit of the magnificent seedlings of his labor that would grow a baby inside of me.

I shut my eyes and prayed.

Chad yanked off his rubber and slung it untidily to the foot of my bed. I looked at the poor spent rubber stretched to a ridiculous and grotesque size. How many babies floated in the triumph of Chad's joy juice trapped at the tip of it? I got up from bed, took the rubber filled with Chad's orgasm, balled it up in toilet tissue, and flushed 400 million would-be babies down into sewage. As I got dressed I wondered if the rubber had a tiny yet invisible hole at the tip that leaked a would-be baby into me. If so, I hoped it would hide until I could get the work done to bring it to the life lived not just on this earth that we call a planet but in a world we call our home.

I took Chad home to his split-level apartment, and dropped him off at his front door. I watched his wide backside disappear into his apartment.

I sped off.

Chapter 3

When I got back home I went online. I found some very interesting Web sites geared to surrogate mothers, adoption, Big Brother, implants, and organ donor programs. There were some sites where research was already underway exploring and testing the possibility of male birth. I came across a Web site that billed itself as "Male Pregnancy: A Study Project Dealing with a New Approach to Parenting and Childbirth." The study was seeking men interested in conception and giving birth to children. There were thousands of links to other sites. One I found made the hair stand up on my forearms. There it was. An invitation for study subjects interested in having a baby. I was stoked. I couldn't wait to tell Chad. I had almost lost my own self-confidence by Chad's doubts. My discouragement turned to hope.

I scrolled down the Web site and found the doctor, Bridgett Ashley, and her report on the delicate procedures, which I read with heart-pounding excitement. If Dr. Wilson could cure Chad's legendary sexual addiction, surely Dr. Ashley could make me one of the few men on the planet to give birth. I sent an e-mail to Dr. Ashley. I asked her to send me an application for enrollment in the study project.

I couldn't sleep that night. I was anxious. Each time I closed my eyes a different baby, sometimes a bubbling little girl or boy, would lift up the covers at the foot of my bed. Then one, sometimes two, of them tickled the bottoms of my feet. I couldn't sleep in a room with giggling babies, so I decided to laugh along with them, and that was how I found my sleep.

The next morning, I rolled out of bed and flipped on the lamp. Got up and went into the bathroom, peed, brushed my teeth, shaved, and took a shower. The warm water put me in a luxurious mood. I toweled dry and flipped on The Baby Channel. There was a young mother swabbing the tender sensitive areas of her son's umbilical cord. I watched her carry out this function with the precision of a surgeon. A nurse came into her room grinning and handed her a book, *How to Care for Your Newborn.* The young mother smiled and waved the woman away. Was that scene choreographed or improvised by the child's proud mother? I envied that mother and made a wish to be as careful and gentle with my own child. As I rubbed body lotion on the dry areas of my body, I caressed my nipples that had grown hard. The mere thought of suckling my baby pumped up my chest. I headed to the office.

As a private investigator, I ran my own business. Amy, my office assistant, was resting her head on the desk.

"Kel, I'm not feeling good. I need to go home. Feels like I'm about to throw up," she said, her face flushed.

"Ah, sorry to hear that, Amy. Go ahead and take off. This work isn't going anywhere fast. It'll be here whenever you get back. Hope you feel better."

"I'm pregnant."

"Pregnant?" I swallowed.

Suddenly, it seemed to me that everybody was either pregnant or wanted to get pregnant.

How could I do business with Amy and me both out on maternity leave at the same time? Maybe I'd take half the time I allotted Amy for maternity leave. Most personnel rules gave three months off. As the owner and operator of my private investigative business it gives me the opportunity to bend the personnel rules as I see fit. I can work as much or as little as I want. I was glad Amy told me she was pregnant. Now I could pick her brain and observe her in a clandestine way.

"Oh Amy, that's wonderful. How far gone are you?"

"Three months; I'm due June sixteenth."

"A spring baby."

"Yeah," Amy giggled weakly.

This gave me time to plot my pregnancy. Here it is the first week of January. If everything worked out the way I wanted it to, by March I would be incubating a little Chad. Amy's news cheered me on. I went over to the water cooler and brought back a glass of water for her.

"Thanks, Kel."

"You're welcome, Mommy Amy," I teased and winked at her.

I decided to call Chad at his office with the news.

"Guess what?"

"Don't tell me the rubber broke last night and now you're pregnant. Didn't I tell you those cheap Trojans were bunk?" he said, laughing.

"Chad, you're only half right. I'm not pregnant yet. Amy is. She beat me to the punch."

"Well hooray for her."

"Don't you see, Chad? This is an omen. I've been thinking all along about a baby. What do you know! It's like boom! Here my secretary is three months pregnant. I now have a sign. A wonderful sign, Chad." I beamed.

"Oh, Lord. What's next, Oprah or Ricki Lake? I can see the show now. I'm gay and having my boyfriend's baby. Why you call me to waste my time, Head? Don't you know some of us get paid to work and not to fantasize all day?"

"I'm not fantasizing about going on a talk show. I'm having my baby."

"All right, Madonna, I've had it. This has gone on long enough," he said and hung up the phone.

When Amy came into my office, she seemed to misread the disappointment in my eyes.

"You look worried, Kel. Don't worry. I'm only off three months on maternity leave. I'll come back to work," she said, turning around and walking back out of my office.

I went online to check my e-mail and found a reply from Dr. Ashley. She had attached an enrollment application form and a medical release that I downloaded. I quickly completed then faxed them to Dr. Ashley. By the time I closed my office and got home, a telephone message was waiting for me from Dr. Ashley. She told me she'd received the completed forms. What made me really happy was when she told me that I'd been preliminarily accepted as a participant in the male pregnancy program. Dr. Ashley told me to make plans for an initial consultation visit with Dr. Fredrick G. Valesco at the project affiliate office in San Francisco. She told me that Dr. Valesco was a fine doctor, the best in the business. She provided me with his telephone number and address, and made plans for me to go to Mercy Hospital to have my blood work done so that the test results could be sent to Dr. Valesco's office ahead of my visit with him. My joy was boundless. I sprinted upstairs, unpacked all the baby clothes, and put them away in a dresser drawer. I then went to work putting up the crib, took the bassinet into my bedroom, and set it up. I was going to have a baby! Damn! I danced like I was at a Mardi Gras carnival in Rio. I left a message on Dr. Valesco's voice mail for my first appointment.

Before I could hang up in peace the phone rang.

"Juicy Head," Chad said.

"Hey, Chad! I've got great news!" I bubbled over with excitement.

"Don't tell me, the rabbit died and it's not Amy who is pregnant. It's really you and you want a boy, right?"

"Chad, I got a call from the Male Pregnancy study project and they've accepted me as a participant. I'm so thrilled. Chad, I'm really going to have a baby!"

"Hold the fuck up, Head. You've only been accepted. That does not mean you are pregnant. Don't put the cart before the horse. Anything can happen in between."

"Chad, this is like a dream come true."

"Ah, don't you mean nightmare? The groom of Frankenstein." Chad laughed.

"Ha ha, very funny. Anyway, I'm going to see the obstetrician soon."

"You mean the mad scientist."

"A doctor, Chad. Give him a chance already. Let's see what he can do. I already saw Dr. Ashley's pregnant man."

"Where, at Sears?"

"He was online. He looked just like I imagined I'm going to look. A thirty-year-old man with a gut or a beer belly. Like the ones we saw in Cancun drooling over us when we were on the beach."

"Those men are typical straight men. They worked hard to get those bellies. What you are doing is bizarre," he threw in.

"Chad, all you've got to do is bear with me. If it doesn't work out, no foul, no harm. The least you can do is stand by me. Goddamn."

"Stand by your man," Chad began to sing and mock me.

"Chad, why does the idea of me being pregnant disturb you so much? I'm the one putting my respect, reputation, health, and life on the line, not you."

"Head, having a baby is a woman's burden, not a man's. This is one of the things she has to go through to become a woman."

"Well, what about all the millions of women who can't or choose not to have children? Are they any less of a woman because of it?"

"Honeydew Head, let's take my friend, Tracy. She separated from her husband, Vince, and moved to Seattle with her six-year-old daughter, Veronica. Tracy sent that child to visit with her grandfather in Memphis. Didn't I tell you that Veronica was visiting her grandfather and both of them got burned up? He fell asleep and left an iron on the sofa—the house caught on fire. Forgot to turn the freaking iron off! They were trapped upstairs on the second floor of the house. He was in one bedroom, she was in the other. Neither one of them could reach one another. To this day, Tracy can't stand the thought of having another baby. That's why she drinks like a fish. That girl makes me fucking sick! Crying at the sight of a fire or when she hears the siren of an ambulance. She thinks paramedics are rushing Veronica to the hospital to save her life. She is so damn weak. She still thinks she's a mother. She's afraid of having another baby because she does not want to bear the pain of giving birth to another one and then lose that one, too."

"Chad, you talk like a woman's only duty is to have and love a man and spread her legs apart and let some man do his business on top of her. It hurts to lose a child. She may be trying to drink the hurt away."

"You did. You lost what would have been your firstborn. Then last year you got sick with God only knows what and now it seems to me that this is your last stand. Do you think having a baby is going to turn back the hands of time? Erase what happened to you? You need to slow your role. The good Lord gives and takes away. What if you get pregnant and have a miscarriage or lose your baby like Tracy lost her daughter?"

We were silent for a few moments.

Chad struck a chord in me that had been out of tune for a long time. If I lost another child, it would open another hole in my heart that would never close. I'd have put that hole next to the one I already got. Maybe, I would turn both of the holes into a pair of eyes so that I'd have double vision and be able to see and understand things better. Chad told me that I was going to make a mess out of my family tree. I've wanted to have a baby since the abortion.

"What would Sister Woman call your baby?"

"If it's a boy it'll be her grandson and if it's a girl, it'll be her granddaughter. Anyway, Tracy is one of the women who would understand me and what I want."

"Head, don't count on it. You know I don't speak to Tracy. I'm too through with her."

"Chad, I'm not mad at Tracy. You don't have to be either. Why you mad at somebody who is not your real sister? You didn't even spend your childhood growing up with her. You two were thick as thieves. You need to find her and make your peace. Besides, she's over three thousand miles away. She's living in New York and if I've got to go there for my implant, I may stay with her during my recuperation."

"Suit yourself." Chad hung up.

Was this my last stand? I mean the truth is that when I became mysteriously ill last year, I came this close to losing my life. I'd have days when I couldn't seem to stop crying because I was scared of what was in store for me tomorrow. Sometimes my hands would tremble when I'd dump a dose of fluconazole in my palms. I knew that it was only my fears. Yet, anyone who looked at my trembling hands would think I was afflicted with Parkinson's disease. Being sick, or living on the edge of death, I want to tell you, are things I wouldn't wish on my worst enemy. I fought back death like a man fighting off a murderer hell-bent on taking my life to see if he could get away with it. I wasn't ready to die yet because I had so much unfinished business I had to get done. Being near death feels as if one's life is like a broken piece of glass, shattered into millions of tiny pieces. I consider myself lucky they were able to pick me up piece by piece. It took a lot of work, but they fixed me up and glued me back together again.

However, the only thing is, when they put me back together again all the pieces don't fit the way they once did. I keep rubbing here and there, finding jagged rough edges, bumps that weren't there before I got sick and stepped over to the other side. I worry when the day will come when those pieces of glass will become unglued. I know that a cracked glass can't hold water but the only thing I don't know is when or what will happen to me to make it spring a leak or crack wide open. I had my wits about me, because the hell if I was going to let the big square toe of the Devil of Death swoop down and take me, not without a battle to end all battles! No way! Death didn't know who the hell it was fooling with. Death had a fight on its hands! I mean that! You think I'm lying! We fought in that hospital room for days. You hear me! Death had the advantage over me because I was flat on my back. But I wasn't down for the count though, and death knew I still had some fight left in me yet. So I fought him the way a man fights when he is caught up against the ropes or he's backed into a corner. There's nothing he can do but get his ass kicked or come out swinging. I beat Death back with ferocious jabs, undercuts, and head butts, and he told me I'd gotten the best of him for now. Then he told me, "Just to show you I can take you out of this world I'm going to catch you with your pants down! That's a promise!" I looked Death dead in his steel-gray eyes and told him, "You think I'm going to be sitting up on my goddamn ass in Mercy twiddling my thumbs waiting for you?" I told Death he better get up out of my face. Death made tracks. Or is he hovering around me somewhere, watching and waiting for me to slip up and fall? Every time I take my pants off at the sex clubs I wonder if Death is going to strike me down before I bust a nut.

Was God in cahoots with the Devil of Death? I wonder if God had looked at my record of giving to other people and decided to spare my life. I wonder if God gives us extra credit for compassion. Can this credit be cashed in like chips in a poker game? Should I want to use some of these credits to cure my sexual addiction and ensure that I would not die during childbirth or have a healthy baby? Would I be able to do it, or is there a penalty for early withdrawal? Maybe He is watching me after all. I worry about how much more I've got left to give to others before I'm left with nothing at all for myself. Is it more important to give rather than to receive in life? Is having a baby the truest or noblest meaning of giving? Would I be helping myself if I were to bring the new life of a child into the world? Or would I be giving help to the child? Would I finally overcome the loss of my would-be firstborn? I wondered if after giving everybody the best of my love and my last dime whether I'd gone bankrupt inside. Think about it: I could never slit the throat of my beloved child because I didn't want it to grow up black and gay. Was I already broken inside like the glued pieces of glass that are my life? How in the world could any man, lost, broken inside, put himself back together to give and bring forth the power to give birth to a child? Is this a daunting task? Was I biting off more than I could chew? I mean, could I really do it? Or is this a pipe dream?

I took a shower, had dinner, and before I could get down on my knees and say my prayers, the telephone rang. It was my mother.

"Kel, you watching the news?" Ma asked.

"I'm about to pull my covers up to my ears and go to sleep. Why? What's wrong? Another re-recount of the Florida vote?" I said, laughing.

"Honey, that minister got a young girl pregnant as a cow and she has a one-and-a-half-year-old baby," Ma said, sucking her teeth.

"Good for her! Everybody can't conceive a child. Don't you think she's blessed?"

"Blessed my ass. All I know is she'll never have to see a hungry day as long as she lives."

"More power to her."

"The good reverend has to pay her ten thousand bucks a month in child support for that love child."

"Is it a girl or boy?"

"Girl. It's the cutest little thing. Looks just like him too. Big old round face with eyes spread further apart than Jackie O's. Where that family get them eyes from beats the hell out of me." She laughed.

"He's not the first old big-eyed Negro preacher to father a child outside of wedlock, and he won't be the last, Ma."

"Who you telling? The mayor of that city across the bay we call Oz been separated from his wife for twenty years and he said his girlfriend is pregnant too. His old ass needs to go somewhere, find a chair in a corner and sit down. All these old babies they bringing in this world."

"They're babies, Ma. Innocent little angels, kicking and screaming up a storm and getting into all kinds of mischief," I said.

"You sure was a big baby. My lord! Twenty-two inches long, eleven pounds with coal-black hair and thick eyelashes. A pretty black baby."

I blushed.

I imagined that my baby would look the way my mother described me when I came into the world.

"Everybody making and having babies, Ma. It's a time to be born. A new century and fresh ideas and to have a baby on top of it is a blessing. A great blessing."

"I cooked some candy yams, cabbage, ox tails, and hot water corn bread. Come over tomorrow after you get off from work and have dinner with me."

"I'll try to swing through tomorrow evening. God willing."

"Good night, Kel."

"Good night."

I flipped off the television and got in the bed. Wouldn't it be a wonder if all of these men getting women pregnant outside the walls of marriage could have their own babies? I slipped into a dream.

It was about three o'clock in the morning. I picked up the telephone and called Chad.

"Baby, I'm ready. My water broke."

"Oh shit. I'll be right over."

"Hurry, Chad. I need you here."

"All right already. I'm on the way there. I won't be long. Relax and stay calm. Remember what they taught us at the Lamaze class."

I was in the delivery room and Chad was sitting in a small chair next to my bed. My hands and feet were tied to the railings of the bed with black leather straps. I was stretched out on a long metal table, my stomach as tight and as round as a water balloon. A thin white sheet was thrown over me. My face and hands were sweaty. Chad was wearing a blue smock. He held my hand. My labor pains were only a few minutes apart. I asked for a glass of water. The delivery nurse, a dark-skinned heavyset middle-aged black woman, her cheekbones high and hair in cornrows, refused me.

"This is Eagle's Nest Hospital. We don't serve water in the psychiatric maternity ward. Especially when the baby's head is crowning." She smiled and fumbled with an electronic heart monitor. I watched her frame disappear through a door.

"Crowning? Psychiatric maternity ward? Why are we at Eagle's Nest? I'm supposed to go to Mercy Hospital. That's where my doctor is. He's the only one who can deliver my baby. What does she mean the baby's head is crowning? I don't have a vagina! I'm supposed to have a caesarian! Chad, get me the fuck out of this place!"

"Honeydew Head. Take some deep breaths. Remember, deeply. Look at me." Chad began breathing in and out heavily and waving his arms like he was a maestro conducting a symphony.

"Chad, how could you let this happen to me?" I asked.

"Shhhh! It'll all be over soon. No pain, no gain," he said after he stopped his mock role as a maestro. He put his hands back in the crevice of his lap. Chad began to sing a little nursery rhyme I hadn't heard since I was in the third grade.

> Last night, not the night before
> Twenty-four robbers came knocking at my door
> I got up to let them in
> And this is what they told me
> I'm your mama
> I'm your daddy
> I'm that big-headed baby in the alley

I opened my mouth to tell Chad to stop playing the dozens with me. My lips moved but I couldn't talk. I'd lost my voice.

"What's the matter, Hothead? The cat got your tongue?" Chad put his hands up to his mouth and snickered.

The nurse came back in the room with what looked like a twelve-inch-long sharp razor blade. She walked over to a sink that had a large white light over it that swung on a thin black rope. I watched her reach up over the sink and pull down a long brown leather razor-sharpening strap fastened to the wall. She slowly stroked the razor back and forth up against it. She then began to sing.

> Mama killed him
> Papa ate him
> Buried his head
> In the marble stone

She let the strap go and it quickly rolled back up the wall, making a cracking noise. She turned and walked over to Chad.

"Excuse me, but are you his husband?" she said, pointing the razor toward me as she spoke.

"You got it."

"I would caution you to stand back. He may hemorrhage some. We don't want the slightest slither of blood to stain that smock you are wearing. We only use the best detergent here, called Fab. Get it? Fab-ulous," she said and smothered a laugh.

Chad stood up from his chair and slowly backed into a corner of the room. He walked like a man who didn't want to turn his back on a woman with a razor. A hot white light just above my head felt warm against my face. Sweat dripped down from my forehead into the corners of my mouth.

"Now Mr. Warren, this isn't going to hurt a bit. Before you know it, you'll be the poster boy for pregnant men all over the world. Isn't that just wonderful?" The woman with the razor grinned, showing a full set of flawlessly white teeth capped in pink gums. She came down with the blade and sliced me from the middle of my chest to my navel. I tried to scream but I still couldn't speak. I could barely see my baby for all of the blood. My instincts told me it was a little boy with thick curly black hair and eyelashes. The woman with the razor wrapped the baby up in a white hand towel. When she walked out of the room with my baby I woke up.

"Help meeeeeeeeeeeeeeeee!" I screamed to the four walls in an empty bedroom.

I bolted up in the bed and switched on the lamp. My whole body was drenched with sweat. It came to me. In the morning, I'd go over to Chad's apartment and tell him that I would abandon any further plans of trying to have a baby. He'd grin and say, "Oh, Head. See, I was right again. You were wrong. It's a scandalous hare-brained idea anyway. God didn't give you a vagina, uterus, or fallopian tubes. He gave you a big dick. Be proud of it." He would call me selfish and insist that I let him take me to see my doctor. Chad would tell me it's the level of fluconazole that I once took that was to blame for my wild flights of fantasy. Let him have his surrogate mom for all I care, I thought. As I fell back into the deep haze of sleep, I knew I had come too far and couldn't turn back even if I wanted to.

Chapter 4

The next morning, I called Amy and left a message on her voice mail telling her that I was taking the day off. I had to make plans to get my implant work done, soon. Every minute was more precious and valuable than the one that came before it. I went to Mercy and had my blood work done. I called Dr. Valesco's office and made an appointment. He had a long waiting list. The earliest appointment I was able to get was two weeks away.

It was sunny and cool outside. The skies were a Caribbean blue and the clouds looked like sprinkled baby powder. Looking at the wonder in the sky above my head, it didn't matter to me that the Bay Area was overdue for rain.

I took advantage of my day of freedom and went to Armor Protective Home, to see my best friend, Atlas, who'd been in hospice. Hospice was situated at the front of the nursing home. Atlas was in the last stages of AIDS. Before I left home, I had called him and asked if I could bring him anything. Atlas told me he wanted his favorite, a box of Godiva chocolates. I've known Atlas since the seventh grade. He was voted most likely to succeed during our sophomore year at Kennedy High. Atlas was blessed with the gift of painting. He had designed and painted the murals for the State Capitol in Sacramento. He sold his work at auctions all over the Bay Area, then later, during hard times, at flea markets in San Jose and Berkeley. Before he became ill, he was an art teacher at U.C. Berkeley. I'd had a crush on Atlas long before we started dating. His strong calves, thighs, small waistline, bulging crotch, and soft step made my mouth water. All of these attributes were hidden behind a mask of determined intelligence. Atlas was out long before it was fashionable (at least in some circles) to be gay. He looked a little like Bill Cosby.

When I arrived at his room, Atlas was looking out of his window through a clump of eucalyptus trees.

"Hey, Atlas," I said and set the small box of chocolates down on a tiny table next to his twin bed crowded with a tray of untouched breakfast muffins, coffee, and Christmas cards. It was lunchtime. Food carts were parked outside of patients' rooms.

"Hey, Miss Thing," Atlas said, making a gallant effort to rise from his bed to hug me.

"Hey, Atlas. Wait. Don't get up. Let me come around there and put these long arms of mine around that hot body," I teased.

Atlas's shoulders jutted out from his dressing gown like two stilts. His cheekbones were like those of the fashion models seen on runways all over the world, high and sharp. I muffled a strong impulse to cry and kept on my dark shades and Raiders baseball cap.

"Look at that heifer up on the pole!" Atlas said, drawing my attention to a grayish-brown cat that looked like a giant squirrel stranded on top of a telephone pole.

"You been up there for two days! Bitch, jump!" he yelled, then burst out laughing.

A short fat man with round shoulders and a deep chocolate complexion came into Atlas's room right on my heels. The man had a distinctive African accent. His upper teeth were capped with gold. I looked at his hands. They were small and as dark as his face, making the silver ring he wore on his right thumb stick out in an odd sort of way.

I pulled his IV monitor out of the way as the man with the African accent made his way around to Atlas.

"Now Miss Atlas. We all know how fabulous you are." He cleared his throat and winked at me. "But we ain't gonna let you go into one of your diva antics this afternoon. Curtain is not at six. It's at twelve. Time to eat." He snapped his fingers and pulled the curtain separating Atlas from his hospice mate, an elderly white man with hollow jaws and a wisp of a beard. He appeared to be living only with the help of an oxygen tank. African accent took what looked like a breakfast tray of untouched food off the table. He put in its place a covered lunch tray. The only things that were obvious on the tray were a small carton of apple juice and an orange. I watched African accent take the uneaten food and set it at the very bottom of the food cart in the hall. He quickly came back into Atlas's room.

"Sister-honey-girl," Atlas said.

"Correction, it's Ms. Sister-honey-girl to you," African accent snapped his fingers twice this time.

"Right, and I'm Whitney Houston. Anyway, Kel, this is Cameroon. Cameroon, Kel."

Cameroon cleared the overstuffed tray and left fruit in a tiny bowl in its place. We shook hands. I told Atlas that I was going to have a baby.

"Girl, you need to quit it. You gonna end up pregnant in your tubes." Atlas laughed. He seemed to show more strength in his laughter than it looked like he had in his whole body.

"I'm going to try to do it."

"Who is going to be the daddy? Don't tell me. Knowing your ass, it'll probably be through osmosis."

"A manchild," I said. I watched Cameroon set some pills in a tiny cup on the table, exchange a couple of brief words with Atlas in French, and walk out of the room.

"Well?" Atlas said. His eyes were big, brown, and watery.

"Chad's, I think."

"You whore! It's going to be mama's baby, daddy's maybe."

"I've already pick up some baby clothes."

"Get the fuck out of here. No shit."

"I kid you not."

"Where did you go? Saks Fifth Avenue?"

"You know me, always the practical one. I went to Sears. They had a half-off sale."

"You mean the frugal one. But that's too cute. How does your thugs-band like the idea?"

"He doesn't like it. Says it's far-fetched and that I'm dreaming. Slipping off the edge of the earth. That I've lost my grip on reality."

"Tell his ass you were dreaming when you met him. And now he's the Freddy Krueger of your nightmares. He better ask somebody. Shit," he said and rolled his eyes upward.

We became silent.

I was visiting my sick ex-boyfriend. Someone who I'd once spent long nights fighting, making love to and wedding plans with. Atlas interrupted our plans, one spring Sunday, during brunch at HS Lordships, when he shut me down. "I want to be free, Kel," he said. I loved him so I set him free. Gave him the freedom a man needs to discover the things that make him tick. I looked in that man's puppy brown eyes and told him, "You're still my friend."

Years later, the same man who wanted his freedom from me turned toward the reckless, murky world of drugs and substance abuse. That man was now in the throes of fighting the greatest battle of them all, the struggle to cheat death. Stop it cold. Lock it up in a space voyager, shoot it ten zillion miles past the stars into that other unknown to anyone born on earth. One can be reckless with sexual addiction too. It's easier said than done, but all it seems to boil down to is that you have to know when you've had it up to here.

Atlas went on, "Me and my mama got into it." He smeared Chap Stick on his thin dry lips.

"What over?" I asked.

"She said I wouldn't be in here if I'd stopped smoking crack. I've been in here three weeks and she hasn't come to see me yet," he said. His face grew sad. He shoved the lunch tray aside, then cracked open the box of chocolates and put a piece of candy in his mouth. He began to chew and looked toward the window as though he'd been waiting for the cat upon the telephone pole to shit or get up off the stool.

"Don't worry. She'll come see you. Hang in there."

"You know, the worst thing about getting sick is I lost my garden. The house, the Lexus, the Mercedes, the boat, my portfolio, my career as a painter, that bunk-ass boyfriend of mine that turned me out to a shit in the first place mean nothing to me. Absolutely nothing! All of that including him was rubbish and will someday perish, turn to dust. My poor foliage is what hurt to watch wither away like the great Roman Empire. All of my poor orchids, *Chionodoxa lucilliae*, narcissus, crocus, *Tulipa* and allium, my little palm trees just destroyed. I should have listened to you when you pulled my coattail and told me that nigga wasn't no good for me."

"All you had to tell me was he didn't have a job and wouldn't screw around with you unless you bought him crack. I knew then that trouble for you was about to last always."

Atlas told me that one night his ex-boyfriend hit him over the shoulder with a poker in a fight they had over a rock of crack cocaine. Atlas let me know that was when he should have run as far away as his legs could carry him.

"Love, honey. It makes you do some crazy shit."

"Atlas, it's always taken a fool to learn that love doesn't love no one. The great stars in your eyes had you as blind as a bat. That's all."

"How the hell do you figure? When you and I were together you didn't love me. You pretended to be in love with me. Now you come all up in here acting like you know what love is."

He caught me off guard. I felt as if I'd suddenly been tossed into the boxing ring and half of my ear was being gnawed off by a brutal, washed-up, baby-talking, once great prizefighter deliberately because he knew that was the only way he could win the fight. Nevertheless, I reminded myself, of course, that I wasn't at a Vegas championship fight. I was at the bedside of an ex-boyfriend. I was compelled to go and see him for the same reason I wanted to have a baby. I was interested. Atlas pulled the thin blanket up to his neck as if he'd developed a sudden chill.

"Whoa! I didn't come to talk about what could have been between us. That's water under the bridge. I'm not swimming in it. I'm in no mood to drown. I want to glide. Fly."

"Well, either go parasailing or get your tall fine ass on a boat and row! Winch!" We both laughed. Atlas's wit and sense of humor were totally unstoppable.

"You know I'm agoraphobic and my arms weren't made to row a boat! These babies were made for hugging," I teased.

"Take them long-ass legs of yours and go stand in the water and push that boat. Push it real good," he laughed. He coughed dryly.

"Tell me, what are they feeding you in here to make you talk so nasty?" I asked.

"It's not what they are feeding me. It's what they are not feeding me. I can't eat this shit. I'm living off of the air in this room and the kindness of strangers," he said theatrically.

We both turned and looked out of his window at the tanned ripped torso of a paramedic who had climbed to the top of the telephone pole to rescue the stranded cat. When the paramedic backed down the pole with the cat and disappeared from our sight, I could hear the roar and hand clapping of people who had gathered underneath the pole. Atlas looked back at me. His sunken face looked like that of a starved East African boy.

"What are you doing off work today? Not just to come and visit the sick and shut in."

"You my boy. I can't up and forget about you. But I did make an appointment to see Dr. Valesco to talk about the implant work I need to have done so I can have my baby."

"Who would have thought? Now here it is. You got dick for days and it's going to be turned into a piece of meat that's in danger of looking like a woman's change of life. You may as well cut that thing off, put it in a pickle jar, and freeze it for future scientific research," he laughed. Atlas wouldn't let up. "Baby, you better get that doctor's curriculum vitae! That's where they dish the dirt, or clone you an embryo. Hummmp! Clone one! Why you want to end up with stretch marks and collapsed tits? Child, you better ask your mama."

"Atlas, those are warrior marks. Not stretch marks. Jeez. War marks and battle scars. Some of the most beautiful artistry after childbirth the world has ever known. Pablo Picasso should have been so lucky to paint such masterpieces."

"I've painted better! Battle scars? Show me a stretch mark on that high fashion model; what's her name?"

"You mean Tyra Banks."

"Yes. I'll show you an unemployed diva. In serious trouble, destined for a life-long career as a welfare queen."

"All I'm saying, Atlas, is that I'm going to try. If it doesn't work out, I'll live with the defeat. But not knowing if I can have a baby is tearing me apart inside."

"Girl, go ahead and do it. Shit. At least you will have the *National Enquirer* doing a story on your ass. I can see the headline, 'Gay Freak Has Perverted Test-Tube Baby from Mars.'" He began laughing and it turned into a rather fierce cough. I handed him a glass of water. He nudged my hand away so hard the glass of water fell, crashed to the cold linoleum floor, and broke into tiny pieces.

"Atlas, want me to get Cameroon?" I asked and he nodded, unable to speak any further. He was bent over with convulsions. I ran out of the room, down the hall to the nursing station. Halfway down the hall, I spotted Cameroon a couple of rooms away, standing over an elderly black woman with stooped shoulders. I stopped in front of Cameroon and the old woman. I was breathing hard, a little out of breath.

"Cameroon! It's Atlas, he—" Cameroon put up his right hand as if he was directing traffic in the middle of an intersection busy with vehicular traffic. I watched Cameroon and the old woman. Instead of getting someone else to come and see about Atlas, out of panic, I froze like a deer caught in the headlights.

"Let me sleep with my husband tonight. Why the hell do I have to sleep by myself? We've been married seventy years! Why break us up now!" she said as she sat at the foot of the bed of a black man who was turned on his side, watching her.

"Now, Mrs. Hill. This isn't your room and this kind gentleman here is not your husband. Wouldn't you like some peach cobbler with some nice cold vanilla ice cream? You know it's your favorite," Cameroon said as if he was speaking to a small child afraid to sleep alone in a dark room. The old woman smiled and seemed to cheer up.

"That would be nice. My granddaddy loved my peach cobbler to death. I made it for him when I was a little girl in North Carolina. His father was the first Negro governor, you know."

"Yes. I remember you telling me about that. How wonderful!" Cameroon said. He took the old woman's arm and gently led her out of the room. I followed them to her room at the end of the L-shaped hallway.

"Now you climb on back up on your bed and I'll have Misty bring you your favorite."

"Don't let her forget. I sure won't."

Cameroon pulled the old woman's door shut, winked at me, and shook his head.

"She thinks Mr. Green is her husband. Every day we have to go in his room and get her out of his bed. Mrs. Hill has Alzheimer's. We haven't served peach cobbler and vanilla ice cream here since the nineteen eighty-nine earthquake. And what can I do you for?" he said, making eyes at me.

"It's Atlas. He's having a coughing attack."

"Come. We must hurry!" he said, sprinting down the hallway. I stayed close to his heels. We stormed into Atlas's room. He had collapsed and lay slumped over in the bed. Cameroon propped two pillows behind Atlas's back, sat him straight up in the bed, and then checked his pulse.

"Oh God! He's gone into cardiac arrest. Code Blue!" he yelled into a microphone built into the wall above Atlas's bed. Then he turned to me. "Sorry, but you are going to have to leave now. Here, write your name and telephone number down on this note pad," he said, pulling out a tiny booklet from the oversized pocket of his white smock. I took the notepad and scribbled my name and telephone number on it.

"You can either call back this evening or in the morning to check on his condition, but now I'm asking you again to leave. I've got to call his family," he said.

"But you don't understand. I'm his family. Don't you see?"

"Blood relations, and I don't mean ex-tricks, boyfriends, or lovers. You know, relatives, that sort of thing. Now please go. You must not remain here any longer," Cameroon said. I watched Cameroon start CPR on Atlas.

My mind told me to pick my feet up one by one and walk away, but I couldn't move. I was stuck. I was frozen in my tracks, in place, in time. I wanted to turn and be able to walk away with the assurance that I'd see this soul again, during my next visit. In addition, listen to his ranting and raving. Consume it and let it consume me. I looked at Atlas and wondered if I'd ever see him again. I could still hear the bubbling up of his laughter that rang in my ears like an echo. I lifted the covers at the bottom of his bed and rubbed his thin-callused feet. My paralyzed feet regained the life I needed to allow me to turn and walk out of Atlas's room. I walked like a soldier shell-shocked after engaging an enemy in fierce battle, only to lose his most cherished buddy out on the battlefield. I passed dozens of rooms with elderly men and women lying in beds, sitting in wheelchairs, rowing walkers, playing checkers, reading, watching TV, or looking out of the window at the world that they left behind.

Atlas seemed out of place among the elderly and infirm, some of whom seemed discarded like old worn-out shoes and cast away from a lifetime of productivity. Flung into nursing homes they didn't choose and in all probability fought courageous battles against, they were banished like eyesores to nursing homes and hospices with fancy names, like Wonder Gardens, Royal Oaks, Tranquil Creek, Sweet Home Cove. Now in the inglorious twilight of life, longevity had no place and they were no longer considered useful in the scheme of things. It seemed to me that life had declared that Atlas at twenty-nine years old, sick with a huge disease with a tiny name, was cast into the deep dark hole of old age. He'd been dumped into a nursing facility that reeked of dried urine, with the name Armor Protective Home that flew square in the face of what he really needed and was neither home, armor, nor protection.

When I got to my car and began to drive away, I began to cry. I stared up at the lush green hills of Richmond, the car lots, supermarkets, gas stations on San Pablo Avenue, and the casino right across the street from the hospice. I'd read a newspaper article once that reported one of the patients at Armor Protective had been missing for a week. They found her in her nightgown one evening, playing blackjack at the casino. Would my newborn child who would grow into adulthood put me away in the twilight of my life? Would the child I'd decided to have stuff me inside of a nursing home where the staff would have to fetch me out of the bed of another man who I believed was Chad? If I were to contract AIDS and wither into a debilitated helpless state, would my mother or Chad, the would-be executor of my estate, not put me away? Was I prepared for any of this? If not, when would I begin to take the proper precautions? Such precautions couldn't be any more difficult than slipping on a rubber when having sex.

Chapter 5

A week had passed since I'd gone to Mercy to have my blood work done. When I got to work this morning, there was a message in my voice mail. Amy had called in sick. I sat down and flipped through my desk calendar. I found the date of my consultative appointment with Dr. Valesco and his address at the bottom of the page. I decided to take off work that afternoon. I gazed at my wall at the pictures of Malcolm X and James Baldwin. My life seemed so complicated next to theirs. Was Chad right? Was this whole idea about me having a baby absurd? Had I lost my grip on reality or did I no longer accept what's humanly possible in this life? Why couldn't I live with the loss of my would-be firstborn? Let it go. I couldn't. Would black men, gay and straight alike all over the world, smack me down thinking I'm harming the image of a virile, strong, masculine black man whose dick stays hard for days no matter what? Isn't this my life? Does anyone pay my bills for me? I thought about my friend Nina, her partner, Andrea, and her two-year old daughter, Shuntria, as cute as a button. I'm her godfather, and she doesn't even know me. I don't go around her enough so that she can get to know me. Then why would I want to have a baby when I don't go and spend time enough with my own goddaughter? Shouldn't Shuntria know me so well that when she sees me coming through the door, she'd jump up and down, squeal, run up to me with open arms and squeeze my neck like she hasn't seen me in years? Shouldn't she pout, kick and scream, throw a tantrum when she sees me leaving her after a visit? Her little fat round cheeks softer than cotton balls, her heart-shaped smile, sparkling brown eyes are treasures to cherish. What she does, like all children when they don't know you from a hole in the ground, is to look at me skeptically, her face shaped like a big question mark, knowing that I fit in the picture somewhere but unsure as to when, where, how, and why. Shuntria is Nina's only daughter. Couldn't I have an only child too? Chad's argument disgusted but didn't dissuade me. I had no choice but to soldier on. The telephone jangled, interrupting my thoughts.

"This is Dr. Valesco's office. We're calling to confirm your appointment for this Friday afternoon. Are you going to be able to make it?" the woman said with a voice at once clear and impersonal.

"Sure I'll be there and on time. Can I ask you a question?"

"Go ahead."

"Would you mind faxing me Dr. Valesco's curriculum vitae?" I asked. She hesitated for a few moments before answering me.

"I'll check with the doctor, and if he doesn't have a problem, I'll fax it right along. Oh, I'll be sending you an informed consent form for enrollment in the program," she said. I gave her my fax number and wondered if she thought my request for Dr. Valesco's curriculum vitae was odd or out of the ordinary. I hung up feeling as if I'd gotten one step closer to my dream. I suddenly began to feel nervous. My heart was racing and my armpits were wet. I left the office, went into the men's room, and splashed cold water on my face before coming back to my office. I spent most of the day reviewing and sending off reports to several insurance agencies and balancing invoices.

The phone rang.

"Hello, I'm calling from Dr. Valesco's, and the doctor has agreed to fax you his curriculum vitae," she said.

"That's great. You've got my fax number?" I asked.

"Yes. I'll send it to you promptly."

"That's fine," I said as though I was already familiar with the verbiage of such a document.

I hung up the telephone and went over to the fax machine. I stood with my arms folded across my chest. Atlas had a knack for spotting scams perpetrated on others but could never tell when someone was trying to run a game on him. The fax spewed out the good doctor's curriculum vitae. I pulled the document out of the machine, walked back into my office, and sat down to read it.

Dr. Valesco's credentials seemed impeccable enough. He was a licensed laboratory director with a PhD in human genetics. He was board certified in obstetrics, embryology, gynecology, and urology. He attended medical school at Stanford, interned at the National Institute of Biology in Maryland, lectured at the American Academy of Medicine in Rome, and graduated from Chicago University. He was an expert witness in malpractice trials, lived in Marin County, and taught at a small private university in Berkeley. I couldn't be more thrilled. Damn! I'm in safe hands! Sent along with his curriculum vitae was a consent form. I quickly stuffed the documents inside of my briefcase sitting in a chair next to my desk.

I felt like beating my chest with joy. Instead, what I did was take a deep breath and exhale. I was relieved that I wasn't going to be seeing some quack. "He's a fine doctor. One of the best in the business," Dr. Ashley had told me. Her tone was smart and confident. I knew that Atlas was going to give me his seal of approval when I gave him the news. "Get his curriculum vitae! That's where the dirt is!" Atlas had told me. I wondered if the CV would help to bring Chad around that long corner of doubt, disbelief, and skepticism. I could see Chad sitting on the sofa watching E! when I'd tell him about Dr. Valesco's stellar, unblemished background and flawless credentials. Chad would put his hands to his face. Frustrated, he'd shake his head and tell me again that I'm loony. That I've totally lost my mind, gone bonkers, flipped over the edge into the zany la-la land of insanity. He'd play devil's advocate and probably find some way to belittle Dr. Valesco and pour cold water on the fire in me that was now raging out of control. A little red warning sign was posted in the square corner of my mind, telling me to proceed with caution. "What might look outside like a shiny red apple could be rotten. Rotten to the core," Ma told me once, after I'd graduated from Cal State University Sacramento and moved back home. Against her advice I'd taken 1,000 dollars, my life savings, and bought a classic candy apple red Firebird. It stalled and broke down on the freeway while driving back home.

I took a lunch break at Spangles in Jack London Square. I sat across the table from a black woman who seemed to glow with motherhood. She had a black mole near the corner of her mouth and shoulder-length dreads that were pulled away from her oval face and roped into a long ponytail. She was feeding a little boy who looked to be about the same age as Shuntria. The kid was dressed to the nines. He wore the tiniest stingy brim hat with a rooster red feather stuck along the side.

"Come on, eat for Mommy, like a big boy," she said, lifting the spoon up to his mouth. The child turned his head away from the food and giggled.

Mother had her son dressed in a pair of midnight-black matching Kani jeans and jacket. His little undershirt had a picture of the San Francisco Forty-Niners pasted on the front. I thought about Shuntria and I missed her. I knew then that I had to get Shuntria to know me. I felt a sense of urgency. I had to devise some kind of plan to get Nina to bring her over without it being so obvious. When I finished with lunch, I paid the tab, scooted from under my table, and went over to mother with child.

"Excuse me, I don't mean to be rude or interrupt your lunch but I've got to tell you how cute your son is and from where I sat all I could see was the look of love on your face. Such a perfect picture," I said, hoping she wouldn't think I was making a pass at her.

"Why thank you!" She looked at me, then back into her son's soft brown eyes. "Tell this gentleman thank you, Jamar," she said.

"Tank you," the child said. He looked up at me, back at his mother, kicked his little feet, and smiled brightly. I waved good-bye to both of them and headed out of the restaurant. A chill wind blew into Oakland from San Francisco Bay. I pulled up the collar of my trench coat. As I walked a couple of blocks down the street, I stopped in front of Babies and Bath. I'd overheard Nina telling one of her friends on the telephone when she was pregnant with Shuntria about going there to buy some things for her baby. Did I have enough time to shop? The least I could do was get out of the frigid chill of the air, go on in, and browse.

Once I got inside of the store I felt the way you feel when you are in a car and it goes real fast up a hill and comes down on the other side of it almost as quickly. It was as though my heart had slipped down into the pit of my stomach. If Babies and Bath were not paradise, then paradise didn't exist at any other time or place on earth. The joy of a thousand joys washed over me. I was in my element that seemed to have been hidden away from me. I wondered if feeling this way was really the truest meaning of freedom. Even my eyes felt new and I was able to see everything so clearly. A wonderland that was so exquisite that it seemed mystical. What I had to do was take a few deep breaths, relax, and concentrate on picking up only a few things—otherwise I'd linger in Babies and Bath for all of eternity.

As I regained my composure, I walked to the middle of the store and found a shopping cart. I found a pacifier, Johnson & Johnson's baby oil gel, receiving blankets, Baby Magic lotion, a baby toothbrush, Huggies Ultratrim, Supreme, and Overnites. Along the back wall underneath a stack of baby cribs and bassinets I found a large box of Q-Tips, diaper rash cream, nursery drinking water, and a Sounds 'n Lights Monitor. I looked at my watch. It was time to hurry. On my way out, at the checkout stand, I decided to pick up a photo album, keepsake box, coin bank, and a sippy cup. The checker, a Coca-Cola-complexioned man with a gold earring pierced through his nose, reminding me of a husky black bull, rang up my purchases.

"My wife bought most our things here for little Grace. This is a wonderful store," he said, smiling and handing me my receipt.

"It's like being in dreamland." I winked at him and pushed my shopping cart out of the door.

Before I could look around, it had come time for me to go home. I locked up the office, slipped down the six flights of stairs, and reached my car, parked in the Jefferson garage across the street from the office. There was a spring to my step as if I was walking barefoot on top of cushions. I made it to my car and headed home. I could feel my insides smile, and it seemed as though my dream of a special kind of fatherhood was moving straight for me. I was longing to caress, stroke, put baby oil gel and soft powder on my baby. Why did time seem to be dragging? Had I not wanted to have a baby, it would have been spring already. I'd be rushing to San Miguel's nude beach on the coast, stalking in a revealing skimpy bikini. I'd have one orgasm piled upon the other, spent before the afternoon sunshine had a chance to warm the sand caught in the shade under the rugged mountains that hid this tiny male paradise. Here naked men frolicked casually, jogged, sunbathed, flirted, made dates, had sex with abandon on the beach.

Climbing down toward the beach from the top of a flat grassy plateau, then walking nimbly along a crooked path that is sometimes rough and exhausting. Might have to stop half the way down and catch my breath before moving on. I imagined only going to the beach during my second trimester. I couldn't risk slipping and tumbling down the path and losing my baby. I'd have to take the utmost care. I'd be living for two. My days of lying on the beach with my member slung halfway across my thigh would be no more. I'd no longer sneak a peek at the musclebound men who'd lie on towels in makeshift coves with bodies glistening with oils, tanning lotion, and sunscreen. No more would a cute Latino man stop by to chat with me and offer to rub and massage my aching muscles, then dissolve into making love the way Adam and Eve must have done out in the open at the beginning of time, shameless and proud.

It was dark and cold when I arrived home. After I parked I was set to do my daily routine, check my voice mail messages, eat a green apple, make a tossed green salad. I twisted the key in the front door and reached down to collect my shopping bags. When I opened the door and flipped on the light I had a full house!

"Surprise!" screeched a throng of party people. Yellow, lavender, green balloons, confetti, gold ribbons filled my living room and a large birthday cake with one tiny candle covered the coffee table. Stevie Wonder's song "Happy Birthday to You" blared above the laughter and the floor began to bounce underneath my feet. I looked at Chad, Ma, Nina, and my neighbor, Mitch, my best friend Naomi, her boyfriend Shorty. Then there was my friend Scott and his partner, Ricky. Cerrita and her girlfriend, Mary, sat like two lovebirds on the sofa. I was more surprised to see Mitch than I was by the birthday party. He's never visited me before. All the same, it was good to see him. Mitch was of mixed parentage. His father was Puerto Rican, his mother black. His hair, spiked, frosted blond at the crest of his forehead, made me forget that he was twenty-nine. It made him seem younger. From a distance, anybody who didn't know any better would swear up and down that Mitch was Brad Pitt's cousin.

I dropped my shopping bags to the floor. I began to feel as if I'd been caught red-handed. Chad took my coat, hung it up in the closet, bent over, and scooped up my shopping bags. I watched him start upstairs with the bags, where I hoped he'd stash them down in the nursery. One by one, everybody took turns either squeezing my neck or pumping my hand. I stood in the same spot right inside my front door and couldn't find the energy to move until I saw Shuntria sitting in a baby chair, a pacifier stuck between her little round cherry-red lips. I brushed past my guests and went over to her. I could hear a chorus of ahs as I picked her up out of the chair. To my surprise, she didn't cry! Had someone spiked her formula with a little champagne? I took her pacifier out of her mouth and set it on the small tray on her baby chair.

"Hey, little lady," I said.

"Happy birthday," she said in a tiny voice.

"Oh, sweetheart, thank you." I kissed her soft dimpled cheeks. She smelled of fresh milk and baby powder. My eyes watered, and since it was my party, I could have cried if I wanted to but I didn't. I had to set an example for Shuntria. I'd made some progress with her and my tears could frighten her and set back our relationship. I held her in my arms as if I was afraid to let her go. She was a warm badge over my heart. Everyone was dancing and I mock danced with Shuntria. After the record stopped playing, I walked over to Nina. Nancy Wilson's sultry voice engulfed the room. Nina planted a tiny kiss on my cheek and smiled. The clink of glasses, the sound of champagne being poured into flutes, and what seemed to be catered snack trays of pink shrimp, Townhouse crackers, tartar sauce, hot wings, bits of celery, tiny round tomatoes, carrots made me think that the holidays were still upon us. The rooms were filled with a low murmur of voices chattering and light but rich laughter. Skylights softened faces, made the African figurines on the mantel above the fireplace seem to come to life. I looked over at Chad and Ma, who were huddled in a corner speaking in hushed tones. Looking at them made me think they were the last two heroes of a football team strategizing before making the next big play.

"Hey, Kel!" Nina said and squeezed my neck.

"Nina, this is such a surprise, and on a Monday night. Where's Andrea?" I asked and slightly bounced Shuntria up and down.

"It's your birthday. Like Christmas, it only comes once a year. Andrea's in Denver, attending a women's conference. She'll be back home in the morning," she said, patted my shoulder, brushed past me, and joined Naomi and Shorty in the kitchen leaning against the counter talking. Her long dreads swung like horsehair behind her back. I held on to Shuntria for dear life as I walked over and sat down next to Scott and Ricky.

"What say, Godfather?" Scott said and laughed. Ricky joined in. Shuntria giggled.

I blushed.

Scott was a sexy mocha-complexion twenty-eight-year-old hotel manager. His hairless face gave me the impression that he was a recent high school grad.

"I'm feeling you guys. I haven't had a surprise birthday party since I was eight years old," I said, giving them both a high-five.

"That long huh?" Scott asked.

"Feels longer. Chad, usually takes me up to Mount Tam the weekend of my birthday and we find a camping spot."

"This time of the year?"

"Yeah."

"Wouldn't it be cold up in the mountains during the winter?" Ricky asked, his olive complexion clear and glowing. He spoke with a hint of a Spanish accent. He'd once told me that his parents named him Ricardo after Lucille Ball's ex-husband, so he decided to go only by Ricky.

"Not when you got a teddy bear for a man to keep you warm. It makes for some snuggling that's out of this world," I said as Ricky nodded, took a sip of his drink, and set it down on the coffee table. He put up his index finger, the way I've seen people do on Sundays in sanctified churches to excuse themselves during the middle of a preacher's sermon. Ricky didn't get up from his seat; he seemed to be trying to get some attention. "I was born in Cancun. I grew up learning how to survive in the heat. We didn't have a mountain as big as Mount Tam but we slept two, sometimes three to a narrow bed. Other times we slept on the floor. That's where I learned how to snuggle," he said, picked up his drink, took another sip, and put it back down.

"Tell me about it. I was born at Chariot Hospital in Sacramento with all the conveniences of medical science. All the camping we did in Sacramento took place up at Clear Lake and that was during the summer. Talk about mountains—you haven't seen so many mountains until you've been up in that country," Scott said and twirled one of Shuntria's tiny braids. She buried her head in my chest shyly. I left Scott and Ricky sitting on the sofa talking of mountains and birthplaces. As I walked I thought about where I would have my baby. Was there a special hospital for gay pregnant men? If so, what would it be called, Gay Side Hospital? Before I made it to the hallway, Ma diverted me to the stairway where she was sitting. I looked across the room and Chad was engaged in conversation with Mitch, Cerrita, and Mary. Ma held out her arms and took Shuntria from me. My arms felt empty.

"Ain't you going to eat something?" Ma asked.

"Yeah, in a bit. I had a big lunch today," I said, sitting down on a step next to her and thinking that I had to buy a child gate for the stairwell.

"Child, you got to eat."

"I will, Ma, in a little while, but right now I'm too excited to do anything but enjoy my birthday party," I said.

"Chad tells me you giving a baby shower." I've never been a Boy Scout but just the same I'd sworn never to tell a bald-faced lie to Ma, so I told her a half-truth.

"My secretary is pregnant. I might give her a baby shower," I said, hoping she wouldn't pry and we'd end up turning out the party. I looked at a pile of birthday gifts in the corner next to a gleaming fireplace. I excused myself and made it over to Cerrita and Mary, who seemed to have disengaged from Chad. Mary sat on the carpet, legs folded Indian style between Cerrita's thighs. Cerrita munched on a celery stick.

"Hey, Goddaddy," Cerrita said as I pulled up a chair next to them. Mary smiled, leaned forward, and patted my leg. As I spoke, I leaned forward, my elbows rested on my knees.

"Cerrita, did you create the catering spread going on here?"

"You got it. I kicked off the business a couple of weeks ago. I sent you an e-mail invitation for the grand opening," she said in a breezy tone. Her black hair was cut short. Cerrita and Mary were decked out in African garb.

"I got it, but I was over in San Francisco watching a great movie, *Before Night Falls,* the story about a Cuban writer, Reinaldo Arenas."

"I heard about the film."

"Chilling, when you think that the country of your birth can keep you under house arrest for the rest of your natural life."

Cerrita was raised in Bermuda. She'd often told me what it's like to suffocate on a tiny island when there's nothing but sand under your feet, wind at your back, and sea after glorious shining sea. It's not postcard picture-perfect. She described the tiny island as a tourist trap. When she came to the States as a twelve-year-old girl, she told me that it was an escape from a life of boredom standing up in a tiny booth at some beach giving directions to lost tourists. She missed her father, who sent her away to be raised by her Aunt Althea in Oakland.

"It's enough to stop the blood cold. The biggest lies are told in the most beautiful of places," she said.

I turned my thoughts to my own country. Ours is a land that is far from being picture-perfect. The farther we advance it seems to me sometimes the farther we retreat. Advance then retreat. Like an army of soldiers losing the battle but too proud to throw up the little white flag of surrender. All too often, sometimes it seems that we too easily accept the things we were born into. I brought before the party revelers some ideas.

"Let's take childbearing roles, for example. As long as we've known, a woman has had to give birth to a baby. Why can't a man do it?"

"Because he so totally don't have the tools, Kel," Mary said. She rolled her eyes.

"Put the childbearing tools inside of him so that he can do it. Let him share the joy, pain that comes with giving birth. See, that's what's wrong with the world. The world is too complacent. Too slap-happy with the status quo. Who says we've got to live the rest of our lives with outdated mores in a world created before any of us were born?" I said.

"Having a baby ain't no joke, Kel. My mother spent three days in labor with me after her water broke. The umbilical cord was wrapped around my neck. My mother died. It nearly strangled me to death," Cerrita said. It seemed as though Naomi had overheard our conversation. She came over and joined in.

"Shit. I'd love for my man to have a baby instead of me. I don't want my insides stretched longer than the highway between San Francisco and New York," Naomi laughed. Shorty joined us. "You'll never get a baby inside of me. I'm too much of a man for all of that. Check it. God put a woman on this earth to bear the fruits of child labor. And that's all there is to it."

"Hummmp, I'm a woman, not a machine. You think that because I've got a uterus that I'm supposed to crank out babies the way General Motors cranks out cars," Naomi said.

"Get the fuck outta here. What you want me to do? Have a Tar Baby?" he said. The whole room roared with laughter.

"If you man enough to make a baby then you should be man enough to have one," Naomi said.

"A real man doesn't fear the things he doesn't understand," I said. I watched Mitch's head slump down to his chest. Mitch was zonked. He had dozed off to sleep and began to snore. I realized that my final chore after the party was over was going to be taking Mitch home around the corner to his mama's house.

"Let's take a vote," Cerrita said. The music changed to Sade's CD, *Lovers Rock*. All the males were now seated in the living room. Had Mitch forfeited his right to vote because he was drunk and unconscious? I wondered if Mitch would suddenly wake up and accuse me of violating his voting rights. I didn't see Ma, Shuntria, and Nina. I wanted to give them the chance to vote. Otherwise, we'd have to do what they did so horribly in the Florida presidential election, a messy recount. After that, then we'd have to do a recount of the recounted votes. We'd end up never knowing who really won the vote.

"Wait! Everybody's not present," I said. I rushed into the kitchen and found Nina changing Shuntria's diaper and Ma standing over the oven re-covering a peach cobbler she'd made for the party. I brought Nina, Ma, and my goddaughter into the living room to vote. Ma looked at the snoring Mitch, went into a closet in the foyer, brought out a blanket, and put it snugly over his shoulders. I looked around the room and counted the potential voters. With Mitch dead to the world there were ten voters in the room. By gender, five males and five females equally divided the room. We decided to use Shuntria's vote only as a tiebreaker. It was only fair to cut up two strips of paper with yes or no written on them and place them inside of a paper bag and let Shuntria reach in and pull one of the pieces of paper out if push came to shove. I went into the kitchen and prepared the ballot bag. Chad got up from the sofa and followed me. When we were out of ear-shot, he confronted me.

"Why you doing this? Big-headed thing. It's embarrassing and it's not going to solve anything," he said. Chad bit down on a raw carrot. He began to chew.

Was I courting public opinion in my own home? If so, would this be a conflict of interest? It seemed to me, Chad felt that it might be. I went into a cabinet drawer and pulled out a pencil and small notepad to tally the votes. I wrote on two separate pieces of paper the follow-ing: *yes, a man should have a baby if he so desires* and *no, only a woman should have the ability to have a baby.*

I shook the bag up.

"Chad, do you think that voting on this issue in my own home is a conflict of interest?"

"Exactly."

"It's a game. We're only having some fun. It's my birthday. Come on. Be a good sport."

"I don't like this game," he said. He followed me back out into the living room to the throng of voters. Chad and I sat down in chairs be-tween Nina and Ma.

"How that baby going to vote? She's not even over eighteen," Shorty said. He looked at Shuntria. The room shook with laughter.

"Shorty, this is real democracy here in action. Shut up," Cerrita said, sounding official.

I took the vote.

"How many people in this house tonight believe that, yes, a man has the right to have a baby if he wants to? Let me see a show of hands," I said. I looked around the room. Five hands went up in the air. Voting in the affirmative were Scott, Naomi, Nina, Cerrita, and I. I tallied the votes on the notepad. I went on with the voting.

"How many people in this house here tonight think that, no, it's sick and wrong for a man to give birth to a baby? Again, can I see a show of hands?" I said. My heart raced. I counted the hand votes. Voting in opposition were Chad, Ma, Ricky, Mary, and Shorty. It was a tie vote! Shuntria's crucial vote was needed to break the tie. Adrenaline rushed through me as I reached down, picked the brown lunch bag up off the carpet, and showed everybody the yes and no answers in the bag so as not to let them think I had rigged the vote. I shook up the bag again. I went over to Shuntria, who was sitting in her mother's lap. I kissed her on the cheek. She giggled and kicked her fat little legs furiously.

"Shuntria, history is going to be in the palm of your little hand. Now reach down in the bag and pull out a piece of paper for God-daddy," I said. I opened the bag and held it in front of her. She put her little dimpled hand in the bag and pulled out her vote. I took her vote to everybody.

"Yes, a man should have the right to give birth if he so desires." I read her vote, setting it and the bag on the crowded coffee table.

"Bullshit! This shit is bunk! Naomi, let's raise up outta here. Kel rigged the freaking vote," Shorty said with a terse grunt.

"Sour grapes, Shorty. A new spelling of your name," I said and the winning voters laughed along with me.

"We got to cut the cake so that Kel can make a wish," Cerrita said. She winked at me.

"I'll go in the kitchen and get the utensils and plates," Chad said. Cerrita got up, slipped her arm through his, and walked with him toward the kitchen. They got back and handed out plates and utensils to everybody. When they sat back down, Chad led the chorus of

"Happy Birthday." I gently got down on my knees and blew out the candle.

"Now make a wish," Naomi said, smiling. I shut my eyes. I secretly wished that on this night in a room filled with people that made my life worth living that I would become pregnant and give birth to the most beautiful child in the world. When I opened my eyes and smiled, I saw Chad rush into the kitchen. Scott got up from the sofa and followed behind him. Moments later, they returned with a carton of Breyer's vanilla ice cream and a knife to cut the birthday cake, and passed out plates, utensils, and napkins. Scott put a scoop of vanilla ice cream on everyone's plate. We all sat down, ate our birthday cake, and listened to a Kelly Price CD, *Mirror Mirror*.

It was getting late. After all, it was Monday. Everyone who had a job to get to the next morning seemed to glance surreptitiously at my grandfather clock. Ma and Naomi gathered the plates and utensils and took them in the kitchen. Scott nodded in my direction and toward the sliding glass door that led to the patio.

The air outside was brisk. Scott lit up a cigarette.

"I think that I know where you're going with this," he said with a twinkle in his maple eyes.

"What do you mean?" I asked. I turned to look at the giant oak tree in my yard. I listened to the whoosh of wind that rustled the leaves.

"Don't be defensive with me, Kel. I'm feeling you. Why don't you come right on out with it? Why beat around the bush?" he said.

"I don't know what you're talking about," I said.

"You want a baby. Right?"

"Yeah, that's only half of the truth," I said.

"See! I knew it. It's written all over your face."

"Not a surrogate baby, Scott. I want it to come from my body."

"I don't think that it's biologically possible. I bet Chad thinks you've flipped out. I saw the bags full of baby paraphernalia when you first came through the door. I thought you'd bought the stuff for charity," Scott said. He took a drag off his cigarette and exhaled. I was surprised at his ease of acceptance.

"Chad's got one foot in the closet and the other one on dry land. Appearances mean more to him than fulfilling life's dreams," I said. I stuck my hands in the pockets of my blue jeans to warm up my cold knuckles.

"Do you think it'll happen? I mean, is it biologically possible? Do you know of all the risks?"

"All I can do is try to make it happen. I've wanted to have a baby since my would-be firstborn was aborted."

"I guess what I'm trying to say here, Kel, is have you thought this thing all the way through, that's all."

I told Scott that I was more interested than ever in making it happen with or without the support of Chad, my friends, and family. This is not some last great gay crossover assimilated dream. When I start letting the world dictate and tell me what I can do then I'm dead.

"I've made it up in my mind that I'm going to have a baby," I said to the cold air outside rather than to Scott. We were standing underneath the orange glow of the security light in my yard. Yet even under this manmade light, Scott seemed to have the look on his face of a man who was harboring the weight of secrets too heavy to bear all on his own.

"I want to have Ricky's HIV," he said. He looked down at the cement covered patio. I felt the tables turn. Scott had slammed the ball down in my court.

"What?" I asked. I waited for Scott's reply that I knew I'd never be able to accept from him. Scott's reply wouldn't make any sense to me because it's so inexplicable.

"He's the man I want to get me pregnant with AIDS."

"Why?"

"Kel, for ten years I've grown increasingly tired of carrying the burden of worrying about infection. Sometimes it feels like I'm being forced to wear a crown. Put the rubber on, it breaks. Take the HIV test and wait two depressing, agonizing weeks for the results. Is it positive or negative? The volunteer studies I've belonged to for over a decade seem to take me nowhere sometimes but to the baths and sex clubs. So that I can rack up even more numbers of men whose HIV status I know absolutely nothing about as they grope in the dark wanting a piece of me. The support groups for HIV-negative men where I sit around in a small circle like some middle-class Stepford wife, consumed with survivor's guilt, smug and bored to death with nothing to say or do. I want to die with Ricky. I don't want him to die and leave me here all alone, Kel. Do you feel me?"

It seemed to me that Scott thought that it was a foregone conclusion that he was going to get sick with AIDS sooner or later. So was he telling me why bother with taking precautions? I shook with chills.

"I'm feeling you. Does Ricky feel the same way you do?"

"At first, he was so totally against it. He thought I was patronizing him. Or poking fun at him. Now he's cool like that. He's down with me."

"What a courageous act. What a sacrifice," I said. It felt as if I was in a dream talking to myself instead of to my best friend, Scott. I looked at the wind rustling the oak tree.

"So. I don't think your idea is a harebrained one at all. Not at all."

I weighed Scott's decision in my mind. I was trying to give birth to a new life. I began to think what Scott was doing was putting his own life, maybe even Ricky's, into jeopardy.

"We are trying to do two different things. Life versus death."

"Kel, now you are being hypocritical. I thought you felt that it's important to live life the way you want to. It seems to me that you're part of the status quo. Remember the status quo you preached so fervently against in your living room a few minutes ago? Lest we forget," Scott said. He sucked his teeth and rolled his eyes.

"All I'm saying, Scott, is to be careful choosing the things you'd be willing to suffer and lay down your life for. That's all I'm saying, baby," I said. I looked in his eyes that seemed so sad. I pulled him close. We hugged, he pressed his rock-solid frame up against me. The warmth from his body, at least for a few moments, blocked off the nighttime chill in the air. We clung to each other like the only two survivors of an earthquake that devastated the whole town and we thought we'd never see each other again after this night. Wasn't I doing the same as Scott, putting my life or the life of my baby at risk? I let him go and we went back inside to join the party.

Prince's song, "I Would Die 4 U" was playing. After I saw Cerrita and Mary to the door and thanked them for coming to my house, the party started thinning out.

"Fairy tales can come true, if you only believe," Cerrita whispered in my ear and kissed me softly on my cheek.

"I believe," I said as though in prayer. I went into the closet and retrieved Cerrita's and Mary's jackets. Nina had gotten up, gathered her baby bag, buttoned down a sleeping Shuntria. She stood at the door with Ma.

"Kel, I got to get home and straighten up my house. Andrea's a neat freak," she said and gave me a tiny kiss.

"I know that's right. Ma, you and Nina need a ride home?' I asked.

"I drove. I'm taking Nina and the baby home," she said and hugged me.

Shorty nodded in my direction with a smirk on his face. He opened the front door and walked out, leaving Naomi behind. Naomi walked up to me and looked me deep in the eyes. She slung her tiny black purse with a long strap across her shoulder.

"Shorty's mad. I don't give a good goddamn. He'll get over it or hit the skids. I am not the one. Okay, I don't take his shit." Then she said, "Kel, I want you to come to church with me this Sunday."

"To your daddy's church?" I asked.

"It's our church, Kel. The church belongs to you and me. The Bible says come as you are."

"Yeah, but what does your father say? Merle Edwards, the great man of the cloth. Let me think about it. I'll call you by Saturday."

"All right," she said and planted a tiny kiss on my cheek and went outside to what she described as a ticked-off Shorty.

Chad and I gave Scott and Ricky their coats and walked them up to the door.

"Scott, thanks for sharing with me and I really enjoyed seeing you guys. It was real," I said, hugging both men. Chad followed suit. I opened the door and they disappeared into the chilly night.

"What are we going to do with Mitch?" Chad asked, standing over Mitch's snoring torso.

"Here, give me a hand. Let's take him upstairs and put him in the daybed in the guest room."

Chad and I got Mitch upstairs, came back down, and cleaned up the living room and the kitchen. I wondered if his mother would put an APB out for Mitch.

"I'm going home, Juicy Head," Chad announced, as he gave me a slight nudge on the chin and kissed my cheek.

"The birthday party was off the hook, Chad. Thanks," I said.

"Head, see how spontaneous I can be?" he said, as if he was about to beat his chest with pride.

"Yeah, I was totally surprised. Especially when I came through the door with all of those baby ensembles I bought this afternoon from Babies and Bath. Where did you put them?"

"I put them in the room next to the guest room." I breathed a sigh of relief, grateful Chad hadn't taken them upstairs and thrown them out of the window.

"What did you think I'd do? Throw the baby clothes out with the bathwater?" he said, laughing. I nodded. I wondered if he would actually. Was Chad beginning to loosen up, or become more comfortable with me having a baby? We went downstairs. He held me for a few moments, then let me go.

"Chad, stay with me tonight. I want to feel you."

"We got to go home, Honeydew Head. I have got to get up at five, and be at work in San Francisco at six. A monster's commute." I felt like someone had taken a tiny pin and poked tiny holes in my birthday balloons. Now all the air was coming out of them.

Chad let himself out.

I went upstairs and took a shower. I finished my shower, toweled off, slid between the bed covers in my birthday suit. I dozed off to sleep thinking about what this birthday celebration unfolded for me. Cerrita told me, "Fairy tales can come true if you only believe."

Chapter 6

I woke up the next morning to the mournful bleating of a foghorn off San Francisco Bay. The strong aroma of coffee coming from downstairs in the kitchen perked up my senses. I went into the bathroom, splashed my face with cold water, and brushed my teeth. I slipped on a pair of briefs. I walked to the guest room and the door was open. The daybed had been made up. Mitch was gone. After I reached the bottom step of the stairs I saw Mitch sitting at the kitchen table, topless. He sipped his coffee, looked at me, and grinned sheepishly. I walked over to him and tousled his hair.

"Good morning," he said.

"Good morning back at you," I said. I was unaccustomed to waking up with a neighbor sitting in my kitchen half-naked eating Ma's peach cobbler and drinking my coffee. I wanted to act like the gracious host but the party was over.

"Kel, I want to apologize about last night. I must have really put on one, huh?" he said.

"You went down for the count," I said. I went over and poured myself a cup of coffee.

"Thanks for putting me up last night. My shirt is in the living room. I feel sort of naked."

"No big deal. I'm not in a rush to kick you to the curb. I've got to get to work before the traffic piles up on I-eighty." Then I joked, "It's not every day I wake up in the morning with an all-American straight Latino hunk sitting at my kitchen table half naked eating me out of house and home." I laughed.

"I'm out of here," he said. Mitch did not return my banter as he scooted away from the table, walked into the living room, and put on his plaid rancher's shirt. He came back in the kitchen and leaned up against the fridge.

"Kel, would you mind if I come over to talk to you sometimes? I have some really heavy shit going down with me these days. I just need someone to listen. I've been living in that geriatric home around the corner from you taking care of my mother for ten years," he said. I didn't see any harm in a neighborly chat, so I agreed.

"Not a problem. Except these days you might be hard-pressed to find me home."

"I'll keep trying until I do," he said.

I saw Mitch to the door and locked it as he walked outside. I clicked off the coffeemaker, rinsed, then put the cups in the dishwasher. I went back upstairs to my bedroom and got ready for work.

Amy was back to work after being out sick. She still looked somewhat peaked, especially with dark circles around her eyes. She barely looked up when I came through the door and greeted her with a chipper good morning. She put her head down on the desk and cradled it between her arms.

I went into my office, remembering what Ma told me happened with her when she got pregnant with me. Besides morning sickness, she suddenly developed a fierce dislike for milk. It didn't matter what kind of milk, powdered, vitamin A, B, C, D, nonfat, skim, or low fat. She told me that thoughts of drinking milk made her nauseous, gave her cramps, and made her vomit. She'd cry sometimes three times a day after looking at her swelling belly. During her first trimester my father would measure the roundness and fullness of her stomach, twice a week. He stopped when he couldn't take her weeping any longer. He bought her a journal at the beginning of her second trimester and her tears wet the pages until they began to look like they'd been accidentally placed in the washing machine with dirty laundry. The black ink from her pen and her tears had smeared the pages so that most of her writing looked like hieroglyphics. Ma said she cried so much during her pregnancy that my father left her for a month. When they got back together, she cried because he'd left her, and cried because he'd come back to her. She cried every time she thought about losing him forever to a woman with a slim waistline, a flat stomach, who craved and drank milk by the gallons. Cried when she'd worry about having to join the long line of single welfare mothers pushing babies in strollers with Daddy nowhere on earth to be found.

She told me that when I was born my faint little wails and screams were like music to my father's ears. He knew what to do so I'd stop crying. I either needed to have my diaper changed; or I was hungry and wanted to be fed; or I wanted to be held and cuddled or spoken to. She said I'd kick my tiny feet. Coo. The dimples in my little cheeks made her think about the sheer wonder of life, of creation. My father didn't know how in the world to stop Ma's weeping and wailing. When Ma's water broke she went into labor. For sixteen hours she never once shed a single tear. Her eyes were Mojave Desert dry.

Amy walked into my office and sat down in a chair.

"Kel, I can't eat anything. Everything I eat comes back up," she said. Amy's head cocked slightly to the side. Amy had been in the United States since she was twelve but still had a heavy Philippine accent. She spoke English only outside of the doors of the home she shared with her husband, six brothers, an elderly father, and another married sibling.

"Have you discussed this with your doctor?" I asked. I tried not to sound like a family counselor.

"Yeah. She told me some women have morning sickness so bad until they can't eat food."

"If you can't eat then how is the baby going to grow?"

"I know, that's what I told her," she said. A worried expression washed over her round face.

"What about the foods you like best?"

"Won't stay down. I bring it back up."

"Do fruits and liquids do the same thing?"

"Uh huh."

"Jeez. Can you drink milk?"

"No," she said.

Then my telephone rang. It made me feel like I was a prizefighter on the ropes. The bell had saved me because I was about to ask Amy if she cried a lot. Did her husband give her a journal? Did her tears turn the words in the journal into hieroglyphics?

"Amy, excuse me. We'll talk in a bit."

Amy got up from the chair and slowly walked out.

I picked up the telephone.

"Hello. This is Helga from Doctor Valesco's office reminding you to complete and bring your consent form during your appointment this Friday."

"The one you sent along with Dr. Valesco's curriculum vitae?"

"That's the one," she said. I could feel a smile in her voice.

I hung up.

I found the form that had been put into my overstuffed briefcase, and began to read it over. It was standard, simple enough. I was pleased that the program footed the costs for diagnostic exams, donor tests, blood tests, implants, and the two-day admittance to the hospital to give birth and brief period of convalescence. I finished reading half of the form and tucked it away in my briefcase. A chill went through me. I went over to the water cooler, poured myself a cup of water, and gulped it down. I walked past Amy, and a series of what-if questions began to swirl around in my head. What if I go through trying to have a baby and it doesn't work? What if the procedure is successful and I get pregnant? Am I going to reject milk, cry (not to say I already don't) like a baby? Turn my own journal into a mass of hieroglyphics from all of my tears? Will I be unable to hold down my food? Get nauseous and have to keep my head rested and cradled in my arms all day at work? Will Chad have me committed as a mental patient at the Center for Gender Disorders in San Francisco? Would I worry about losing my twenty-nine-inch waistline? Would Chad leave me because I'd grown fat and dowdy? What would happen to all of my poor baby ensembles? Give them to the Goodwill, the Salvation Army, to Naomi's church? Enshrine them, making a permanent baby room in my house where I can go and think myself into pregnancy? I sank down in my chair. I sighed.

"Kel, I go home. I'm sick. I'll call you tomorrow, all right?" Amy said. She already had on her coat with a backpack slung over her shoulder.

"Hope you feel better, Amy," I said to her back as she opened the door and trudged out of the office. I turned my attention toward getting some paperwork done. I finished the paperwork and locked up the office. By the time I was done, the nighttime skies were starless raspberry black. Thousands of orange lights lit up the East Bay hills like tiny candles blowing in the wind. The temperatures hovered somewhere in the high forties. The wind was brisk and cold enough to make you walk faster than usual, or wonder why you hadn't put on thermals and a turtleneck shirt.

I pulled up in front of my house, grabbed my briefcase, and climbed out of the car. Across the street, there was Mitch sitting behind the wheel of his car. The motor hummed, and smoke jetted out from the exhaust pipes. He turned and looked at me. I nodded and waved at him. He put up his hand, motioned me over. I walked over to his car. I should have ignored Mitch, walked into my house, double locked the doors. Yet I was curious.

"Hey, Kel. You got a few minutes?" he asked.

"Sure. What's up?" I asked and set my briefcase down at my feet.

He sat in the car smoking a cigarette. He was wearing the same plaid shirt he wore at my birthday party and faded blue jeans. His speech was slurred. Mitch was drunk. He sat his cigarette down in the ashtray and he grabbed the steering wheel. His knuckles were white.

"Oh, man. I feel so fucked up. My girlfriend just left me," he said. Mitch told me that he'd lost two jobs in one year and got busted with a DUI. He was fired from one of the jobs for showing up at work drunk. He was under investigation by the DA for unemployment insurance fraud. Mitch threatened suicide. "You got a gun?" he asked. His head bobbed halfway between the seat and the steering wheel. He picked up his cigarette from the ashtray, took a puff, and blew smoke out of his window that smelled of tobacco and beer.

"Mitch, I suggest you go home and take a shower. It'll clear your head. It's just your emotions getting the best of you right now," I said. I picked up my briefcase off the ground. The cold air made my lips dry and chapped.

"Man, I just need someone to talk to. Can I talk to you, man?" He wept.

"Well, yeah, Mitch, but not right now. Maybe later. I've got to get inside my house. We can talk later when you've sobered up," I said. I turned, walked back across the street, and entered my house through the garage.

As I clicked the button and listened to the garage door come down, I thought about how long I'd known Mitch. I pieced together what he'd told me during casual conversations over the past five years that we had been neighbors. We'd wave at each other in a neighborly way and share yard and gardening tips. I hadn't seen Mitch too much after I moved around the corner from him about two years ago. He'd keep in contact, dropping by every once in a great while to talk about garden ideas. Recently, he bought a car and told me that he rarely tended his mother's garden, the way he once did. He told me that his mother, Rita, had picked up where he'd left off. I would see her in her yard supervising Mitch's gardening work, her movements slow yet deliberate. She wore a wide straw hat pulled over a shock of brilliant white hair. Rita was very old. Her face had lifelines that reminded me of a road map that went in thousands of directions all at once. Mitch had told me that he'd lived in the same green box-shaped ranch-style house since he was a two-year-old boy. He was the eldest of two children. His sister, Consuela, lived in Denver with her husband, Nick, and a German shepherd they called Moon. Mitch moved back with his mother, after the Oakland Hills fire made his tiny apartment in Oakland uninhabitable. His father had died one year after Mitch returned home.

After eating leftovers from the party, I went upstairs to my bedroom, disrobed, and took a warm shower. I stepped out of the shower and dried off. I sat on the foot of my bed buck naked and rubbed lotion all over my body. I wished that Chad were there, to rub the lotion on my back. I thought about calling and inviting him over; then just as quickly thought against it. I looked at my flat stomach. How round would it be when a baby set up residence? Would I have stretch marks like Atlas warned? Would my muscular chest grow into breasts bigger than any Dolly Parton ever imagined, making it necessary for me to undergo breast reduction surgery? My nipples perked up, grew hard at the thought. My loins felt the chill of death.

I got up from the bed, found a pair of boxers Chad had given me last Valentine's Day and slipped them on. I stared at my briefcase leaning up against the wall across from my bed. Instinctively I went over, picked it up, and took out the half-finished consent form sent to me by Dr. Valesco's office. I looked it over this time, carefully. There was an indemnity clause. I could not be involved in any other program or similar study sponsored for the purposes of male impregnation. I could not bring civil damages for any temporary or permanent injuries suffered as a result of the experiment. My survivors could bring civil charges, should the program result in my death because of medical malpractice. My child, should the program result in my successful pregnancy and birth, would be my sole parental responsibility. I had to agree to become a poster boy of sorts for other researchers involved with the program should my participation result in the birth of a healthy child. Should the project result in my pregnancy, I had to forswear interviews with the news media and the television and film industries. The program would own the rights to my story from beginning to end. I could, if I chose to do so after the child was born, accept invitations for interviews from any source. I would seek no monetary reward. My payment would be in the form of giving the world its first black pregnant male to give birth to a child, then live to talk about it. Something inside of me pulled back a little. The guidelines seemed so severe, so strict, and so narrow. Had I misread the consent form? Had paranoia slithered into my consciousness? Had study participant remorse come to set up permanent residence in my mind? What was I getting myself into? I signed the application, feeling torn between a sense of joy and concern. I put the consent form back in my briefcase, reached over to the lamp on my nightstand, and clicked off the light. I drifted off to sleep.

The doorbell woke me up. I looked at the red digital clock on my dresser. It was 1:30 a.m. I couldn't imagine who would be paying me a visit at that time of morning. What was so important that it couldn't wait until the next day? I went down the stairs, flipped on the light in the foyer, then on the porch, and looked through the peephole in my front door. It was Mitch. He was leaning up against my house, hands tucked in his pockets. I opened the door and the cold wind flew inside.

"Mitch? What's up? Don't you know what time it is?"

"I'm sorry, man. I need someone to talk to. You told me I could talk to you."

"Yeah, but not before day in the morning," I said as a wave of sympathy washed over me. I relented and reluctantly let him in. He stood in the foyer as drunk as a Dean Martin character in a feature film. I took his elbow and led him to the bottom step of the stairs where he sat down. I went to the kitchen and began to run some water for coffee.

"Would you like some coffee, Mitch?" I yelled from the kitchen.

"It'll only make it worse," I could hear him say in the distance.

I turned off the faucet, and went back and sat down on the stairs next to him. Mitch was looking down at the carpet. Then I said, "Mitch, I'm going upstairs to get dressed so I can take you back home, to Rita."

"My girlfriend, man, she did it. She made me lose my job. That whore! I need somebody to hug, man. Can I hug you?" he said. He put his callused, cold hands around my shoulder. I hugged and patted his back as if he were a child who'd fallen down off a bike and scraped his elbow. You want to reassure him that it's all right to fall down sometimes but you must always pick yourself back up. Mitch went on with his spiel.

"We were together for a year. Met her one Sunday at the Lutheran church after services in the community room. She was a big woman, man. She has long brown hair and big tits. I like tits, man. Do you like tits? She's got a five-year-old daughter, Chelsa, who thinks the world of me, man. I take her to Great America, to Marine World. To the Disney Store up at the mall and you know what? She fucking thinks that I'm her dad, man. I swear to God. I never was able to have a child. Doctors say my sperm is shot to shit, man. Chelsa, she's like my own little girl. I bought her a fucking Ken and Barbie doll last Christmas, man. That's what she asked me to buy for her. I filled her stocking with all kinds of shit, man. Her mom is a whore. I saw her tonight, man, sitting in this dude's car, man. You know what she did? Went down on him and sucked his fucking cock, man," he said, and began weeping. He regained his composure and looked at me forlornly.

"Are you gay?" he asked and sniffled.

"No, are you?" I laughed. I looked down at the carpet.

"How can you be gay and work for the FBI?"

"Mitch, I don't work for the FBI."

"Well, you carry a gun, don't you?"

"Yeah, some private investigators carry guns for security and protection. Mitch, don't you remember what I told you years ago? I'm a private investigator under contract to provide investigative services for various insurance companies."

"Oh man, you did. I'm just fucked up."

"Mitch, have you ever had sex with another man?" I asked. I was curious, not interested.

"Yeah."

"Really. Go on," I said.

"I was sixteen years old and he was my football coach. That's when my parents sent me to live with my Aunt Rose in Miami. He would take me after practice to his second home in a little house that sat right on the beach. We'd spend hours sitting at the beach watching the waves, seagulls, and the sunset behind the ocean. He didn't hurt me. What hurt me is when his wife found out about us and divorced him. He changed, stopped coming to school to teach physical education. He disappeared like a fugitive on the run. Why couldn't I have learned from him?"

I patted his knee. He turned, hugged me, and sobbed in my chest. His warm tears ran down my shoulder. Mitch began to caress and massage the nape of my neck and shoulders. I felt my member grow and lengthen each time he groped me. I tried to think about the consent form I had to turn in, during my appointment at Dr. Valesco's office on Friday; or about Atlas, and whether or not I'd make it back to see him before it was too late. I thought about all the wonderful baby ensembles in my nursery. By the time I decided which thought to concentrate on to divert and stem the rising tide between my legs, he had my manhood in his warm mouth. I was caught between my ecstasy, guilt, and the ferocious agony of Mitch's hunger, his cry for help. Like a soldier assigned to guard a duty post, I left the gate open for someone to come in and touch me. Hold me and release the pas-

sions that only those who are not afraid of truly living can feel. A pang
of guilt bubbled up inside of me, and I gently pushed his head away.

"What's wrong? Don't you like it?" he said as he brushed his hair
back with his hand and then pushed my arms down to get back at me
again.

"Mitch, this isn't right. You are drunk and don't know what's going on. Besides, you are my friend and a straight man. This is going to
throw a monkey wrench in our relationship," I said, pulling up my
boxers. My member was still throbbing, half-erect.

"Don't you want to fuck my ass, man?" he said and yanked a rubber out of his jacket, tore it open.

"Mitch, this is not going to work out," I said. I got up from the
stairs and walked in the living room to turn on the light. Before I
could reach the lamp, Mitch jumped up on my back and we tumbled
to the carpet. It became a wrestling match. The smell of his sweat
made me erect again. We tossed and turned. We grunted, strained
against each other. He held me down and I flipped him over, reversed
roles. It went on like that for more than half an hour. I lay on my back
spent, naked. My erection was stiff and as hard as Bethlehem steel.

He unbuckled his belt and took off his jeans. Mitch's penis was
hard and small. He rolled the rubber on me.

Mitch sat down on me and bucked like a pony. I wanted to push
him off of me. It was too late.

"So this is what you want, huh? All these years! Watching me!
Waiting! I figured as much! Well, man, I'm going to let you have it
once! Then I want you to stay the fuck away from me! I mean that!" I
said. I stood up with Mitch straddling me on the stairs. I took him to
the kitchen and propped him up on the kitchen counter, the floor and
the kitchen table. I took him into the living room and he bent over the
sofa where I rode him like a man who just discovered the joy of sex. I
thrust my member in and out of Mitch with a lust that shamed and
delighted me.

My soul was unable to command my body to stop. I was a body and
soul. Had I discovered two warring competitors in one dark body?
Body and soul, the equivalency of flesh and spirit had disconnected
from each other, gone their separate but unequal ways. In pitch-black

darkness, Mitch's tight buttocks clapped against my thighs joyfully. I imagined Mitch as a construction worker who had slid down a long pole. Not finding a bottom, he kept descending. Down, into the rich black earth. After two hours of fucking and three orgasms, Mitch spurted his warm juice on my chest. As his movements slowed I galloped like a black stallion to the finish line and came for the fourth and last time.

I shoved him off of me.

"Get out of here, Mitch. Go home. You got what you came here to get. Now leave," I said, as I got up from the carpet and walked into the kitchen, tossed the rubber in the trash, and grabbed a paper towel, wiping his juice from my chest. I walked back into the living room and clicked on a lamp. Mitch went over and sat catty-corner on the cold gray leather sofa. He began to flick his nipples. I went and stood over him, wanting all of this to be done and over with.

"You're wonderful," he said. He half smiled as a tear rolled down the middle of his cheek.

"Come on, Mitch. I told you that it's time for you to go home now," I said. I went and picked up his clothes off of the carpet and handed them to him.

"We're lovers," he said. He stood up, pulled on his briefs, jeans, shirt, and jacket.

"Correction. We had sex, Mitch. Chad is my lover."

"You black bastard!" he said. He took his fist, swung at me, and missed.

"Don't even think about it, Mitch." I charged and grabbed him by the neck. I brought my balled fist down like a hammer but I didn't hit him. I began to choke him. We were eye to eye.

"I can't breathe! Kel, you're killing me, man! Let go!" Mitch gagged and struggled to break free.

"I should kill your goddamn ass!" I said.

Breathing hard, my heartbeat quickened. Then it came to me. I had a chokehold, not so much on Mitch, but a man who was lost. Lost, like I found myself when I'd wandered through the narrow corridors and cubbyholes at the sex clubs. It was the liquor; the loss of his job, the loss of his girlfriend, the loss of his Oakland apartment years ago and the loss of his virginity at sixteen, to a married man at a Florida beach house, that made him curse me. Mitch was adept and nothing about our escapade appeared to suggest that it had been a dress rehearsal for a virgin. Was this his way of striking back at me? Was he taking revenge on me, for rejecting his invitations over the years to join him at his house during the football season to watch "Monday Night Football"; or was it a secret desire five years in the making that had now bubbled up like hot lava uncontrollable in its terror? Had he masturbated on his little cot in a small room at the back of his mother's house thinking about how and when he'd seduce me? Did he hide surreptitiously at night behind the tall hedges in his mother's front yard, videotape and watch my boyfriends slip into my house right under Chad's nose? Did he believe that now it was his turn to bow down between my thighs? I didn't punk out. Hitting Mitch would not have been cathartic for me. Neither would it have been fair play, since he was drunk and maybe not fully aware of his brazen and reckless proclivities. To smack him down would've been akin to pushing a blind man out into vehicular traffic, hitting a man when he's down, spitting on the grave of the only person in the world who ever really cared about you in life. Where would I have ended up? In jail; sitting behind a long steel table in a cold room, with a two-way mirror interrogated by two baby-faced rookie cops for weeks before being afforded counsel; convicted of assault and battery, on someone who spent years talking to me about gardening tips and soil fertilization. When I gave birth, I wondered if Mitch would volunteer to take my own child to Disneyland.

"Look, you don't want to fuck with me, Mitch," I said. I let go of his neck. I led him to my front door, opened it, shoved him out of it.

I shut the door.

"You fucked me!" he yelled at my door. I opened the door. He turned and walked away.

"Go home, Mitch, to your mother. Get some help!" I said. I shut the door and went upstairs trying to make sense of what had happened. I went into my bathroom and took a shower. I soaped up, scrubbed Mitch's sperm off of my chest; rinsed, but nothing could wash away the utter regret I felt. When I got out of the shower and began to towel off, I feared for Mitch's safety. My conscience began to bother me. Had my escapade with Mitch pushed him over the brink of suicide? I climbed beneath the sheets on my bed and watched the red light on the digital clock on my dresser pass away the hour. I couldn't find my sleep. I hopped up and quickly got dressed.

I drove by Mitch's house and spotted his car parked in the driveway of his mother's house. I turned around and went back home. I groped through my dark house, found my bed. It was over. I should have never let Mitch come in my house. I remembered Dr. Ashley's comments about Dr. Valesco. "He's a fine doctor. One of the best in the business." I had to see this doctor, this man of all work in a few days about having a baby, I thought, as I finally drifted off to sleep.

Chapter 7

Dr. Valesco's office was on the thirty-second floor of a high rise, across the street from the Hyatt Regency, at the foot of Market Street. I had taken an elevator that shot me up to his floor nearly as quick as lightning. The rush made me feel as though I'd left something behind. I entered the lobby, found a sign-in sheet, and scribbled my name, date, and time of arrival. I was the only patient waiting in the lobby to be seen. I sat on a sofa next to a magazine stand stuffed with pamphlets, medical journals, and periodicals all having to do with pregnancy and prenatal care. I finished reading the consent form. I could see the bobbing red head of a woman who sat behind a smoked-glass window. She was on the phone, then hung up and slid the window open. She looked at me, smiled, and fingered the sign-in sheet.

"Are you Mr. Kelvin Warren?" she asked. A small fan whirred above her head. She was wearing a white lab coat.

"Yes, I'm Kelvin Warren. You can call me Kel. I'm somewhat early for my appointment but I don't mind waiting until it's time for me to see Dr. Valesco," I said. I got up from the sofa, forced a smile, and tried not to look or sound as anxious and nervous as I felt. I walked up to the counter. I looked at the name tag pinned on her lab coat. Helga Bosner, nursing assistant. So she was Helga. Helga Bosner, the one I'd made my appointment with, who sent me the informed consent form.

"Fine. Dr. Valesco will be with you shortly, Kel. Meanwhile, did you bring your completed consent form for research?" she said.

"Sure," I said and fished through my briefcase, yanked it out, and handed to her.

"Great. Now if you don't mind, Dr. Valesco would like you to complete this medical questionnaire," she said, taking the consent form from me and handing me a pen and a two-page questionnaire stuck to a clipboard.

"Thanks, I'll get this done right away and give it back to you," I said.

"We've still got some time yet before Dr. Valesco is ready to see you. So please don't rush through it. This is the most tedious but important part of the process," she said, yanking a thin tissue from a box of Kleenex on her desk and dabbing it at the corners of her flaming red mouth. I went back and sat down on the sofa to complete the form.

The questionnaire was comprehensive. After reading through it, I decided its purpose was to find out if I was a suitable candidate. I was no novice when it came to doctors and examinations. When I was in the trenches suffering from a mysterious illness last year, I'd become a human guinea pig and pin cushion. What man hadn't at least heard about the pain of childbirth, the labor, the misery, and the worry some women had about bringing the life inside of them to the eyes of the world?

I finished the questionnaire, then watched the nursing assistant through the smoked-glass window get up from her chair. She disappeared out of my view. I picked up an eight-year-old issue of *People* magazine. On the cover of the magazine was a grinning barefoot and pregnant Arnold Schwarzenegger promoting his movie *Junior*. When I sat back on the sofa and cracked the magazine open to read the movie ad, I looked up and Helga was standing at the door that led into the examination rooms.

"Kel?"

"Yes," I said, and set the magazine down on top of the table in front of the sofa.

"Dr. Valesco will see you now. Please come this way," she said, stepping to the side before letting me through the door. She took the questionnaire and stuffed it inside of a thick medical chart that she held between the crease of her arm and chest the way a secretary holds a legal notepad on the way to a conference board meeting. She led me down a long hallway with small rooms along each side. I walked as if I was already going to see my doctor and get the results of a pregnancy test. We stopped halfway down the hall and walked around a short corner. The room had a window that looked out on the San Francisco Bay Bridge and Treasure Island.

"Strip to your waist and hang your clothes on the rack over in the corner. Dr. Valesco will be in to see you in a few moments," she said, and went over and opened a drawer under a sink and took out a thin cotton dressing gown that had three sets of strings that tied from the back.

"Here, put this on. It gets a bit chilly in here these days. We are still under a Stage Three energy alert. Like everyone else we've been asked to conserve energy. Luckily, hospitals and doctor's offices won't have to suffer the rolling blackouts. Dr. Valesco wants a sperm sample, urine, and blood test done." She went over to the sink and picked up two little plastic containers the size of Vaseline jars. Then she said, "Let the first stream go, then fill this one up to here." She pointed to the line halfway up the container and set it back on the top of the sink. "We need your sperm to go in this other container here. Then when you are done, bring both samples back into the examination room and set them up here. We'll do your blood draws before we're done. The blood draw nurse will come in a little later. Have fun," she said, patting the top of the sink.

"Where are the rest rooms?" I asked.

"Oh, right across the hall. You can't miss it," she said. She winked at me.

"Thanks," I said, as I watched her walk out of the door and pull it closed. I quickly got undressed and slipped on the gown. I went over and got the containers, opened the door and went to the rest room, and peed in a little plastic container. I dropped my boxers, sat down on the toilet, and fantasized about Dr. Valesco to get an erection. I imagined that he came into the room to examine me and all he had on was a white smock and a stethoscope. He was about my age, only an inch or two shorter, with no facial hair. His body was cut almost to perfection. His chest was firm with smooth black hair that gathered from his navel like a stream of black ants. As I lay on my back, he opened his smock and began to feel my abdomen, and my dick got hard and throbbed uncontrollably. He took my member in his warm mouth and swallowed me whole. I writhed and moaned. After a few moments, he stopped and pulled out a rubber and broke it open with his white-as-toothpaste teeth. He hoisted me further back up the examination bed, and my dick broke through millions of hairs outside of his ass and found its way to glory. Dr. Valesco beat my chest as he came and shot his warm liquid that looked like thick lines of white string across my chest. When I came in the container, my fantasy had come to an end. I cleaned myself up.

I didn't think that Dr. Valesco was dragging his feet about getting in to see me. Being a patient means having patience, realizing that you are not the only one a doctor has to practice medicine on. A doctor can work only so many hours in a day. Some doctors would like to think of themselves as God, to be everywhere all the time, but most of them are nowhere around when you really need them for something.

A tall, clean-shaved man with a high forehead entered the room. His hair was a little bushy, gray at the temples. It came down to his forehead in the shape of a V. He had the same kind of biracial olive-colored complexion as my first cousin, Tasha. Tasha's mom, Susan, is white and her dead father, Sonny, my uncle, was black. Of course, appearances mean absolutely nothing in the scheme of things. Whether or not we want to be, we're a sometimes-reluctant melting pot that's making it nearly impossible to handcuff people and throw them into narrowly defined racially and sexually cramped categories.

"Kel, I'm Dr. Valesco. How's it going?" he said. He sounded hoarse. He grinned, reached out, and pumped my hand.

"I'm doing all right."

"Oh, I see the little vampires have made their way to you, judging by the look of things," he said as he held in his hands what appeared to be my medical chart and walked over to me. I studied his face. It's interesting when you anticipate meeting someone you've never met before, because they never look or seem to be what you imagine. Dr. Valesco wore a gold band on his left ring finger, suggesting that he was either married or in a long-term relationship.

"I've looked over your chart. It includes the recent test results of your blood work at Mercy Hospital. Everything looks good. All of your tests are negative, particularly HIV. Before I make a preliminary decision, there are a couple of minor questions I'd like to go over with you. Do you mind?"

"Not at all."

"Are you allergic to any medication?"

"No."

"I see here in your chart that you were taking a thousand milligrams of fluconazole on a daily basis last year. Are you still taking it?"

"No," I said, as a feeling of triumph washed over me. I felt that I'd overcome my mysterious illness last year.

"Why were you taking fluconazole?" he asked.

"I was misdiagnosed with valley fever," I said.

"Did your doctor ever determine the nature of your illness?" he asked.

"Not to this day."

"How are you feeling now?"

"Like a million bucks."

"It says here on your questionnaire that you are in a long-term relationship," he said and flipped through my answers on the questionnaire.

"We just don't live together by choice."

"Interesting. How does he feel about your decision to have a child?"

"He's against it and thinks it's a foolish and dangerous idea."

"It says here that you are thirty years old. Is this correct?"

"Yes."

"You go to the gym?"

"I try to when I can find the time to go."

"Do you smoke cigarettes or use any recreational drugs? Cocaine, uppers or downers?"

"No."

"Never?"

"Never in my life."

"It says here that you are a law enforcement officer. Who do you work for? What do you do?"

"I'm privately contracted to do investigations for insurance companies."

"So does this mean that you are self-employed?"

"That's right. I'm self-employed. I pick and choose the companies I want to work for and cases I agree to handle."

"How do you feel about taking further medication?"

"I'm scared as hell."

"Of what?"

"I once worried that the medication I was taking may have caused some internal damage, but not anymore. I feel like I'm in good shape."

"Do you have any issues surrounding infertility?"

"No."

"So you gave me a good sample of sperm?"

"It was one of the best orgasms I ever had," I said. I blushed and looked away from him to suppress my laughter.

"Ever thought about adoption, the Big Brother program, fertility or surrogate programs?"

"Sure," I said. I heard someone knock on the door.

"Come in," he said.

"Excuse me for interrupting you, Dr. Valesco, but I need to see you for a few moments," Helga said.

"Excuse me for a moment, Kel. I'll be right back," he said. Dr. Valesco followed Helga out of the room.

I leaned over and picked up a magazine called *Fertility* from a small stand. I flipped through the pages and stopped halfway through when I saw a young black woman who looked like my childhood sweetheart, Cookie. When her mother, Leona, would go to work at Wal-Mart every morning, I'd sneak into Cookie's house by climbing through Cookie's bedroom window. First we'd play house, then doctor, graduating to spin the bottle. Winter was in full swing when I started having sex with Cookie. Cookie's period stopped cold by the end of March. By the time all the blooms on the pear trees in my back yard turned to ripe green pears in June, Cookie was three months pregnant with our baby.

We never got totally naked because we were both afraid of getting caught "doing the nasty," as we called sex before we knew it by any other name. We just knew that doing the nasty made us feel good, and if you got caught doing the nasty it could get you into a whole lot of trouble. I'd take off my pants, socks, and shoes. Cookie would take off her panties and pull her dress up to her nipples that looked like tiny acorns. I'd rub my hard dick across pubic hair so straight that it looked like it belonged on the head of a doll.

Her mother, Leona, took her to get an abortion. After the abortion, it wasn't that I knew I'd never love or need anyone that way again. I accepted that and went on. What I was unable to accept, though, is the way I felt after she aborted the child. I felt so left behind, with a heart broken into so many tiny pieces that for the next year, I had trouble breathing. After that warm summer day when Cookie had the abortion, I didn't eat anything for weeks. Crying about it did nothing but make me feel like I'd been robbed of my manhood. I kept stumbling, falling, tripping all over myself. I had to keep getting right on back up.

Right after the baby was aborted, when summer was still in its infancy, a thin milky-white substance began to ooze from my nipples and didn't stop until school began in the fall. Before school began, I went to Evergreen Holy Tabernacle Church to talk with Naomi's father, Reverend Edwards, to ask him why God took my baby. Reverend Edwards told me that God never gives us more than we can stand. I remember telling Reverend Edwards that one of these days I'd have my own baby, before I stormed out of the church. Look at me today. I'm not sitting in the crushed velvet pews at the front of Evergreen Holy Tabernacle Church. I'm propped up on a semihard examination table in a strange doctor's office, a man trying to get pregnant because a young girl I once loved killed my would-be firstborn. I prayed. Mercy Lord. Have mercy on my tortured soul.

I heard someone knock on the door. I set the magazine back down on the stand.

"Come in," I said. Dr. Valesco came into the room and picked up where he had left off.

"Sorry about the interruption. Now where were we? Oh, yes. I was asking you about your involvement or consideration of other reproduction programs."

"I've never been involved in any of those programs. My partner, Chad, and I have considered using a surrogate mother."

"What do you think about that program?"

"I'm concerned about legal issues, not ethical ones. A mother can make a claim to joint parental rights. That would be messy."

"Do you have any biological children?"

"Not living."

"You lost a child, Kel?"

"Yes."

"How old were you then?"

"Fourteen."

"How old was your girlfriend?"

"Twelve."

"Twelve years old?"

"She was three months pregnant when she had the abortion. After she had the abortion, my nipples began to run with some thin milky stuff. "

"Interesting," he said as I watched his eyebrows come together. He seemed to be taking notes, jotting down my responses in a chart.

"Well, I was pissed off. I'm not interested in having another woman carry my baby in her womb. Not this time. I can't risk taking that chance. This time I want to do it myself."

"Are you familiar with a hormone called prolactin?"

"I can't say that I am. What does this have to do with me?"

"Well, it explains why you developed breast milk after the abortion. Prolactin is a hormone that women secrete to produce breast milk."

"But Cookie was the one having the baby. Why would I be the one to develop breast milk?"

"One theory is that you have a higher than usual level of prolactin in your bloodstream. So when conception occurred with your mate, your body did what a nursing mother would have done and that is produce breast milk. A reversal of sorts."

"I see."

"Apart from that, have you considered adoption, the Big Brother program, fertilization and surrogate programs? These are not inferior choices, Kel. Do any of these programs appeal to you?"

I never told Dr. Valesco that I thought these other programs he mentioned were inferior. They simply were not one of my choices. Was he trying to tell me in a polite sort of way that I wasn't a suitable candidate for his program?

"If you don't think I qualify for the project, tell me now and I'll get the hell up out of here. Find someone who is interested in working with me. Don't bullshit me." The silence between us felt awkward.

I looked past him and out of the window across the bay at the green grass and the eucalyptus trees on the slopes of Treasure Island. A ferryboat sailed upon the bay with a swirl of water that followed behind it like a long fishtail. I turned and looked at the wall next to the sink. There it was, a diagram showing the growth of an embryo from conception to birth. It was the first time I'd ever seen how developed my aborted child looked, and it made me realize that Ma hadn't told me every bit of the truth. She told me at the hospital after they pumped three bottles of aspirin from my stomach, "Kel, that wasn't a baby Cookie was carrying. Child, that was nothing but a clump of blood. Let's go home." Was Ma trying to spare me further humiliation?

Dr. Valesco stuck his stethoscope in his ears and listened to my breathing and lung ventilation. He took the stethoscope out of his ears. Then he said, "Lie back as far as you can on your back."

He pulled out the extra length at the end of the bed for me to rest my legs on. He then began to squeeze down on my abdominal muscles. His hands were warm and gentle. I was glad I wasn't attracted to Dr. Valesco, otherwise I'd be fighting off an erection.

"Does that hurt?"

"No."

"How about here. Does this hurt?" he said, massaging under my ribcage.

"No."

Dr. Valesco examined the two scars on my shoulder and the one under the nape of my neck where a surgeon biopsied half a swollen lymph node.

"Battle scars from your illness last year?" he asked.

"Yes," I said as he took his finger and drew a line under my navel.

"This is where we'll make the incision when you have your caesarean. Your baby will have to be surgically removed. You'll have another battle scar. Does that bother you?"

"My great-great-grandfather was a Cherokee and he had battle scars all over his body. So I think I'm long overdue to pick up where he left off," I said.

"Nice analogy. You can sit up now." I sat up like a man waiting for his doctor to give him a clean bill of health.

"I can tell you that based on my exam of you this morning and the test results, I've decided to allow you to be a participant in our program. Have you read our policy about research-related injuries? The risks involved in your participation and the background and purpose of this program? Kel, I want to be straight with you. This is not going to be easy. Probably even more dangerous since you were recently ill and never diagnosed with a confirmed malady," he said.

"I've got some materials, but if there is more I'd like to get that too."

"Have you considered or selected a suitable female to donate the mature egg?"

"I have someone in mind. Only we haven't talked it over yet. Will it cost her to donate the egg?"

"No. We handle all of the costs. But make that decision within two weeks because you are, after all, thirty years old and your biological clock is ticking," he said, laughing and putting me at ease. Then he said, "Do you have any questions or concerns, Kel?"

"Some."

"Go ahead, please."

"Well, I mean, I know this isn't going to cost me anything. What I want to know is that without going into any long, drawn-out details, how is it going to work? What I mean is, how does the basic procedure work?"

"The practice is standard for all male pregnancy programs. The first stage is in vitro fertilization. If your latest blood work is good and your sperm is fertile it will be mixed with the donated egg and fertilized outside of the female donor's uterus in a test tube, and that will complete the initial phase. Then I will surgically implant an organic artificial uterus and uterine lining made from live tissue in a laboratory and not manufactured out of nontissue material. The artificial uterus will be placed on your pelvic floor. The placenta will form inside the uterus when a specialized part of the fertilized egg, called the trophoblast, embeds the wall of the artificial uterus. Kel, at the end of twelve weeks the placenta where your child will grow becomes a separate organ. One of the sticky side effects during male pregnancy is the near or in some cases total loss of facial and pubic hair. We are working to correct this problem, but this is one of the necessary evils of our program.

"You see, the difficulty with male birth is that there is no natural uterus development so a child doesn't have anything to firmly attach itself to. That's the reason for the implant of the organic artificial uterus. Then the fertilized egg will be injected into the artificial uterus through a surgically implanted permanent catheter underneath your ribcage. Since you don't have ovaries, taking hormones would do you no good whatsoever. So we created a special therapy especially developed for men that we will inject into the catheter over the course of your pregnancy. You will constantly need the injection of fluids from our special therapy once a month, and depending on how things progress, perhaps more often than that to assist with the growth of your pregnancy. Yet, one treatment on a monthly basis should do the trick. Obviously, there are uncertainties and major risks involved," he said. Dr. Valesco sat down on a low backless swivel stool that squeaked.

"Dr. Valesco, I don't need to know this level of detail. I read your CV and trust you or I wouldn't be here. I know that this is an experimental process and that there are risks and uncertainties. You've explained that to me and I appreciate it. And you have given me the basic information I needed to make a prudent decision as to whether to do this or not. Beyond that, I leave the details in your hands. I want to do this; I understand the risks and I trust your competence and your commitment," I said.

"That's understandable. I've scheduled implant surgery for you in one week. As I said we'll also catheterize you for easy injections. If all goes well, the baby assisted by the special therapeutic injections should develop its own hormones to sustain itself. Are you still interested in participating in the program, Kel?"

"Well, yes!" I said, sounding a bit overexcited. Dr. Valesco chuckled and patted my knee. Then I asked, "Has any man anywhere else ever given birth to a child?"

"Kel, as you can imagine in San Francisco, I have a lot of men involved in the program. Some of these men are a lot farther along than you are."

"You mean some of them are actually pregnant?"

"The program is only a couple of years old. There's a fair amount of interest. One of the participants is now at the end of his second trimester. He's the first. His baby is due around Easter. Regrettably, we've also had some heartbreaking failures."

"Jeez," I said. My eyes widened. "What about the pregnant guy in New York?" I asked.

"Dead. He died in the third trimester," he said. His face looked grim. I wanted to put my hands over my ears. I felt the blood rush to my head from excitement. Why had I ignored the part he said about heartbreaking failures? Shouldn't I have at least asked Dr. Valesco why these men failed? Or did I really want to know? I put my fears aside.

"I'll ask you once more, are you still interested? If not, I can make some referrals for you to get involved in the other programs I informed you about earlier. You are a very brave man, Mr. Kel Warren," he said. He sounded like he'd just handed me a check for a million dollars.

"I'm interested," I said. I waited for Dr. Valesco to ask me if this was my final answer, the way I've heard the host of that game show ask contestants on *Who Wants to Be a Millionaire?* Is my life one big sacrifice? Or am I a fool who don't know when he's had it up to here? A wave of sadness went through me. I shook it off.

I sighed.

"Then good. Until next time, take care and don't forget to see Helga out front to make your next appointment. Also, have your egg donor contact my office to complete the in vitro fertilization stage. Is she ovulating?" he said. I was glad I remembered from biology that an egg matures every twenty-eight days.

I was about to say, "I don't know. We're not fucking."

Instead I told him, "She's my friend and we talk openly."

"Then good," he said again, with a tone of voice that suggested that our session was over. He shook my hand and left the room.

I got dressed and imagined sitting down with Naomi over dinner and asking her when she was going to get her period. The rain hit the narrow panes of the window like musicians beating on steel drums. I leaned against the bed, looked out the window at the expanse of the San Francisco Bay Bridge that cut into Treasure Island. Mankind had cut into the great mountain that was Treasure Island to make way for a bridge to get to the other side of the bay. Why couldn't someone cut into my belly, after my pregnancy reached full term? And connect me to the other side, where my maternal instincts waited to meet me with open arms and a warm heart. I picked up a magazine called *Baby Boomer* on the stand under the window, a department store for infants and children at Fisherman's Wharf. I flipped through the pages and naturally decided to go shopping. I sat the magazine down, slipped on my overcoat, and left the exam room. I picked up an appointment slip at the reception area from Helga.

"Here is your appointment. We've scheduled surgery at Mercy Hospital. Drive carefully, Kel. We want to see you again and again," she said, smiling.

"Thanks. I feel like flying."

"No, no, no. Aren't you afraid of getting those black shiny wings of yours wet? It's raining rather heavily out there," Helga said, playing along with me.

"Rain has never stopped the California eagle from flying. I'll be goddamned if I'm going to let it stop me." I laughed, feeling like my doctor had told me that I was three months pregnant.

"Bye, Kel."

"Later."

I drove straight to a deli and bought a tuna sandwich and bottled water. I sat at a table at the back of the deli and wolfed down the food. By the time I left the deli and found a parking place at the foot of Aquatic Park, the rain had stopped. I walked half a mile to Pier 39 to get to Baby Boomers. I walked past a throng of tourists; mothers with babies, their little heads wrapped snugly in knit caps, gloves, and overcoats; fathers hoisting their babies up to see the marvel of science at the Discovery Store. Parents rolled babies in strollers up to the windows outside the House of Wax, so that they could see the body doubles of the rich, the famous, and the scandalous. I looked at the ruddy cheeks of the toddlers being held by their parents with awestruck faces as they kicked and screamed at the sea lions who had taken over a pier, defying any human being to come anywhere near their babies.

I marched to Baby Boomers thinking about my first trip to Disneyland. I was six years old. When Ma took me to Disneyland for the first time, the overgrown size of Donald Duck, Snow White and the Seven Dwarfs, Mickey Mouse and company scared me so badly that I hid behind her coattails. That was when I realized that my favorite cartoon characters seemed larger in real life than on the small screen of the television at home. This revelation disappointed me. I'd thought they weren't as funny in person as they were on television. I never looked at any of them the same way again.

As I walked into Baby Boomers, I knew that I'd never look at my life the same way again. I know that nothing ever stays the same. But I was going to have a baby even if it killed me. It came to me this would be my last stand, my everlasting desire. The store was filled with so many wonderful things for a baby that I didn't know where to begin looking. I grabbed a shopping cart and I was on my way. What caught my eye first was a hand-carved, solid mahogany rocking horse. I walked over and rubbed my hands over the shiny wood. I gently picked it up and set it in my cart. Then, I found baby candles that smelled of peach; a *102 Dalmatians* bedding set; a white christening blanket; a bathtub and floating thermometer. I wanted to play it safe, so instead of only picking out the cute little pink Easter dress bonnet and black patent leather shoes for a baby girl, I shopped for a little boy too. I found the tiniest blue double-breasted suit, and the brim hat I'd seen the little boy wearing at Spangles restaurant in Jack London Square. I was on fire! I found a powder blue necktie and a pair of miniature diamond cufflinks. I found a pair of one-caret diamond stud earrings that would make a little girl into a perfect angel. I pushed my cart full of valuables up to the checkout stand and set them up on the counter. The cashier rang them up.

"That'll be six thousand thirty seven dollars and nineteen cents. Do you want to pay by cash or credit card?" he asked.

"Visa," I said, whipping out my wallet and handing him the card like it was nobody's business but my own.

"Would you like some assistance with your bags?" the cashier asked. He was a tall and somewhat lanky blond young man who looked like he could be in his second year at any one of the many universities in the Bay Area.

"That'll be great. I'm only parked less than a mile away. But yes, a strong hand and a cab would do the trick," I said, putting my wallet back in my pocket and buttoning my jacket.

"Hold 'em up. Juan!" he turned and yelled across the store to a muscular Latino who was propping up boxes against a wall next to bassinets.

"What's up?" Juan said. I watched him stack the last box up against a wall. He walked over to me. He was a brawny man with dark brown eyes, wavy jet-black hair neatly combed to the back. His moustache was slight. He had a tattoo of a scorpion between the thumb and index finger of his right hand.

"This gentleman needs a hand with his merchandise," the would-be college student said.

"Hi," Juan said. He had a sly grin on his face.

"Hi. I'm not that far from here. It should only take a few minutes, actually."

"Not a problem. It has stopped raining for now but we'll have to jet, before it starts again," he said. He rolled the cart out of the door for me. I watched Juan's upper back muscles strain against the tan sweatshirt. His buttocks looked like two firm cantaloupes, stuffed into a pair of soft blue jeans. I wasn't trying to be flirtatious, but my member began to involuntarily fill my crotch with restless desire. I blamed the rain and cold weather for making my dick hard. It had gotten down into the low thirties with a severe wind chill factor. It was so cold outside, it felt like I was wearing shorts or bathing trunks.

We stood at the mouth of Pier 39 and waited a few minutes for a cab; but after several minutes, I began to feel like every cab in San Francisco was busy picking up people elsewhere. I imagined cabs were picking people up from flats, the financial district, Chinatown, the Sunset, the Richmond district, North Beach, Lake Merced, anywhere but Fisherman's Wharf, where all the action seemed to be in the midst of an incubating storm.

"Check it out. Where you parked?" Juan asked.

"Not far. Right up the street."

"You game?"

"I'm ready!"

"Let's do this," he said. He pushed the cart along the sidewalks, as my erection refused to abate.

When we reached my car, and loaded the bags and boxes in the back, I could feel the wetness of pre-come; that was the evidence of my desire for Juan. I went into my wallet and pulled out a twenty-dollar bill to tip him.

"Thanks, Juan," I said. I patted his hard-as-steel forearm and handed him the money. He refused to take it.

"No charge. But what you can give me, Sweet Pea, are the digits," he said.

"Got you covered," I said as I went into my wallet, took out a private business card with my telephone number on it. I gave it to him. He took an extra one, wrote his telephone number on the back, and gave it back to me.

"You married?" he asked, looking at the silver band with a diamond on the top on my right hand.

"In the soul mate sense, not legally."

"When is the baby due?"

"If everything goes the way that I want it to go, it'll be here by November. In time to celebrate Thanksgiving," I said, feeling a sense of pride. Then I said, "I'm getting ready for the day I bring my baby home from the hospital. It's going to be great," I said. I volunteered only enough information to pique his curiosity.

"I'll bet. Well, I better get back to the store before we both turn into human icicles," he said. He looked at my card and stuffed it in his upper shirt pocket. He took off running.

"Later," I said to his massive back and watched him sprint off like Carl Lewis. His backside bounced like two firm basketballs. I climbed in the jeep feeling like a high school junior who'd just made plans to take his one and only love to the prom.

Chapter 8

Before the early morning fog rolled in off the bay, then evaporated, I had gone to the gym and worked out, and every muscle in my body was tight. I went home and cooked salmon croquettes for lunch. I made dinner plans with Chad and spent the rest of the afternoon carting my soaked patio umbrella, wet table, lawn chairs, and barbecue pit from the backyard to the garage. Then I pruned my rosebush, picked lemons off my lemon tree, and dug a hole near the side of my left fence where the city had agreed to plant a palm tree. As I plowed the shovel into the rich black earth, I thought about the nature of planting and growing things—about seedlings that burst into magnificent spectacular growth as if by osmosis. I imagined that the seeds of a child had already been implanted in me, and that the birth of my baby would be my way of giving back to the world the life it had given me, the way we must all give back the gifts of our lives; surrender to the earth when the time comes to lay our bodies down. This earth, the doer and the maker of all feasts and famines is the original home of every single living creature that strolls across the face of this planet. I imagined that as it is in human relationships, the earth has a family tree. The soil, the lakes, the rivers, the oceans, the ponds, the lagoons, the mountains, the hills, the valleys are brothers, sisters, mothers, fathers, aunts, uncles, nieces, nephews, cousins, godmothers and fathers, grandparents. Is the sun the god of earthly things, the omnipotent ruler? The moon: is it the watcher and the provider of infinite light to guide and see us through the darkness of the world by night? I finished my gardening and went back in the house to take a shower. As I showered, I looked at the soap rack Atlas had given to me as a housewarming gift when he had better days. The aftertaste of salmon croquettes in my mouth made me realize that Atlas was the one who taught me how to cook them. I hadn't been back to see Atlas since Cameroon booted me out of the nursing home during my last visit.

Oh, my God! Had Atlas died since then? I had to hurry! I got dressed quickly. When I got downstairs to the kitchen, I took out some of Ma's peach cobbler, put it on a paper plate, and wrapped it with foil.

Before making it to the Armor Protective Home, I stopped off at Albertson's. I went in and bought half a gallon of vanilla ice cream. When I reached the nursing home I didn't find Atlas in his room. I quickly went and found Cameroon. He was standing at the nursing station.

"Oh, it's you. How are you?" he said in a sing-song voice that didn't sound real.

"Not bad. I've come to see Atlas and I brought some peach cobbler and vanilla ice cream for Mrs. Hill," I said.

"Mrs. Hill?"

"Yeah, you remember, the old woman who wanted peach cobbler and vanilla ice cream the last time I was here."

"You mean you've bought her dessert."

"Well, yeah. Is there anything wrong with that?"

"It's against hospital rules. We don't allow our patients to eat food brought in by non–family members."

"Oh, here we go again! Jeez, so what would you suggest that I do with it?"

"Here, let me have it," he said. He bent down and placed it in a small refrigerator next to his desk.

"Anyway, I've come to see Atlas."

"Atlas?"

"Yeah. Atlas."

"Atlas was transferred."

"Where, to another wing of the hospital?"

"He's in the intensive care unit at Mercy Hospital across the street. He suffered a coronary. I don't think that the last time you visited with him was particularly helpful. He's incoherent. He doesn't recognize anyone. Not even me."

"Why would he recognize someone anywhere remotely close to being like you?" I asked sarcastically.

"That's not a nice thing to say to me. I was his caretaker."

"He deserved better."

"Are you suggesting that I was derelict in my duties?"

"If the shoe fits, baby, wear it! That is, if those big—" I was interrupted by a patient. I turned around to see Mrs. Hill sitting in a wheelchair.

"Cameroon. Where's my peach cobbler and vanilla ice cream?" she whined. I walked around the counter into the nurse's station. I went into the refrigerator and took out the dessert. I took the foil off the pie, flipped the lid on the carton of ice cream, and handed it to Mrs. Hill.

"Cameroon, I told you my husband would bring me what I want," the old woman said, smiling.

"Cameroon, good food is a terrible thing to waste. Of all people, you should know that. With all those starving babies in Africa who'll never live long enough to ever see a peach cobbler or ice cream," I said. I watched Cameroon's face flush with anger.

"Leave these premises before I call security," Cameroon said. He seemed to be pissed off. His cheeks puffed out as if he had a mouthful of cotton.

"Cameroon, give me a spoon and take me to the cafeteria. I want to eat my peach cobbler and vanilla ice cream. Oh, goody," the old woman said. She clapped her hands like a little girl.

I left Cameroon, the old woman, the peach cobbler, and the vanilla ice cream I was certain he would've never given to her, and rushed out of the nursing home. I shot across the street to Mercy Hospital and sprinted up three flights of stairs.

"Are you his next of kin?" a bleached blond nurse asked after stopping me at the nursing station.

"I'm his friend, Kel," I said. She looked at me skeptically. Her perfume was strong, irritating my nostrils.

"We've restricted his visiting time. So you must not stay for more than half an hour. Atlas is a very sick man," she said.

"Why else is he in the hospital?" I said. The nurse backed away from me as if she had walked up to quicksand, become fearful of the danger, and decided to turn back. I walked into Atlas's room. He was semiconscious, with a respirator stuck in his nostrils. I pulled up a chair next to his bed near a wide window and sat down. I kissed and held his bony hands, stroked his cheekbones that looked as if they were going to burst clear through his face. I sat and watched over him like the Pope.

"Atlas, it's me, Kel," I whispered.

"Kel, is that you?" Atlas said weakly. His hand gripped mine as his other hand flew in the air like the broken wing of a blackbird.

"It's me, baby. How you feeling?"

"Girl, girl, girl, girl, girl! This is my last hurrah! How does my hair look?"

"It looks good. Give us that seventies Michael Jackson Afro! I knew if anybody could bring back the seventies you could, Atlas," I laughed. I hoped to cheer him up.

"Kel?"

"Yeah."

"You still here?"

"I'm still here, baby. I'm still here. Now I don't want you to be afraid, you hear."

"How does it feel to die?"

"I think to die is to surrender your body to the earth. But your spirit lives on."

"Where will my spirit go?"

"It'll linger in the air around the people who were in your life who meant the most to you. Or it may converge with a new spirit being born in the world."

"Will they know that I'm there? Will I be able to see and hear them?"

"Not right away, but they'll know and feel something familiar that reminds them of you. You'll be able to see and hear them. Only if you want to."

"Heifer, how do you know all this?" He smiled weakly.

"I know life and I know death. I've lived between both of them as if they're older and younger siblings. I guess you might say I'm in the middle, born between life and death. I once crossed over to the other side."

"You mean when you got sick last year and the doctors couldn't figure out what was wrong with you?"

"Absolutely."

"But you came back, Kel."

"Halfway. But I'm in a hurry because I got so much work to do and not a lot of time to do it in. The next time I cross over, it's for good. I won't be coming back, not to this life."

"Well, isn't halfway better than no way?"

"I'll be all the way back this year. Before I leave for good. You see, the next time when I cross over to the other side, I'll be traveling light."

"Girl, how you going to get all the way back?"

"I got good news yesterday. When I went to see Dr. Valesco, he told me that I could have a baby. He's going to implant an artificial uterus inside of me that the baby will be able to grow in. When I have my baby, I'll be all the way back. A new start."

"Shut up! Dr. Valesco? Say what? Who told you that? Isn't he your gynecologist?"

"No, he's an obstetrician helping me to conceive my baby."

"Do me a favor?"

"What?"

"Give him the name of a great African king."

"What would you suggest?"

"Solomon."

"King Solomon?"

"That's it."

"What if it's a girl?"

"Give her the name of Sheba."

"Like the African queen? Those are great names. I haven't picked out a name yet. I'm going to wait until my second trimester."

"I'll say."

"Me too," I said. I smiled.

"Kel?"

"Yeah."

"Mama still didn't come to the hospital to see me."

"She'll be here, trust me."

"She's got to hurry, Kel. I can't hold on forever."

"Hold on, Atlas. If I've got to bring her here kicking and screaming, she's going to get here. I can promise you that," I said. I looked at the lines on the heart monitor next to his bed.

"Do it for me, Kel."

"You have my word on it," I said. The nurse came into the room.

"Your time is up. He needs his rest. He's a very sick man," she said, as if I didn't already know.

"Oh, Miss Thing, please," Atlas said, snapping his fingers weakly.

"That's all right, Atlas. They've got hospital rules and we've got to live within some of them. For now," I said. I let go of his damp hand as I bent over and kissed him on the cheek.

"Don't stay away so long."

"I won't, Atlas. I won't."

It's never ceased to amaze me to realize that when you sit next to the bed of a man who is dying, it's always like he's your last friend. When I made it back home, I got in touch with Naomi. She picked up on the first ring.

"Hey, Sista."

"Hey, Brotha. You give any more thought to going to church with me tomorrow?" she asked.

"It's a go."

"Really?"

"Yeah. What time do you want me to pick you up?"

"Service starts at about eleven o'clock. Let's do brunch at HS Lordships at the Berkeley Marina after services. Or do you have plans with Chad?"

"No, but there are a couple of little favors I'd like for you to do for me."

"I'm listening."

"Didn't you tell me once that Atlas's mother, Olivia, is an usher at your church?"

"She was formerly an usher. Now she's a missionary. She's there every Sunday. That woman doesn't miss a beat. Kel?"

"Yeah."

"Kel, I keep telling you not to say my church."

"Naomi, I don't know what else to say. I left the church a long time ago."

"That's it. It's simple to understand. You left the church but the church didn't leave you. A church can be anywhere you put it as long as you believe in God. The church is inside of you. Anybody can throw up a shack and call it a church. It's the spirit inside of us that counts," she said.

"You got a point, Naomi. Anyway, Reverend Sista, I've got to get Olivia up to the hospital to see Atlas. He's dying and she hasn't stepped a foot in his hospital room. I want to see if you can talk to your father about it tonight. You don't have to mention her name to him. God knows how well that man can preach some gospel. I was wondering if you could call him up and ask him to talk about obligations of parenthood, being lost and found. Fellowship and redemption, rebirth since it's the first Sunday of the month."

"I can't tell my daddy what to preach about. But I'm his only child and I take care of my daddy. He listens to me."

"Then if Olivia is delivered through your daddy's gospel, we'll take her up to the hospital after services to see Atlas."

"What if she doesn't get it? Then what?"

"I'll let the spirit, as you say, that's inside of me move me."

"So it's a deal?"

"A couple of other things."

"More?"

"If we miss brunch, let's do dinner at the Outback."

"Sounds like a plan," she said.

"See you tomorrow," I said and hung up the phone.

I picked up Chad for dinner at Hotel Mac in Point Richmond. The crowd at Hotel Mac was festive. Christmas lights were strung above the awning where people sat, sipped on cocktails, and chatted. Fresh blood-red poinsettias looked as if they were naturally grown at Hotel Mac. The bar on the first floor was packed with revelers who seemed to be still in the midst of toasting a year that was a little more than one month old, still in its infancy. There were eleven more months to go before the year reached its full term. That is how I thought as I sat at a table with Chad. I held my glass up in the air and gave a toast to a brand-new me.

"Chad, I'd like to propose a toast to life, to love, and to the birth of all things big and small," I said as I watched the candlelight that sat between us flicker, casting Chad's dark face in a warm glow.

"My, aren't we the chipper one tonight? Come on, Head. Spill it. I know when you got something up your sleeves," he said. He sipped his drink.

"Chad, it's possible. I can have a baby!" I said. I felt like standing up from my chair, hopping upon the table and dancing in celebration.

"Oh, Head. Keep it down before somebody hears you in here. You want us to get kicked out on the street?"

"How are we going to get kicked out of someplace unless we eat and don't pay? I pay my bills, Chad."

"Let's not go there."

"That's not what I mean. I mean, these people don't know us from a hole in the ground. What should they care if I have a baby or a tumor?"

"Most people would believe you if you had a tumor because it's not something anyone would dream of wanting but it's a normal part of life. Like this white tablecloth on top of this table," he said.

I fingered the tablecloth.

"Chad, don't trip, but the doctor told me I've got to have an artificial uterus implanted inside of me."

"Artificial uterus! Oh shit! Now I know you've gone fucking bananas. What the fuck do you hope to prove?"

"Chad, tone it down. We're not exactly outside on the basketball court shooting hoops."

"If we were, I'd beat your ass until you came to your senses. Do you know what this is going to do to my sex life?"

"What do you mean, your sex life? You're this close to converting to full-time asexuality."

"Oh, Head, stop it, please. Stop. You poor thing. I don't see how you could have made a decision like that without talking to me about it first."

"Chad, are we not talking about it right now? Or am I having dinner alone at Hotel Mac with the ghost of Chad Smith? Open your eyes, Chad. You can see much farther than that."

"All right. Let's go over this again."

"We already have, Chad. Until I'm turning purple in the face."

"So in about a month that dick of yours is going to look like a split pink grapefruit. Is that right? Or we'll be bumping fuzzes to the break of dawn?"

"Not even."

"Well, what then?"

"Chad, look, Naomi has to agree to donate me one of her eggs. If she doesn't, I'm stuck. It's over. Wham, like that."

"You haven't talked with her about it yet?"

"We're going to church tomorrow. Then after services we are going to brunch at HS Lordships."

"Head?"

"Yeah."

"You know what?"

"What?"

"This shit is so funny. I swear to God."

"Why?"

"HS Lordships is where we once kicked it at five years ago. It's also where I dined with Atlas for the last time."

We talked about how we first met. Chad was at the salad bar piling lettuce, tomatoes, chipped cucumbers, carrots, diced bacon and raisons, and Thousand Island dressing on a small plate. He walked around the bend not paying attention to where he was going, bumped into me, and spilled that plate of salad smack dab in my crotch. I couldn't believe it when he took his napkin, bent down, and began to wipe the mess from between my legs. The more he wiped the harder I got. Chad stood up, we looked at each other, and laughed. Later, he came over to the table Atlas and I had at a window. I introduced Chad to Atlas. Chad apologized for the mess he made between my legs and dropped me a note with his telephone number on it.

"I still got those slacks with permanent stains that won't go away. The rest they say—" I said. Chad interrupted.

"Is history," we both said at the same time and laughed.

"How is Atlas?"

"I went to see him this afternoon in intensive care. He's hanging in there but he has only one more wish. He wants to see his mother one last time before he dies. I'm going to help him to make it come true. His mother, Olivia, goes to Naomi's church. "

"No shit," Chad said and sipped his cocktail.

"I feel kind of guilty because I haven't been back to see him but once since he had convulsions one time I visited. Suffered cardiac arrest." I looked at my empty plate.

I listened to the clank of glasses and rustle of tablecloths. I didn't even know if Atlas was dead or alive. To be honest, I didn't want to know. I didn't think that I had any room inside of me to accept what I feared the most, that Atlas wouldn't live long enough to ever see his mother again. It seems so old-fashioned for anyone to come down with full-blown AIDS with all the drugs and medication we have to stop it from happening. It's not like all we've got is AZT. Atlas told me once that the only cocktail he wanted to take was that belonging to a man with a twelve-inch Zulu dick and an asshole tighter than one belonging to an eighteen-year-old virgin boy. Atlas is my friend, not someone who didn't want to take cocktails. It was his choice.

"Earth to Head. Do you copy?"

"I was just thinking about Atlas. He made a choice not to take cocktails to prevent getting sick."

"Well, there you go. He made his own bed. Now he's sleeping in it."

"All I can think about these days is getting fat and pregnant. I'm going in for implant surgery soon, Chad. Atlas thinks I'm a whore for wanting to do it. Do you think that I'm a whore, Chad?" I said as I stuffed a slice of roasted chicken in my mouth and began to chew.

"Not a whore, Head, but you are stubborn. I hope to God that you realize that you're dreaming the impossible, Honeydew Head. I'm not taking you to the hospital to have the operation either." I looked at Chad's face. What would it take for me to tell him that I'm sexually addicted too? As quickly as I thought about telling him, I just as quickly thought about not doing it. This wasn't the time. God only knows that Hotel Mac's wasn't the right place. Unless I had an obscene desire to see Chad rack up thousands of dollars in property damage after he'd take a chair and smash out every window in the restaurant.

We finished eating dinner in silence; and I watched couples sitting at tables, chattering, oblivious to anyone who was not a part of their inner sanctum. The silence was broken when the waiter brought back the check and set it down in front of me.

"I'll take care of the tip, Head," Chad offered.

I paid the check and we got up from the table, and walked down a short flight of stairs and left the restaurant.

I drove Chad back to my house. When we got inside, Chad sat down on the sofa, picked up the remote from the coffee table, and flipped on the television. He began watching E!. I sat down next to him. E! was showing a man's fashion collection designed by a popular East Coast rap star.

"That shit is fucking crazy off the hook!" Chad yelped. I got up from the sofa and decided to light some candles. I went and sat back down next to Chad. Chad watched E! as if the fashion police had kidnapped, handcuffed, and forced him to watch the rap star's line of clothes if he wanted to stay alive.

I wasn't interested in watching television.

"Chad, I've got a long day tomorrow. I'm going to turn in for the night. Coming with me?" I asked. I rubbed the inside of his strong thighs erotically to get him in the mood.

"See, that's what I mean. How would you be able to have a baby when you go to bed early like an old man?"

"Chad, don't you want to climb up in my bed and hold me? I'm not asking for you to fuck my brains out."

"Yeah, Head, but once we hit the sheets it's on! Let me watch E!. I'll be up in a shake."

I got up from the sofa and went upstairs to my bedroom. I stripped and climbed underneath the sheets. I dozed off. Chad's snoring woke me up. I turned and looked at his naked back. I took my forefinger and drew a picture of a three-month embryo shaped like the one I saw on the chart in Dr. Valesco's office on Chad's back. Shaped like my three-month-old embryo Cookie aborted. As I fell asleep, I wished for two things, a baby and for Atlas's mother to see him one more time before he died.

Chapter 9

I drove to Naomi's home at the Richmond Marina, made it there fifteen minutes before services were set to start at church. When I arrived, Naomi was waiting for me out on her doorstep. She was wearing a silky turquoise dress, a wide white brim hat, matching seashell earrings, and elbow-length gloves. She clutched a small black purse.

I unlocked the passenger door and she climbed in.

"Hey, Kel," she said, giving me a slight peck on the cheek.

"Hey, back at you," I said, smiling.

"I like that suit. Armani?" she asked.

"Chad's. It's his suit," I said. We both laughed.

"I spoke to my daddy last night. He going to say a little something. Something."

"He's cool like that?" I asked. I felt like I'd stepped across one bridge but that I had a long ways to go before getting over to the Promised Land.

"Kel, you looking at Daddy's girl."

"I'm feeling you."

We parked, got out, and walked up to the wide swinging front doors of Evergreen Holy Tabernacle Church in North Richmond. The house of the Lord stood in front of railroad tracks, separating the black north from the white south. The church was long and narrow. The benches were covered in crushed red velvet.

Naomi sat next to me in the front pew where we had sat since we were small children. No sooner had we sat down than the youth choir began to sing "Climbing Higher Mountains." Sitting on the other side of me was a pregnant young girl. She looked at me and nodded. She was fanning herself with a church bulletin. Naomi leaned forward and looked a little past me at the woman. Naomi scooted closer and leaned into my ear.

101

"That's Cayleen sitting next to you. My daddy's girlfriend," Naomi whispered. I could hear her suck her teeth.

"Say what?"

I turned around and looked over in the next pew. Naomi's mother, Sugar, seemed to be staring at Cayleen's back. She had the look on her face of a woman who wished that she was anywhere but sitting in church getting ready to hear her husband preach.

"They tell me she's pregnant by my daddy. That heifer got the nerve to step into a house of God. Look at my mama sitting back there smoldering." I turned around and looked at Sugar again.

"Jesus."

I leaned slightly forward and looked across the aisle. There was Atlas's mother, Olivia. She was wearing a snug white full-length dress and white gloves. Her hair was pulled back into a bun, fastened with a gold barrette. She was fanning herself with a small cardboard fan with a short handle.

The Reverend Merle Edwards, in a dusk gray suit, lavender tie, white shirt, and black patent leather shoes, stepped through a door right across from the altar. He graced the pulpit. He walked with a slight limp. His thin black hair was cut close on the sides and busy on top. I looked at a portrait made of terry cloth, hung above his head, of a bronzed Jesus, wearing dreadlocks, sitting in the middle of his twelve disciples of African descent. Jesus and his disciples were draped in red, black, lavender, and gray dashikis. Their sandals were flat and black. Reverend Edwards' large hands gripped the pulpit. When the choir finished singing, the missionaries and elder members shouted amen and clapped; some praised the Lord. Reverend Edwards opened his sermon.

"Before I fell asleep last night, a voice came to me. Told me to speak to you this morning of redemption and fellowship. Of being lost and found. Rebirth. You know God has blessed me with one child. The birth of my daughter showed me the sheer wonder of the Lord God's work. Somebody sitting in this church doesn't hear me this morning! Somebody in this church got a child laid up in a hospital bed wondering where is his mama! Why she won't come to sit with him and rub his tired feet. Stroke his sweaty brow. Tell him what a joy it was the day her womb stretch forth, after her labors, and God brought him through her during childbirth. He is wondering why his mama won't come to hold his hand. Hands she tended to when he was a little boy when he'd cut himself playing in his backyard. Wondering why his mama won't come to see him and look in his eyes and tell him God's will be done. That child is wondering if he is a motherless child. Somebody doesn't hear me in this church this morning! Until he sees his mama again, that child can't travel to God's mighty kingdom where he will be reborn. That child is lost without the love of his mama. He can't be found until his mama does right by him. The church is for sinners and the saved. We redeem ourselves, when we join in the fellowship of the Lord. You got to love the flesh of your flesh, blood of your blood. If you don't, there is no redemption."

"Tell it like it is, preacher!" shouted an old man wearing dark sunglasses, sitting next to Naomi. I watched him get up from the pew. His clenched fist punched the air.

"It is these times that God has to stretch forth his mighty hand and make a bridge to reconnect that mother with her dying baby. Somebody isn't listening to me this morning! To know the glory of God, we must be merciful. To bear a child and bring it forth, in this world full of the devil's work, is a blessing. A blessing because everybody's not able. God is a just God. He knows and sees all things. Oh, you can run but you can't hide from God. He knows what you thinking about before you know about it yourself. This world is full of men and women with babies who call themselves mothers and fathers. Giving birth to a child doesn't confer motherhood or fatherhood, because your egg and sperm came together during conception, and now a baby is being born. What does it mean to abandon a child whether it's sick or healthy? What it means is that God's eyes are wet with tears. Because something he gave us the ability to do has been cast away. Forsaken. Somebody isn't listening to me this morning!" The preacher wiped the sweat from his brow.

"Well, all right!" yelled a tall dark-complexioned woman sitting next to Olivia.

"Hallelujah," said the woman next to her.

"If you knew the blessings of God, you wouldn't leave your child to die alone among strangers; no more than you would kick a man on the ground in the teeth. If you knew God, you wouldn't push an old woman down a flight of stairs and break her neck. If you knew God you wouldn't turn your back on the life that came from your womb and from your body. Somebody say amen! Y'all don't hear me this morning! Some of us got our eyes wide open but can't see a lick. Blind as bats! A child is your wealth! Money can't buy a child. Can't make or raise one either. That child you brought in this world didn't ask to be brought here. A child belongs to you in sickness and in health. Even when he stands out on the corners, holding a rusty tin cup begging for change; standing outside in front of some liquor store with a bottle wrapped around his lips. Drunk! With a needle stuck in his arm or a crack pipe to his mouth. With all the things he ever owned in this world stuffed in a pushcart. His hair matted and nappy, but that's still your child. His clothes pungent and dirty but he's your child. Somebody isn't listening to me here this morning, church! That's still your child. Your child may be sitting in some lonely jailhouse doing life. Sitting on death row."

"Well," I heard a woman's voice say behind me.

"Or sitting in some courtroom with handcuffs fastened so tight around his wrists until it stops the blood cold! Your child may be blind, crippled, or he may have lost one of his legs to diabetic-induced gangrene. All glory is to God! That child may not be able to read or write good enough to spell his own name. What are you going to do? Turn your child away? Jesus didn't turn away the afflicted. He cured the sick, welcomed them to his table of fellowship. Somebody in this church here this morning got a child in the hospital holding on until he's able to look one last time in his mother's face before he makes that long journey to cross over to the other side. Somebody needs to say amen."

Clatters of voices echoed off the wooden paneled walls and stained glass windows and hung in the warm air of the church. The congregation was on its feet shouting. The church was awash with the spirit of gospel music. Tambourines, bass guitars, drums, and a staccato piano merged into a melody that reached a crescendo. The youth choir began to sing "Let Us All Go Back to the Old Landmark." The floor rocked beneath my feet. Naomi and I got up from our seats. I looked at the congregation.

"Glory be to God! Glory be to God!" said a middle-aged woman standing next to Cayleen. The woman walked over and handed me a sleeping baby girl with white ribbons in her hair. I took the baby and watched the woman dance. Naomi and I sat in the pew, like a married couple with a toddler. I began to sway and rock the child in my arms.

"Say it, Reverend!" shouted a man about thirty years old with a white toothpick dangling from the corner of his mouth. It seemed as though the man had come from the back of the church. He danced. His hands were on his slim hips. He was sweating and seemed to be lost in the rhythm of the church.

I watched a smallish woman, with short black hair, wearing a yellow dress get up from the front pew, waving her hands. She began to dance and beat on a tambourine. I looked down the aisle at Olivia. She was up on her feet shouting.

"Oh, Father! Hallelujah! Hallelujah. Mercy! Mercy on me! Glory! Praise the Lord! Amen! Glory be to God!" Olivia yelled and danced in frenzy. Naomi looked at me and nodded. Reverend Edwards came down from the pulpit. Two elders, who were very old men, followed behind him. I watched three missionary women walk up to Olivia. They all joined hands and surrounded her. She danced, wept, smiled, and laughed.

"Make a joyful noise for the Lord!" Reverend Edwards said as he walked up to Olivia and put his hand on her forehead. The missionaries stood behind Olivia. The preacher continued, "Get out of her, Satan! Take your grip off of her throat! Release her in the name of Jesus! Leave, Satan! Leave her body!" he commanded.

"Reverend, my son! My son is dying! My baby, my precious baby! My pride and joy, my one and only child! God knows how much I love you, Atlas! I didn't mean it, baby! Mama didn't mean to do you no harm! Oh Jesus! I love that boy so much! Lord have mercy. Have mercy on my soul. For the love of God, somebody take me to see my child again," she shouted and fell into the arms of the missionaries. A collective gasp went through the church.

"Take Mother Olivia to see her baby again! Hurry," the reverend declared. He walked over to Naomi and me. I kissed the baby on her little fat cheek and handed her back to the dancing woman. Naomi and I went up to the altar and got Olivia. I put her arms around my shoulders, and as I walked her out of the church Naomi fanned her with one of the cardboard fans. We helped her into the front seat of the car. I was taking Olivia to see Atlas. Naomi patted Olivia's shoulder and handed her a handkerchief from the backseat.

"It's all right, Olivia. It's going to be all right," I said as I watched her regain her composure, just to lose it all over again. Before I could start the engine, I heard a woman screaming. I looked back, out of my rearview mirror, toward the front of the church. Sugar was all over Cayleen, choking her and hitting her face.

"Naomi, look!" I said. She followed me out of the car. We ran over and separated the two women.

"You got a lot of nerve to bring your pregnant self up in this church with my husband's baby in your belly. You bitch!" Sugar broke loose from Naomi and struck Cayleen's face again.

"Please don't hurt my baby. In the name of God, please don't hurt my child."

"I'll beat that baby out of your ass. Right here on the steps of this church, so help me God!"

"Somebody, help me!" Cayleen yelled and put her hands out in front of her. She seemed to be protecting her baby.

"Mama, stop! Don't, Mama!" Naomi said. She pulled an angry Sugar away from Cayleen. I watched Naomi take her mother around to the side door of the church and disappear through it. I put my arms around Cayleen, tried to soothe her and tell her it was going to be all right. Cayleen wept.

"We are on our way to the hospital. Climb in. You need some help," I said. I led her to the Jeep and opened the back door for her. Olivia sat in the front seat humming "Climbing Higher Mountains," as though she hadn't seen or heard a thing.

"Hurry, Kel! I got to see my baby," Olivia said and rocked a little side to side.

Naomi came back to the Jeep and climbed in beside Cayleen.

"You all right?" Naomi asked Cayleen.

"I got to see a doctor. I tell you, something wrong with my baby," she said. I looked at her through the rearview mirror holding her stomach. I prayed that she wasn't having a miscarriage.

"Kel, what room is my son in?" Olivia asked.

"He's on the third floor. In room three oh six," I said. I remembered because it was the same room I was in at Mercy Hospital when I was sick last year.

When we got to Mercy, Cayleen had settled down. Naomi and I took her to the emergency room. I watched Olivia walk briskly up to the elevator and press the button to go up. After making sure that Cayleen got seen, we found Olivia, who was at Atlas's bedside. Atlas was propped up in the bed, on two pillows, barely conscious. Naomi and I stood back and watched. It seemed to me that I was watching the precious last moments between Atlas and his mother.

"Atlas, baby, it's me. It's your mother. See, I'm here now. You don't have to suffer no more, baby. It's all right to let go. God will take care of you from now on," she said and kissed him on his cheek. She took his hand into hers.

"Mama?"

"Yeah, baby."

"Kel told me he'd bring you to me," Atlas said.

"Well, he made good on his promise. Mama's here and so is the spirit of God," Olivia said and wiped a tear that rolled down her cheek.

"I'm so tired, Mama. So tired. I tried to—" Olivia cut him off.

"Don't talk if it's taking away your energy. I want to tell you that I'm sorry. That I should have come sooner and I hope that God will forgive me. I love you, sweetheart. Love you with every inch of my very being."

"You need not apologize, Mama. God will understand," Atlas said. He took a deep breath that brought his body halfway up off of the bed. I looked at the heart monitor. A straight blue line on the monitor told me that Atlas was no more. Gone.

"Oh, my baby! My precious baby! As long as . . . as long as I live you'll always be my baby. If I had to give birth to you again . . . I'd do it, so help me God," she sobbed, gripping his body and laying her head over his still frame. Naomi put her head on my shoulder and I grabbed her around the waist. We walked over to Olivia.

"No more pain, no more weeping, no more wailing. He's gone on home," I said. I walked over to Olivia and looked into her bloodshot eyes. I rubbed and patted her back.

"Let me stay here for a little while. I'll be out directly," she said. Naomi and I left the room and waited on a small bench next to the elevators just outside the nursing station.

"Naomi, would you wait here for Olivia? I'm going down to emergency to see about Cayleen," I said.

"Brotha, go ahead. I'll wait right here," she said.

When I got to emergency, Cayleen was in with the doctor. I sat in the waiting room flipping through an old *Jet* magazine, half-reading. I watched Cayleen come out of a door next to the triage nurse's station. My nerves that had been jumping all over the place since that morning relaxed when I saw a smile on Cayleen's face.

I sighed.

I went up to Cayleen. "How's the baby?" I asked.

"The doctor examined me. She said that the baby is fine. We were just a little shook up. That's all," Cayleen said.

"Well, that was enough. It's good you and the baby are all right."

"You got that right. Your name is Kel. Naomi's friend, right?" she asked.

"Yeah, Naomi, she is my friend."

"She's so lucky to have a friend like you."

"I think Naomi and I are lucky to have each other as friends."

"Kel?"

"Yeah."

"Thank you for coming to my rescue. You didn't have to do anything. I won't forget it. Can you do me a favor and drop me off at home? I live over on the Southside near Kennedy High."

"After I go and get Naomi and Olivia upstairs. Olivia's son just died," I said. I looked at the floor.

"Oh, I'm sorry to hear that," she said. She patted my hand, went with me to get Olivia and Naomi. When we got up to the third floor,

Olivia was sitting on the small bench with Naomi, smiling. She seemed to be at peace. I hugged her.

"I want to thank you two for bringing me here to see my baby, for the last time."

"It's what he wanted, Olivia. To see you one more time," I said.

"I'll always see him. Atlas was my heart," she said.

"Can I get you anything?" I asked.

"No, baby, I need to get home to make arrangements for his memorial service. Atlas wants to be put away simply. I'm his mother and that's what I'm going to do for him."

"I understand," I said.

After we dropped off Cayleen and Olivia at home, I felt the kind of quietness inside that comes with the loss of something you know you'll never find again, no matter where you search for it or how hard you try to find it. Atlas was gone and I had one less friend in the world. Naomi was sitting with me in the front seat.

"Naomi, you still want to do brunch?"

"I'm starved. It's been a long, interesting day. How about you?"

"I'm hungry too. Eating is going to be good for both of us."

At HS Lordships Restaurant, we found a table near a floor-to-ceiling window that looked out on San Francisco Bay. From where we were seated, I could see the gray steel beams of the San Francisco Bay Bridge and the Golden Gate Bridge that loomed like a great golden arch. We got plates and I piled so much food on top of it that I didn't know where I was going to put it. My eyes felt bigger than my stomach. Naomi ate like the semivegetarian that she is. She made a tossed salad. Naomi picked at her food.

"Everybody knew my daddy was seeing Cayleen. Mama knew it. She invited her over to their house in the first place. Cayleen was my mama's friend. Mama was going to Reno for months, leaving Cayleen to spend all weekend long with my daddy. Mama never gets back from Reno before Monday morning. One thing must have led to something other than Cayleen and Daddy sitting up in that house sharing the same bowl of popcorn. Next thing you know she knocked up, solid."

"Oh, well. You don't let a fox into a henhouse."

"Or you don't let a hen loose around a fox," she said.

"Sugar going to be all right?" I asked.

"When I took her back in the church, I told her to go home, pack her things, and come over to my house, stay with me for a spell. Until things cool off."

I thought about Atlas.

"By now, Atlas probably has snatched up one of the finest angels standing outside of Heaven's gate," I said, smiling.

"One angel? Try a trio of them. They tell me that Atlas's appetite for men was insatiable," Naomi said.

"He told me he had his first boyfriend when he was six years old. I could barely aim my dick and piss in the toilet straight when I was six years old," I said, laughing.

"That's too funny," Naomi said. She giggled.

I watched an Asian woman feed her toddler as he sat in a high chair. It made me think about how it was going to feel, to bring my baby here and feed it. Would Chad look on, as proud as any parent can be?

"Naomi, remember when I fell in love with Cookie?" I said. I looked out on the bay.

"Yeah. Everybody remembers that. Because you tried to kill yourself after she aborted your baby. Silly," Naomi said.

"Well, as time went by I got over Cookie. Not losing the baby," I said. I confessed to Naomi that unless I had another child I'd always be a man whose baby was aborted. I made her understand I could easily get a surrogate mother to have my child; but it wouldn't be the same as it would if it came from me. Naomi reminded me about what happened to Cookie after she aborted the baby.

Cookie got married two years later, to a man twice her age. Every time she got pregnant, he'd beat the baby out of her. Cookie had just got her nails done the day before. A lot of people say that when he broke one of her lavender-colored nails, that was the last straw. When he smacked her down that morning, something inside of her broke too. She crawled to the kitchen, reached up to the counter, and found a butcher knife sharper than a razor blade. Cookie cut her husband every which way but loose. When the police finally did get to her house, a couple of hours later, they found Cookie on her knees with the knife still in her hand, bent over her husband's dead body.

"You know she's a big-time talk show host now," Naomi said.

"Bigger than Oprah?"

"They don't talk about the same things. You'd know her by her face, not by her name. You can find her magazine easy because she's always the only one on the front of it."

"Maybe she'll invite me to talk on her show when the baby is born."

"You mean you'd like to give birth to a child. From your—" I cut her off.

"Not my loins. My urethral canal is too small. The baby's head would never make it through. The child would suffocate."

"From your ass?"

"No."

"Where, pray tell?" she said. She nibbled on half a stick of celery.

"My belly."

"That would be great, Kel."

"I need an egg and that's what I want from you."

"One of my eggs?"

"Only one of them."

"Where would I go to get you one of my eggs? Do you already have a doctor in mind?" Naomi asked without seeming to think twice.

"I do. Dr. Valesco. His office is across the bay in San Francisco," I said. I pointed out of the window toward the San Francisco Bay Bridge. I looked out of the window as if I could see his office from our dining table. I went into my back pocket, took out my wallet, and found one of Dr. Valesco's business cards and gave her one.

"Who is footing the bill for the procedure?"

"It's a male pregnancy project, Naomi."

"How did you find out about it?"

"I did some research. It's totally legitimate."

"You sure?"

"Look at me. Have I ever lied to you?"

"Well, I remember that one time you told me to watch for a total eclipse of the sun after the ten o'clock news on Halloween," she said and rolled her tongue around in her cheek.

"Naomi, I never told you that."

"Psych!" she said, and laughed.

"I've also got to have surgery to get some implant work done."

"Lord, Kel. You mean to tell me you going to get a period? Baby, getting cramps, let me tell you, it isn't a whole lot of fun. I rather watch paint dry."

"Not even."

"PMS?"

"I don't think so."

"How does Chad feel about it?"

"Pissed."

"Why? He's not going to have it. Lord only knows he's not going to take care of it. You're going to be a single mom. I mean dad. This is going to be so cute! I bet your baby is going to be a knockout. Have you thought of any names yet?" she said.

"Not yet, but no Lolethas, Pineathas, or Tangarays, please. No Lonzells, no Tuffies, Doggers, or Willies; none of that."

Naomi doubled over with laughter.

"What about a little Chad Junior?"

"I just want to have a healthy baby."

"You not worried about losing that twenty-nine-inch waistline?"

"I'll have the beer belly I've always wanted," I said sarcastically.

"Have you told your mom yet?"

"Not until I get to my third trimester."

"Can I be the mama, Kel? Shorty wants me to have a baby. I'm scared to death," she said in a tone that reminded me when I'd played house as a little boy and my girlfriend would want to be the mama. I'd play the daddy.

"Naomi, you would be the mother since it's your egg. But let me ask you something. How are you going to have Shorty's baby? A caesarean?"

"Who ever said that I am? Shorty has two boys from his first marriage. Anyway, he's not divorced. If he wants a baby, I'll give him one of my eggs and he can have his own," she said. We laughed.

"Naomi, girl, you too much."

"Who? Miss Naomi loves her some dick. But anything bigger than the one going in or coming out of me isn't going to work."

"For now."

"Forever, shoot."

"Well, that's that. Everybody don't want a baby."

"Kel, if I ever tell you I want to get pregnant, would you please do me a favor?"

"What?"

"Slap the shit out of me!" she said. Naomi doubled over again with laughter. Naomi was in a joyful mood. Before we got done with brunch, I talked Naomi into taking me to the hospital to have the implant surgery work done.

I took Naomi home and we sat out in her driveway in my Jeep. I looked at her front window and I could see Shorty peeking at us through her drapes.

"Naomi, I'll talk to you later," I said.

"All right. Wow! It was quite a day. Holy rollers and all that mama drama made me kind of feel like I was watching the *Ricki Lake Show*. Kel, I'd invite you in but you'd probably have to beat Shorty's ass. Can you believe he's still pissed about being on the losing side of the vote we took the night of your birthday party about a man's right to choose?" she said and shook her head in disgust. Then she said, "I've got some news for you too."

"What?"

"I'm ovulating!"

"Really! That's wonderful!" I said. We gave each other a high five.

"I hope that the good doctor can see me by Tuesday."

"I'm sure he'll be able to. He wants to move quickly."

"Good. I'll call his office tomorrow morning and make the appointment."

"Thanks, Naomi, for coming through for me with this and putting that bug in your father's ear," I said and gave her a tiny kiss on the cheek.

"That's what sistas are for."

"Want to go with me to Atlas's memorial?"

"You don't think Chad would like to go with you?"

"Chad don't do funerals. Funerals give Chad the creeps. Give him nightmares. He skipped his mother's funeral. Told me he didn't have any money for airfare. I offered to pay for his trip and then he said he was sick with the flu and couldn't make it."

"What's up with that?"

"He won't talk about it. I've been trying to pull it out of him for five years. He's not saying a peep."

"That's interesting," she said and climbed out of the Jeep.

"Call me," I said as I watched her get out of the car and walk up to her front door and go in the house. Before pulling off, I waited for a few moments in case she ran back out in distress. I didn't want to have to beat Shorty's ass.

Chapter 10

Five days had passed since I'd last set foot inside Evergreen Holy Tabernacle Church. The church wasn't as filled with mourners as it had been with worshippers last Sunday morning when Reverend Edwards' sermon drove Olivia to Atlas's bedside to look into her son's chestnut eyes and tell him it was all right to let go. Including the Reverend Edwards, Naomi, Olivia, and I, there seemed to be about two dozen mourners. It was a closed casket. I was a pallbearer. I sat at the front of the church with five other pallbearers. Three of the men were Atlas's uncles, William, Gains, and Joseph. I sat between my friends Scott and Ricky. Olivia sat next to Naomi in the first pew. I didn't cry the day Atlas died and decided not to at the funeral either because I promised myself to be strong for his mother. I watched Reverend Edwards erupt from the same door on the side of the church that he came out of last Sunday. He sat between two deacons.

I went up to the podium. I delivered a eulogy.

"Atlas, you were my friend. You were born a child who became a man. So it's fitting that you are the child of every mother and father who walks the face of this earth. So it's fitting that you became a man and the man of many a father's, son's, and young man's dreams. You were my friend, Atlas. I say this again because I want to hear these words deep within my mind. I want to hear them ring like the great clocks in the cathedrals at the top of every hour that passes away the time. From every hill, mountainside, valley, and meadow on this black earth. Atlas, you took the bitter with the sweet. I once wondered who taught me how to have a friend. I don't have to wonder anymore. It was you, Atlas. Your nature was fierce and underneath the canvas of the portraits you created was a quiet strength. I told you, Atlas, not long ago that your spirit would be free the day your last breath floated from your body into the timeless winds. See, I told you, Atlas, and now it is so. I feel you hovering around us as I speak

115

these very words in your name. Spread your wings like a black butter-
fly. Fly, baby. Flit lightly through the skies with grace and the candor
that is the stuff of legends. You are now as free as the breeze. So long,
baby."

I turned to look at Olivia. She was slowly nodding her head. I
watched Naomi gently pat her thigh. After a few spirituals sung by
the choir and speakers remembering Atlas, it was time for his burial. I
got up from the pew and formed a line two deep with the other pallbearers. We rolled the casket up to the front door of the church. We
then carried Atlas's body down a short flight of steps, into the air outside that was cold, warmed only by a distant sun. Scott, Ricky, and I
gripped one side of the casket. Atlas's uncles took the other side. We
hoisted the casket inside the back of the white hearse.

Olivia interred her son at Rolling Mountain Cemetery. The sky was
streaked with thin silver and smoke-gray clouds. The grass at the
cemetery was soggy. The rain had left small puddles at the curb. The
smell of magnolia was in the air. Atlas's plot was under a great oak
tree, on a hill that sloped half the distance from the top of the hill to
the street. All you could hear were the lazy drone of bees, the chirping
of sparrows, bluebirds, and robins. I stood between Olivia and Naomi
in front of sprays and baskets of white lilies, yellow and red daisies,
pink and purple gladiolas, carnations, white and pink baby's breath.
Reverend Merle Edwards delivered the last rites.

He read from the Book of Romans.

"For I am convinced that neither death nor life, nor angels, nor rul-
ers, nor things present, nor things to come, nor powers, nor height,
nor depth, nor anything else in all creation, will be able to separate us
from the love of God in Christ Jesus our Lord."

He then brought the formal ceremonies to an end after reciting the
Lord's Prayer.

I turned to Olivia.

"Is there anything I can do? Or do you need anything at all?" I
asked.

"Kel, you and Naomi have been so good. So wonderful to me, I
think I got a new son. And a daughter I spent no time at all going

through labor with, no time at all. A smooth, painless, uncomplicated birth," she said, sounding a bit reflective. Then she said, "We're having some food back at the church. Y'all welcome to come and join us if you like." She smiled.

"Thank you, Ms. Hacker. But I would like to ask you for one little favor. If you don't mind," I said. I watched Scott and Ricky come over and join us.

"What, baby?" she asked.

"Can I have one piece of the pink and white baby's breath that's on the top of Atlas's casket? That would mean so much to me," I said.

"Baby, go on ahead and get it. Atlas would be so flattered. He loved flowers. Sometimes when I'd go over to Atlas's home to visit, I'd think that I was in a greenhouse. It was like I'd given birth to a botanical garden. Atlas loved him some plants, I'm telling you," she said. I went over and plucked two flowers off of the spray of baby's breath.

"Kel?"

"Yes, Ms. Hacker."

"Don't start calling me Ms. Hacker. I'm Olivia, or call me Mama if you want to," she said. She laughed. Scott, Ricky, Naomi, and I joined her laughter.

"Can I call you Mama, too?" Naomi teased.

"Yeah, you can."

"Can I call you Mama?" Scott said. Before she could answer, Ricky chimed in.

"How about me? I want a mama too," he said. We laughed, turning what could have been a very solemn occasion into one where we made light out of darkness.

I walked with Naomi, Scott, and Ricky down the slope of the hill of Atlas's new home. We arrived at my Jeep.

"Scott, are you and Ricky going to meet Naomi and me at the church?" I asked.

Scott looked at Ricky, who nodded.

"Yeah. We'll meet you guys there in a few," Scott said.

"Then I'd like for all of us to meet at my house for a little while. To kick it," I offered.

"I'd love to come over, Kel, but my Shorty's patience with me is wearing like his name, short," she said.

"What's up with that?" I asked.

"I'll put a bug in your ear later about it," she said. I watched Scott and Ricky climb into a truck and take off. Naomi and I met them out in front of the church. We went in and the missionaries fixed us plates. After eating, Scott, Ricky, and I were ready to leave. Naomi wasn't.

"Kel, my daddy's going to take me home," she said. I sensed something different in her mood. It was distinct.

"Call me, Naomi," I said, giving her a tiny kiss.

"I will, soon," she said.

Scott and Ricky were standing outside of their car, in front of my house talking. We went inside. I took their coats and hung them up in the hall closet. I took my baby's breath out of the inside of my jacket, and set it on the kitchen table. I watched Scott and Ricky sit down together on the loveseat. I took a jar out of the cabinet, ran some water, and put the baby's breath inside of it. I found a log in the living room, put it in the fireplace, and lit it. I put Rachelle Ferrell's CD *Individuality* on.

"Can I get you guys anything?"

"I'd like a beer," Ricky said.

"What about you, Scott? Can I get you something?"

"A brandy. Straight up."

"One beer and a brandy. Coming up," I said, as though I was a seasoned bartender. I went into the kitchen and came back out in the living room with their drinks.

"So what is this great news you got to tell us about, Kel?" Ricky asked.

"Well, Scott has probably already let the cat out of the bag. I know how lovers enjoy laying up in bed and dishing," I said and sneered at Scott playfully.

"You know I can't hold ice water," Scott said. We laughed.

"I'm trying to get pregnant."

"Scott told me that already, but are you really pregnant yet?"

"Not yet. Naomi's going to donate me one of her eggs. I also got to have a little operation."

"Well, I'll be damned! Don't tell me that they are going to cut your shortie off," Scott said.

"Hell, no! I've been given assurances by my doctor, although he told me about the risks involved."

"How does Chad feel about it? I mean, I know you guys don't live together."

"He doesn't approve of it, no more than Jerry Falwell would. But it's not his decision to make. It's mine. Because it's my body, not his. It's all very simple, really. Look at it this way. If I can determine what goes inside of it, shouldn't I have the right to determine what comes out of it? It shouldn't take a rocket scientist to figure that out."

"Damn! So that's why when you came home the night we threw you a surprise birthday party, you had tons of bags of baby clothes and shit. I thought that you had a pregnant girlfriend on the sly," Ricky said.

"Ricky, you're talking to a father-to-be. I'll probably be called bi-parental. Come on upstairs. I want to show you guys my nursery," I said with pride. I started up the stairs. Scott and Ricky followed behind me.

"Sweet Jesus!" Ricky said as he stepped into the room.

"My God! Where in the world did you find such a tiny chair?" Scott said.

"I found it at Babies and Bath in Jack London Square. It was a steal. Everything was half off. I couldn't pass it up," I said.

I showed them the baby bed that was already put up and covered with *102 Dalmatians* blankets and pillowcases. Ricky liked the rocking horse I got at Baby Boomers at Fisherman's Wharf the best. Scott liked the Scooby gowns, bibs, pajamas, slippers, and undershirts and Pampers. Ricky walked over and climbed upon the rocking horse. He rocked back and forth.

"This shit is dope!" Ricky yelped.

"Ricky, get off of that horse before you break it. You know you way too big to be up on that thing!" Scott admonished. "Kel, you got it going on up in here! I don't think that I had half the shit you got here."

"How would you know? You were just a baby," I said.

"I know because my parents kept all my baby shit as a keepsake. When I was a little boy, I used to go out in the garage where they hid it. I would find the baby bed and I'd climb up in it, and jump up and down on the bed. Until one day, the frame broke in two," Scott said with a mischievous grin.

"Scott. How could you?" Ricky said. He sucked his teeth. Ricky went on, "Kel, what do you like most about the nursery?"

"The thing I like the most about the nursery hasn't been put in here yet. My baby," I said.

"God almighty. Will you be the first one to do it? I mean, the first man to have a baby?" Ricky said, leaning up against the wall.

"My doctor told me that one of his patients is due to have his baby by Easter."

"This is unbelievable! Like a dream," Scott said. We started back downstairs and sat around the fireplace like Boy Scouts.

"Ricky and I got some good news too. You want to tell him, Ricky, or do you want me to do it?" Scott said and sipped his brandy.

"Go ahead, baby. You tell him," Ricky said, in deference to Scott.

Rachelle Ferrell's voice lilted and swayed like the flames in the fireplace. I watched Scott's face.

"Wait! Don't move! Let me go pour myself a glass of wine so we can toast the news!" I said. I hurried into the kitchen, took out a bottle of wine, poured some in a flute, and came back out to join Scott and Ricky. I sat back down across from them both.

"I'm pregnant with Ricky's HIV!" he said. We tapped our glasses in celebration. I'd given some thought to Scott's announcement to me, during my birthday party, that he wanted to get pregnant with Ricky's HIV. I still wasn't entirely happy about it. Was my choice to get pregnant superior to his choice to get pregnant with HIV? As much as it hurt, I couldn't pass judgment on Scott's decision to get pregnant with Ricky's HIV, any more than I would want either one of them to disrespect my own decision to get pregnant with one of Naomi's eggs. Anyway, if you really looked at it, Scott and I were both seeking pregnancy, in one form or the other. Both pregnancies carried with them calculated risks and danger. Were Scott, Ricky, and I all freaks of nature? I didn't think so. What is life if we don't have a choice in how we want to live it?

"When did you find out you were positive?" I asked. I took a sip of my wine.

"Last Friday, wasn't it, boo?" Scott said. He turned to look at Ricky.

"Yeah, it was last Friday because we stopped off at the DMV in El Cerrito to get my driver's license renewed," Ricky said. He snuggled in closer and took one of Scott's hands and kissed it.

"What a phenomenon!" I said.

"Now we don't have to use all those rubbers, which should save me a ton of dough," Scott said, like he'd already figured out a cost-savings benefit long ago.

"Should either one of you get sick, are you going to take any cocktail therapies?" I asked.

"If Ricky gets sick before I do, we decided that he'll take them until I come down with full-blown AIDS. Then he'll stop taking the cocktails and he'll join me in my illness."

"So you both will be sick at the same time? Like a joint project?" I asked. I scratched the back of my head.

"Yeah, I hope this doesn't still sound too kinky to you, Kel. 'Cause here it is you're trying to bring a new life in the world and Ricky and I are doing something that is going to take life out of the world," Scott said. He looked at Ricky, who nodded in agreement.

"Do you think that you guys will change your minds about any of this?" I asked, trying not to sound like a therapist. I remembered the argument Scott and I had out on my patio at my birthday party about his decision. Since then, my own quest to get pregnant had taught me to be more accepting of other people's life choices.

"The only way we'd change our minds is if a cure is found for AIDS. Then all bets are off," Ricky said. His hand sliced the air horizontally for emphasis.

"Oh, I see. If there is a cure, then what you guys have decided to do would be reduced to a moot point, right?" I said. I took it all in.

"That's right, because a cure would defeat the purpose of having to worry about the fear of infection from the get-go," Scott said.

"In that case, you both would live," I said. I was worried about losing more friends to AIDS after burying one today.

"Forever," Scott said.

"And a day," Ricky said. He finished Scott's sentence.

"So what it all boils down to is one word, hope," I said, more to my own self and the burning flames in the fireplace than to the two men sitting with me in the aftermath of Atlas's death. I got up, went into the hall closet, and took out the Scrabble game. We played Scrabble until Scott and I both got tired of Ricky beating us hands down game after game. Night had fallen by the time they decided to go home.

"Well, guys, it's been real," I said.

"Revealing to say the least," Scott said. He got up off of the floor and then pulled Ricky up by his hand.

"It really has been something," Ricky said. I walked over to the closet and fetched both of their jackets. They put on the jackets and gave me a hug. I went with them to the front door.

"You guys take it easy," I said. I opened the door.

"Let us know when the rabbit dies," Scott said. They laughed as they stepped outside.

Chapter 11

It was Tuesday. Three days had passed since I'd heard from Naomi. A week had gone by since Naomi went to see Dr. Valesco and donated her eggs. It wasn't that I was growing impatient or nervous. I was anxious about getting the work done, to get the pregnancy on its way. Naomi is very strong willed. Once that woman sets out to do something, there's no turning her back. Shorty was another story. He worried me. I doubted but was concerned that he had attempted to talk Naomi out of donating one of her eggs to me so that I could get pregnant. I decided to ring her up.

"Kel, Shorty trippin'," Naomi said.

"What about?" I asked.

"I told him that I gave you one of my eggs and you know what that nigga told me?"

"What?"

"If you have the baby and something happens to you, I've got to take care of it. Since it's my egg you're getting," she said, sucking her teeth.

"What did you tell him?"

"I told him if that happens then I would be the one to take care of it because he don't even take care of his own kids. How is he going to take care of any of mine? Anyway, I made the appointment last week and the procedure was done the next day."

"Did it hurt or anything?"

"I'm a little sore."

"What?"

"But now I've got to put Shorty's big dick ass on hold for a month. Locking the kitty cat up," she said, laughing.

"So it's done."

"Done. Shorty can take his fat ass to hell. I don't know why I still put up with him," she said. She sounded serious.

"It's called love, Naomi."

"Well, excuse the hell out of me. If this is love, I hope I never start to hate his ass. When I do it's going to be on. Okay? Watch me," she said.

"Sista, you are something else."

"What happens now with you?"

"I've got to wait until my sperm fertilizes your egg."

"Hang in there, Brotha. Dr. Valesco told me that in three weeks your sperm will fertilize my egg."

"When that happens, it won't be long before I conceive."

"You've got to show me the baby clothes and stuff you bought for the baby. Don't buy anything else. Otherwise, we're not going to be able to give you a decent baby shower," she said.

I found out that Naomi hadn't told me about donating the egg because of all of the drama surrounding the death of Atlas and her mother smacking Cayleen down. As I had suspected, Shorty had tried to talk her out of donating one of her eggs to me.

"Naomi, thanks, Sista."

"You don't have to thank me, you know you my brotha."

"Naomi, I'm going into the hospital tomorrow for the implant work I need to have done. Do you mind picking me up?"

"Who? I don't even know how you can fix your mouth to ask me that. You know I'll be there to get you. What time do you have to be at the hospital?"

"At eight in the morning."

"Damn. That's early, but I'll be there to get you." I hung up the telephone feeling like I was coming closer to a dream come true.

I was lying on a table at Mercy Hospital, being prepped for my implant surgery. I was nervous as hell. I thought I'd never live to see another hospital, at least until the baby was born. Had I slipped into a paranoid state? Was the male pregnancy study a front by the government to prey upon unsuspecting gays; inject them with poisonous chemicals or a new virulent strain of AIDS? Was the study being covertly funded by the Klan, the John Birch Society, or the Moral Majority in a plot to exterminate blacks and gays as a way of killing two birds with one stone? Was Dr. Valesco in on the scheme too? Was he the chief ringleader? Dr. Valesco didn't waste any time doing the surgery. Before I was able to let my wild thoughts of conspiracy theories take hold inside of me, it was too late. Dr. Valesco put me under. He took me in the operating room. The next thing I knew, I was in the recovery room. I woke up groggy. When I finally was able to focus, I found myself looking up in Dr. Valesco's face.

"Kel, how are we doing here?"

"A little sleepy."

"Does anything hurt?"

"Underneath my ribcage is a little sore."

"It'll all go away in a few days. The surgery went well. We did the implants and put the catheter in. It's a good thing you've got such a large torso, because you got enough room below your ribcage to grow a six-pound baby."

"Are you sure everything went well?"

"So far, so good. Look, I need to see you in my office two days from now to begin the injections. Can you make it?" Before I could answer, he said, "Oh, you've got to stay one more night in the hospital to make sure you don't develop complications."

"All right and I'll be there."

"Take care," he said. I watched him disappear through the door.

I picked up the phone and called Chad, but there was no answer. I'd already told him about the surgery. I didn't expect for him to come and see about me. Especially since he'd told me he wasn't going to take me to have the operation. So I didn't trip. But at least he could have picked up the telephone, to call me and see how I was doing. I called Naomi. She picked up on the first ring.

"Naomi, it's me, Kel."

"Hey, Brotha. How did the surgery go?"

"Dr. Valesco said everything went well. I can go home tomorrow. Can you come and pick me up from the hospital?"

"You know I'll be there. What time?"

"Come about nine o'clock in the morning."

"Do you need anything, Kel?"

"Home. I want to get out of here, Naomi."

Less than twenty-four hours later, she picked me up and took me home, where I convalesced for two days. I'd forgotten how uncomfortable it was to have a catheter stuck in my body. Once a week I had to go to the hospital to have the catheter cleaned and disinfected.

I'd made my peace with the implant, which didn't bother me too much until I had to reach up to get things out of shelves or closets. The catheter was another story. It pulled my skin and made the area surrounding it red and sore.

I locked up the house and went to visit with Chad and share my good news with him. The day after Atlas's funeral Chad told me that he felt some remorse about not attending the memorial service with me. After many years of being with him, he finally told me why he didn't attend his mother's memorial. Chad's mother was a religiously conservative fanatic. Much of his life, at least until he turned eighteen, he had to suppress his sexuality. He had grown to hate standing on corners, holding the magazines that his church promoted, and especially knocking on people's doors early on Sunday mornings, either waking them up or interrupting their breakfasts. Chad would never identify or name the church he grew up in. As long as I'd known him, he always referred to his religious background as "secular but different" when I'd ask about his church affiliation.

Chad would take a few minutes to ponder the question, as if he was taking a multiple choice examination, where all the potential answers sounded the same to him. All he ever told me is that he had grown up in the church. All in all, he had taken the religion that he called the church in stride. Chad told me that being in the church prevented him from associating with anyone other than other church members. He told me that he felt as if the church had put him under constant surveillance, like being watched twenty-four/seven by the FBI. All of his telephone calls, before he turned eighteen, were screened. He had to go to bed at nine o'clock every night, regardless of whatever plans he already made for the evening. He told me that the church picked out his girlfriends for him. These girls, with long dresses and stiff hats, frightened him. His parents picked out all of his clothes and shoes and decided what books he could read and those that he could not. He told me that the food his mother cooked sometimes made him sick to the stomach and that he developed bulimia by the time he made it to the tenth grade. Every Sunday, he told me that he had to sit through Bible study. He said he would look at pictures of families, in the Bibles and magazines that his church promoted, who seemed to live in a kingdom neither in heaven nor on earth. The pictures of the women always showed them with long stringy hair, the men with slim waist-lines; and the children were pictured as happy-go-lucky.

Once on the way home from school, Chad's curiosity got the best of him, and he ventured into an adult bookstore. He told me that he spent hours in that bookstore, flipping through pornography maga-zines. He had picked out a huge black dildo and a skin magazine that had sweaty, musclebound men with erections. He decided to buy the dildo and the magazine and take them home. He told me he would lock himself up in his tiny bedroom and discover the thrills and de-lights of fantasy. Once he told me that he put some Vaseline on the dildo and, after several attempts, was unable to get it all the way in. The part that got in did the trick. He told me that was when he real-ized that he was gay. He lost his virginity, and he waited for the day he turned eighteen, to leave home and move to San Francisco, a city he called Oz. He told me that when his mother died a couple of years ago, he had all but forgotten that she had given him birth and brought him into the world. As far as he was concerned, a stork could have dropped him down on his parents' porch. Chad told me that he felt no familial connection to his parents whatsoever.

When I slipped my key in Chad's front door, I looked at him sitting on his sofa watching E!. From what I could gather, from a glimpse of the television screen, he was watching *Mysteries and Scandals*. A man stood in near darkness, out on the street, wearing a long black trench coat, narrating the story of a legendary actress who was speculated to have killed her gangster husband and let her only child take the rap.

"What's up, Juicy Head?" Chad said without turning away from the television show and looking at me.

"Naomi donated the egg and I've had my operation. It won't be long now," I said and remembered the little joke my mother had told me once when I was a little boy about the cat's reaction to a dog that had got his long tail cut off—"It won't be long now."

Chad turned to look at me.

"Head. Look at your face! Come with me!" he said as he took my hand and led me into his bathroom. We stood in front of a mirror.

Chad went on, "Look at your fucking face! Your moustache and goatee are as thin as a spider's web! Oh, Head! You've got nothing left on your face except thick eyebrows and eyelashes. You remind me of a camel. Big old headed thing. See, I told you this shit was going to fuck you up." I looked in the mirror. My face was as smooth as ice cubes. There was still a trace of my thick moustache and goatee. All Dr. Valesco had done was put the catheter inside of me, but I'd started having to shave right after the operation because the thick hair on my face began to itch. Then I had trouble sleeping because it would hurt when I'd roll over in bed on the side of my body where Dr. Valesco put the catheter. I began to get nervous, sit up at night and worry about whether the operation would work. My face was puffy and I had bags under my eyes. I wondered if something went wrong with the implant. I wasn't concerned about the doctor's work because I totally trusted his medical expertise. I decided that the itch of my facial hair was due to worry and stress over having the catheter stuck inside of me.

"Chad, I can always pencil in a moustache. It's not a big deal. Some men never grow them at all. Look at Michael Jackson," I said.

"Yeah, look the fuck at him! Do you want to look like that? And where is that big dick of yours? Has it shrunk down to the size of a peanut?" he said as he reached down between my legs and grabbed my member and began to massage it.

"See, Chad! It's still there and more sensitive than it was before. Sometimes it springs to life if the wind blows too hard on it," I said and rubbed his thigh.

"Let's test it," he said, taking off his undershirt, jeans, socks, and sneakers. I stripped. We got busy making love like it was the first time our bodies ever explored each other's. I flipped Chad over on his belly. I climbed him like I was hiking up Mt. Tam. The closer I got to the top, the farther my love came down. Chad found erotic zones in my ear, armpits, toes, and scrotum that seemed like they'd been touched for the very first time. When we got done I lay in Chad's arms, my nipples hard and tingling.

"Well, did I pass the test?" I asked.

"Is everything a test with you, Head?"

"Chad, you were the one wanting to put me through a test."

"I'd give you high scores, Head. But we're not exactly at a preseason San Francisco Forty-Niners football game. What is that thing stuck under your ribs for?"

"It's a catheter, Chad. That's where Dr. Valesco is going to put the fertilized egg and the other stuff. Why? Are you interested?"

"Hell no! Honeydew Head."

"Chad, I thought that you might be considering having our next baby. All I want is one child."

"You'd be lucky as hell to have one," he said.

"Chad?"

"What, Head?"

"I'm a little afraid. My whole body is changing. I can't go work out like I did before I had the operation."

"Be careful, Head."

"Chad?"

"What, Honeydew?"

"If something should happen to me and the baby, I don't want you to sell my house. Keep it in the family."

"All right, Head. Stop talking like it's the end of the world."

I got up from the bed and went back into the bathroom. I looked in the mirror. I wanted to say mirror, mirror, on the wall, tell me, is he going to love my baby? Or am I living in a dream? I wanted to ask the mirror on the wall if Chad was going to have me committed to the psychiatric ward at Armor Protective. I pictured my new neighbor, Mrs. Hill, who would get up in the middle of the night, wander into my room, and get in my bed thinking that I was her husband. I looked at the stitches that still had not been taken out yet and the catheter.

I stumbled back to Chad's bedroom and slid underneath his cool sheets. I snuggled into Chad's firm chest, feeling warm, as I pictured my baby, feeling, growing inside of me. I fell asleep and had a dream that I had a little boy who looked like Jamar, the toddler I'd seen at the restaurant in Jack London Square, before I went shopping at Babies and Bath. Chad and I had taken him to Marine World Africa U.S.A., and on a tour of the wine country in Napa Valley. We had named him Chad Jr. His fat little cheeks made everybody we ran into want to pinch him. We came back home and I put Chad Jr. to bed. Before he fell asleep, I told him a fairy tale about a man who always wanted to have a baby; and after wanting it so much, all of his life, his dream came true. I told him all you have to do is believe and it will be done.

Chapter 12

Ma was standing over the kitchen counter, running water into a huge pot, slicing sausages, cutting up chicken pieces and celery sticks, and shelling jumbo shrimp. She was making gumbo. I'd chucked up all of my dinner last night. I had been on the telephone, talking to Ma about how I thought California did such a lousy job with handling natural gas and energy when my dinner, a tossed salad, fried drumsticks, steamed rice, and celery sticks turned sour on my stomach. I dropped the telephone and got into the bathroom just in the nick of time. I was concerned that now Ma was going to start calling me every night to see if I was all right. Now everything that she cooked, she made extras for me. If I wasn't at home, when she'd call me, I'd have a message on my voice mail from her. "Kel, come on over to the house and eat or get you a plate."

She had finished mixing all of the ingredients in the pot of gumbo. She sat down at the dining table and nursed a glass of Christian Brothers brandy. She looked at me.

"Kel, I know your sickness cleared up, but maybe they should have kept you on that medicine. That's what I kept telling that daddy of mine. Told him the same thing. He dropped out the chemotherapy program on the last day. Told me he wasn't nobody's test-tube monkey. Little old legs looked like black shoestrings. He was too old. Daddy was seventy-five years old with colon cancer. He got poor as a snake. All he did was sleep and have the worst nightmares. I heard him one night in his room. He woke up screaming about his dead brother being dragged to death one night on a dark road right outside of Dallas, when he was a little boy. He told me it happened so fast, all he could see riding in the truck was the redness on the back of the two men's necks and the hair on their heads, blowing out of the windows of that truck like the hair of two witches riding on broomsticks."

"They never found out what was wrong and ended up giving me medication for a condition I didn't even have, Ma," I said, and tried to avoid looking her straight in the face. I wondered whether I was somebody's test-tube monkey.

"Child, something done made you lose all the hair on your face. Lord. I'll say," she said getting up from the table and walking toward me.

"Medicine can do that to you, Ma. You know that." I wasn't lying; some medicine has that kind of effect. Only in my case, it just so happened to be a combination of bad nerves and worry about how everything would turn out.

"Kel?"

"Yes."

"Look at me. I'm your mother and I know when something's not right. I know my child. I gave birth to you," she said as she gently took my face in her hands and looked at me gravely.

"Well, I'll be goddamn! Child, when you start taking hormones?"

"Ma, I'm not taking hormones."

"You sure those little old pink things the doctors gave you last year when you were sick didn't mess you up?" she said, picking up the medicine bottle once filled with fluconazole and looking at it. She half shook the empty bottle.

"Ma, you told me about Bernice," I said. I wished I knew how to tell her that I had an operation so that I could have a baby, but I decided to stick to my guns and wait until I was into my third trimester. I walked over to the sink and began to run cold water over a head of lettuce. I could feel Ma's eyes on my back.

"Your ass done got just as plump as a cantaloupe. I know because you always had a narrow behind. And it sure is good to see you get your color back. You got so dark when you and that Chad went on vacation to Cancun. Are you bleaching?" she said, looking at me now with even more interest. I cut up cucumbers, turned the water off, put the diced lettuce in a salad bowl, and set it in the fridge. I dried my hands on a soft white cloth that hung from the handle of the fridge. I went over to the kitchen table and sat in a chair in front of Ma. I was exhausted. She looked at me and sipped her drink.

"Ma, you the one had me. As far as I know, I was born a black baby. I was never what anybody would call high yellow or a redbone. And I'm not bleaching. I think having a built-in permanent tan is great. I feel blessed," I said. I made it over to the sink, ran water over the to-matoes, and started to dice them. All I could hear was running water, the slow bubbling stew of the pot of gumbo that simmered on top of my stove. I was in agreement with Ma, but it wasn't that the Cancun sun had toasted my skin. It was because the fluconazole I was taking when I was misdiagnosed with valley fever had darkened my skin. When I stopped taking fluconazole my skin tone had gone from the color of dark mahogany to the color of light oak brown. I hadn't ex-pected this to happen to me. It was just one of the ways I had reacted to the fluconazole. Now I was regaining my original skin tone and color.

Recently, I had grown a small paunch which had nothing to do with the fluconazole. My solid rock-hard abdominal muscles had become slack because I couldn't do crunches anymore, not with the catheter and implant stuck inside of me. I didn't even try to hide my belly from Ma.

I began to look back on the day I rushed over to Dr. Valesco's of-fice. He told me that the second phase of the plan was successfully completed. My sperm had fertilized Naomi's egg. Dr. Valesco went over the initial injection procedure he told me that he was about to perform on me during the third phase. He told me to get up on the examination table, take off my shirt, and lie on my back.

"Now lie still and don't move," he said.

"All right," I said as I lay on my back. I imagined being curled up like the fetus inside of its mother's womb, pictured on the wall just above my head. I looked at the picture. I identified myself with the picture, hoping to find, if not comfort, then inspiration. I didn't lose focus that I was a man who wanted to have a baby. But was I sharing in a great work that would distinguish the new millennium from the twentieth century? Or had I become a guinea pig willing to sacrifice my own life to conceive a child at any cost? Or was I allowing doctors and researchers to practice genocide on me? Dr. Valesco took a sy-ringe and stuck it into the catheter. A strange cold feeling washed over me, as if someone had poured a bucketful of ice water over my head. My body shivered and shook like Jell-O. My eyes rolled to the back of my head. I became light-headed. It felt as though I'd received a high-voltage electric shock treatment.

"Sorry, Kel. Now keep still. Take a couple of slow, deep breaths," Dr. Valesco said.

"All right," I said and pictured myself at the gym lifting weights and taking deep breaths to lighten the load of the barbells. The pressure from the fluid going inside of me was like the heavy foot of an elephant resting on my chest. I felt a warm tear roll down the side of my face into the corner of my mouth.

"That's it, we're done. I've injected the fertilized egg mixed with the special therapy. If things go as planned, you should have a near normal full-term pregnancy. You can relax and sit up, Kel," Dr. Valesco said and patted me on the back.

"Yeah, we are done," I said as I still sat up on the table. I stared out of the window at the lush green hills of Treasure Island. Was I paralyzed? I wondered if I'd be able to get up off of the table and walk without falling down. Or would my legs buckle under me? I felt like a man who had been out at sea for months and nothing on land felt steady anymore.

"Well, what would you give me on a scale of one to ten?"

"Huh?" I asked. I struggled to regain a sense of full equilibrium. I looked down at a copper-colored substance on the paper sheet that spilled over from the injection.

"Where do I rate?"

I was too out of sorts to give Dr. Valesco a grade, so all I asked was, "Dr. Valesco, has my baby been conceived?"

"That's right, Kel. Conception of your child took place in a test tube. The fertilized egg represents conception and I just injected it inside of you through the catheter. In eight weeks you'll come back for an exam, to see how the development and growth of the fetus is progressing. The tricky thing about male pregnancy is that it's experimental and sometimes prone to scientific error. I'm cautiously optimistic about you being able to carry the baby to full term. We've got to do a confirmatory pregnancy test to validate the success of the implantation. Only then can we say that you have a viable pregnancy. There must be a successful interaction between you and the unborn child.

You've got to be receptive to the growth of the baby. So for now, consider these results as preliminary until your follow-up examination. But for all intents and purposes you are pregnant. The worst case scenario would be that you could suffer a miscarriage. Then we'd have to start over again. The next eight weeks will be the most dangerous period of your pregnancy. Some women have a very difficult time with pregnancy. Our male pregnancy study subjects have a higher pregnancy failure rate than women. Anytime you inject a foreign object inside the body it is vulnerable to attack by your immune system, which may try to reject the implant. Remember, no turning and twisting your abdominal section and waistline. Don't bench press at the gym. It might interfere with the growth of the child. Your condition is very delicate. Walk. Walking will help you to relax."

"When my baby is born, Dr. Valesco, I'll give you a final rating. Until then, think of your treatment of me as unfinished business. We never count the eggs until they are hatched," I said.

"You're wise to think that way, Kel," he said, waving good-bye to me and leaving the room.

After I'd diced the tomatoes, Ma walked over to me and put her hand on my forehead.

"Child, you got a fever. Lord, I hope to God you not getting sick again. All them months you stayed in that hospital and letting them people stick holes in you like a pincushion. It's a wonder everything you drink don't just pour out of you like a sprinkler."

"I don't have a fever, Ma. It's hot in the kitchen because you got the stove on cooking the gumbo, that's all," I said. But my body was warm and it felt like my jeans were too tight around my waist. I pulled up my undershirt, unbuttoned my pants, and let my zipper down halfway to my crotch. Ma walked over to me.

"Child, your stomach is as round and tight as a pregnant woman's. You must have quit doing them sit ups," she said, walking over to the stove and looking into the pot of gumbo. She took a long-handled spoon out of my cabinet drawer and began to stir the gumbo. I went and sat down at the kitchen table. The smell of the gumbo was starting to make me feel nauseated. I went into the bathroom right off of the kitchen and vomited. I must have stayed in the bathroom longer than Ma wanted me to because she began knocking on the door. I got up off of my knees, rinsed my mouth out with cold water, and splashed some of it on my face. Suddenly, I had to urinate. I got done and washed my hands.

"I'll be out in a minute, Ma. I'm taking a piss," I yelled at the door.

When I opened the door, Ma was standing with her arms folded across her breasts, looking as worried as she did when I was sick last year and didn't know what was wrong with me.

"It took you that long to piss? Child, it ain't but so much piss in anybody's bladder. Want me to take you to the hospital, Kel?" she said, taking my elbow and sitting down next to me at the kitchen table.

"I'll be all right, Ma. It's probably one of those forty-eight hour viruses. It'll pass through me in a day or so," I said, trying to reassure her that everything was fine so that she wouldn't lay up at night worrying about me.

"You'll feel better after you eat some of this hot gumbo," she said, and got up from the table, went back over to the pot, and began to stir. I watched Ma stand over the pot of gumbo with one hand on her hip.

"Ma?"

"Uh huh?"

"I don't feel like eating gumbo today."

"Don't feel like eating gumbo today? I've never seen you turn away from gumbo except when you got that Cookie pregnant. You couldn't even stand the smell of it. Puked all over that new comforter I'd bought for you at Macy's white sale. I knew then that somebody was pregnant, especially when I had been dreaming of rain and for days it had been hotter than the heat coming from hell's kitchen."

"Ma?"

"Huh?"

"Did you ever want grandchildren?"

Ma told me that anybody with a mind and wants to keep a family going would want offspring. It's the natural order of things. Long ago, she hoped that God would bless her with a grandchild; but she put away such foolish wishes. But she believes in God's blessings and one of them is the miracle of birth.

"So if I believe in blessings, I suppose a miracle is something that I also believe in."

"If I got pregnant, Ma, would you respect and accept me and my baby?"

She laughed. "Child, where's that thermometer at? Poor thing! If it ain't a fever got you talking out your head, I don't know what it is," she said, picking up the lid of the pot off of the kitchen counter and covering the pot of gumbo. I went into the medicine cabinet in the bathroom and got the thermometer. I came back out and stuck it underneath my tongue the way it's done at the hospital. After a few moments, I took it out and showed it to Ma.

"See, Ma. I don't have a temperature. You still think I'm talking out of my head?"

"Baby, you been working too hard, that's all. Kel, I've always told you that God never gives us more than we can carry. I mean that and you should understand it. Everything in nature happens according to God's divine plan," she said and walked over to me and gently rubbed the top of my clean-shaven head.

Hours later, when the gumbo cooled, Ma helped me put the gumbo and Uncle Ben's Converted White Rice into ten Ziploc freezer bags. After we got done, we set them in the fridge. I had to argue with her about cleaning my house, but lost out because I couldn't muster the energy to do it myself. I was sensitive about Ma coming over to my house, tidying up and cleaning things, because I remember when I was growing up, I would sometimes leave a sink full of dirty dishes or a basket of soiled clothes for Ma to wash up. She'd roll her eyes at me and say, "I ain't nobody's maid, hell! The more I do the more I have to do! Shit!"

My legs felt like they were going to buckle out from under me and I had to sit down on the sofa in the living room and rest. I flipped on the television. Chad's channel, E!, was on. A controversy was swirling around the heads of Elton John and Eminem, a rapper notorious for bashing gays in his songs. The reporter, a Tammy Faye Bakker look-alike with thick black mascara around her eyes, seemed to deliver the news with glee. The two singers performed together at the previous month's Grammy Awards. At the end of the performance, Eminem had flipped a bird to the fans, telling them to go and fuck themselves.

I muted the sound.

Ma came out of the kitchen and joined me on the sofa. She leaned over and went into a mid-sized basket lined with terry cloth and pulled out purple, lime green, red, yellow, white, beige, orange, and gold scraps of cloth. She grabbed a little box full of needles and began to stitch the patches together. She was making a quilt. We sat in silence. I watched her delicately pull white thread through the cloth, connecting one color, one patch, to the next one. She'd rub the wrinkles until the cloth was smoother than anything I'd ever seen her iron in my life. The seams were invisible. She'd sink the needle softly into the cloth, then pull, without ever so much as missing a beat. She began to hum a song to herself. If only she'd utter the words, then I'd know what she was singing about. I pictured Ma giving the completed quilt to me one Sunday afternoon, after little Chad's navel cord had fallen off. I'd just given little Chad a warm bath and he was cooing and swinging his tiny hands and feet. Ma would start up the stairs heading into the nursery. Ma would rub Johnson's Baby Oil on little Chad and rock him to sleep. She would give little Chad to me before she left my house. I would put little Chad on my chest where he would fall asleep.

Ma stopped quilting and my daydream ended. She looked at my hands. My fingernails had grown longer than she'd ever seen me wearing them before. All of the thick hair on my forearms was gone and if she could have seen my armpits she would have noticed that the hair was gone there too. All of my pubic hair had disappeared after Dr. Valesco injected the fertilized egg and therapy into me. My electric shaver was sitting in my bathroom underneath the sink, gathering dust by the hour. I no longer needed to shave because my skin was as smooth as a baby's bottom. Now I knew that the change my body was going through was because I was pregnant.

"Kel, look at your nails, child. You must be getting a lot of protein. I sure wish my nails would grow like that. But I can't grow them anymore for biting them off. Look at my nails," she said. She held out her cranberry red fingernails that were stubbed but polished to near perfection.

"I guess. My body has changed. I got a little molehill for a stomach now."

"Child, if I didn't know any better, I'd swear on the Bible that you is pregnant. But I must be dreaming."

"Ma?"

"Yeah, baby?"

"Just for fun. If I were really pregnant, what would you do? Would you trip out on me?" I asked.

"Child, didn't I tell you a few minutes ago that I believed in miracles? God's will be done. Don't talk like that because it's all right. God gave me you. God could have made me a barren woman. Instead He blessed my womb."

I wasn't going to press Ma. Not for now and maybe not ever as it regarded my pregnancy. It was my decision, as I told Chad. Neither Ma nor Chad is going to have my baby. Was it that selfish of me to expect for them to help me raise my baby? I'd prefer, though, that they offer me support and be in my life. I just wasn't going to stress out and lose sleep over it. Millions of single parents are raising their children alone and doing as good a job if not better than two parents. I don't think that it's freakish or strange to want the best for your children.

Ma gathered up her basket of soft cloths, quilting needles, and thread, and I saw her to the door.

"Kel, you sure you're going to be all right? Lord, I feel something about you that I can't name. It's like having something on the tip of your tongue but you can't say it. Oh, it'll come to me by and by," she said as she gave me a peck on the cheek.

"I'll talk to you later, Ma," I said, opening the door for her. I went to the kitchen window and watched her towering figure of strength climb into her car and drive away. As I watched her, I thought to myself, "You are going to be a grandmother, Mrs. Warren. A grandmother one of these old days."

Chapter 13

I sat in Dr. Valesco's office feeling fatigued, anxious, and tired. I was constipated. I'd been throwing up so much the last couple of weeks I worried that if I wasn't pregnant then something was going on inside of me that I could feel but couldn't see. It was as if my stomach would churn and reject everything I ate. I'd lost about five pounds and even bottled or tap water tasted bitter to me. I'd come to Dr. Valesco's office for my follow-up examination. Before I came to the office I'd talked to Helga over the telephone about what kind of tests Dr. Valesco was going to run on me to see if the baby was developing normally. She said, "Kel, you've got to have an ultrasound and a urine test to confirm your pregnancy."

I sat in the lobby of Dr. Valesco's office along with two twenty-something men. The men sat in identical French colonial high-back chairs reading magazines. One of the men had spiked blond hair and a hint of a goatee. The other man looked like he went bald prematurely. The top of his head was bald and shiny. I sat on a multicolored sofa that had a portrait of toddlers from every racial group you could possibly imagine. They were playing with building blocks and wore Pampers. I watched these two men and wondered what stage of the program they were in, or if they were like me, here to pee in a cup to see if they were pregnant.

Helga had led me into the examination room, through a side door in the reception area. She walked ahead of me and opened the door to a rest room.

"See that little cup over there?" she said, pointing to a plastic cup half the size of a jar of Vaseline. She went on, "We need you to give us a sample right up to here. Leave the cup up on this ledge. And come across the hall to this room here when you're done," she said, waving her arm and smiling like one of the women pointing to a door with dream prizes locked behind it on *The Price Is Right*. She drew my attention to a small ledge that had a box-shaped door cut around it. She closed the door. After rushing into the nearest rest room for the last two weeks, dumping piss in the toilet like a pregnant water hose, I was so nervous I was barely able to pee. I set the sample on the ledge and left the rest room, hoping for the miracle that Ma told me she believed in.

I went into the exam room and hoisted myself up on the examination table. I looked at the Bay Area skies, a checkerboard of gray clouds, patches of blue sky and sunshine. Suddenly, it began to rain heavily. I thought about what Ma had once told me, when I was a little boy, that when it rains while the sun is shining the devil is beating his wife. The wind blew the cypress trees on Treasure Island. I watched a tiny tugboat on the bay struggle to pull and bear the weight of a vessel that seemed to be overloaded with cargo.

I heard a knock at the door.

"Come in," I said weakly as I watched Dr. Valesco's face, wishing that I could read his mind.

"Kel, how are you doing?" he asked, his face still not betraying what was about to come out of his mouth.

"Well, I've been sick."

"What's the matter?"

"Well, for starters I've lost weight. I can't seem to hold down my food. My stomach does flip-flops and I get dizzy. I'm constipated. I get tired real easy and pee a lot. All of my hair is gone. All I got left is a big dick and a tiny paunch for a stomach."

"Whoa! Kel, settle down," he said, laughing. He gently put his hand on my shoulder. Then he said, "Take off your shirt and lie back. Let's see what's going on here." Dr. Valesco put on his stethoscope and asked me to take even, deep breaths. He put the stethoscope on my stomach and listened.

"Sit up, Kel," he said, his face still unreadable to me. Maybe I did have a tumor inside of me like Chad had been telling me all along. Why hadn't I listened to Chad? What he told me made perfect sense. How could a man have a baby anyway? Was Ma's belief in miracles an old wives' tale? Was the belief in miracles something that was left over from the vestiges of our slave past? Was Cerrita wrong about fairy tales coming true? Was it a tumor I was growing and not a baby? I was dying to know. I steeled myself.

"Break it to me gently, Dr. Valesco. Or I'm going to crack like a plate," I said, looking down at the shiny white floor and freezing the tears in the back of my eyes.

Dr. Valesco took an office Doppler, a hand-held ultrasound listening device, from the hip pocket of his white smock. He placed it on my stomach for a few moments. Then he smiled and looked up at me.

"Kel, I hope that you believe in dreams, because I can hear a heartbeat in your stomach. Not only that, the urine test came back positive. Mr. Kel Warren, congratulations! You're eight weeks pregnant! You are going to have a baby," he said, taking off his glasses and wiping his eyes. A million thoughts converged in my mind; collided all at once. I couldn't speak. I rolled my tongue around in my mouth, to see if I still had teeth. I took a deep breath and exhaled. I was still breathing. This wasn't a dream, after all. I was sitting upon a hard examination table, in Dr. Valesco's office, in the flesh. I wanted Dr. Valesco to unwrap a sterilized needle and poke it into me, anywhere, just to see if I was alive. I remembered getting circumcised, when I was twelve. I was dating Nicole, a neighbor who lived around the block from me. I'd told her that I was going into the hospital to get circumcised and would let her know how it went, after I came back home from the hospital. A couple of days had gone by after the surgery before I decided to venture out of my house to see Nicole. My member had swelled to the size of a hot link. It was wrapped up in a bandage that looked like a burrito covered with thick ketchup. I didn't want to show Nicole my new dick, because it didn't look the way it did the last time she'd seen it. Nicole insisted that I show her what they'd done to me at the hospital. "I want to see your thang," she demanded. Nicole wouldn't take no for an answer. She led me by my hand, out into her backyard, into a clubhouse that her brother Gilbert had made for the two of them to play in. When she unbuckled my belt, pulled down my pants, and saw the bloody bandages on my dick, she screamed and ran away. I imagine that she's been running ever since, and has never stopped to think anything else about the untidy consequences of male circumcision at all. I didn't talk to anybody about getting circumcised for two weeks after I'd watched Nicole bolt and run away from me like somebody had yelled fire in a crowded movie theater. When I did talk about it, what came to mind was that I couldn't sleep on my stomach for a very long time after the surgery. That's when I began sleeping on my side in a fetal position. I've slept that way ever since.

Let's say I had hearing loss, moments before Dr. Valesco came through the door to tell me I was pregnant. I still would have been able to see his face well enough to read his lips. I felt the water freeze behind my eyes, gather like storm clouds, but held it back like a dam. The tears probably would've soaked the thin white paper that was the sheet on top of the hard bed I was sitting on. After all of my obsessing about getting pregnant, here it was. Now I didn't know how or what to feel. Dr. Valesco tried to reach me again.

"Kel, did you understand me? You're pregnant!"

"A baby?" I asked as if I was hearing him tell this to me in a dream that had come to life.

Dr. Valesco spoke to me as if he wanted me to make no mistake about it. "You are going to have a baby, Kel, you are pregnant," he said. To let Dr. Valesco tell it, this was much more than he'd even anticipated or ever imagined.

He went on, "Frankly, I didn't think that conception would take hold in you. Despite our best efforts, very few men go on to conceive a child."

"I'm feeling like I'm in another world. I prayed to God for one child and now He's answering my prayer. Good grief."

From now on until the baby is born, I was to see Dr. Valesco once a month. Dr. Valesco gave me some prenatal information to take home to read. After Dr. Valesco listened to my complaints of frequent urination, nausea, weight loss, and fatigue, he told me these are common symptoms of pregnancy. "So please don't be alarmed," he said and handed me a guide called *Pregnancy & Prenatal Care for Men.* I looked at the front jacket of the book. Dr. Valesco was the author.

"Like I said, it's important that you come to see me once a month for regular checkups and injections. This is still a delicate yet remarkable condition that you are in. Don't take any other medication before consulting with me. Not so much as aspirin or Tylenol. Again, congratulations," he said as he gently slapped me on the back.

"Dr. Valesco?"

"Yes, Kel."

"When do I go in to have my baby?"

"Sometime right around Thanksgiving Day," he said as he leaned over, opened up a drawer, took out a pregnancy calendar, and handed it to me. He went on, "We'll schedule the caesarean."

"Will you take this catheter out of me before long?"

"You still need monthly injections, Kel. Up to the end of your third trimester. That's the down side. I know how unpleasant they are. But they are a necessary evil. The child needs to keep growing in the sack, hence the reason for the injections." I watched Dr. Valesco disappear from the room.

I rubbed my warm round belly, in small circles, and a sense of exhilaration washed over me. I felt like getting down off of the table and making a joyful noise. Shout, dance, and testify like the people at Evergreen Holy Tabernacle Church do on Sundays. But I was dizzy and lightheaded, and I wished that Chad were here with me. I'd nestle my head in his barrel chest after looking in his chestnut eyes, and feel a sense of contentment and jubilation. I got dressed, and before I left Dr. Valesco's office, I went up to the reception area, found Helga, and picked up my appointment slip.

"Congratulations, Kel. You must be ecstatic. Dr. Valesco told me that you're having a baby. How wonderful," she said, smiling. She scribbled down the date and time of my next appointment on a thin slip of paper and handed it to me.

"Thanks. I feel like I'm on the top of the world!" I said with a smile as bright as the sun peeking through the window just above Helga's head.

On my way home, it wasn't very easy for me to decide that Chad would be the first person I'd tell that I was pregnant. I thought that Chad would be so happy about my pregnancy, and all of his foolish notions that I had gone over the brink of insanity could now finally be put to rest. He'd be delighted that once and for all we were going to be the fathers of a lovely baby. I hoped this would stop him from ribbing and poking fun at me as if I'd lost my mind.

Chapter 14

"Chad, I've done it, baby. I'm eight weeks pregnant! Isn't this great news?" I said, sitting down next to him on his sofa. Chad was watching E!. The show was ragging on an eccentric male celebrity who once paid another man millions of dollars to go to bed with him. After a tabloid newspaper exposed the celebrity, he went into seclusion. Now he lived alone on a tiny island in the South Pacific, surrounded by a jungle and the sea.

"Oh, Head. Why do you always have to do things the hard way?" he said. His eyebrows came together in the middle of his face.

"Chad? Guess what?"

"Oh, so don't tell me you are having twins and the stork is going to drop them down on your doorstep in the rain," he said, shifted away from me.

"Chad, I haven't lost my mind. And a stork won't be dropping down a baby on my doorstep, Chad. It's coming out of me."

"Poor Honeydew Head!"

"Chad, Dr. Valesco told me that being sick during the first trimester of my pregnancy is nothing unusual or to be concerned about. Chad, feel my stomach," I said. I pulled up my undershirt and took his hand and placed it on my round belly. Chad kept his hand on my warm stomach for a few moments and then gently pulled it away.

"Head?"

"Yeah."

"That's only gas. Men thirty years old get bloated all the time. Don't you know the difference? Gas, Head, it's only gas. Jeez."

"Chad, I want you to be as much of a father to my baby as I will be. Do this for me, Chad," I said, stopping short of getting down on my knees like I'd seen once in a movie when a man got down on his knees crying, begging his estranged spouse to come back to him.

When I realized that Chad seemed to be more interested in watching E! than talking to me, I got up from his sofa and decided to go home.

"Chad, I'm tired. I'm going home to rest," I said, giving him a small kiss on his unshaved face.

"Bye, Juicy Head."

"See you, Chad."

It seemed as though the telephone was waiting for me to step through my front door before it decided to ring. It was Amy. She was going through a very difficult time with her pregnancy. One morning she called in sick and told me that she was spotting. By the tone of her voice I knew that she was worried that she was having a miscarriage. She asked me if I was sitting down. I told her that I was. That was when she gave me her resignation. She had no other choice. The way she explained it to me was that she'd planned to take extended maternity leave after her baby was born and that staying home she'd get the rest needed that would save her baby. I told her not to worry about the clerical things I needed done. I'd already decided to close my downtown Oakland office and have my furniture moved to my house. The California energy crisis had brought with it rolling blackouts and tripled the costs to heat my small office on the twenty-seventh floor of the Kaiser Building that looked out across Lake Meritt. So Amy's resignation, as bittersweet as I felt it was, could not have come at a better time. I told her to keep in touch and let me know how things went with her pregnancy. I hung up the telephone. I set about hiring a moving company to put some office equipment in storage and take only what I needed to do my contractual work home. By the end of the week, I hoped to have my office set up at home in my study.

The next morning, I called Naomi and told her that I was pregnant. I told her to get over to my house right away. When she got over to my house, she laughed, then cried, when I told her that she had helped me make my dream come true. Her laughing and crying sort of reminded me of the rain coming down with the sun shining all at the same time. She kept getting up from my sofa, walking into the kitchen, and bringing me back saltine crackers. She told me they would hold me over until I became able to hold down solid foods. Naomi told me that when I had called and told her I was pregnant, she hung up the phone and began to yelp. She told me that she must have drawn the attention of Shorty, who she said was in between jobs and spent most of his time these days sitting in front of ESPN watching sports highlights. A little air had been let out of my balloon of happiness when Naomi told me that Shorty had been secretly working on a joint custody agreement that he thought she should get, protecting her rights as a surrogate mother. Naomi had brought the document over to my house with her and set it on my coffee table. She stared at it like it was an African sculpture she thought might look good in her house but would not know where to put it. She told me that the five-page agreement was Shorty's idea and that she had nothing to do with the contents or language. She wanted my advice because she said we were friends, but we were also sort of like a project within a project. The way she explained it to me was that a project had certain rights, responsibilities and obligations, as do the biological parents of children. Since getting pregnant I'd become able to pick up on slight nuances. It seemed that my mind's eye had become more discerning. Everything I looked at now was focused, keen and sharp. My memory was precise. Aromas were stronger, intense, and lingered in the air longer than they ever did before. The grass was greener, the sky was bluer, trees were taller, the air was fresher, and life seemed to be worth living again. Would I let Shorty burst my bubble? Naomi sat down next to me and began to sip a can of beer through a long red and white straw. I got up and plopped Whitney Houston's greatest hits CD in the stereo. I sat back down next to her.

I watched her face.

"Shorty thinks we both need to sign these papers. In case something happens to you when you go in," she said.

"We never talked about signing papers, Naomi, when you agreed to donate me your egg. This is all rather sudden."

"I know. And I don't totally agree with Shorty, but he does have a point. What if you die during childbirth?" We were silent. I listened to Whitney Houston belt out her song, "The Greatest Love of All."

That was a question I hadn't come up with an answer to. I didn't have a cover or a backup plan. That was an area of vulnerability. Who would step in and take my baby? When I was a small boy I had a friend named Seth. His mother died during childbirth. Seth's father was unwilling to step up to the plate and raise him after his mother died. Seth was bounced like a Ping-Pong ball from one foster home after the other. I didn't want that to happen to my child.

I was in a quandary. Maybe I should tell Ma before the end of my second trimester. Yet Ma was a woman to whom appearances really mattered. Would she even accept my child should something go terribly wrong with me? Anyway, wouldn't asking Ma to raise my child be equivalent to dumping it on her like so many of the crack mothers do to their mothers these days? Ma raised me and maybe she wouldn't be interested in raising somebody else's child. I could hear her mouth. "Hell. I'm sick. I don't feel like raising somebody else's child. I got my own life. Shit. Everybody grown need to raise they own kids." Or she'd ask me, "Is that all you know how to do is have a belly full of babies?"

Didn't Naomi tell me not so long ago, "Kel, if I ever tell you I want to get pregnant, would you do me a favor? Slap the shit out of me?" But didn't she mean getting pregnant and not raising babies? Or did she feel the same about both sides of the equation? I needed for Naomi to tell me the difference.

"Naomi, do you remember telling me to slap you if you decided to get pregnant?" I asked and bit down on a cracker.

"Uh huh, and I meant exactly what I said. I think it's real cute for you to be having a baby," she said and sipped her beer.

"Well, did that also mean that you wouldn't be interested in raising a baby either?"

"Why are you asking me that?"

"Only because if something should happen to me and you had to raise my child, I want to know if it would be wanted and treated right. Nothing destroys the life of a child more than when it's abused or feels unloved or unwanted. I'm not tripping, Sista. I need to know where it is that you stand on this. Especially since you told me that this whole surrogate mother agreement idea wasn't yours but Shorty's."

"Is this all about Shorty's homophobia, Kel?"

"That's another issue that I'd have to work out in my mind before I commit to signing any documents that may result in my child being under his care and supervision. If Shorty talks about me like I'm some sort of biological error, I can imagine what he'd do to my child. I'd rather have a miscarriage than have my baby ending up abused and mistreated. I'm sorry, Sista."

"Kel, don't talk like that. Do you hear me pressuring you?"

"I'm glad you're not. Let me hold onto this agreement and sleep on it. I'll let you know my decision in a few days."

"Cool."

I took Naomi upstairs and gave her a tour of the nursery. Naomi told me that she had heard about Three Little Pigs, Babies Plus, and Scooter's stores that sold baby clothes and furniture. Naomi said that she'd never seen a home that had a nursery so filled with the joy of anticipation of a new life to come. Every once in a while, Naomi would playfully pull up my undershirt, gently rubbing my belly. She'd giggle girlishly, pull my undershirt back down, and smooth it over my tight round belly like she was ironing the wrinkles out of a pillowcase. I showed her a gold-plated treasure chest that I bought a few weeks before at Babies and Bath. Naomi's eyes sparkled when I told her that I would keep the baby's birth certificate, immunization records, first pair of shoes, first photographs, first report cards, and a lock of my child's hair in the treasure chest as keepsakes. Naomi touched all of the furniture in the nursery. She went into the dresser drawers, took out baby clothes, and gently caressed them against her face. I looked at the face of my friend and I was glad that she was in my life. During moments like this, I believed that Naomi was my flesh and blood sister. Yet at the moment, I was basking in the glow of our relationship knowing full well that what the good Lord gives He can just as easily take away. We started back down the stairs and by the time I reached the bottom step, I got dizzy, stumbled, and crashed into the sofa.

"Kel, baby, you all right!" she said, sitting down next to me with a look of concern upon her face.

"I'm fine. I get winded sometimes though. Dr. Valesco told me it's common during the first trimester," I said, hoping that she wouldn't get worried.

"Can I get you anything?"

"Well, you can help me get my ass back up the stairs and into the bed," I said. I reached up, grabbed her around the shoulders, leaned on her until she got me back upstairs and into my bed. I slid beneath the covers. Naomi sat on a corner of the bed.

"Kel, you need to eat something. That baby can't grow in your belly on air and the joy in your heart."

"I know, Naomi. But I can't hold my food down."

"You've got to try, Kel. Wait. I'll be right back in a minute," she said. I watched her disappear into the hallway.

A while later, Naomi returned with a bowl of hot chicken noodle soup and crackers.

"Naomi, it's not going to stay down. I'll just eat the crackers."

"I'm not leaving this house until you eat at least half of this soup. I mean that."

"Yes, Mommy dearest," I said, trying to cheer up.

I impressed Naomi and ate the entire bowl of soup and all of the crackers that she spoon-fed me.

"Us going to be having us a baby. Us got to eat and stay strong," she said, sounding like an old soul.

"Naomi, girl, you are a mess." I managed to smile through my dizziness.

"You haven't seen a mess. Just stop eating and I'll show you a mess. That's my egg you carrying, Mr. Warren. Okay!"

"You got it, Miss Naomi."

I lay back in the bed with the covers pulled up to my belly. Naomi pulled the cover back and again began to rub my belly. Her hands were soft and smelled of roses.

"Kel."

"Yeah."

"You are the only brother I ever had. I love you and I don't want to see anything happen to you or our baby. I know this is a little weird but I didn't tell you, but I've been feeling kind of sick lately too. So when you told me that you were pregnant I knew it before it was true. A mother knows when her eggs are fertilized and a baby is conceived."

"Isn't that something. Naomi, are you pregnant?"

"Not hardly. Baby, you the one pregnant. We don't want a double pregnancy. Since you're having a baby, you got enough pregnancy to share it with me. Shorty knows that it ain't no love without the glove. He's got to come correct. That is, if he's going to come at all. Okay! Now get some rest and don't do any work tomorrow. Stay home and rest."

"Yes, Mommy dearest."

"Kel."

"Yeah."

"Shut up!" she said, laughing.

"All right already!" I joined Naomi in laughter.

I could hear Naomi double lock the front door with the extra key I'd given to her. As soon as Naomi left, I went to the bathroom and upchucked. I flipped the switch on the lamp and found my sleep. I had a dream.

I was in the recovery room at Mt. Vernon Hospital in San Francisco. I was propped up with two pillows behind my head. Chad brought to me a baby boy with a mocha smooth face, thick eyelashes, and coal-black hair. He set the baby in my arms. Naomi came in with a baby girl with a golden tanned complexion and chestnut eyes. She set the baby in my other arm. Ma came in holding two babies. One of the infants had blonde hair with a tiny red ribbon gathered at the top of her head. The other infant had tight slanted eyes and skin as yellow as sunshine. Scott and Ricky came in the room with one baby each. Scott was holding a baby that had slick black hair that cascaded down below his forehead. The baby had an olive complexion. Ricky held a baby that had blond hair and ocean blue eyes. Cerrita and Mary came in the room holding a baby. The babies were wrapped in Spanish-style receiving blankets. I looked around the room and counted ten babies. At the very top of their lungs, they all yelled, "Congratulations, Kel!" Dr. Valesco came into the room grinning as though he'd hit the lottery. He walked over to me and asked, "Kel, now how would you rate me?"

"I see ten babies in the room. I guess I'll give you a perfect ten," I said, smiling.

I woke up the next morning and got my pregnancy calendar. It was three days away from April Fool's day. Was I a fool for going through with this? Or was I suffering from an obsessive-compulsive complex? I was having cramps in the backs of my legs. They were so bad until I walked stiffly to the bathroom to pee. I rubbed my stomach. I hadn't eaten a full meal in weeks, but my stomach had the early signs of stretch marks. Little squiggly white lines that looked like tiny road maps had formed vertically around my stomach like a permanently attached weight belt. I got in the shower and let the warm water splash up against the backs of my legs. I turned around and aimed the water at my stomach. As I kept rubbing my stomach I began to feel the cramps go away. I felt soothed.

As soon as I twisted the shower off, I could hear my telephone on my nightstand ringing. I grabbed a towel off the rack and wrapped it around me before picking up the telephone. The voice on the other end of the phone sounded like Scott's.

"Kel, what's upppppp?" he said and I pictured his face, contorted tongue lapping out the side of his mouth like you see men do in some beer commercials.

"What's upppppp?" I teased, putting my tongue out of the side of my mouth. We both laughed.

"Nothing much. I'm calling to check up on you. See what's moving on the baby-making front."

"I've got some excellent news I'd like to share with you, Scott."

"Oh, boy. Check it. What say we hook up for lunch this afternoon? That is, if you feel like it?"

"I'd like to see you, Scott, but I'm in the family way."

"You knocked up?"

"Yeah, buddy."

"Get the fuck out of here! Here it is I was thinking that I'm probably the only man in America deliberately pregnant with my boyfriend's HIV and you get pregnant as a cow on a Georgia farm like it's nobody's business. I can't wait to tell Ricky."

"I bet you can't," I said and chortled.

"Oh, boy. You know what I mean."

"Yeah, I do."

"Well, you must be eating everybody out of house and home. Right?"

"That's the kicker. My diet is a little weird. I can eat but everything comes back up later."

"Is that shit normal? I mean, it's not happening to you because you are a pregnant male, is it?"

"Nah. It's one of the things about being pregnant you got to deal with. It'll pass, but in the meantime I sure miss grubbing. All the foods I used to love now make me sick as a dog. Sometimes even thinking about food makes me want to go to the bathroom and puke."

"That doesn't sound too cool."

"Scott, I've just stepped out of the shower. Why don't you come over to my place and I'll make you lunch?"

"Sounds good," he said and hung up the phone.

I got dressed, went downstairs, and looked in the fridge. Ma's gumbo stared me in the face. I looked the other way. I had to eat something before I starved to death. As Naomi told me, my baby couldn't grow on air and the joy in my heart. I took out a bowl of green grapes, a carton of orange juice, and a jar of dill pickles. My baby must not have been happy with my selection because by the time Scott arrived for lunch I had thrown everything back up. I was going over the surrogate mother agreement when he knocked on the door. I had a TicTac in my mouth.

"Kel, look at you, man. Damn! I got to admit it, I'm proud of you but I'm also a little jealous," he said and sat down on the sofa.

"Why?"

"Oh, boy. 'Cause, shit, look at you peeps. You black, gay, and male. The original version of the three strikes law. Now you representing but there's only one problem."

"What is it?"

"You a cop."

"Correction. Private investigator."

"So you working with the same assholes who'd just as soon lock your black ass up for the hell of it and throw away the key."

Scott's words, as true as they were, annoyed me. They floated around in my head like a bad dream. I've screwed my share of the same assholes that would lock me away. I wondered if I was betraying

Scott or my people. I'm black and I'm blue. I didn't tell Scott that I was often pulled over by the cops for no other reason than I'm black. The only thing that stops them from beating my ass down like they did to Rodney King is the raging bulge between my legs and my badge I never leave home without. I carry my badge to let the good old boys in blue know that if they fuck with me somebody's going to have hell to pay. To the good old boys in blue, without my badge I'm just another nigga let loose out on the streets. My badge doesn't do the trick all the time. Before I can show my badge good, some of the good old boys in blue make other plans. Lure me out to deserted back streets, where they take my member in the warmth of their mouths, and swallow millions of would-be babies down the pipes of throats hot and hungry with lust. I've slipped the tight blue pants of cops down to their ankles, slapped handcuffs around their thick wrists, and made them assume the position. I ride them long and hard. I once told a rookie cop fresh out of the academy with a baby face and a virgin asshole, "I ain't giving up nothing but hard dick! Now spread 'em!" Could I tell Scott that the hottest three-way I've ever had was in the back of a paddy wagon one Fourth of July night with two black horny cops with asses tighter than vice grips? The fireworks that went off in the back of that paddy wagon made the ones bursting in the skies that night seem pale and dull in comparison. We made love to each other until the early morning sunlight told us that a new day was dawning.

Scott had a point.

"Check it out though; this ain't slavery time. I'm not working for free."

"Well."

"I want to have a healthy baby with normal body parts and be a good father, Scott. That's all there is to it," I said.

I made Scott understand that the last thing I wanted was a trophy or consolation prize. Or have my face plastered on the front cover of *Ebony, Newsweek,* or *Time.* I wanted Scott to realize that what I was doing was something that I believed deep in my heart was the right thing to do.

"You starting to show yet?"

Before I could answer him, he pulled up my undershirt and took a peek at my pregnant body. He shook his head and rubbed my belly. He frowned at the catheter.

"Your hands are freezing!" I said, getting goose bumps and laughing. Then I said, "You hungry?"

"You damn Skippy! I want to chow down."

I popped a bowl of gumbo in the microwave and defrosted it. I served the hot bowl of Ma's gumbo to Scott. The smell of the gumbo didn't bother me but my stomach got queasy just the same. Scott did his best to coax me into eating a bowl myself. I half-relented. I went into the fridge, took out half of a cantaloupe, and poured myself a small glass of milk. I sat down at the kitchen table with Scott. I was about to ask Scott how he would deal with a surrogate mother contract if he were in my shoes. When the rest of my breakfast and my half-eaten lunch made other plans, I got to the bathroom just off the kitchen. Everything came back up out of me. I could hear Scott knock on the door.

"Kel, you all right?"

"Yeah. I'm all right. Give me a few seconds to wash up. I'll be out in a shake," I said, running water, splashing it on my face, and brushing my teeth. I went back in the kitchen. Scott was standing over the kitchen sink washing out his bowl. He'd taken all of the dishes that had piled up in the sink over the last week, ran water over them, and was setting them in the dishwasher. He dried his hands on a washcloth, turned, and walked over to me. He gently put his hand on my shoulder and rubbed my back.

"Oh boy, Kel. I see what you mean. Being pregnant ain't no joke, huh?" he said as we walked over to the sofa and sat down. Then he looked at me and asked, "Do you want me to do anything to help?"

"Well, I can't take any medication other than aspirin. But what I need today is some help cleaning up my house. I can't get all the way through it without having to stop and take a break."

"Consider it done. When you need me to give you a hand, let me know. I'm still working nights as hotel manager at the Renaissance Hotel, so my days are free. Now let's get you back upstairs and into bed. Us going to have us some babies now," he teased and laughed. I smiled weakly and leaned on Scott's massive shoulder as we started upstairs. I thought to myself, all right, Naomi number two.

I must have slept all afternoon because now it was dark outside. I got up out of the bed and walked around the house. Scott had cleaned the house from top to bottom, watered the plants, took out the garbage, dusted and scrubbed countertops and floors, vacuumed, washed clothes, folded them up into neat little stacks, and separated the white laundry from the colored. He left a note sitting on top of the surrogate mother agreement. Scott's note simply said, "I know Naomi is girlfriend. But please be careful. Things could get a little messy. I'll talk to you later." Scott's note implied that he had read the agreement. Scott would be the first one to say, "You know I can't hold ice water." If Scott knew about the surrogate mother agreement, then that meant the whole world knew about it.

Spring was right around the corner. During the day it was sunny and warm, but at night I was still turning on the heater to stay warm. I had made a great deal of improvement in being able to eat food and keep it down without feeling that I needed a bib to catch the onslaught of regurgitation. I hadn't grown accustomed to feeling fatigued, but I had no choice but to move over and make some room for it in my life right now. I made a decision to hold on and let patience and time become my guide.

When I got up the next morning, I found the surrogate mother agreement. I decided to pore over it. The document in its present form needed a lot of work to make it presentable and acceptable, not only to me but to Naomi too. Shorty had written the agreement for Naomi as though she couldn't read and write. I was going to do my own version using terms that protected the rights of my child and to which Naomi and I would agree. It pissed me off that Shorty had written up the agreement as if he was the one who was pregnant and not me.

I'd become like a locomotive engine with plenty of steam and I'd come way too far to turn around now. I could see the light at the end of the tunnel that shined as bright as the light I was going to see in the eyes of my newborn baby.

Chapter 15

On the last Sunday morning in May I went to my bedroom window and looked out at Mt. Tam. It had the shape of someone pregnant. Each morning I awoke to the chirping of robins courting in my oak tree. I could eat just about anything I wanted to. I'd gained back the weight I lost in the past few months. Dr. Valesco told me during my last visit that I had to be careful about my blood sugar level. He thought it was a little high but felt that he didn't need to put me on any medication to bring it down to normal levels. Dr. Valesco kept stressing diet as the way to go. I had had a scare about one month before. I started bleeding from my urethra very heavily one morning. Surprisingly, Chad came over to my house after I called him and took me over to see Dr. Valesco. I'd lost so much blood that I didn't have enough strength to ball up my fists. I thought that I was having a miscarriage. As it turned out, I'd developed an adverse reaction to the monthly special therapy injection. My urethra had become irritated. To let Dr. Valesco tell it, I lost about two test tubes of blood. He told me it was nothing to shake a stick at. Dr. Valesco modified the injections to an acceptable level. I was relieved to find that the baby was not harmed. Dr. Valesco admitted me to the hospital for observation and put me on an IV until I got strong enough to leave and go home after a couple of days.

Over the past week I'd finally worked out the bugs in the surrogate mother agreement. It went like this: My baby would receive legally my surname at birth. My name and Naomi's name would appear on the birth certificate as the father and mother respectively. As the childbearing parent I would have the sole responsibility for my child's financial support and health care. My child would reside in my custody full time and would be told as soon as it became old enough to understand that Naomi is the biological mother. Upon oral request

from the surrogate mother, visitation rights would be allowed when it
didn't interfere with the childbearing parental rights to raise and care
for the child in a logical, responsible manner. Upon the death of the
childbearing parent, by agreement between surrogate mother and childbearing parent, custody would be given to whoever the court decided
was in the best interest of the child. The court would then decide who
should become the legal guardian of the child. It was a document with
no frills, low balls, or surprises. It was only fair. Naomi was meeting
me for dinner that night to go over the agreement and raise any objections before we were due in civil court next Monday to sign off on the
document and legally file it with the court.

Naomi arrived at my house moments after I'd popped the hot muffins out of the oven and plopped them into a bowl. I had whipped up
salmon croquettes, steamed white rice, a green tossed salad. I made
Naomi's favorite, a low-fat banana pudding for dessert. The dining
room table was set with flatware, goblets, white candles, and Chardonnay. I pulled up a chair and Naomi scooted into it.

We sat down to dinner like a husband and wife celebrating our
twenty-fifth wedding anniversary. The growth of my pregnancy seemed
to make the table appear farther away from me than it used to be, so I
had to really use my arms to reach for a lot of things. Dr. Valesco had
warned me against twisting and stretching. So I only reached for
things that were at arm's length.

"Oooooh! These salmon croquettes are slamming! Child, you know
you can burn! Damn! I wish Shorty's fat ass could cook," she said,
munching on the three salmon croquettes that she had mashed into
her rice, making it look like Hamburger Helper.

"Sista, you just like good food. That's all. When I was a little boy
and hid behind Ma's skirt tails I learned how to cook from the heart.
That's where good food comes from. The heart."

"You ain't never lied. I can't stand pretty food. A plate of food that
looks like it belongs on the cover of *Sunset* magazine," she said.

"Sista, did you get a chance to go over the new agreement I wrote
up for us?"

"Yeah, I did. Consider it a done deal," she said and bit into a corn muffin.

"Cool. Then we'll meet up at the courthouse tomorrow morning. At nine-thirty a.m. sharp."

The telephone rang.

"Kel?" Ma said.

"Hey, Ma."

"What you doing?"

"Having dinner with Naomi."

"Aw, that's sure nice. She's such a nice girl. How come you won't go ahead and marry her?"

"Let's not go there, Ma. You know we're only friends. Like brother and sister."

"But just the same. Anyway, I won't interrupt your dinner, but I was wondering if you watched the news lately."

"I've been listening to the news on the radio, Ma."

"You hear about that poor girl who got pregnant by her football player boyfriend?"

"I heard about it, Ma."

I'd heard it all before. It shook me up. Ma told me about the celebrity athlete who had his girlfriend and another woman pregnant at the same time. When she told him she was pregnant, he told her to have an abortion. Ma felt that his girlfriend should have turned him in to the police. Ma went on to tell me he put out a contract on her life. The newspaper could not have told it better. Ma reminded me that he sandwiched his girlfriend's car between his car and a hit man's car. Ma described the all-American star athlete as a low-down bastard for shooting his girlfriend through the head.

"They tell me that on her deathbed, she told the doctors he was the one that shot her. I was so glad the hospital saved her baby, but child, that poor girl dead. I couldn't believe that piece of swine got off without being put in the electric chair. Kel, you hear me?"

"Yeah, Ma. That was sad. Sometimes I wonder why we treat each other worse than dirt."

"Anyway, I didn't mean to bother you and Naomi. Tell her I said hello. You hear?"

"I will, Ma." I hung up the phone.

"Was that Mommy dearest?"

"Yeah, that was my mom. Always with some kind of news or something she's stewing about. She sent you a greeting."

"Is everything all right, Kel?"

"Everything's fine. She put a bug in my ear about that girl whose boyfriend had her murdered because she didn't want to have an abortion."

"Oh, Kel. I heard about that. That was a goddamn shame." We ate listening to Avant's CD, *My Thoughts*.

Again, was this the image of the black man this country wanted to put forward? As someone who was a taker, not a giver of life? Was I worried about Chad doing this to me? If he did, then I only hoped that Dr. Valesco or whoever was charged with the task of saving my life would save my baby first. Longevity has its place, but I would sacrifice my own life to save the life of my child. Isn't sacrifice the real test of true love? Since Cookie aborted my first baby, years later, all I've been able to do is ask myself this question. Why? A question that to this day floats around in my head like an unsolved murder mystery. I know that as long as there's a moon above and stars in the sky I'll ask new questions, search for new answers. Yet I fear that I'll keep circling back like a boomerang groping to discover the rhyme, the reason why sacrifice must be the real test of true love.

"You know, I could eat like food is going out of style and still sometimes I wake up in the middle of the night with hunger pangs," I said, laughing.

"With five and a half more months to go, don't get like that guy Professor Klump in the movie Eddie Murphy played in," she said, giggling.

"Can you imagine?"

"You? Uh huh. At the rate you are going that baby is going to be the picture of health. I don't see a preemie in your nursery. I can see you now on the cover of *BabyTalk* magazine, holding one fine baby in your arms. I'm so proud of you, Brotha."

"I'm proud of you too, Sista, because without your egg I couldn't have conceived," I said. Jill Scott's CD *Who Is Jill Scott* was serenading us, making me think of Chad.

Naomi wouldn't let me clean up anything in the kitchen. She cleared the dining table, rinsed the dishes, put them in the dishwasher, and started it. Then she put the leftovers in Handi-Wrap and set them in the refrigerator. She took out the Scrabble game and we played until I got sleepy and any word that came close to sounding like "bed" made me doze off like I suffered from sleeping sickness. After a couple more games of Scrabble, Naomi took off for home and I went upstairs and got in the bed. It was a curious dream I had after I fell asleep.

I was sitting in a chair as wide as the bed of a 4 X 4 pickup truck. My hair was in two long thick braids that fell down to the middle of my chest. I had eaten so much food that I'd grown to the size of a six-hundred-pound man. I'd ballooned to a size that made it all but impossible for me walk through the front door of my home. The roof of my house had to be cut open so that I could be lifted out by a crane. I was wearing a smudged dowdy housecoat, flat pink slippers, and my head was covered with a red head rag. I fumbled through an over-stuffed baby bag, fingered puke, chipped rattles, sour bibs, mismatched booties, Johnson's Baby Powder caked with baby oil, wasted at the bottom of the bag. *Where is my baby? What in the world is this?* I wondered as the huge crane struggled with my weight and lifted me up through the roof before dropping me down in my backyard.

I took off early Monday afternoon and met Naomi at the county courthouse between Macdonald Avenue and Thirty-Seventh Street. We sat in the courtroom on the second floor on a long wooden bench. It was only a formality, but at the suggestion of the California Bar Association, Naomi and I both had hired attorneys to represent our individual interests. We had agreed during dinner last weekend that this was done not in any way to suggest that we were adversaries. It was a routine legal practice that was common in surrogate mother cases. My attorney, Randall Huntington, was a family law attorney whose work I was familiar with. He had played a key role in protecting the rights of adopted children whose parents, after giving them up for adoption, reneged on the agreements and wanted to reverse the decision and claim full custody rights. Randall and I belonged to the same chapter of Black Informed Gays (BIG). Naomi was a sometimes guest member. Shorty wasn't interested. I didn't know Naomi's attorney. She had told me during dinner that her attorney, Casey White, was the first black woman to successfully sue the city of Richmond for racial discrimination in the city's adoption policies.

I turned around to see if there were any visitors seated in the courtroom. To my surprise, Nina, Andrea, Shuntria, and Cerrita sat next to one another. They all waved at me. Cerrita waved a tiny gay rights flag in the air like she was at the Gay Olympic games, happy to see me come in first across the finish line. I grew warm inside and wondered who told them about the hearing. I leaned forward a little and Naomi was turned around waving to them. Naomi turned back around and winked at me.

"It's not a big deal, Kel. I invited them. We need a cheering section!" Naomi said, threw her head back, and laughed.

"Girl, you too much," I said, and grinned.

Naomi was dressed casually in a soft white cashmere sweater and khakis. I wore a large undershirt that covered my belly. I was grateful that I had not graduated to extra large sizes yet. I watched Naomi fumble through her appointment book that she told me always seemed to be crowded with more daily schedules than she had room for. She was juggling multiple careers, one as a life insurance agent, the other as a hair stylist. She owned a small chain of beauty salons in Richmond. Naomi snapped her appointment book shut.

The court clerk, a thin Asian woman with black hair styled in a beehive, snapped to attention as the judge entered the courtroom from a door behind the bench, wearing a long black robe with a gold-studded AIDS awareness pin stuck in her lapel.

"All rise," the clerk called out as the judge stepped up to the bench. "The Superior Court for the County of Contra Costa, Department 15, is now in session, the Honorable Lucinda Day Coolie, presiding. You may be seated," the clerk concluded as Judge Coolie settled in behind the bench. The courtroom became hushed as we all took our seats again.

The judge was a heavyset black woman appearing to be in her mid-forties who rarely blinked when she looked over her courtroom. She cleared her throat and adjusted her eyeglasses.

"Good morning, ladies and gentlemen," the judge began. "We have a full docket this morning, so let's get started. The first matter this morning is the case of Naomi Edwards versus Kelvin Warren. Petition to confirm surrogate mother agreement. Are counsels present?" I was a little taken aback by the judge's characterization of the hearing, pitting me against Naomi. Randall looked at me sheepishly.

"Present, Your Honor. Casey White, counsel for plaintiff Naomi Edwards," announced Naomi's attorney before taking her seat at counsel's table.

"Randall Huntington appearing for defendant Kelvin Warren, Your Honor." Randall remained on his feet in anticipation of addressing the court first.

"Let the record show that both parties as well as their attorneys are present in the courtroom this morning," the judge proceeded. "Mr. Huntington, are you ready to proceed?"

"Yes, Your Honor," Randall replied. "Prior to this morning's hearing, Ms. White stipulated to the form of the surrogate mother agreement. Does the court have a copy of the agreement?"

"The court does have a copy, signed by both parties. Ms. White, do you have any objections to the confirmation of the agreement in its current form?"

I watched Naomi's attorney, a smallish black woman wearing a two-piece beige pantsuit with a white blouse that exposed her cleavage. She stood up to address the court.

"We have no objection to confirmation of the agreement, Your Honor," Casey responded, and then sat back down.

"Let the record show that both parties have stipulated to confirmation of the surrogate mother agreement submitted to this court. Anything else, Counsels?" The judge peered down from the bench over the rim of her glasses.

"No, Your Honor," Randall said, standing up again briefly.

"Nothing further, Your Honor," Casey echoed Randall's response and then again took her seat.

"Very well, then," said the judge. "The surrogate mother agreement will be confirmed. Mr. Huntington, will you prepare the order?"

"Yes, Your Honor," Randall quickly replied as he picked his papers up from the counsel's table. "Thank you, Your Honor."

"Thank you, Your Honor," added Casey as she turned toward the door at the back of the courtroom.

I took a deep breath and exhaled slowly as I followed and waited for Naomi to pass before I stepped into the aisle and joined the procession to the rear of the courtroom. The judge had already called her next case.

Once in the corridor, Randall and I briefly said our good-byes to Naomi and Casey, then turned toward the side exit from the courthouse.

"Randall, I was a little nervous at first. I thought Naomi's attorney was going to throw a monkey wrench in the works."

"So did I. It went off without a hitch," he said, as Naomi and her attorney came over and joined us. Naomi and I hugged and Randall and Casey greeted each other with a nod and shook hands. Nina, Andrea, Shuntria, and Cerrita were huddled around Naomi. I watched them kiss her on the cheek and offer her congratulations. I watched Nina hand the baby to Naomi. Naomi turned to look at me. She was smiling. She seemed to be so at ease holding the baby. It made me feel warm inside and I pictured her holding our baby, making a fuss over it. She brought her entourage over to me. Naomi handed the baby to me.

"Hi, Goddaddy!" Shuntria blurted out and giggled.

"Hey, little lady! How's my little lady doing today?"

"Fine."

Shuntria was dressed in a cute little navy blue pants outfit with matching cap. Three gold buttons snapped her jacket closed. I bounced her up and down.

"Hey, Kel," Nina and Andrea said almost at the same time and mobbed me with kisses.

I blushed.

"My heroes," Cerrita said, and again waved the gay flag and laughed.

"Kel, I'll talk to you all later. Casey and I have to get going," Naomi said.

"Call me," I said and waved good-bye. I watched her disappear with Casey down a flight of stairs.

Before Nina and her family left the courthouse, I'd made plans to take Shuntria to Marine World Africa U.S.A. Shuntria had grown so much since I'd seen her at my birthday party. Cerrita and I made plans to go to the gym during the week.

"You know I can't pump iron like I use to. I'm leaving it all up to you, Ms. Cerrita."

"Not to worry, Mr. Kel. I got your back. I'll pump the iron in your name," she said, posing like she was in a Miss America bodybuilding contest.

"Where's Mary?"

"We've got to talk about that one."

"Kel, would you like me to get you a cup of coffee or anything?" Randall asked.

"Randall, no you won't. You stay your fine ass right here with this man and talk. Remember, BIG don't have no small secrets. We family, honey. Everything we do is kept in the family. Okay Kel, we'll talk at the gym. Don't forget," she said and squeezed my arm. She patted Randall on his broad back.

"I won't. I promise," I said.

"Cerrita, don't forget about the BIG meeting coming up soon," Randall said.

"Who? I wouldn't miss it for the world," she said. We watched Cerrita disappear into an elevator.

"Well, you seem to have quite a cheering section going on." Randall grinned, flashing a mouth full of chalk white teeth.

"I'm blessed," I said as we walked down the hall and started down the stairs.

"Yeah. You blessed and then some."

I invited Randall to lunch at Marline's restaurant in North Richmond. He accepted the invitation in the blink of an eye. I wasn't nervous about going to lunch with Randall. But as I drove to Marline's I wished that it were Chad I'd invited to lunch. I arrived a little ahead of Randall and met him outside of the restaurant. Marline's was the oldest soul food restaurant in Richmond. Marline's grandson, Andy, took over the restaurant after his mother, Louise, died a couple of years ago of a heart attack while she was on a cruise to Jamaica with her partner, Molly. Marline's opened during the 1940s, the heyday of the Kaiser Shipyards that employed skilled black boilermakers and welders who'd escaped from Jim Crow working conditions in the South. We sat at a cozy booth in the back of the restaurant. For a Monday afternoon, the foot traffic at Marline's was thick. They only played old school jams at Marline's. Bobby "Blue" Bland's song "Turn on Your Lovelight," washed over me like warm rays of sunshine.

I'd been reading in the newspaper over the past month about a group of pregnant twelve-year-old girls hiding out at the old Richmond pier down at the Shipyards. Instantly, they reminded me of Cookie. I couldn't do anything to save my baby that Cookie aborted. I knew that I couldn't save the whole world, but I could do something to help these young girls save their babies. I decided to make a proposal at the next BIG meeting to get the group involved in community outreach and get these young girls prenatal health care, testing, and counseling.

"Kel and Randall! What's up, peeps!" Andy said loudly with a grin that revealed a mouth full of teeth capped with silver.

Randall nodded.

"I'm all right, Andy. What's cooking?"

"What's cooking, man, you know Andy is throwing down up in here! We got specials for days! Greens! Beans! Cabbage! Yams! Mountain oysters! Tripe! Hot water corn bread! Ribs! Rib tips! Fried chicken! Baked chicken! Peppered steak! Check it out! Today's lunch special is red snapper! All of that! Then some! You better ask somebody!" he said and passed menus to Randall and me.

"I hear you, Andy. My mind is stuck on hungry," I said and eyed the menu.

"Ain't nothing like good food for thought! Good to see you two brothers! Enjoy your meal! Hey, Sarah! Sarah! We got some hungry men up in here! Make tracks, girl!" Andy yelled and disappeared like a flash of hot air through a door that led into the kitchen. Randall looked at me and smiled.

I ordered red snapper, smothered potatoes, and black-eyed peas. Randall ordered meatloaf, steamed vegetables, Boston baked beans, and corn muffins. The waitress, a thin black woman who introduced herself to Randall and me as Sarah, wore a tall colorful African head-dress. She set our plates on the table.

We began to eat.

Randall talked to me about setting up a living trust for my child. Before I could give him an answer, he shot off to go to the rest room. "Excuse me, Kel. I'll be right back." When he got up and headed for the rest room, I looked at his backside that was so voluptuous and tight that it looked unreal. Randall was about Chad's height, only a bit thicker with skin the color of maple and rippling muscles that seemed like they were about to break out of the tailored suits he always wore, even during our quarterly meetings at BIG. I would be telling a colossal lie if I said I didn't lust after Randall. He'd moved to the Bay Area about five years before from Atlanta, Georgia. He went to U.C. Berkeley and played football with the Cal Bears. Later, he transferred to Stanford, where he got his law degree. He was single, uninvolved, and lived alone in a Victorian on top of Russian Hill in San Francisco. The attraction between the two of us was mutual. One night, last year, toward the end of winter, we held a BIG meeting at his house.

After the group dispersed, Russell invited me to join him on the rooftop of his home for a barbecue. We ate, drank beer, talked, and watched a happy morning sun come up and sit like a fat orange ball in the middle of the Golden Gate Bridge. The sun warmed my face, but the wind on the roof was cold. Randall went and got a blanket out of his house and we snuggled together spoon fashion. I lay next to him between blankets warmed by the passion that I was barely able to contain. I fantasized that Randall and I ended up making love all morning long. I imagined that Randall made my body shiver from the top of my head to the bottom of my feet.

My daydream ended when Randall returned from the rest room and sat back down in the booth.

I looked into Randall's ginger brown eyes and felt so safe, so secure. I wondered when I had stopped feeling like that with Chad. It was like huge parts of my life with Chad, although lived, had been lost and unaccounted for. I was ready to give Randall an answer to his question about having a living trust. Was he going to ask me to be his one and only too? What would I do with Chad? Why couldn't I have both of these gorgeous men? I understand rules, but most of the rules I follow are the ones made for me by someone else. Shouldn't gay men make their own rules? Rules that don't look at everything we do as marginal or on the fringe of society? Or rules that don't punish and stigmatize us for being what and who we are? Is this asking too much?

I took slow, slow sips of lemonade.

"I hadn't thought about getting a living trust. Do you think that it might be a good idea?"

"Under these circumstances, I think it would be an excellent idea. I can assist, that is, if you need help with drawing up the documents. It's really very simple," he said, licking his full purple lips. We finished eating and made a plan to get together soon and work on the living trust.

"Kel, what are you doing tonight?"

"Just going home and resting."

"The reason I asked is that I'd like to come over and spend some quality time with you. I've got to be honest. I've never known a pregnant man before. Don't laugh at me, but I looked at your stomach and I want to rub it so bad."

I blushed.

I wanted to say, "Be at my house at seven p.m. sharp!" But all I said was, "I can't be responsible for what happens when you come over to my house, Randall."

"Let me take full responsibility for that. All of it."

"You promise?"

"Cross my heart."

"And?"

"Hope to die."

We paid up and left Marline's. I watched Randall's tall frame disappear around the corner. I headed for my Jeep and home. I was out in the world. Chad hadn't made love to me in months. He barely touched me anymore. It was as though since I'd gotten pregnant he treated me like I'd become a pariah or had a contagious disease that he didn't want to catch. When I tried to get close to Chad, he'd tell me, "Head, you have changed." Or he would tell me, "You've got to meet me halfway." How in the world can you meet a man halfway when he doesn't even come around? Many a night I lay awake hoping that I'd get a surprise ring of my doorbell. I'd run down the stairs, open the door, and it would be Chad. He'd be standing there with one red rose. He'd take my hand and we'd start up the stairs to my bedroom, where he'd lay my pregnant body down, caress my swollen ankles, massage my sore lower back, gently kiss and rub my growing belly. Tell me that he loves me but loves my unborn baby more. I'd take Chad, kiss his dark face while scented candles lit up the room. The silhouettes of our bodies would merge and become one. I'd slowly undress him, taking one stitch of clothing off of him at a time until he'd be as naked as my baby will be the day I bring it into the world. He'd put his warm head on my stomach, try to listen to my baby's heartbeat. Tell me what a blessing from God it is for me to be able to have not one heart but two hearts beating all within one dark body all at the same time. He'd tell me what a wonder! He'd tell me that he feels like the luckiest man alive. That he's overcome with so much happiness because he is going to be a cofather to my baby. He'd be a shining example of black fatherhood, show the world how to raise a child, teach it to choose love over hate, peace over war, joy over pain, happiness over sadness, life over death, hope over despair, kindness over meanness, forgiveness over remorse. He'd tell a child never to rob, kill, cheat, steal, abuse alcohol, or do drugs. To believe in the spirit, honor its parents, worship its ancestors. To take life one day at a time, live every day like a dream come true. Try to change the things that could make this world a better place for all of us to live. To find triumph underneath the failures life sometimes brings. Teach a child what I've learned is that fairy tales do come true if you only believe.

When Randall rang my doorbell, I was at the kitchen table eating a Marie Callender's cheesecake topped with fresh strawberries. I went to the door and let Randall in. I took his jacket and hung it in the foyer.

"Jesus H. Christ! Would you look at these houseplants! I've never seen houseplants so huge. What in the world do you use to grow them like that?" he said and went over to finger an eight-foot palm tree in front of the sliding glass door.

"Crushed eggshells ground up into a powder so fine until it looks like dust."

"Amazing!" he said.

I invited Randall to have some dessert. He thanked me but declined. He went into the living room and sat down on the sofa. I went into the kitchen and put my dessert in the refrigerator. When I came back in the living room, Randall had taken his shoes off and he seemed to be comfortable.

I got nervous and erect.

"I'm glad you came over, Randall."

"I couldn't resist coming."

"Why?"

"Because I want you, Kel. Ever since that night we slept together up on my roof I've felt that I had to feel you. Even if it means ending our friendship."

"Randall, you know that I'm in love with Chad."

"I'm not telling you to leave Chad for me. I'd never break up a happy home. Chad's cool like that. He's not the one I'm interested in, though."

"Why me and why now? Why now when I'm all fat, barefoot, and pregnant? What if he found out? Or walked in and saw both of us with the look of love in our eyes?"

"You can't hide love, Kel."

"You know, life is weird. Here it is I'm pregnant and big with a baby and I still need me a man."

"Is Chad not man enough for you?"

"He's man enough but not all of the man that I need. I don't think anybody can be everything for everybody. That's not the way love goes."

"Tell me. Tell me how does love go, Kel?"

"Now that I'm in the family way, I've learned that love is something you can feel moving, growing inside of you. You get scared sometimes because anything that grows can go into a different direction. When you think it's going one way you find out it's not going the way you want it to go. That's the way I think love goes, Randall."

"Can I touch you, Kel? Can I hold you?"

"Only if you don't hurt me."

"I promise."

"For true?"

"For true."

We went upstairs and got undressed. Randall held me in his arms as though his massive black body was a warm blanket. Randall did all the things Chad had not done to me over the last two months. Everything that I'd imagined that he'd do and things I didn't think he'd do. I pictured myself getting deeply infatuated with Randall, almost on the brink of falling in love. Sort of like a man who stands teetering on the edge of a cliff with the wind at his back. He can see the bottom but doesn't want to fall, so he fights the wind, struggles to hold back. I imagined not worrying about Chad coming in the house and finding me lying with Randall. I thought about what my rationale for sleeping with Randall would be. If Chad were to walk through my bedroom door and look at me curled up into Randall's barrel chest, I wouldn't freak out. I'd tell him to take off his clothes and hop in the bed between Randall and me. I pictured the three of us in the bed, black men loving one another. Isn't that the ultimate goal of black gay unity? To help each other step to the plate and speak our name? We took a shower. Randall was unable to keep his hands off of my belly.

"This is so awesome! I've never had any pregnant dick pussy before," he laughed.

"As far as you know."

"Well, I'd heard how good it is. Now I know for true."

"This is as good as it gets."

"Kel?"

"Yeah."

"Don't let this be the last time we kick it."

"Promise."

"For true?" Randall said.

"For true," I said.

My making love with Randall had gone from fantasy to the real thing. Was there really, like people say, nothing like the real thing? Could I have it all? Could I have a soul mate in Chad? Multiple and explosive orgasms with Randall? Could I have a smooth transition into parenthood with my baby? What about day care, public versus private school? Did I think that the move to give vouchers to parents was a harebrained idea? How would I react to the nasty attitudes people were bound to give me because I'm a man who had a baby? Would my child's classmates taunt, tease, and shun him the way people did to Ryan White when they learned that he was a little boy infected with HIV attending public school? Would I have to take my child and move to a deserted island in the South Pacific for the sake of safety? If I went to the oldest civil rights organization on the planet asking for legal help, would that organization come to my defense? Or would they tell me to go to hell? Or accuse me of being politically incorrect? I'd been independent since I left home to attend college. How would it feel to have a young life dependent upon me for care? I looked at Randall and wondered if he had at least one answer to the thoughts that swirled around my mind.

I studied Randall. He was bent over the bed pulling on his black socks.

He invited me to the BIG meeting next month. He told me that everybody had been asking if I was all right. I felt a little funny about not coming to the BIG meetings for the last three and a half months. When I finally did show up I'd be in good company with my friends, yet I wondered how useful I could be given my pregnant state. But I had to get my proposal for some community outreach work to BIG.

Randall slipped on his black loafers. I gave Randall a heads up about my proposal.

"I can't wait to hear more about it. Nobody's going to trip. Besides, you know everybody there anyway. Come to the meeting planned next month."

"It's a deal," I said and slapped Randall on his firm bottom. We went downstairs and I got his coat.

"Kel, it's been real."

"The pleasure was mine, baby boy. All mine," I said, giving him a hug and letting him through the door.

Chapter 16

"Everything is fine, Kel. You sure about not wanting to know the gender of your baby?" Dr. Valesco said, pulling the stethoscope out of his ears and placing it back in his lab jacket. It was getting toward the middle of June. I was a big man. I looked at Dr. Valesco and pondered a decision.

Then I said, "I like surprises, Dr. Valesco."

Dr. Valesco told me he thought that if I were aware of the infant's gender then it would be easier for me to plan and shop. What I had to tell Dr. Valesco was that I bought things either a boy or girl could wear. Then some of the stuff I got was gender specific. Dr. Valesco seemed pleased when he realized that I'd bought my share of androgynous gender-neutral baby outfits too.

"All right. You've informed me. The sonogram results are available if you change your mind. Anyway, I think you will be pleased," he said and winked before he left the room.

On the way home from Dr. Valesco's office I went to Big and Tall and bought some clothes that would fit me. Every pair of pants at home in my closet that I tried to put on was either too tight or I was only able to pull them up halfway to my thighs. All of my weight gain had settled in my midsection. I bought extra large undershirts and, as much as I hated it, larger boxer shorts because they were more comfortable. At least for the moment my skimpy-G-string-thong-bikini-brief days were put on hold. I was utterly fascinated with my stomach. All of my buddies at the gym told me to stop drinking beer because they thought it was why I couldn't pump iron anymore. Some of them told me that was why my waist had thickened and I had a bloated belly. I'd nod and wink at the ones who told me that if I thought that they were cute.

When I got home I called Nina. I told her to pack a little travel bag for Shuntria. I was making good on my promise to take her to Marine

World Africa U.S.A. On Saturday afternoon, I told Nina that Chad
had agreed to go with us to Marine World. I was excited about going
to Marine World with Shuntria and Chad by my side. I thought it
would be like a dress rehearsal for the day when Chad and I would
take our child there for the first time. Nina told me that she'd have the
car seat ready, some Pampers, baby wipes, a small blanket, and two
bottles of milk, among other things, in Shuntria's baby bag. Nina
seemed to be glad that I'd started to spend more time with Shuntria as
her godfather. She told me that when I had my baby, Shuntria would
have a permanent playmate. Nina was already calling my baby Shuntria's first cousin.

The weather was picnic perfect. The high noon sun was warm and
the skies a deep blue, not a cloud to be seen for as far as the eye could
see. I was wearing an extra large undershirt, khaki shorts, and sandals.
I walked slowly and was glad to pick up Chad so he could give me a
hand with Shuntria. Shuntria had a lot of energy and I got tired easily
those days. I'd walk some, then breathe heavily, and have to sit down
and rest. Climbing up and down the stairs at my home sometimes
completely wore me out. Everything but food I kept upstairs either in
my office or bedroom, and it was an excellent idea when I decided to
work out of my house at my own pace.

I picked up Chad. He was watching E!. He was fuming over having
missed a segment E! had done on Sade. He told me that he was taking
a shower and when he got back downstairs to the television, the only
part of the cover story he was able to see was when she was talking
about doing an international concert tour.

We picked up Shuntria about half an hour later. Nina had her
dressed in a cute little white two-piece matching short pants outfit.
Shuntria had on the tiniest pair of sneakers I've ever seen. She ran up
to me.

"Goddaddy," she beamed and hopped up in my arms like a little
ballerina.

Nina and Andrea stood just inside the front door of their apartment
grinning and chatting with Chad. Andrea gave Chad the baby bag
and car seat. I held Shuntria.

"Kel, she's not too heavy for you, is she?" Nina asked.

"Well, I think I'll let her walk to the car on her own two little legs," I said, laughing.

"I know that's right," Nina said as she and Andrea stood in the doorway and waved Chad, Shuntria, and me good-bye. I stopped and rolled down the window.

"We'll have her back home by four, if she doesn't wear me out before then," I said laughing.

We got to Marine World and found a grassy knoll where we set up camp. Chad and I took Shuntria on the carousel; after riding it, I let that be my only ride at the park. It was difficult getting my legs up around the seat of the pony so I sat on a bench that went around in circles. I got dizzy. I came close to upchucking.

"Oh, Head. You ain't no fun. Shuntria and I are going to get on the train. You coming?"

I waddled behind Chad and Shuntria, who seemed to have more energy than the little train I watched slowly coming around a bend.

"Baby, you and Shuntria sit in a car together. We all can't fit in one car. I'm too big."

"Old big-headed thing, you ain't no fun. No fun at all."

"I'm having fun, Chad. My feet and knees are bothering me. We've walked all over the park. I'm a little winded."

"You tired, Goddaddy. I carry you," Shuntria said, hugging my fat calves like she was going to try and pick all 215 pounds of me up.

"Baby, your little arms too short to carry me," I said, patting her little shoulders.

"Shuntria, that big-headed old thing ain't tired. All he need to do is lose some weight."

"Don't you see I'm pregnant, Chad? Pregnant, and you still got your head in the sand."

"That ain't nothing but a tumor. Nothing but a great big old tumor that has spread to that big old head of yours."

"Come here, Shuntria," I said. My eyes swelled with tears. To keep from crying, I turned and looked at a couple dressed like Bugs Bunny and Daffy Duck. I took Shuntria's hand and we went back to the camping spot we'd found. I left Chad standing out in front of the train that still hadn't quite made it around the bend yet. I went to a stand and bought corn dogs, candy apples, and pink cotton candy. Shuntria didn't like the corn dogs and her teeth weren't strong enough to bite the hard candy apple. She was crazy, though, about the pink cotton candy that we ate.

"This good, Goddaddy."

"You like it, Shuntria?"

"Yeah!" she said, bouncing up and down.

By the time Chad came to join us, I had stuffed myself with five corn dogs, two candy apples, and two large bags of popcorn. I'd drunk enough water to fill a baby tub and bathe Shuntria in it. The two corn dogs I'd bought for Chad had gotten cold. The red candy apple had melted in the sun. His popcorn was stale. I handed the snacks to Chad. Chad dumped everything in the trash can.

Chad seemed to be lost in his own thoughts. We took Shuntria to find booths with games that gave prizes to winners.

"I want a Tweety Bird, Goddaddy. That one," Shuntria said, her little finger pointed to a stuffed bright yellow Tweety Bird.

"That one over there, honey?" I asked.

"Yeah! Yeah!" she said. She clapped and jumped up and down.

"Let's see what Goddaddy can do to get you a Tweety Bird," I said and looked at Chad.

"What you looking at me for?"

"Come on, Chad. Give it a try. I can't be reaching like that. Dr. Valesco told me when I first got pregnant not to twist, stretch, or reach too far. Shuntria wants a Tweety Bird."

"Shhhh! Before somebody hears you. Farfetched Head."

I handed a woman with thin blonde hair money to play. You had to get three basketballs into a hoop that was attached to a tight fishnet. It took six attempts, but Chad managed to get three balls in a row in the hoop. Shuntria was delighted. The woman with the thin blonde hair smiled and handed Shuntria a Tweety Bird. I told Chad to carry Shuntria and Tweety Bird back to the car. We drove back to Nina and Andrea's apartment. Had it not been for Shuntria singing her ABCs and "Farmer in the Dell," it would have been totally quiet during the drive back.

"Y'all have fun?" Nina asked as we delivered Shuntria safe and sound. I couldn't help but remember that Shuntria's father, Riggs, died in a train wreck and Nina met Andrea. Ever since his death, Andrea has been like a mother and father to Shuntria, the way Ma was for me.

"Shuntria is a sweetheart. I think she liked Marine World."

"Yeah, Mommy," Shuntria said, dragging Tweety Bird by one of his legs up on the sofa.

"Did you tell Goddaddy and Uncle Chad thank you?" Andrea asked.

"Tank you, Goddaddy and Uncle Bad," Shuntria said and we all laughed. I looked at Chad, whose laughter I hadn't heard in a long time. I'd forgotten the way he laughed. It took Shuntria to make him laugh again.

"Not Uncle Bad, baby. Uncle Chad," Nina corrected Shuntria.

"Oh," Shuntria said, squeezed Tweety Bird, rocking him back and forth.

"Thanks, guys. Looks like she had a good time," Nina said as she and Andrea showed us to the door.

"Bye, Shuntria. Goddaddy see you later, all right?" I said and waved at her.

"Bye, Goddaddy," Shuntria said and giggled.

"Shuntria, you be a good girl. You hear? Bye-bye," Chad said.

"Bye Uncle Bad."

"She's just a baby, Chad," I said as we climbed in the car and drove away.

"Head?"

"Yeah?"

"I want to apologize for how I've been acting toward you. Since you got pregnant and all. I must admit something."

"What?"

"The thing that bothered me the most was that you used your own sperm. Not mine. I thought we'd agreed on us using my sperm or yours with a female surrogate mother."

"You're absolutely right, Chad. That was the agreement at first. I reneged on it because of what happened to me years ago with Cookie. I couldn't go through the threat of having another baby aborted."

"But you never talked to me about how I felt about using my sperm."

"Not really."

"Why not?"

"After you told me that I couldn't use your sperm to make the baby, I didn't press the matter. I'm the one who suffered the loss of a child, Chad, and not you. I'm the one who has an old wrong to right, not you. So it made sense for me to do it this way. Don't you see?"

"I guess so, Head. But I want a baby on my own too."

"Well, get pregnant like me."

"Hell no!"

"Why not?"

"I don't want to go through all the crap. I'd rather have a surrogate mother donate an egg and fertilize it with my sperm. Keep it simple and stupid. Head?"

"Yeah."

"What are you going to name the baby?"

"Well, I was going to tell you that I called Dr. Valesco and he told me the sonogram shows I'm having a boy. At first I didn't want to know, but what the hell. I'm going to name him Chad Junior."

"Oh, Head." Chad wept. It was the first time I'd ever seen him cry since we'd been together.

"I love you, baby," I said.

"I love you too, Big Head."

We stopped at a traffic light. I felt the baby kick. I pulled up my undershirt.

"Chad, feel this."

Chad put his hand on my belly.

"Oh shit. A little knot punching up in your stomach. You all right, Head?"

"I'm fine. My baby is kicking me."

Chapter 17

It didn't take long to get used to little feet kicking inside of me. One time when it happened I was on the phone with Ma. She was telling me about how difficult it was becoming for her to pay the energy bill from her small Social Security check. I had started up the stairs to get my checkbook when I felt something pressing up against my belly. I sat down on the bed, pulled up my huge undershirt I'd bought from Big and Tall. I looked at the little impressions my son's feet had made in my stomach and laughed. Ma thought that I was entertaining Chad.

It was sunny and windy. I'd called Chad and invited him to the BIG meeting but he had a schedule conflict. Chad was closing escrow on a real estate deal with a client, then meeting with other clients to show multiple listings. Over the last few weeks I'd been finalizing my proposal for BIG to get involved in helping the unwed pregnant pre-teens sleeping under an old pier at the Richmond Shipyards. I'd made a mental note to get BIG involved in doing some community work with the church to help get the teens decent prenatal care and social assistance.

The skies over San Francisco were azure blue. In the far distance as I drove across the San Francisco Bay Bridge and approached the city, I could see the Transamerica pyramid. It marked San Francisco like a badge of honor. I'd been invited to Randall's home to attend one of the first BIG meetings I'd been to since I got pregnant. I could tell that I was a little nervous because my underarms were wet with perspiration. I couldn't tell what made me more nervous, seeing Randall again after we slept together or facing the other BIG members who understood an unspoken rule that it was acceptable to debate but not engage in sexual activities with other local chapter members, a rule that Randall and I had broken not so long ago. Past BIG meetings were open forums. A table was covered with a dish and refreshments that each member had brought to share. I'd baked two sweet potato pies last night to bring to the meeting. I told myself before I left home I wouldn't stay too long because my ankles were swollen. I couldn't wait to get back home and soak my feet in warm water filled with Epsom salts.

Sometimes the meetings grew intense, yet there had never been any physical violence. We all agreed to disagree.

I'd spoken to Randall over the telephone several times since he came over to represent me in the surrogate mother hearing. I still had a crush on Randall, but my heart beat for Chad. I had a soft spot for Randall.

After parking down the slope of a hill a block away from Randall's home, I knew that by the time I got to his front door I'd have to sit on the sofa at least half an hour to catch my breath.

"What's up, Kel?" Randall said as he stood at the door, grinning broadly. Randall planted a kiss on my lips. He smelled of pineapple. He invited me into the house.

"Hey, Randall. Didn't mean to be late. I'm not as nimble as I used to be. Are the folks here?"

"They are up on the roof. I'm glad you got here. Can I get you anything? Something to eat or drink maybe? Come on, let's go over to the buffet," he said, raising his voice above the stereo that filled the room with the smooth jazz sounds of Paul Hardcastle.

"Well, I would like a little something," I said looking over at the spread of food set out on a long glass table.

"All right, Kel, let's get you something to eat."

"I'd like that a lot."

Randall led me to the end of the table where I set my two sweet potato pies next to a pasta dish. I found a plate at the end of the table. I piled cheese, crackers, and cole slaw on top of it. Scott and Ricky came out of a door at the top of a rather steep flight of steps.

"Kel! Hey man! What's doing, dude!" Scott said, giving me a peck on the cheek.

"Hey!"

"Hey, Kel. Wow! You big, man. Gosh!" Ricky said and blushed a little.

"Where's Cerrita, Mary, Nina, and Andrea?" I asked and put a piece of Swiss cheese in my mouth and began to munch.

"All of them up on Randall's roof. All except for Mary."

"What happened to Mary?"

"Well, they went to . . ." Scott was about to explain but was cut off by Ricky.

"Scott, let Cerrita tell him what happened. She might not want all of her business put out in the street," he laughed.

"I feel you," I said.

"Well, pupa Kel. When do you go in?" Scott asked and sipped on a glass of wine.

"The baby is due in November."

"You got a name for it yet?"

"Dr. Valesco told me I'm having a boy. I'm going to name him Chad Junior."

"Congratulations, Kel," Ricky said.

"Oh boy! Yeah, man, congratulations," Scott followed suit.

Randall came over and sat down next to us. I watched Nina, Andrea, and Cerrita descend the staircase. They came over and sat down next to us. We sat around the living room in a small circle.

"Randall, I've been thinking about getting BIG involved in outreach work with homeless, pregnant preteen unwed mothers. They are homeless, living at the old pier at the Richmond Shipyards. I can get Naomi to interest her father, the Reverend Edwards, to get involved. We can use some of our membership dues to open a charitable account that's co-owned with Evergreen Holy Tabernacle Church. We'd use the money to start rescue work for the girls from the old pier. I sent the proposal by e-mail to everybody belonging to BIG. Here's a draft copy of the project proposal," I said and passed it around to the members.

"That's good. I haven't checked my e-mail, but I think it's a good idea," Randall said.

"We had so much luck with the gay teen HIV project. I think this will be just as successful as the other project turned out to be," I said and watched everybody nod in agreement or tell me that they thought that my new proposal was a great idea. Yet underneath the polite smiles and tactful agreements there seemed to lurk an undercurrent of unrest floating about the air of the room. Nina threw in the first few punches.

"I want to know why Shorty is tripping off of Kel being pregnant. He acts like it's his fat ass that's got to go through labor. He is so jacked up," Nina said.

"Not only that, they tell me that he forced Naomi into court to sign that surrogate agreement," Andrea added.

"Shorty hates gay folk," Scott piped up.

'They tell me that his father was gay," Cerrita said.

"His brother, too," Scott offered.

"So what does that make him?" Ricky asked.

"An odd bird?" Randall topped it off. So I thought.

"Shorty's breath stank!" Nina said. She got in the last punch as a roar of laughter went through the room.

"Look, y'all, we didn't meet to talk about and read Shorty for pure filth. Dumping on Shorty has nothing to do with my proposal. I thought we came to meet to come up with some specific goals for BIG. I'm inviting Naomi and Shorty to the Juneteenth picnic at Blackberry Farm," I said, trying to bring the meeting to some kind of calm. I looked around the room and a blanket of silence had fallen. I heard a few people gasp. I sensed that we could have gone on all night talking about Shorty and people like him that hold intricate lifelong homophobia that they carry with them to the grave. Instead, we got down to business and went over the project proposal. Each one of us was delegated a specific task to get the project off the ground. It was my job to oversee the work and make sure we met all of our objectives. I was delegated to canvass the shipyard area. As a first step, I would take the girls to the free clinic for checkups and prenatal care and get them set up with other organizations that assisted unwed pregnant girls.

We all agreed to meet next at Blackberry Farm on Juneteenth, June 19, for a potluck barbecue and fun in the sun. Cerrita didn't seem to be her usual self. Mary and Chad's absence from BIG was conspicuous. Chad told me why he couldn't make it. Yet nobody asked me why he didn't come with me. Randall, Scott, Ricky, Nina, and Andrea began playing Scrabble. I sat on the sofa next to Cerrita.

"Kel, let's go out on the balcony. I want to talk to you about something," Cerrita said.

I remembered about a month ago, I began spending some evenings at the day care center at the gym, singing nursery rhymes with toddlers, teaching some of them how to tie their shoelaces for the first time. One Saturday afternoon I ran into Cerrita. She was on the Stair-Master and I was on the one next to her. Cerrita took a shower at the gym. I didn't because I was afraid of catching athlete's foot in the shower. Some of my workout buddies had claimed that they got athlete's foot after taking a shower at the gym. I couldn't afford to get stuck with that problem. I didn't want to do anything these days that might harm my baby.

After we were done with our workout I invited her over to my house for dinner that evening. We had a lot of catching up to do. A couple of weeks before, Cerrita had sent me a postcard from Bermuda. She was visiting her father's side of the family and thought enough to show me some love. We'd been playing telephone tag ever since. She made a note in the postcard that she fell out with Mary after she accidentally dropped one of Cerrita's diamond earrings in a large fondue pot when they attended a fondue festival in San Francisco a couple of months ago.

Cerrita leaned over the balcony. She seemed to be far away, lost in her thoughts.

She picked up where she left off. "Look at you! Just glowing up a storm! I couldn't talk freely in the room tonight because I've got my mind on Mary. I kept seeing her dark dreamy eyes," she laughed. Cerrita's eyes were crinkled and watery.

"You hear from Mary, Miss Cerrita?"

"When do you go in?" She ignored my question.

"In November."

"Are you going to, like, have an ultrasound done?"

"I already know. It's a boy. Gender doesn't matter with me. I want my baby to be healthy, that's all."

"Mary and I are going to adopt. Neither one of us wants male sperm in our bodies. The thought of something as big as a baby coming out of me gives me chills. I don't relish the thought."

"To each his own. Cerrita, I asked you where is Mary?"

"We split up."

"Say what?"

"It's a trial separation. We speak over the phone."

"Over the lost diamond earring in a vat of fondue?"

"Those diamond earrings were special to me. They were the only things I had left belonging to my mother. Shoot."

"Poor baby," I said and pulled her close. I felt her body shiver with sobs. Moments later, she regained her composure.

By the time we got back inside Randall's home, everybody had left. Randall was sitting in a reclining chair. He watched us come through the sliding glass door.

"Where did everybody go?" I asked.

"Home. It was getting late. They all went home. Everybody." He said the last word slowly.

"I'd better scoot too," Cerrita said, giving Randall and me a hug before walking out of the door.

Randall's apartment smelled of coffee. It seemed as though he had planned to be up rather late. My plans were to come to the meeting and then go home afterward. I didn't plan a sleepover with Randall. He walked up to me and looked me in my eyes. My loins began to swell, but in the mirror of my mind I realized that I didn't have a reason to go to bed with Randall. Chad was treating me right. After we'd come back from Marine World, Chad had softened his attitude toward me. He was spending more time at my house. He brought over a ton of clothes and spent weeks with me without the slightest interest in going back to his apartment. To have sex with Randall now would be wonderful but it wouldn't mean anything to me.

"Would you like to go up on the roof and get comfy?"

"I'm having some stomach pains, Randall," I lied.

"Oh, can I get you a seltzer or an antacid?"

"Nah, I think I'd better get along. I've probably had too much excitement for one day."

"You like to go in my bedroom, lay down, and let me rub your stomach?"

Randall's offer was tempting, but I didn't want him to put his hands on my naked stomach anymore. That was Chad's territory. I hoped Randall would back off. I hoped that he'd understand that I was vulnerable and lonely when we had had sex. Was I running the risk of losing his friendship? Why couldn't we be platonic friends? Check our big hard dicks at the door. Randall grabbed a handful of my member. I gasped. I couldn't let him do this to me. I thought about Chad and his medium-sized hands on my stomach, rubbing it in slow small circles. Randall's hands were extra large and manly. I had to find the strength somewhere to resist Randall. I thought about Chad and his chestnut-brown eyes staring into mine as though he was pleading with me to consume him with my passion. Randall's thighs were hard. Chad's thighs were rock hard. Randall's member was thick and long. Chad's was huge and harder. His erections lasted longer. Chad would be waiting for me at my house. He'd be worried if I stayed out all night and made it home barely before sunrise. Coming home worn out, dragging my ass with the fragrance of Randall's sweat buried deep in the tiny crevices of my crotch. I could probably wash and scrub away Randall's sweet fragrance but I couldn't hide the deceit in my eyes. Visine wouldn't do the trick. Chad would shut me down for sure. Could I risk it for old time's sake? Tap Randall's tight ass for the good times? Hit it and quit it. We'd hit the sheets and make fierce love. We'd fall asleep until around 2:00 a.m. in the morning, when Randall would tap me on the shoulder wanting some more. He'd climb upon my member, ride it like a cowboy on a wild bucking horse and moan for the next four hours. I'd slap that ass while he tweaked my nipples, making my member harder by the second. I'd thrust my tongue so deep down in his throat I'd feel his tonsils. Could I afford the price I'd have to pay for lying up with Randall?

I looked at his face.

"Randall."

"Yeah, baby."

"You feel good. God knows you do. I've got to go, really."

"Why?"

"I don't want to be a player no more. I'm living with Chad now. I've decided to settle down. I've got to get home to my baby."

Randall pulled back from me, went over to the sofa, and slumped down in it. I looked down. I grabbed my knapsack and made for the door. He got up and came over to me. Randall stood in front of the door, his large frame blocking me from leaving his house.

"I understand. When you need me, call me."

"If and when I do, Randall, I will call you."

Randall stepped to the side of the door and I left hastily.

Driving home from Randall's house, I almost had to pull over along the side of the road. Damn! It was as if someone had taken a veil from across my eyes. I perked up. For the first time in my life I had controlled my libido. Now it was crystal clear to me why I'd become a sexual addict. So simple that I could have slapped myself for not knowing. After my firstborn was aborted, I found myself going to bed with dozens of women. I was looking for two things, my lost child and manhood. I remember the fine passionate ones, Rhonda, Tonya, Nellie, Shellie, Juanita, Chalice, Lattice, Doreen, Dorothy, Candy, Alesha, Gladys, Wanda, and Savannah. I'm not even lying. My mind doesn't fool me. I was hell bent on trying to get somebody pregnant and reclaim my manhood to make up for the double losses I suffered. Somebody may have ended up hurt, but as far as I know, nobody got pregnant by me. But by the time I reached my early twenties I came out of the closet because I realized that I was born gay. Discovering that I was gay didn't mean that I'd found a cure for my sexual addiction. Truth is, it may have fueled the fire. Instead of slowing my role, allowing myself to choose one man to love for life, I began going to bed with just as many men as women. The brothers were hotter than fire. Sensuously gorgeous guys like Ronnie, Bobby, Richard, Mike, Herbert, Lonnie, Kevin, Lorenzo, Alfonso, John, Sean, Maurice, Akiem, and Rhiem. Men whose cute faces and voluptuous bodies I remember, but their names never meant anything to me. Had I become an equal-opportunity whore? The only difference was that I knew none of the men I made love to could ever get pregnant by me. Was this the reason why I learned to love so hard that sometimes my partners would tell me that I made love like a man ready to move on to his next piece of ass? I knew that any of the women I made love with could have easily become pregnant. Did I think that if I had sex with a different man every single day of the week that maybe one of them would get pregnant by me too? Here I was riding across the San Francisco Bay Bridge and I cured my own sexual addiction without paying anybody so much as a red cent. I rolled down the window and laughed out loud. I imagined my sexual addiction tumbling down the side of the bridge and falling to the bottom of the ocean.

Chapter 18

It was Juneteenth, the day African Americans celebrated being freed from slavery. It was also one of those days when it was so hot you could crack an egg open and fry it on the sidewalk. We drove in a caravan to Blackberry Farm. Chad and I led the way. We had easy conversation these days. Chad had moved most of his clothes into my house and was gradually moving some of his furniture into the second half of my house. Chad and I had never spent more than a week together at one time. Now we seemed to get along effortlessly. He'd come home from work to a hot bath and dinner by candlelight and the fragrance of jasmine. He gave me massages nightly followed up with the best lovemaking I have ever had in my life.

Over the past two weeks, I'd received irate telephone calls from everybody who complained about Shorty coming on the trip during the BIG meeting at Randall's house. Yet it seemed that in the spirit of Juneteenth there was a sense that it was best to let bygones be bygones. Much had been accomplished with the unwed preteen project BIG was putting on. Naomi and I had gone down to the Richmond Shipyards and rescued three homeless unwed preteens and got them into prenatal programs and housing owned by Evergreen Holy Tabernacle Church. When word got out about how we'd done with these three preteens, the telephone at my house would be ringing off the hook with people calling to make referrals.

For the picnic, we had a potluck. Chad put together a mouthwatering pan of hamburger patties. I'd made a couple of sweet potato pies, sautéed a couple of sides of ribs, a dozen hot links, chicken, and T-bone steaks. It was good to see Mary and Chad join us at the picnic. Randall was kind of standoffish. When Chad and I went for a swim in the pool, my baby started moving around a lot. He loved the water! Chad and I were splashing water like dolphins. We got out of the pool and let the sun dry us off before we headed into the locker room and took a shower. After barbecuing the meat, we took out the Scrabble boards and played. I looked over at Shorty and he was playing against Cerrita. They were both laughing and strategizing. I watched Chad go into the back of the Jeep for a basketball. Chad, Scott, and Ricky went over to a basketball court and began shooting hoops. I went over to Randall, who was sitting on the edge of a bench sulking. He rested his elbows on his knees and looked at the ground.

"Randall, what's up?"

"Sup, Kel."

"You tell me?"

"You see anything wrong with this picture?"

"Randall, Chad is here. I can't do anything about that. Chad and I are a couple."

"Apparently, neither can I. My only problem is that I've fallen in love with you, Kel. But you don't even see me. You are treating me like I'm some kind of invisible man and shit. Played me like a fucking fiddle."

"Randall, you're not being fair to yourself. We mean more to each other as friends than lovers. I love you, man. As a brother."

"I got a brother. I don't need another one. I want me a man. Not just any man. You're the one for me."

"I'm not free fucking and kicking it with anybody these days but Chad. I don't know. Since I got pregnant all I seem to do is think about the baby and Chad. I don't feel empty anymore. I'm letting the streets go, man. I've had enough."

"Hooray for you."

"Randall?"

"What?"

"We've always been friends. Don't let what happened come be tween us. Let's be bigger than two people who fucked and went their separate ways," I said, gently patting him on the back.

Naomi came over, bringing Nina, Andrea, Cerrita, and Shuntria.

"Anybody want to play volleyball?" Naomi asked.

"Come on, Randall. Get your tall black ass up off of that bench. I'm going to show you a thing or two," Nina said, her laughter spilling over to all of us. She handed Shuntria and her baby bag over to me.

"Hey, Goddaddy!"

"How's my little girl doing this afternoon?"

"Fine," she said in a tiny voice.

"Yeah, Mr. Baby Johnny Cochran. We want to see you show your stuff on the volleyball court," Andrea said.

"I know you ain't about to chicken out on us," Cerrita said, grabbing one of his huge hands and pulling him along.

"Where's the rest of the team?" Randall asked.

"Waiting for you," Naomi said.

I was sitting in the shade of a very old, huge redwood. The shade helped me stay cool, but my heart was warmed to see Randall smile. He seemed to understand where I was coming from.

"This is going to be the battle of the sexes!" Andrea announced, and gave a high five to Nina before going over to join Naomi, Cerrita, and Mary on the volleyball court next to the swimming pool. I looked at the team configuration. The men were Chad, Scott, Ricky, Shorty, and Randall. The women were Naomi, Nina, Cerrita, Mary, and Andrea. Before they began to play, I watched them take a straw vote to elect team captains. From where I sat on the bench, I heard a faint applause that rose up in the air when Chad and Naomi were named team captains.

In between tending the meat on the grill, I watched Randall play next to Chad. I looked at both of these wonderful men and thought, if it were possible, I'd have them both for lovers. Randall would be like my spare tire when things between Chad and I got flat and we were at odds with one another. Chad would remain my main squeeze and the cofather of my child. The only problem with that is they wouldn't have it. I'd have to split up my love between the two of them. How could I love myself, two men equally, and a baby too? In the end, I wouldn't love anybody as much as I would be juggling people's lives around, giving little of myself, getting even less back in return.

The gray smoke from the grill stung my eyes, made them burn. I lowered the cover over the grill and let the meat smoke for a while. I sat down on the bench, found a bowl of potato salad Cerrita had brought, and piled it on a paper plate. Made myself a couple of hot dogs. The weenies were the first things to get done on the grill. I cooled off one for Shuntria, who shook her head. She only ate small bites from the hot dog bun. I watched both teams play with the vigor of world class southern California volleyball champions. Naomi served the ball hard over the net. Shorty returned the ball forcefully. Cerrita jumped and slammed the volleyball over to the other side of the court. Chad caught it and hit it only hard enough to set up a slam of the ball to the other side that was blocked by Andrea and spiked by Nina over to Chad's team. Ricky caught the ball and popped it in the air lightly, setting up Scott for a hard slam back over the net. It went on like this for nearly an hour. I watched them finish; both teams gave each other high fives. It was unclear to me which team had won or if winning had been the ultimate goal. All of them trudged back over to where I was sitting on the bench.

"Well, who won?" I asked Chad, who was walking between Naomi and Shorty.

"Who else? We the man!" Shorty announced and gave Chad a high five.

"No doubt!" Chad said, laughing.

"It was a tie game. We asked for a rematch. But Mr. Chad, the esteemed team leader, turned us down," Naomi said.

"For now," Chad said and sat down next to me.

The rest of the group made it back to the picnic table. They mingled, ate hot dogs, played cards. The boombox blared Jill Scott's CD. Her poetic ballads filled the park, bringing soft rhythms to the outing. Randall had taken over tending the grill. A couple of hours later, we all sat and devoured the food in celebration of the holiday.

I ate again. I couldn't seem to get full. There was always room for one more hot link or a steak or two. My weight gain had become more gradual. Naomi came over to me.

"Kel, let's take a walk in the park," she said.

"Cool," I said, getting up from the bench and taking Shuntria over to Nina. We went up a short hill to the other side where there was a blue lake and sat under the shade of an oak tree. The birds chirped and boats were drifting on the lake. I watched others casting out fishing poles along the bank and every now and then a child would burst into laughter running down the grassy knoll.

I turned to Naomi.

Naomi told me that she was looking for an attorney to represent Sugar in filing for divorce against Reverend Edwards. The way she explained it to me was that Reverend Edwards was being a jerk about sharing his community property with Sugar. Reverend Edwards owned a barbershop, real estate all up and down California, and acres and acres of land in Georgia that he rented out to a shopping mall. Naomi's attorney didn't do divorce cases. She wanted me to ask Randall if he would represent Sugar in her case against her husband. I was interested in finding out how in the world Sugar found out that Cayleen and Reverend Edwards were rolling in the sack. The spin Naomi put on it boiled down to this: Reverend Edwards told Sugar that he wanted a son, somebody to carry on his name. Sugar couldn't have any more kids. She had a hysterectomy right after Naomi was born. Sugar was at home one morning, sitting on her bed, and talking on the phone. Her cousin Elnora was giving her the phone number of a cousin that lived nearby that she didn't know anything about. Sugar didn't have a pen or paper to write on, so she went into Reverend Edwards' briefcase looking for a pen and paper to jot the number on real quick. What she found instead was a letter that her husband wrote to Cayleen telling her how much he loved her, how happy he was that she was carrying his child. Then that Sunday, all hell broke loose in front of the church and Sugar smacked Cayleen down.

"Oh shit," I thought, wondering if I should get up and jet back over the hill to stand between Randall and Chad. What if Randall, to get back at me for rejecting his advances, spilled the wine and told Chad that we'd made some serious love not so long ago? I had to beat Randall to the punch. I couldn't do it then though. It wasn't the right time. Watching those two women go at it made me think that *The Jerry Springer Show* was being taped that day in front of Evergreen Holy Tabernacle Church right before my very eyes.

I told Naomi that I would ask Randall and see if I could get him interested in representing Sugar.

"We better get back before they eat up all the food," I said. I got up and we went back to join the group. When we made it back, everything was the way it was at our departure. Peaceful, and everybody, even Shorty, seemed to click. We hung out at the park for a couple more hours. Then we all decided to leave the same way we arrived, by caravan. Chad piled in all of the leftover food, extra trays, blankets, backpacks, and chairs. Cerrita and Mary agreed to lead the caravan back home. Randall drove alone behind them. Nina and Andrea were driving behind Randall. Naomi and Shorty were driving behind Chad and me. I had taken over driving.

When I got home, I found a message waiting for me on my voice mail from Amy. My heart raced. The last thing I needed right now was more heartache or drama. Yet Amy's news was inspiring. She'd had a six-pound, eight-ounce baby boy. Mother and child were resting fine at home. I called my ex-secretary to congratulate her.

"Amy?"

"This is Amy."

"It's Kel. Congratulations, Amy!"

"Thanks, Kel. It was a little scary. Sort of like being on a roller coaster without a seat belt. I'd do it again, but next time I hope I don't have any problems," she said. I could hear the smile in her voice. She sounded clear and confident.

"Amy, I'm pregnant."

"What?"

"You heard me right. I'm having a baby. I go in this November."

"Really!"

"You darn tooting!" I said. I was proud.

Before I hung up the phone with Amy, I went through more than the whole nine yards. I told her my reasons for wanting a baby, the gender of my child, and how with the blessings of God I was going to make the sacrifices needed to raise my son. Amy didn't trip at the news. She wished me well and gave me her new address. I sent her a gift for her son that I had bought for her months before at Babies and Bath.

After I was done talking to Amy, Chad invited me to take a shower with him. He soaped off all of the charcoal smoke that had settled in my skin like vapors. Afterward, he gave me a Johnson's Baby Lotion massage that put me to sleep. I slipped into a dream.

Chad Jr. was a teenage freshman at Richmond High. I was driving home from visiting with Ma, listening to the radio. A news flash came on that a teenager at Richmond High had gone berserk and shot up two teachers and fourteen students. *Oh God!* I thought. *I hope my son isn't one of the victims.* I stepped on the gas. I made it to the school. Ran through a throng of grieving students, parents, and faculty. I called for Chad. I yelled at the top of my lungs until my voice became hoarse. I could only whisper little Chad's name. When I couldn't find my son, I fell to my knees, put my face in my hands, and wept like a baby. I looked up and Chad was standing before me.

"What's up, Pops? I'm all right," he said. His baggy blue jeans fell halfway down his narrow waist.

I got up from my knees, held my son in my arms, and rocked him back and forth. *My boy is safe,* I thought. *My son is alive.*

Chapter 19

The following month during my regular visit to Dr. Valesco's office in mid-July, he told me that another man involved in the study gave birth to a healthy baby girl on Easter Sunday. This was wonderful news, but Dr. Valesco spoiled it. He told me that the man died of a rare blood infection the same day, after giving birth. Dr. Valesco told me that he didn't mention this when it happened because he didn't want me to become worried. I was dismayed, but I half shrugged this information off of me like raindrops falling off a raincoat to the ground. I couldn't let this part of the news get me down. My ancestors would chant as they marched through the valleys of death, "I ain't gonna let nobody turn me around." I had to keep on marching too. Had Dr. Valesco told me instead that his baby died, then Chad would've had to come pick me up off of the floor of Dr. Valesco's office and drive me back home. I wouldn't have had enough room inside of me to take that kind of news. God had given me my own life and even if it was tarnished by a misdiagnosed illness, I was grateful. Yet it was the new life blooming inside of me that meant the most and everything in the world to me. It was all that I was living for now. It was what I went to sleep and woke up each and every morning thinking about. A man knows of many truths. My baby was the truth. I knew my child was the truth because I felt it growing inside of me. Should God spare the life of my child and take mine, then I think that His work will have been done. This was what I believed and felt that it was so.

Labor Day was one week away. It was Indian summer in the Bay Area. The days were long and hot, the nights warm and short. Chad was at work when I called Randall's office. Randall's secretary Tish picked up. She asked me about the baby and when was I going in. I told her the baby was fine and I had about two and a half more months before I went in to have my baby. She put Randall on the line. I told him that I was sorry I had not told him how much I appreciated the help he gave Naomi's mother in her divorce case. He told me that he understood and accepted my apology. He sounded like a man in a hurry to get somewhere.

It had to be less than five minutes after I hung up the telephone with Randall when Ma called. She asked me if I was doing all right. I told her that I wanted to come over to her house and talk to her about something.

"What's wrong?"

"We'll talk about it when I get over to your house."

"You sure everything is all right?"

"I'll be over in a minute, Ma," I said.

I hung up the phone.

All of Ma's red and pink roses planted underneath her kitchen window were in full bloom. Her lawn went up a small incline that made a line leading to the front door. The grass in the front yard of her cottage was fresh green, neatly trimmed. The California sun warmed my face as I made my way up the walkway. I'd stopped at Subway and picked up a foot-long tuna fish sandwich. I walked underneath a great oak tree in Ma's yard.

Ma came to the door and let me in before I was able to ring her doorbell. She was holding what looked like the quilt she began stitching together the last time she visited with me at my house. I sat down at the dining room table and finished eating the other half of my tuna fish sandwich.

"Child, you look swollen."

"I'm pregnant, Ma. I'm having a baby."

"A baby?" She laughed. "Kel, you a mess, child."

"I'm serious, Ma."

I told Ma the whole story. I told her about finding Dr. Valesco. I told her I got pregnant after Dr. Valesco implanted the artificial uterus and injected the fertilized egg inside me. I told her about the regular monthly injections through the catheter to keep the baby healthy and growing. Showed her the catheter high upon my stomach. I told her that now that I've got a uterus, I'm going to have contractions and labor pains when the baby is ready to be born. I told her that I had gained at least fifteen pounds through my fourth month, but now my weight gain is more gradual. I told her that I'm blessed with a high metabolism rate and I could eat just about anything I wanted to. I told her that so far, I've been lucky not to experience the discrimination many females do when they get pregnant. I told her that there's nothing unusual about my actions—it was just that I'm involved in an experimental male pregnancy project with an uncertain outcome. I told her that Chad's actions sometimes puzzled me, but we seemed to be turning the corner and resolving some of the conflicts in our relationship.

Ma sat down at the table and looked at me and tilted her head a little sideways, like she hadn't seen me in many years. I told her about the surrogate mother agreement Naomi and I filed in superior court.

I'd never before looked so closely at Ma's face. Now, looking in Ma's face sitting across from me at her dining room table made me see her age. What the years had done was to sculpt her face into that of a woman who had really lived life. Now she understood the complexities of human nature. She had the face of my ancestors now.

"Lord, Lord, Lord, Lord, Lord. I should have known it all along. I've been dreaming every night of fish for the past six and a half months. I knew somebody was pregnant. I thought it was my niece Betsy that was pregnant. All that running and ripping. That child is as hot as cayenne pepper. I knew it had to be somebody in the family. I've been calling my folks all over Georgia and Tennessee, but nobody could tell me who was pregnant. They'd tell me, Ester, it must be somebody on your end. It all makes sense to me now, all those questions you asked me about accepting your baby. All them baby clothes you brought in the house at your surprise birthday party. That's why you sitting up at my dining room table as big as a house out in the Georgia woods. Pregnant and right under my nose. Hummmph! Kel, I sure wish you had told me that you wanted to get pregnant. I could have saved you some grief."

"Ma, the Bible says multiply and be fruitful."

"I know what the Bible says. I don't sleep with it under my pillow every night to rest my head on it. What in the world are you going to do with a baby, Kel?"

"Love and raise it. Teach it right from wrong. Be a father and a mother all at the same time."

"On your own?"

"You raised me on your own."

"Yeah, Kel, but I'm a woman."

"I'm a man."

"Child, don't get up in my face telling me what you are and what I did and didn't do, Kelvin Maxwell Warren. We're talking about a man going into labor and having a child. Why did you wait so long to tell me? What did you think that I was going to do, be talking you into getting an abortion?"

"I was scared."

"Kel, you can't be scared of me, child. I'm your mother. I'm the one who suffered through labor pains to bring you into this world."

"All I want you to do, Ma, is stay in my corner. I mean, accept my child as your grandchild, Ma. You taught me that when I was a little boy sick with colds and stuff that we couldn't avoid suffering because Jesus suffered on the cross. Don't you remember telling me that, Ma?"

I watched her face.

"Does Naomi's daddy, Reverend Edwards, know about all of this?"

"Reverend Edwards has his own problems. He got Cayleen Griffin pregnant and Sugar has filed for divorce."

"I'm sure glad Sugar did. I don't know what's wrong with these holy men these days. Talking about God telling folks to live a clean holy life all the time while doing the very things they preach against. That's why it doesn't pay to believe in anybody other than God more than you believe in yourself. People sure got a lot of nerve. All of them need to have they own babies!"

"I know they do, Ma. I've never met a saint. We are all sinners."

"Kelvin?"

"Yeah."

"Why didn't you just court that Naomi and get her pregnant? The right way."

"The last woman I got pregnant with my baby flushed it down the toilet. It'll kill me dead to have that happen to me again. Don't you understand, Ma? It's the only way."

"You mean it's the only way for you. Child, it's not the only way."

Ma got up from the table and went into the kitchen. I could hear her taking a plate out of the cabinet and putting food on it. I heard the jingle of silverware. She came back out, sat down a plate of food and utensils in front of me. The plate was piled high with pinto beans, rice, fried chicken, yams, and corn bread. Ma invited me to sit to dinner with her.

I had already finished eating my foot-long Subway sandwich. Ma told me that now that I was eating for two it was important to eat a lot.

"What'll you know? I'm having me a grandchild. The good Lord sure moves in mysterious ways."

I watched Ma get up from the table and go into her bedroom. Moments later, she returned and sat down next to the quilt she'd started making at my house when she came over to fix me some gumbo. The quilt was a patchwork of colors as brilliant as a rainbow. I spooned up the yams and pinto beans. I put the food in my mouth, chewed slowly, swallowed. I took a bite of the fried chicken and corn bread. This food was good. Ma set the quilt on top of the table in front of her.

"Ma?"

"Yeah, baby."

"Is that the quilt you started working on when you came over to my house and made me some gumbo?"

"This is the quilt that's going to cover my grandchild. Keep my grandbaby warm and help to protect that child from the little evils in the world. Lord have mercy," she said and began to weep.

"Why you crying, Ma?" I asked, taking a handkerchief out of my back pocket and handing it to her. Ma quickly regained her composure and laughed.

"Child, these are tears of joy. Tears not of weariness or pain. God has blessed us, Kel. A blessing and a miracle, baby. This is God's fine work."

My baby began to kick me. I pulled up my undershirt.

"Come here, Ma! My baby is kicking! Feel this!" I said as Ma got up from the table and came over and sat down in a chair next to me. She rubbed the tiny little molehill my baby made in my stomach. Ma's hands were as warm and as soft as they were when she'd issue warnings to me when I was a child not to run too fast. As warm and as soft as they were when she made chicken soup for me when I was sick with a cold, when I was flat on my back in the hospital with a mysterious illness with a 106-degree temperature for five days. These were the same hands that took a switch or belt to me when I'd disobeyed a rule as a little boy. Now Ma's hands were on my belly pregnant with a new life soon to be brought into the world, the way that a new dawn greets us every waking day God gives us the chance to see.

"Well, I'll be! Ooooooooh! Child, would you look at this! Mighty! Mighty! Kel, you going to have a boy."

"Why you think that?" I said and stuffed a spoonful of pinto beans in my mouth.

"Because your stomach is high up in your chest. If you were having a girl you would be carrying the baby lower in your stomach."

"Oh?" I said, pretending like I didn't already know.

"Lord, I got to go shopping."

I told Ma about my nursery. I wanted her to know that I'd bought a lot of things already. I let her know that all I needed from her was her love and blessings. "That won't cost you anything. Not a dime," I said as I watched Ma get up from the table and take my empty plate into the kitchen. I heard running water, pots rattling. Ma came back out with another plate of food. This time the food was stacked higher than the last plate she had brought out to me. She sat the plate down on the table in front of me.

"Doctors are funny people. You got to stay on them. The one you saw when you got sick last year lied, telling you that all you had was bronchitis. Then he lied and said that it was pneumonia. Gave you fifty AIDS tests and they was negative. Then they said that you had valley fever. If God hadn't stepped in to save your life, you would've died."

"I know, Ma. Dr. Valesco's different. He knows what he's doing."

"I hope so, child! We want us a fine great big old healthy baby! I bet he's going to look just like you. You were twenty-two inches long. I didn't think that you'd ever get all the way out of me."

"Ma?"

"Yeah, honey."

"They going to have to cut my baby out of me. A caesarean, Ma, and I may bleed a lot because my abdominal wall is so thick," I choked up. My eyes watered but I didn't cry.

"Jesus. He bled upon the cross, baby."

"I'm not going to cry, Ma."

"Jesus wept, sweetheart."

"Will the labor pains hurt, Ma?"

"Child, you ever wonder why God put a womb inside of a woman rather than a man?"

"Do tell, Ma," I said. I was interested.

Ma told me that the pain of childbirth could cut a man in two. She thought newborn babies were the strongest people in the world. Ma put it this way: "A man, he can put up skyscrapers, build bridges across the oceans, sometimes find a cure for some of the things that make us sick as a dog. But it takes a special kind of man to conceive a child. Everybody ain't able. It takes a man whose backbone is strong enough to carry the world upon his shoulders. That man is sitting at my dining room table eating my food. I'm looking dead in that man's face. I know him because he is my son. I've always lived to see you do some wonderful things, Kel. Child, this is a blessing. A real blessing."

"That's all right. And don't you be scared. God didn't bring you this far to leave you alone. He will be by your side and I'll be next to Him. Just praying like it was the first time I ever got down on my knees and prayed to God in my life. God may not be there when you need him but He is always on time."

"You've always told me that, Ma. Is it for true?"

"Why sure! I told you that a long time ago. Your memory is about as long as an eyelash," she said.

"Ma, I'm still a little scared for my baby."

"Child, put your worries in the hands of God. He knows all things. He made it so that you can conceive a child without a womb. This is a great getting-up day!" she said, softly slapping her palms down upon the table as if she was about to get up from the table and begin to dance and shout.

"Ma, if I was ever happy before I must have slept clean through it. It's almost as if I'm in a dream. One of those kinds of dreams you have when you've won a lot of money and you don't want to wake up from it."

"Child, that's because the real truth is a dream. Baby, it's a dream that brings true meaning to life, Kel. Listen to me. I'm your mother," she said and came over and kissed my forehead.

Chapter 20

Chad and I spent a quiet Labor Day holiday at home. We set up the picnic table, chairs, and umbrella in my backyard. I started the grill. I put on a sautéed slab of ribs, skinless chicken breasts, a half dozen ears of corn wrapped in aluminum foil, hot dogs, link sausage. Chad had prepared Boston baked beans, a potato salad, and macaroni and cheese casserole.

I'd received the living trust Randall had prepared for me to read and make any changes I thought were important, like who would be the executor of my estate. I sat out on the patio, my stomach high and legs naked. I had on a pair of Bermuda shorts and a faded oversized undershirt I'd picked up years ago during a visit to the Florida Keys. As I read the living trust, I was flooded with a sense of guilt about having slept with Randall. Maybe what did it was the way that Chad had confessed to me last night when we were lying together in bed after making love that he'd never slept with anyone else since we'd been together for five years. I couldn't tell him at the Juneteenth picnic. I had to tell him now. It was time. I turned the other way, then looked at my swollen belly. My baby kicked as if he was telling me that this was my chance to come clean with true confessions of my own. It wasn't as if I was going to sleep with Randall ever again in life. I felt that on the night I left Randall's house after the BIG meeting I had conquered my sexual addiction. I tossed it out of the window of the Jeep. I had to confess to Chad. Hadn't he complained to me about not meeting him halfway? What would be the risks? Were there any advantages? What would be the costs? Would I be able to afford to pay such costs? All these questions were still swirling around in my head when Chad came out on the patio. He had a tray filled with a cold glass of milk, a green tossed salad, and a pitcher of water. He set the tray down on the table and sat across from me. Chad took a sip of his cranberry juice spiked with vodka and propped his long legs upon an empty chair. He took a long drag from the cigarette, and his smoke mingled with the smoke from the barbecue pit. I shifted. I looked through the smoke at his face.

"Chad?"

"What, Head?"

"There's something I got to tell you."

"I'm waiting."

"A while back, I slept with Randall," I confessed.

"Why didn't you tell me this last night when I told you I've never had sex with anyone else since we'd been together?"

"I wanted to come clean about it at the Juneteenth picnic, but I was just afraid to do it, as I was last night. It happened when you were giving me a hard time about being pregnant. I was weak, vulnerable. You wouldn't touch me. I needed something, Chad. You treated me like I had a contagious disease."

"Well, I'll be goddamn! So you slept with that nigga after all? That's why he's so short with me now when he calls the house."

"I'm telling you this, Chad, not to hurt you but to lay all of my cards on the table. So that we can begin fresh with the baby coming and all," I said, hoping to strike an accord.

"So you slept with that nigga after all?" Chad repeated. He looked at the ground, shook his head, and stabbed his cigarette out in the ashtray.

"Doesn't my confession mean anything to you, Chad? I didn't have to tell you, but it would have made me seem like I was deceitful."

"How many others have you slept with, Kel?"

I froze.

I listened to the barbecue on the grill sizzle. A fuss of robins and bluebirds were noisily chirping just above my head in the oak tree. I imagined that the birds were fighting over who had slept with mates, friends, and partners after the sun went down. Everything, including my kicking baby, came to a standstill. Did I have the courage to tell it all? Would this add to the price that I already knew I would have to pay? I hadn't had sex with anyone else, other than Mitch and Randall, in the last six months. I'd sworn off the sex club. My sexual addiction was over. Could I abbreviate my confession? Select dates, times, places that didn't make it seem as though I was a slut? Only count the men I was orgasmic with? Would this minimize the damage? Or had I let way too many cats out of the bag already? I went over, lifted the top of the grill, and flipped the meat over. Took a fork and broke off the end of a slab of ribs. I blew on it a couple of times before putting it in my mouth, chewing it into pieces. I swallowed. I sat back down at the table.

"There were others, Chad."

"How many?"

"What do you want, a score card?"

"What I want to know is why did you cheat on me, Kel?"

"Chad, I never considered it cheating. You were sometimes difficult to reach."

"So you had to reach out for someone else?"

The truth was that I did have to reach out for someone else to hold me, even if that someone else was asexual. Not someone who was the opposite of Chad and wanted to fuck my brains out every chance he got. Or maybe someone I could hold that wouldn't shoo me away like I was a puppy too frisky for his own good. Or maybe someone who took the time to listen to me. Not talk at me, but to me. In the case of Chad that had to be the reason, so I thought. I guess what it really boiled down to was that Chad showed me two faces. One of his faces was that of a man who wanted a long-term commitment with unconditional love. The other face he showed me was that of a man who didn't want anyone to discover that he was gay. I poured gas on the fire when I got pregnant. Had I pushed too hard? To Chad, being black is one thing. Being gay and black is another. I've fought the same internal war all of my life. It's a war that I've had to fight with little or no help from anybody but God. I've come to understand that it doesn't matter if you are black and gay. The only thing that matters is that you still got good enough sense to keep fighting, marching ahead against racism tinged with homophobia. I'm not afraid to look back over my shoulder to see who's watching me. Anybody can watch me, as long as they don't get in my damn way to try to stop me from doing what I want to do and make out of my life. I only know one God. I haven't met Him in the eyes of any man or woman I've ever slept with. Every time I look at my pregnant belly in the mirror and feel my baby kick, that is when I know that there is a God. So this was how I felt when I gave Chad my reply.

"Chad, I did what I had to do," I said.

"All this time I thought that we were a sacred gay black couple," he said.

Chad told me about going to the Castro, that regardless of how thin it seemed to be in the number of men of color represented in the neighborhood, men could kiss, hug, walk openly hand in hand. Even so, there were isolated incidents of violence, vicious youths roaming the streets like wild dogs swinging baseball bats and smacking down a cornered gay man. You'd see restaurants, retail outlets, and boutiques representing every racial culture in the world except African-American gays. On top of all of this, for miles upon miles you wouldn't see a black couple any place in sight. When you did see a single black man, he would give you shade. Acting like he was scared to even open up his mouth. As if his shit didn't stink. Looking at you with an expression on his face that seemed to ask the question: How did you get in?

"Doesn't that tell you just a little something? Black couples are as rare as a four-leaf clover. You've blown what was sacred between us into tiny little bits. All of it! Pick the fucking pieces up off of the floor by your goddamn self!" he said, getting up from his chair and making for the patio door.

"Where are you going, Chad? Are you going to run out on me and the baby?" Then I said, "Wait, sit back down. I'll be right back."

Chad sat back down in his chair.

I went in the house. I started up the stairs to the study and took the book *Sexual Addiction: A Black Gay Man's Guide to Sexual Health* off the shelf. I climbed back down the stairs and went back out on the patio. I handed the book to Chad. I asked him to do me a favor and open the book to the dedication section and read the inscription for me out loud.

He flipped open the cover of the book and began to read.

"For Chad Smith, my first love, whose legendary sexual addiction cured my own."

Chad flipped to the photograph section of the book. He seemed to be looking at the picture of himself and the tanned face of Roger.

"See, you were there too, Chad. I was too. Are you playing holier than thou with me? You didn't think that I knew this about you?"

"Kel, I wasn't hanging out in the Castro. I wasn't with you in those days. I was with someone else. Besides, that man is dead. Dr. Wilson is dead. I struggled with my addiction. I had a doctor who took the time to care."

"See! That's my point, Chad! Just like you were with someone struggling with sexual addiction. I was with you struggling with it. You got over it. Now it's my turn. Can't you meet me halfway, baby? Care about me, baby, the way Dr. Wilson cared about you."

Chad went up the short concrete steps and slid open the patio door. He turned around and looked at me.

"Kel?"

"Yeah, baby."

"I'll be back."

"For real?" I asked, but I didn't inquire as to when.

"Trust me. I promise."

"Chad?" I said to his back.

"What?" he answered without turning around to look at me.

"Don't leave me, not right now. Please don't go. I'm sorry, Chad. If you don't want to stay because of me, do it for the sake of the baby. You don't have to stay for me, Chad, but for the baby," I cried.

"I'm fucking out of here!" he yelled.

I didn't cry at Atlas's funeral because I wanted to be strong for Olivia. I even held back my tears when Dr. Valesco told me, "You did it, Kel. . . . You're a pregnant man . . ." I told myself to hold on, remembering that Reverend Edwards told me after my firstborn was aborted that God never gives us more than we can stand. I told myself, *Don't even think about it.* But it was my heart that hurt and my eyes that made me cry, not the smoke coming from the grill. I would have run after him but I couldn't move. So I hung my head down. I wept.

I let the barbecue on the grill burn to a black crisp. I couldn't stand the thought of eating. I felt guilty. I regretted hurting Chad. Had I fooled myself into thinking I wanted to raise my baby all on my own? Who in the world was going to help me raise my baby now?

Chapter 21

One week after Labor Day, Scott and I went down to the docks, at the Richmond Shipyards, and found two more unwed pregnant pre-teens. We enrolled them in the prenatal program cosponsored by BIG and Evergreen Holy Tabernacle Church. Scott and I found these two girls huddled together on a thin blanket underneath an old rickety pier that I used to fish off when I was a little boy. The strong smell from the sea filled my nostrils and quickened my senses. The girls told us that they'd been there for a week without any food or shelter. We got them into the Jeep and took them to the church where they were to be fed and clothed by the missionaries. As we were about to climb in the Jeep and drive away, Naomi pulled up behind us.

"Hey, Brotha. Hey, Scott," she said.

"Hey, Naomi," Scott and I said in unison.

"What brings you guys to church today?"

"We brought two more unwed preteens from the Shipyards to get hooked up with the program we got going between Evergreen and BIG," I said.

"Cool. Kel, we've got to talk. Call me tonight," she said as I watched her disappear inside the church.

I took Scott home. He invited me inside his apartment. It looked like a house on the inside. Scott's living room was sunken. He had a refurbished bar and jukebox that you had to put a dime inside of to play records. One wall was dedicated to CDs, DVDs, videocassette tapes, and a stereo. He had tiny speakers stuck in all four corners of the room. His apartment was sparsely furnished with a hint of art deco. A long beige flat sofa, a glass end table with chrome legs, life-sized sculptures of old African kings. The two mahogany African masks he had picked up at a swap meet in Berkeley several years before were my favorites. A tall lamp in a corner, shaped like a cup you'd put a snow cone inside of. His kitchen table was tall with a glass top and two high-backed black leather chairs. From Scott's living room window, I looked at the red arches of the Golden Gate Bridge, and it made me think about Chad. I decided not to miss him too much because he promised that he would be back. So when he took off up those short concrete stairs that led up to the patio door, I cried but made up my mind to be patient with him. Give him some time because he promised he would be back. What worried me though was this: I had made a promise to Randall the first time we made love that we would hook up and kick it again. I reneged on my promise to Randall. Had the tables turned? Was turn about fair play and as American as apple pie? Was Chad going to do to me what I'd done to Randall?

I sat down on the sofa. Scott went into the kitchen. When he came back out in the living room, he handed me a cold glass of milk.

"So, dude. Two more months. Are you ready?"

"I'm ready. I been ready," I said, the way I used to talk when I was a kid and someone on the playground challenged me to a fight.

"Well, it won't be long now."

"I still want to go shopping for a few more things at Three Little Pigs. They've got some of the best baby clothes in the Bay Area."

"Say what?"

"No doubt."

"Kel?"

"Yeah, man, what's up? You seem to be a little distracted."

"Well, that's because Ricky's in the hospital. He came down with AIDS," he said.

"What hospital? When did he go?" I asked.

"He went in yesterday. He's at Mercy Hospital. His doctor told me he'll be coming home tomorrow."

"Ah, man. I'm sorry to hear that."

"Well, don't worry about it. You've got to focus on having your baby. This is something I've got to deal with. Ricky's going on cocktails. He'll be fine."

"I know that he will, Scott," I said and hugged him the best I could.

"You know, life is funny. We live some, then we die forever. It's like wham! Just like that."

"Who you telling?"

"You know, Ricky has a two-year-old son in Mexico."

"You told me that a while back."

"Well, he wants to see him real bad."

Scott told me that Ricky's ex-wife, Dina, is a strict Catholic. For over a year, she had refused to let Ricky see his only son, Miguel. I was cheered when Scott told me that after he told Dina that Ricky was sick, she planned to let Ricky visit his son for a while in Mexico.

"Wow. What an incredible story," I said. I swallowed hard.

"I'm picking up Ricky from the hospital tomorrow."

"Do you need me to do anything?"

"I'll let you know if I do, but we'll be fine."

We sat a while listening to an Anita Baker CD, *Rhythm of Love*. By the time I left Ricky's apartment the sun had slipped behind Mt. Tam. The skies were streaked peach with only a few low clouds.

Chapter 22

Seven whole days had gone by and I had not heard a single word from Chad. I was sitting at the kitchen table marveling over the success BIG had had with rescuing ten unwed preteens at the Richmond Shipyards. We'd placed some of them in safe homes and families connected with the church that took them in. The girls were counseled by volunteer social workers that were members of the church. BIG plugged the girls into grassroots programs that led the ones who'd dropped out of school to get reenrolled. The short-term goals were to get them off of the streets, into prenatal care, and open the lines of dialogue between young people, their families, and facilities that offered developmental support. The long-term goal was to provide these preteens with specific job-training skills to steer them away from the cycle of welfare dependency.

I looked around the kitchen at the things Chad left behind: A chrome toaster, a small microwave, a tiny television that he'd fastened underneath the cabinet; a cookie jar shaped like a *102 Dalmatians* puppy; a "Things to Accomplish" notepad he stuck on the front of the refrigerator; two crystal glass candleholders he'd bought at Macy's during the first weekend he'd moved in with me; an old pair of mountain boots that sat in the same place they always had next to the china cabinet right off of the kitchen; a postcard from me that I'd sent him when I went to Aruba two years ago. I included my pregnant body in the things Chad left behind. It gave me comfort seeing the things he left behind. Maybe because I thought that when you leave things behind it means that one day you just might want to come back to get them. My thoughts gave me hope.

The doorbell rang.

"Hey, Brotha!" Naomi said, grabbing me around the neck. She smelled of carnations.

"Hey, Sista!" I hugged her back.

She was right on time for dinner. I had cooked smothered pork chops covered with brown gravy, accompanied by cabbage and blueberry muffins. The intoxicating smell of cooking food made me hungrier by the minute. So Naomi's arrival made me happy when she came through the door. It meant that it was time to chow down.

"Has Chad come back home yet?"

"I think Chad has a lot of soul searching to do on his own. All of his clothes are still up in my closet. That's a good sign, I think," I said. I smiled and felt warm all over.

"Kel?"

"Yeah."

"I want to be a mother to our baby. I told Mama about it, and she was upset that I hadn't told her about it earlier. She's already bought a truckload of clothes and toys."

"Really?"

"I ain't lying! She's even talking about taking him to her new church to have him baptized."

"Say what?"

"Who? You don't hear me, though. She took the money she got in her predivorce settlement from Daddy and opened up a bank account. Put the money in the baby's name. Randall ain't no joke. He's something else. Quick! Don't let an inch of grass grow under his feet. Move his ass," she said, put a forkful of cabbage in her mouth, and washed it down with a glass of milk. She stared at the smothered pork chop.

"Ah, Randall. He's quite a mover and shaker. He doesn't play around," I said and sliced off a piece of pork chop.

When Naomi and I got done eating, she took me out to see the film *The Brothers.* Every single one of the men starring in the film reminded me of Chad in some way or other. One of the guys had chocolate skin, high cheekbones, teeth as white as pearls. Then there was another guy that had a goatee that seemed to be painted on. There was still another one who wore his hair short on the sides with the top cut short into black waves that looked like the slow tide rolling on top of the bay.

After the movie, Naomi took me to Swanson's Ice Cream and Cookie Parlor. I bought a double large strawberry milkshake. When I got done with the milkshake I ordered a banana split covered with hot chocolate, cherries, walnuts, and whipped cream. I topped it all off with a loaf of cinnamon bread that I sliced and dipped in a small cup filled with honey. Naomi shared her Oreo Cookie ice cream in a tiny tray with me after I told her it was all right to go ahead and eat it herself. She didn't take no for an answer. Naomi shoved the tray under my nose and promised not to take me home until I gave the bowl back to her empty.

About three months before, I had begun to crave oranges. By all accounts, I'd probably easily eaten over a crate if not a truckload full. I'd lost count. We came out of Swanson's and I saw a stack of oranges across the street on a stand outside of Farmer's Market. Naomi trailed behind me as we went over to Farmer's Market to get some. Naomi put a big sack in a pushcart, rolled it up to the back of her Lexus, and dumped the oranges in the trunk. I was still below the thirty-five extra pounds that Dr. Valesco told me I could gain without harming myself or the baby.

We drove to Three Little Pigs in Berkeley. Naomi picked out some of the coolest baby clothes imaginable. She found the tiniest navy blue matching cap sailor suit with gold buttons down the front. Naomi fell in love with a pair of tiny blue mittens and earmuffs. She zeroed in on a pair of shades. I'd never seen a pair of shades so small in my life.

I looked at Naomi and said, "Now, Naomi, honestly."

She said, "I want my son to be cool. Okay!"

All I could do was give her a high five. By the time we got done, Naomi had rung up a small fortune's worth of purchases.

Naomi took me over to her house. I wasn't surprised to see Shorty sitting up watching *Who Wants to Be a Millionaire* with Sugar. What surprised me was when he grinned and hugged me as I came through the door. Sugar started to fawn over me. She tried to get me to spend the night over at Naomi's so she could tell me about when she was pregnant, what she'd gone through. I told her I'd love to hear about it but I had to get home. What I had to do was get some rest. It had been a long, exhausting day and the bottoms of my feet were sore from walking.

Naomi took me home, unloaded the sack of oranges, and took them in the house for me. She set the sack of oranges upon the kitchen table, pulled the string on the large sack loose, and put some in the fruit bowl in the middle of the table. Then she separated the rest into groups of six. She placed them in mid-sized plastic bags at eye level within my arm's reach into the fridge.

"I'll talk to you later, Brotha," she said and gave me a slight peck on the cheek.

"Bye, Sista. I'll call you, all right?" I said and watched the red lights on the back of her Lexus disappear into the Indian summer night.

I took a shower and checked my e-mail voice messages. Chad still hadn't called or sent me an e-mail. I pulled the blinds open on my bedroom window and cut the lights out in the room. I lay with my hands cupped behind my head and looked at the moon. My baby kicked. Right before I was about to fall asleep, the telephone rang.

"Kel?" a voice said that clearly wasn't Chad. Whoever it was had a Spanish accent.

"Is this Ricky?"

"Nah, dude. This is Juan Diaz. I met you a while back at Baby Boomers at the Wharf. Remember, you bought a ton of baby toys one afternoon. I helped you get the things to your car. You gave me your telephone number."

"Right! Now I remember. What's up?"

"Well, man, I'm thinking like if you're not too busy that we can hook up tonight. I got a little free time. It's a hot sweaty night. You want to play, Papi?"

My member stood at attention like a soldier standing stiffly in line under the glaring eyeballs of his superior officer. I had to find some way to make it go away. It wouldn't. I began to think quickly. What if this was the night that Chad decided to come back home, get down on his knees to tell me what a fool he'd been? That he was wrong to act as if my sexual escapades put our relationship at the risk of dissolution? Or that he wanted to ask me to forgive him for leaving me with nothing but odds and ends belonging to him in my kitchen, mountain boots, a closet full of his clothes? Maybe Chad wanted to rub my belly, massage my aching feet, and lay with me spoon fashion between thin white sheets under an Indian summer moon. Or maybe Chad would come back home, tell me that he had found himself someone who was not having a baby. That the pressure I'd put on him to be a father wasn't fair to him. That after all it wasn't his sperm I used to fertilize Naomi's egg to get me pregnant. Or maybe Chad simply wanted to sit down in front of E! or listen to some soft warm jazz. All of these thoughts flew through my mind, making the speed of sound slow in comparison. Then it came to me. I had a doctor's appointment tomorrow at Dr. Valesco's office. I could meet Juan for lunch. What did I have to lose?

"Juan?"

"Yeah, Papi."

"I'm a little exhausted tonight. But I'll be in the city tomorrow. Would you like to, say, like, meet for lunch?"

"Where? What time?"

"What about at the Grotto at about one o'clock?"

"You got it, Papi."

"I'll see you there," I said and hung up the telephone. I lay flat on my back. When I fell asleep my member was still standing tall. My loins seemed to be reaching for the sky.

Chapter 23

Before I was able to get out the door to see Dr. Valesco, Ma called. I told her that I was doing fine. She wanted to know if everything was all right with the baby and me. I told Ma I was on my way to the doctor's office.

"You blessed, baby. God brought you back from the grave."

"You sure got that right. Ma, I've got to run. I'll talk to you later, all right?"

"Bye, son."

Luckily the San Francisco Bay Bridge toll collectors had turned off the metering lights. That made it a lot easier to get across the bridge. I sat in the waiting room of Dr. Valesco's office with two other men. One of the men was a brother. His moustache was neatly trimmed to perfection. His eyes were large and brown. He nodded to me. I smiled. The other man looked like he was about six months pregnant already. His sunburned face was half-buried in a magazine. He never stopped reading his magazine to look up to see who had entered the waiting room. After about an hour, Helga led me back to one of the tiny examination rooms. I sat on the examination table looking out of the window on San Francisco Bay. It wasn't noon yet, but already sailboats seemed to glide upon the water like snow puffs. A great naval ship was docked at a pier. The sky was a dazzling blue that went on forever.

Dr. Valesco came into the examination room. He took a blood sample to check my blood sugar level. I lay on my back on the table. Dr. Valesco took the Doppler ultrasound device, listened to my breathing, to my baby's heartbeat. He showed me a monitor that was shaped like a television screen that showed the full body of my baby. He pointed out all the parts of my baby, the head, eyes, hands, arms, feet, nose, sex organs, and his tiny mouth. Dr. Valesco took out a surgery consent form for me to read and sign. Signing the consent form implied that I understood the risks involved with having a caesarean birth. He reiterated the possibility of hemorrhage several times. I didn't like that part of the examination. I kept thinking about what Ma had told me about bleeding. She said, "Jesus, he bled upon the cross." I never retorted to Ma that Jesus also died upon the cross. Dr. Valesco didn't mention death or dying. He'd pronounce the word "risk," leaning rather heavily on the "S" in the word. It was as though he wanted to make this absolutely clear to me so that I understood what this word meant. I felt like a student under the tutelage of a teacher who had discovered that I had potential for days. Dr. Valesco told me predicting the day a baby is born is not an exact science. He told me that a baby might decide to come into the world sooner or sometimes later than expected. He made it clear to me that I could go into labor before he gave me the caesarean. I didn't know what worried me more, pain or the thought of having the caesarean. I looked at this man who I swore could have passed for the fraternal twin brother of my first cousin.

"I'd be careful about having sex at this late stage. In particular, stay away from the missionary position. That's the most problematic. Try having sex on your side so as to avoid adverse outcomes."

"For real?"

"That would be my suggestion. We've come so far in this project and have done such an excellent job on you. We've rebuilt you from the ground up," he said, took off his glasses, slipped them in the small pocket of his white lab coat.

"You think so?"

"Oh, by all means. Kel, have you been resting a lot and getting along with your partner?"

"Well, things could be a whole lot better between us. Chad's made a lot of progress and now supports my pregnancy. I've been busy, but I'm going to slow down."

"Excellent. You want to minimize the stresses. Rest even more. Your baby is your body too. Whatever emotions you feel, so can the child. You are at a crucial point in the development of the child. The C-section we're going to give you won't be easy. They are never easy for women either. So try not to obsess about it too much. What amazes me is that out of all the project participants, you seemed to have as close to a maternal instinct as any man I've ever known. You know what it is that makes you tick. A poster boy for male pregnancy."

"It's never easy, Dr. Valesco. I try," I blushed.

Dr. Valesco's face changed the way the sky does when all of a sudden a dark cloud floats in front of the sun, casting a shadow. He stood at the window and seemed to be looking out upon the San Francisco Bay. Dr. Valesco spoke with his back to me.

"Kel?"

"Yeah."

"Did you have any early symptoms or warning signs before you got sick last year and were misdiagnosed with valley fever?"

"Not until I started having really bad headaches, high fevers, drenching night sweats, and weight loss. I thought that I was coming down with AIDS, but I'm HIV negative. So I kept thinking, *how would this be?*" I said.

"I want to tell you a little story. It won't take me very long. I never had any warning signs before my recent incident. Unlike you, I wasn't totally left in the dark. There were warning signs along the way. I hope that this doesn't disturb you. But before I tell you, I want to ask you another question," he said, as he turned around and looked at me gravely. Then he went back to looking out of the great window.

"What?"

"What do you think I am?"

"You mean on a scale from one to ten? Two months away from having my baby, I'd give you an eight," I blurted out.

"I don't mean to suggest I'm asking for a rating," he chuckled gently. He kept his face to the window. I watched his back. "What I mean is, what race do you think I belong to? Not that it matters in this day and age like it did maybe forty or fifty years ago."

"You're white!" I said, quickly confident that I'd picked the right answer, hoping that I'd made up for not giving him a rating of ten on his level of medical care and expertise. I've been wrong before playing the worldwide what-race-do-you-think-I-am guessing game. It's always so tricky. My biracial cousin had chosen to be black, at least around the African-American side of her family.

Dr. Valesco laughed. "Kel, I'm no more white than this wall here. I'm black, Kel." He thumped his knuckles up against the wall and turned around to face me. I wondered what Dr. Valesco had chosen to . be around the African-American side of his family. Did he consider me a brother? Or as a project participant who only incidentally happened to be black? Was I selected in the male pregnancy program as part of an affirmative action baby plan the study had been forced to adopt by the government?

"It doesn't matter to me, Dr. Valesco, if you're white or black. All I'm interested in is getting through my pregnancy. Is anything wrong? Did something happen?" I said.

"Nothing that I can't overcome. I'm coming out, that's all."

"As gay?"

"No, I'm coming out as black, Kel. As African American."

"Wow. I knew that you looked like my first cousin. She is biracial. So it makes perfect sense to me. But why now?"

Dr. Valesco told me that he dated a gorgeous, wonderful white woman for a year. Fell so deeply in love with her that he'd get dizzy and couldn't see straight at times. From the beginning, she made no qualms about her hatred of blacks. He loved her so much that every derogatory word you can think of she'd use to describe blacks would do nothing to offend him. He thought of himself as white, as special, as different. Then the other night they were making love and she said to him during the middle of his orgasm, "Fuck me like a big black nigger." He said he rolled off of her and hadn't been able to climb back on top of her since. That night when he took her home he decided to come out as black. He told me that he dumped her.

"Good for you, Dr. Valesco. But how do you know that she was white?" I asked, my brows coming together into the middle of my face. "I mean, if I thought that you were white or possibly black, couldn't you think that she's white but could possibly be black? What if she's really black like you, only she hasn't decided to come out as black yet? See what I'm saying? Until you find out what she is, wouldn't you be doing to yourself what you tell your patients not to do? And that is not to throw the baby out with the bathwater."

"You have a point. Oh well, buddy. What's done is done. It won't be long now. Here, let me give you my new pager number in case anything goes awry in the next few months," he said, jotting down his number on a small piece of paper and handing it over.

"You are a lucky man, Mr. Warren," he said. "A lucky man, indeed."

I watched Dr. Valesco disappear through the door. I got dressed and drove over to the Grotto to sit down to lunch with Juan as soon as I could. On the way over to the restaurant, Dr. Valesco's coming out weighed on my mind. I thought that it was a very courageous, brave thing to do. Now he seemed to have a spring to his step as though he had a thousand pounds lifted from his shoulders.

I spotted Juan. He was sitting at a table in front of a huge picture window that framed Telegraph Hill. He hopped up from his seat quickly and pumped my hand. His smile was infectious. He was a very sexy man. His black hair had a tiny little flip in the front. Juan was wearing a white tank top that exposed a column of biceps and forearms. It looked as though he'd worked out at the gym all morning, never once stopping to drink water or take a breath.

"What's up, Papi!" Juan said, grinning.

"Sup, Juan!" I said.

We sat down.

"You looking healthy, man. Big. I like it big, dude."

"Thanks, Juan. I want to be straight with you though."

"Go ahead, man. What you think?"

"I'm involved, Juan. I got a man."

"No problem, man. Me too. I'm not looking for a boyfriend. Just somebody to kick it and chill with. We can keep it on the down low," he said, sliding his hand under the table and rubbing my inner thigh.

A waiter came and took our orders. I ordered crab cakes, a crab, and a Caesar salad. Juan ordered a platter of deep-fried crawfish, a baked potato, and mustard greens. We took turns slicing the garlic bread that sat on the table in a banana-shaped porcelain dish.

"There's something else, Juan, that I think you should know."

"What, Papi?"

"I'm seven months pregnant."

"I know. That's why you came to Babies and Bath. Check it. I knew it when I first saw you walk in the restaurant."

"It doesn't bother you?"

"Is it supposed to?"

"Well, it's not every day that a man decides to have a baby."

"It's no big deal, but you, like, want to kick it with me or what? Pregnant cock is dope. It's the bombs."

"I don't want sex right now, Juan. I'm extremely attracted to you. But what I need the most right now is someone to be with. Sex is not going to make me happy, Juan. At least not at the moment."

Juan looked at me with a big question mark written across his rugged brown face.

I looked out of the window at the ocean. I missed Chad. Randall was the end of a long line of men I'd slept with out of uncertainty. He signaled the end to my sexual addiction. Juan ushered in the beginning of my relationship with men as friends and associates. Yet what if Chad decided to close the door on our relationship forever? Would all bets be off? Should I keep my options open? Would I end up right back where I started from, being flipped then flipping men over on their backs in return? Would I forget that I'd become sexually addicted in the first place because I lost my manhood after the abortion and was trying my best to get somebody pregnant?

"So, Papi. It's like there's no chance that we can hit the sheets? Or what?"

"Not as long as I'm involved with Chad. My days of sex for sport are over and done with. I want you as a brother, a friend. Would you be my friend, Juan? Man to man. I need you as a friend or an ally. Can you deal with that?"

"I don't know, dude. I'm hot. I may not be able to keep my hands off of you."

I finished my lunch and stood up to leave.

"Juan, I appreciate your honesty. But when you need a friend, call me. All right?"

"You got it, Papi."

We'd gone Dutch. I paid for my part of the lunch and Juan paid his part. I felt tired, as if I needed some fresh air. I craved to be near the sea.

It wasn't long before I found myself driving along the coastal highway, taking in the great blue vistas, the white-capped rush of the ocean, surfers, sunbathers, the green slope of mountains, bursting yellow sunshine. I parked my Jeep right off Half Moon Bay. In spite of the beauty that lay before my eyes, the first thing I watched for was a clearing on the half-crowded beach. I found a landing at the end of the beach, near a blowhole. The fine mist from the ocean sprayed my face like expensive cologne. I unbuckled the straps of my overalls, folded my arms across my belly. I listened to the great roar of the sea. I could hear Chad's voice in the rush of the waves. "Head? Are you there? Can you hear me?" I stood up. I spoke back to the waves. "Chad! Chad, I'm here! I'm right here, baby! Yeah, I can hear you. I can hear you as loud and as clear as a bell!"

Chapter 24

It had gotten to the point where I couldn't go down to the Richmond Shipyards with Scott and rescue any more of the unwed pregnant preteens. I'd get tired too quickly. So I decided to take Dr. Valesco's advice during my last visit to his office to get more rest. I was having pains in the small of my back, and my stomach always seemed to be smack dab up against the steering wheel of the Jeep. I began to worry about the seat belt I had to put around me. It wouldn't take much for someone in front of me to make a sudden stop, making me do the same. My stomach would end up smashed into the steering wheel. Or what if I was driving on a narrow two-lane street and had a head-on collision with another car that made the air bag activate? The air bag would probably save my life, but the sheer power and force of it would probably take the life of my child. I decided to drive only short distances, even then only under the most pressing circumstances. It didn't seem to matter sometimes what position I slept in, I still had discomfort. It felt like when I got circumcised and couldn't sleep on my stomach anymore. I learned how to curl up in a fetal position, slept close to being balled up into a knot. The only way I could go to sleep now was on my back. I'd always dreaded sleeping on my back even before I got pregnant. I thought sleeping on one's back would make one's ass flat. It wasn't as though anybody looking at me walking down the street in jeans would say, "Damn, baby got back!" Yet I was never flat as a board either. I've always had something back there to hold on to. I had enough ass to shake it if pushing came to shoving.

It was a little after one o'clock in the morning. I'd fallen asleep in Chad's huge, soft chair. It reclined and had a way of lulling me into a deep sleep. I'd sat down to dinner last night and eaten lima beans, a baked chicken, and corn muffins. The last thing I remember doing was eating three oranges and turning the television to E!. I watched and listened to some Oscar winners talk about where they were when they learned that they'd been nominated for an Oscar. What pleased me the most was when the actor who played Reinaldo Arenas in *Before Night Falls* was nominated. I felt somehow that I had played some minor part in his getting the nod. In reality though, I knew that I had nothing at all to do with the actor's nomination. But this still didn't stop me from taking small credit. Neither did it stop the smile that rose up in me. I missed Chad. Yet it was my hope that he'd come back home that kept me emotionally stable. I had fallen asleep in Chad's favorite chair that smelled of fresh evergreen. I had slept for only four hours. I got up from the chair and went upstairs to my bedroom. The telephone rang.

"Kel?"

"Ma?"

"Yeah, it's me, baby."

"Ma, are you all right? It's after one o'clock in the morning."

"Child, I know that. I couldn't sleep. I had to hear your voice and to see that you're doing fine. How did your doctor's visit go with Dr. Valesco? Are you and the baby doing fine?"

"Yeah, Ma. He examined me. Told me that everything is fine. That the baby is on schedule to be born on time."

She had read in the newspapers what BIG and Evergreen had done to help the unwed preteens hiding out at that pier at the Richmond Shipyards. She told me that her father worked at that very shipyard the youths hung out at. He was so proud of his job as an unskilled laborer at the shipyards that all he would do when he got home was kick off his shoes. Then he'd go on for days talking about how the Negro was about to bust the union wide open. Colored people were going to be treated with respect for a change, he'd tell her. She lived in a little one-room house in North Richmond. She told me that she would wash clothes in a big old steel tub. She would boil water, then put it in a great big old cast iron pot. She'd help her father take that hot water in that great big old cast iron pot and pour it over the clothes. She told me that she got so much joy hanging out her daddy's clothes on a clothesline that went from that little house to the outhouse.

She gave birth to me late in life. She had to be every bit of thirty-five. It wasn't an easy childbirth because my pops, Frank, got sick when she was six months pregnant with me and died from a heart attack two months after I was born. She explained to me that was why I didn't get a chance to make my acquaintance with him. She doubted if I even remembered him. For two months she had a time trying to tear me out of my father's arms. My father didn't even want to get up and go to work for wanting to be with me all day long. All he wanted to do was hold me in his arms. She told me that my father bottle-fed me and changed my diapers. He made sure that my navel healed the right way.

"I'm telling you all of this, Kel, not to preach to you. Lord knows there's nothing wrong with preaching to anybody. The only folks hate to hear somebody preach are devils and their children. I'd been laying up here in this bed all day long just a-tossing and turning. I wasn't going to be able to sleep until I heard your voice to see if you were all right."

"I'm all right, Ma. You get some sleep. I'm fine. Don't sit up and worry about me. Don't you worry about a thing."

"Good night, son."

"Good night, Ma."

I fell asleep. I had a dream to remember.

Chad, Naomi, and I were sitting with about twenty other parents in the auditorium at Richmond High School. I'd been invited to come and see Chad Jr. receive a 100,000-dollar Martin Luther King Jr.-John F. Kennedy scholarship to attend Howard University in the fall. Chad and I passed each other a handkerchief to wipe away the tears of joy watching our son receive the award. After walking up to the podium and receiving the scholarship, Chad Jr. made a small but important speech.

"I want to thank my parents more than anyone else for believing in me. They taught me to believe in myself, that anything is possible. If only we believe, then fairy tales can come true." Chad Jr. came down from the podium and we all embraced him. As I looked into the eyes of my eighteen-year-old son, I thought, he's a living testament to my own belief that we can make it if only we push a little harder and give ourselves half the chance. We could fly.

I got up late the next morning. By the time I finished taking a shower and sat down to breakfast I had three voice mail messages on my telephone. At first, it wasn't clear when the calls were made because I didn't hear the telephone ring. When I played the messages back I realized the calls were made while I was in the shower. The first person to call was Chad. Then Naomi had called, and Scott Chad's message was that he was coming home tonight. I kept punching the button on the telephone to replay the sound of his baritone voice. Eventually, I saved the message to listen to again and again until I saw him standing at my door grinning like a man who'd come back home from a war that took many lives but somehow spared his own. Naomi had left a message inviting me to church on Sunday. The only message Scott left was that he'd gone and picked Ricky up from the hospital.

I busied myself with making my house tidy. I'd only had myself to look after, so there wasn't a whole lot to do. I marinated a rack of lamb, and set it in the refrigerator to let the spices sink in clear to the bone. I made quiche. Chilled a bottle of Chardonnay. Chad's favorite fragrance was the smell of peach, so I decided to put tiny peach-scented candles cupped in small glasses on the dining room table and watch him swoon over the lights. If I didn't know any better, I would think I was beginning to feel the way I felt when we first dated.

Resting at home gave me more time to think things through with regard to making decisions about my paternity leave after the baby was born. Luckily, I worked out of my home now. This allowed me to select and take on less complicated cases that didn't require air travel, spending long hours driving up and down the coast. Rather than go on traditional maternity leave, I decided to take on less work. I decided to take six months off after the baby was born before taking on any new clients. This would give me time to bond with my baby and think about finding child care when I had to go away on business. Both Ma and Sugar had agreed to watch Chad Jr. when I was traveling. For that I was grateful. For my participation in the male pregnancy project, I'd receive fully covered medical care. That included hospital admission costs and pediatric care for the first five years of my son's life. This was comforting to know because I didn't have to lie awake at night worrying about how I was going to pay a mortgage and health care bills that my insurer had already told me they wouldn't cover because I was a pregnant male. Otherwise, I would have flipped. Those were my thoughts when I went into the living room and sat down in Chad's favorite chair.

Before I could drift off to sleep I heard someone opening my front door. When Chad walked in the house, the first thing he did was come over and hold me the best way that he could. My stomach made it impossible for our crotches to bump up against each other. My belly that had been sitting high and pointed had started to drop a little bit. He put his hand on my stomach and rubbed it in small circles. We sat down on the sofa and he lay his head in my lap. That was when little Chad kicked. Chad laughed because he didn't know if that was a good sign that my baby was glad to have him back or if he was trying to kick him out of the house. Chad smelled of peppermint.

During his two-week hiatus, he told me, he had gone and put flowers on his parents' grave. He thought that this was a big step toward accepting sickness and ultimately death. He'd also made his peace with his friend Tracy. To let him tell it, he accepted Tracy's grief as a mother whose firstborn died leaving her with empty arms. He got Tracy into an alcoholism treatment program. He expressed pride in having put her on the road to recovery.

Chad seemed fit. His chest was broader, tighter, and he'd shaved off his goatee. I looked at his hands. Chad was wearing the ring on his right index finger that I bought him one year after we first met. He seemed calm, as if he was ready to tackle any issue, take it on, get it squared away. He had an air of confidence and seemed ready to compromise with me for the sake of our mutual longing to be together. I told him about hearing his voice when I went to the beach a little while ago. He didn't deny that it was him and thought that he felt me even when I wasn't lying next to him.

We sat down to dinner. The only sounds in the house were the distant voices that came from the television in the living room. It was good to have this man back in my house, in my arms, close again to my heart. I watched his face.

"Chad?"

"Yeah, Head."

"It's great to have you back home, baby."

"I'm glad to be back, Head. I had a lot of demons to unleash. When you told me about you and Randall, it took me back to when I was with Roger, my first lover. I was terribly addicted to sex. I was more angry with my memory than with you."

"Why?"

"Head, you made me think about a part of my life that I'd given up. It was difficult, but I got through and over it. What I realized in the past two weeks is that I'm a survivor."

"Nothing wrong with being a survivor, Chad. As long as you don't have the guilt to go along with it."

"Head, I want to be a father to little Chad. All the little petty things about you not using my sperm are bullshit. This baby is going to be ours."

I felt water settle underneath my eyelids but I didn't cry. I had to be strong. That's what little Chad would want too. For me to be strong. Chad was back and I took it as a sign to go forward. When he told me he wanted to be a father to the baby, those words rang in my ears as loud and as clear as his voice I heard on the beach. Had he finally come to grips with his ambivalence about being a coparent to little Chad? It sure sounded like it to me.

Chad cleared the table. He rinsed off the dishes and stuck them in the dishwasher. We flipped off the television and went upstairs to the bedroom. Chad ran me a hot bath. I disrobed and slid into the bubbly water. He soaped my back and massaged the nape of my neck. I nodded off to sleep a couple of times before he helped me out of the water and into a huge towel to dry off. Chad rubbed little handfuls of Johnson's Baby Powder on the bottom of my feet that tickled and made me laugh, and the baby kick. I remembered that somewhere in the back of my mind, before I got pregnant, I was apprehensive about getting back into shape once I had my baby, but that didn't matter to me anymore. I'd fallen in love with my body and what was growing inside of it more than I had when my muscles pumped, rippled, swelled as if I was training for a professional weight lifting contest.

Chad climbed underneath the sheets. We lay in the bed spoon fashion, until lying on my side became uncomfortable and I turned over on my back. As soon as I found sleep, I had a dream that I will never forget for as long as I live. Or maybe it was a vision.

After years of taking fluconazole for valley fever (a medicine I didn't really need), it had irreparably damaged my liver. I lay in my room in the bed with excruciating abdominal pain. Chad Jr. was in his senior year of college. My son had fallen in love with his high school sweetheart and he'd told me that they'd split up. Chad Jr. was stressed about the breakup when he came to see me.

"How you feeling, Pops?" Chad Jr. asked as he gently leaned over and kissed me on the forehead.

"Oh, fair to middling," I said. "Son, congratulations. I'm so proud of you. You know if I could have made it to your graduation, I would have. I don't know how much longer I'll be around. So I need to talk to you about some things."

"Pops, quit talking foolishness. You're going to be around here for a long time. I can feel it in my bones."

"Naw, son, my time in this life has run out. The good Lord has beckoned for me to come home. I've already told Him that I'm on my way and I'm ready to go. First of all, son, your father Chad loves you dearly. God only gives us one father, and the fathers of this world are a precious blessing. Promise me you'll always love and take care of him."

"I promise, Pops. I promise."

"Second, I know you still love that gal Alliyah crazily but you can't love a memory, son. It'll kill you dead. Because when you really look at it, too much of anything ain't good for the soul. That includes love! Learn to drink sparingly from the cup of love. When you fall in love, cry a little sometimes. Tears never hurt anybody. It sure ain't nothing wrong with good loving, though. It's just that not many people in this world learn how to love. Seems to me, it's easier for people to hate than love someone. Just save a little love in a tiny place in the corner of your heart for yourself. So that when old man fate come a-knocking on your door, kicks you to the curb of life, you'll have something to hold onto. You'll still suffer, but the magnitude of your suffering won't be so great! The darkness won't be so black. A little light will shine in your heart and beckon you back to life. Then you won't have to rush to the bottle, to dope, or to a shrink. Think of love as an old habit that is hard to break, Chad Junior, and you'll realize that habits, like hearts, were meant to be broken. Break the habit, though. You can do it, son. Promise to do that for old Pops. You hear?" I managed to smile through my pain.

Chapter 25

October had rolled around the Bay Area, turning the falling leaves brown. Everybody seemed to be trying to squeeze out what was left of summer. More than just a few people were still dressing in shorts, tank tops, open-toe sandals, and flocking to the beach. The cool breezes that blew the fog in off San Francisco Bay did little to convince the Bay Area that summer had come and gone. I had one month to go before I had my baby. I was ready to have my baby. I'd been putting off going to church with Naomi for nearly three weeks. I still couldn't separate Reverend Edwards the minister from Reverend Edwards the formerly married man. Yet could I afford to cast stones at someone else when I was living in a glass house? It was a good thing for Reverend Edwards that I believed in forgiveness. The other thing I had to consider was that whether I liked it or not, Reverend Edwards was Chad Jr.'s grandfather. Regardless of how I felt about him as a man, this was a biological fact that I couldn't change.

I was peeling an orange when Naomi rang my doorbell. Chad was out with clients showing listings.

"Hey, Sista!"

"Hey, Brotha! You ready?"

"I'm ready! Let's go!" I said, locking the front door and slowly following Naomi out to her car.

Naomi and I sat where we always had, in the front pew. I looked around the packed church. The membership seemed to have increased since the last time I was there. I thought it was because more young people were coming because of the work BIG had done on rescuing unwed pregnant preteens. I recognized at least ten of the girls sitting in the church. I waved across the pew at all of them. They smiled and waved back. Reverend Edwards stood tall in a long purple robe that was open at the neck. He took the pulpit, held on to it for dear life, it seemed. The choir was singing in low tones, "I Want to Be Ready When Jesus Comes."

I got goose bumps.

I watched Chad Jr.'s granddaddy stand in the pulpit and speak.

"Church. Let us all say amen. If these words I lay before you here this morning in the house of God don't move you, then nothing can move you. What I'm about to unfold here in this church is a miracle of God. Sitting before me is a man. Oh no, he's not what anybody would call an ordinary man! He's a miracle! Because God has blessed this man with pregnancy! Every two thousand years or so, the Son is born unto the Father!" I heard little gasps from the congregation. I sat with a lump in my throat.

"Church, you don't hear me this morning! I say God has blessed this man with a child! This child is from the seed of my daughter," he cried, beaming. "Some of us live to see miracles. Some us are blind to miracles. But right here this morning in Evergreen Holy Tabernacle Church we got ourselves a miracle right before our very eyes! You can live a lifetime without ever seeing a miracle. God is a miracle. Oh, yes! Remember Mother Mary gave the world a miracle of all time when she brought forth the birth of Jesus through Immaculate Conception. Church, you don't hear me this morning!" He began to slowly bounce up and down, moving his head with the rhythm of his words.

"We got thousands of unwanted babies brought into this world by accident without the blessings of God. Sometimes we read in the papers about a baby dumped in the trashcan like some old piece of garbage. Sometimes we read about babies born addicted to crack cocaine or infected with AIDS. Sometimes we hear about babies being sold into slavery right under our very eyes. And here it is a new millennium! Babies kidnapped and raped by some sick lunatic! Sometimes we hear about mothers going to school to learn how to care for a baby. Leaving their babies in the hands of those who would put a child in harm's way. We got doctors, politicians, even judges all up in a woman's womb telling her what to do with her unborn child.

"In the name of the Holy Spirit, we got a great seed getting ready to spring forth the promise, the dream of justice. God gives us life! Who are we to judge someone else's life! Church, the good word teaches us to be fruitful and to multiply. Great nations all over the world have honored God's work to show us a path out of darkness. Church, the conception, the birth of any child can't be belittled, shunned, cast aside, whether it's in the body of a man or a woman. We are the fruits of a union between woman and man. Brought forth from that coupling are variations of that union. Your son or daughter isn't gay or straight! That's your child! A seed God created, that whoever carried the seed had to nourish so that it could be brought to life! Church, you don't hear me though! Kel wasn't born into this world by divine creation. His mother conceived him in her womb. Church, we know that God didn't give a man a womb. But what a glorious miracle the Holy Spirit did by giving this man a way to bring forth a life unlike no other that the world will ever see again.

"Church, this man sitting in the front row of this church has always longed for a child. The Bible teaches us to seek and you shall find! I remember this young man when he was a small boy. He came to me when he lost his firstborn child. He asked me why God had taken away his child. He didn't understand me when I told him that God never gives us more than we can stand. Church, I meant that then and I mean that right now. We baptized him right here in this very church. I remembered him last year. His mother, Ester, had come to the church asking me to pray for her child who was laying up in the hospital on his deathbed. With tubes stuck in every part of his body the doctors could find a hole to stick them in. He lay up in the hospital caught in the grip of death for two months! Somebody needs to say amen! His mother stood up in front of this church and told us that her son's mouth was so weak he couldn't chew his food. His body racked with fevers high enough to kill a normal man! She told this church that they had her son up at the hospital turned upside down five hours a day for two weeks to get the medicine through his body. I want to tell you this morning here at Evergreen that the same Holy Spirit that saved this boy's life is the same one that has given him the life growing inside of his body. This is his blessing! Behold God's creation!" He paused and wiped the beads of sweat from his forehead.

"I gave his mother a prayer cloth and she took it to that hospital, wiped his body down until the fever was no more. This man has suffered the way Jesus suffered when they nailed him to the cross, stuck nails in his hands, his feet. Put a thorny crown on the top of Jesus' head. Church, do you think this is only a man carrying a baby? This is a blessing and one of God's true miracles! Somebody ain't listening to me here this morning! Somebody ought to say amen! I've heard people say miracles are hogwash. Miracles are old wives' tales. I tell you to look and behold a miracle right here under our very eyes. A miracle unlike no other, and this is our flesh and blood church! We may live another two thousand years and never again will we witness an event as glorious as this one. Somebody don't hear me though! God has given this young man through the conception of a child, a new life. Church, I want to tell you again, this man has risen from the dead and been reborn! Can't nobody tell me that God ain't real! Can't nobody tell me that He doesn't hear us when we speak his name. Can't nobody tell me that He is not a wonder, a sight to behold! God gives life! Anybody ever wonder why you always hear people say He can make a way out of no way? Well, look at this man here in this church. Then you will find the answer to your question. Somebody say amen." Reverend Edwards got down from the pulpit, and I watched him go sit among the four deacons of the church.

With that sermon I was redeemed. Set free! The three great burdens of my life—the loss of my firstborn, my sexual addiction, and the mysterious illness that nearly took my life now seemed easier to carry. I'd found my way back to the church. I'd found my way home. My body rumbled and shook. Tears flowed from my eyes like a faucet. I looked at Naomi. She had tears in her eyes. I wiped away the tears from my eyes. I'd made my peace with Reverend Edwards. He'd done right by me. The floor of the church began to rumble under my feet. The congregation was up dancing, shouting, yelling. People slapped tambourines, and the choir swayed back and forth in jubilation. I watched Naomi get up from the pew. I followed her. She seemed to be drawn by a force she couldn't control. I watched her dance and speak in a tongue I'd heard before but didn't understand. Naomi's body lurched, bent over and straightened, then bent again. I began to dance with her. My movements were quick. I felt weightless. I watched the congregation pass a cordless microphone around the church. Everybody took turns singing. An old woman with a sad smile passed the microphone to me. I began to sing, "I Want to Be Ready When Jesus Comes." After I finished singing, something inside of me broke away. I uttered the words of the song as though I'd never sing that way again in this life. It was as though I'd come to the crest of a great mountain that stretched deep into the blue heavens where my soul was at rest. I felt like a man who without clothes on his back, a roof over his head, or food to eat was being welcomed back home to the church. It was then that I came to believe Naomi when she told me, "The church belongs to everybody, Kel."

Services went on like this for about a half hour. Then members of the congregation stood up and testified about a baby they lost or a baby they wanted to have but couldn't have. A great many came over to me and showered me with hugs and pecks on the cheek. Naomi seemed spent, yet there was an inner calm about her. It was as though she had found something that she'd lost so long ago. Whatever it was she lost, it had now been reclaimed, and she was holding onto it this time forever, not to let go of it ever again.

I passed the microphone to one of the unwed preteens, a twelve-year-old girl who, out of all the ones I'd rescued from the pier, reminded me the most of Cookie. She took up the chorus of the song. I sat in the pew. Reverend Edwards had clearly surprised me. I wondered if Naomi had put a bug in his ear like she did with Olivia, or whether Reverend Edwards' sermon had come straight from his heart. I didn't have the nerve to ask Naomi, so I took it for what it was, an acceptance of my baby as his grandchild. It was such a wild thought that I felt like pinching myself to make sure that I wasn't in a dream. We stayed in church until services let out a couple of hours later. Outside of the church, some members of the congregation followed me as if I was the pied piper. Many of the women surrounded me. They seemed to look at me like I wasn't so much pregnant but a sign from God. Many of the women told me that for years they had been Christians but never really believed, that I had finally made them believe not only in miracles but also in themselves. Naomi had to pull me away from the crowd because I was getting tired and needed something to eat.

After getting to her car, we took off for home. All I could think of was eating and then taking a warm bath.

"Brotha, didn't Daddy speak the word today?"

"Sista, he tore the roof off of that church. I was surprised. I wasn't expecting unconditional support."

"Well, he knows that this is as much his grandbaby as if I was having it myself."

"You got that right."

Naomi rolled her car up in my driveway. We got out of the car and I stuck the key in the door. I jumped back at the loud sound of "SURPRISE!"

I had stepped into my baby shower.

I looked around the living room decorated with pink, red, orange, green, and blue balloons. Everybody I could think of that I'd been close to and some that I wasn't that close to were there. The living room, kitchen, and patio were packed to squeeze-through capacity. Chad walked up to me followed by Ma. They both gave me hugs and kisses. Andrea, Nina, Shuntria, Cerrita, Mary, Randall, Ricky, Scott, Sugar, Olivia, Juan, and Mitch were there. The only two people I was really surprised to see were Juan and Mitch. Mitch was somber.

I turned to Naomi and gave her a big hug. I watched her go over and join Shorty on the sofa. A pile of gifts was stacked up against a wall next to the fireplace. The living room was abuzz with the clink of glasses, conversation, and hypnotic jazz vocals from the likes of Shirley Horn. Ma was wearing a T-shirt that had written on the back, "Midwife on Duty." She brought me a bowl of her Irish stew that had little chunks of lamb, cabbage, carrots, and potatoes in a sauce that was off-the-hook delicious. We went out on the patio. I looked back at Chad, who was in deep conversation with Randall. I couldn't help but think about what it would be like to have Randall snuggled in bed with Chad and me. I just as quickly thought how mischievous it would be but a lot of fun. I looked at Ma's face.

"Kel, I'm going to be with you. I mean that."

"Well, all right, Ma."

"Anyway, that Chad know he be doting on you some. Kept calling me about your baby shower this and your baby shower that. I was scared he was thinking I was going to tell him to go and pound sand. You know me, I'm dignified, child. The last man I told to kiss my ass was an old jealous boyfriend I had back in the day. I'm not having a man tell me what, when, and how to do what I already know how to do," she said, reminding me of Naomi.

"I'm feeling you, Ma," I said, when Chad and Ricky came out on the patio.

"Sister Woman, can you come inside for a moment? Somebody would like to talk to you," Chad said. He pointed at one of the deacons from Evergreen in a corner in the living room.

"Oh, not one of my ex-boyfriends," Ma teased. She was in rare form this afternoon. She held her glass of brandy waist high and stepped up through the patio door.

"You never can tell; it might be a man bearing gifts," Chad teased.

"If it ain't worth more than gold, he can take it and stuff . . ."

"Ma?"

"Child, I'm just having me a little fun. It's so warm in here." She walked over to the deacon and started a conversation.

Ricky stood on the banister and watched us.

"Chad, you didn't have to throw me this baby shower. You know that I've got enough clothes as it is."

"Head, I thought that it would be good to get all of your friends and what not together to kick it a little bit. And that Juan! He's a cute little thing!"

"Well, you know what they say about small men?"

"They carry a big stick. Juan and Mitch both called you a couple of times when you were gone. I invited them to the shower. Head, while you still got your wits about you, I'm going to go back inside. I think Ricky wants to talk to you about something." I watched Chad disappear through the patio door.

"Oh no, don't mind me, Kel. It's nothing really important. I want to holler at you, that's all," Ricky said.

"Slick Rick! Sup man?" I said as he hugged me around the neck.

I invited Ricky to come and sit down with me at the small patio table under a large umbrella with blue and white stripes. A couple of days before, Scott had called me to ask if he and Ricky could stop over.

Scott told me that Ricky really wanted to see me. Right after Scott had called I waited for them to make it over, but they didn't show up. I was already tired from having to go up and down my stairs all day, which Dr. Valesco had told me was good exercise since I wasn't getting out as much anymore. After a couple of hours passed I became convinced that they had either forgotten or made other plans. I sat down to dinner, then went to bed.

Ricky looked good. He was only a little thinner, but he was always thin, so it was difficult to tell if he'd lost any weight after his diagnosis. Scott was so good at making you think that he was only going to tell you a little something and then let it go at that. By the time he got done, you realized that he'd told you everything, including some things he promised he wouldn't tell. He'd always say, "Well, as long as we're on the subject." Then he'd lapse into his spiel. So when Ricky came out on the patio and sat down in a chair, I already had been given clues about just what it was that he wanted to talk to me about.

"Kel, there's something I need to do. But I don't know if I should do it or let it slide," he said, nervously twisting the ring on his finger.

"What is it?"

"Well, for starters, since getting my diagnosis I've begun to think about tying up all the loose ends in my life. I want to start by seeing my son in Mexico. Scott thinks I should either let my ex-wife send him to me or act like he's dead. But I can't, man. Something inside of me won't let me do it."

I looked at this man's face. I didn't have to think long about what I'd do given the same set of circumstances. I've been good at advice giving, so I jumped at the chance to give some of it to Ricky.

"If it was me, I'd listen to my partner first. Then I'd make the decision with my heart to go get my son. Ricky, I think that we both know that when you fall asleep at night we're not promised to wake up the next morning. He's your child. Go and get him. Quick! You must hurry!"

I didn't have to say any more. I could tell by the smile on Ricky's face that he had made up his mind. The only thing I didn't know was which airport he was going to fly out of, Oakland or San Francisco International.

We went back inside the house. I sat next to Naomi and Shorty. Cerrita and Mary sat on the other side of me. I looked across the room at Ma bouncing Shuntria and fussing over my goddaughter's hair, which was styled in long braids. Chad came into the room. He went over to the stereo and turned it off. The room became quiet. Chad took a fork, gently smacked it up against an empty champagne glass to get everybody's attention. He set the glass and fork down upon the coffee table. Chad came over to me and got down on his knees.

"Head?"

"Yeah, baby."

"Will you marry me? I want you for my husband."

"Yes, I'll marry you, Chad. I want you to be my husband," I said.

The whole room broke into loud cheers. I looked around the room and some people were crying. Scott went over to the stereo and put on an old school jam James Brown song, "Try Me."

I got up and slow danced with Chad the way I'd seen couples do on *Soul Train*. I looked deep into his chestnut eyes. It felt as though we were the only two people on the floor dancing, even though there were at least five other couples with us swaying to the old school jam. As the jam came to an end, the room erupted again with cheers that rang up against the fine crystal figurines that stood on the mantel just above the fireplace.

"May I cut in?" Ma said and laughed. Chad surrendered me to Ma.

"Hey, Miss Ma," I said, smiling.

"Oh, baby. I'm so happy for you. God has shined his light on you, I mean."

"I believe it, Ma. I really believe that He has. I can feel it right here," I said.

"I know you do, baby. I'm your mother."

I danced with Ma for a few more moments, then somebody put on Brandy's CD *Sitting on Top of the World*. Ma broke away from me and began to shake her body down to the floor.

"Ahhhhhhhhhh! Shiiiiiiiiitttttt!" Ma wailed. Everybody circled around Ma and me.

"Work, Ma! Work it, Ma!" I yelled.

"Go Ma! Go Head! Go Ma! Go Head!" Chad led a chant and every-body yelled. It went on like that for at least five minutes. I began to give thanks to everybody for coming over and bringing the gifts and lots of love. Ricky came over and whispered in my ear.

"Dude, thanks. I knew that you'd have the right answer," Ricky said.

"What's going on here? Kel, your man has just proposed to you. Let's not be greedy. Ricky belongs to me," Scott said, laughing. He gave me a peck on the cheek and slipped his arm around me before going out the door. I told Nina and Andrea to tail Ma home. Shuntiu was crying because she didn't want to go home.

"I want to stay with Goddaddy and Uncle Chad," she whined.

"Don't cry, sweetheart. We're going to take you to Great America the next time, all right?" I consoled her.

"All right," she said as I watched her disappear down the walkway with Nina and Andrea.

Ma caught up to them after she wished Chad and me well.

"I'll talk to you tomorrow. You need to get some rest." Ma slipped back quickly into the role of mother.

"I know, Ma."

"Bye, baby."

"Bye, Ma."

Naomi and Shorty were the last ones to leave. I felt that I owed half of my life to that girl. I mean that.

Chad gathered all of the gifts and lugged them upstairs to the nurs-ery. I was hungry. By the way my baby kicked, he was too. Chad set the table. We sat down to dinner. I nearly went crazy happy eating la-sagna Ma had cooked. It was so good it brought tears to my eyes. Chad munched on a tuna casserole Nina and Andrea had brought over. There was so much food I didn't think that I had enough room in my refrigerator to store it. Chad cleared glasses off of the table, put the remaining food in freezer bags, and set them in the freezer. I watched him rinse off dishes then put them in the dishwasher.

After Chad got done with his kitchen duties, he led me upstairs. I watched him go in the bathroom and run a bath.

"Come on, Juicy Head. It's time for you to let Calgon take you away."

"My hero!" I said, disrobing.

I sat in the tub while Chad soaped me all over. Chad was naked by the time I reached the bed.

"The good Lord may not have blessed men with a womb, but he didn't make a mistake when he gave us this!" Chad said, flashing a huge hard-on.

"He didn't make a mistake when he gave us a mouth," I said.

Other than the strawberry whipped cream–covered cake everybody had bought me for my baby shower, Chad was the most delectable dessert I'd tasted in a very long time. I licked him from his head to his toes. I didn't leave one square inch of his torso untouched by the natural hot warmth of my lips. Chad moaned softly, making me teeter on the brink of a near explosion. The more I held back, the stronger my juices erupted like a tiny volcano held back. Now it found release from pressure and freedom to flow until it was spent, satisfied that it had had enough for one day.

By the time we were done making love, the October night had blanketed the Bay Area. We lay back on the bed. Outside my bedroom window the sky was starless, but the moon lit up Mt. Tam. In the far distance, I could hear the lonely whistle of a train. I had my hands folded behind my head.

"Head?"

"Yeah, baby."

"Let's give our own vows, Head."

"All right. When and where do you want to have our wedding?"

"Why not right here in our house?"

"Shouldn't we invite some friends over to witness our matrimony, though?"

"Yeah, Head, let's invite over our friends."

"Should we get married next week?"

"Next Sunday, Juicy Head."

"Come Sunday, we'll be wedded as man and man. Damn, that sounds good to me, baby. Real good."

"Me too, Head. It sounds good to me, too."

I turned to Chad and kissed him on the forehead. I then drifted off to sleep.

Chapter 26

I took the BART train to Dr. Valesco's office. Before I left home I called Ernest, a friend who was a part-time minister. Ernest had married Scott and Ricky two years ago. It was as if Ernest had been at my baby shower when Chad got down on his knees and proposed to me. He didn't hesitate to marry Chad and me. Ernest told me that he would be honored. I didn't want to press Reverend Edwards to marry Chad and me. He'd done enough already. Besides, Naomi had told me that the preacher was off on a rendezvous in Jamaica with Cayleen Griffin.

"When would you like me to marry you guys?" Ernest asked. I could hear the smile in his voice.

"This Sunday."

"One fine wedding, coming up," he said, as casually as if he was a waiter in a fine restaurant asking me how would I like my steak cooked, well done or medium rare.

I sat on the train and began to write my wedding vows, invitations, and acknowledgments to all of the folks who'd come to my baby shower. I'd made clip-art monographed thank you cards and wedding invitations a couple of days before. I finished our wedding invitations and salutations by the time the train rolled into the Embarcadero station. I'd completed a first draft of my wedding vows. Once I got aboveground I dumped the cards in a mailbox on the corner of Market and Beale Streets. I walked the short distance to Dr. Valesco's office.

As I waited in Dr. Valesco's office, Helga came over, bringing me a dozen fresh orange slices.

"Helga, who told you that I was nuts about oranges?" I asked.

"Let's say that a little black bird plopped down on the corner of my desk and told me. Enjoy, Kel. Leave the plate on the end table, I'll get it later," she said, smiling.

Dr. Valesco did another ultrasound. He listened to my breathing, took my temperature, and looked at the baby on the monitor. I'd given a urine and blood sample before he got around to examining me.

"Now, about the labor process. A fair number of women have natural childbirth. Some have caesareans. As you know, you'll have to undergo one too. It's a surgical procedure that can can cause a great deal of anxiety, especially because you've got to be put under anesthesia." Dr. Valesco told me that his staff would schedule the caesarean, that I would go in for the operation on November fifteenth at Mercy Hospital in San Pablo. Suddenly, my heart began to thump so loud in my chest that the baby kicked. This time his kick hurt.

"Dr. Valesco?"

"My partner and mother want to be with me in the operating room. Is that all right?"

"Kel, your partner and family can come to the hospital to give you emotional support. If we were going to be in the delivery room, I wouldn't mind them coming in, but it's major surgery. Would you mind if they just waited outside the operating room?"

"All right, as long as everything looks good. Does my baby look fine?"

"We're expecting a very healthy baby, Mr. Warren. A very healthy baby, indeed," he said, patting me on the knee as a signal that he was done with the examination. I watched him disappear through the door. I got dressed.

I was back on BART heading back home. I took out my wedding vows and started to work on them. Every once in a while, I'd look up to see a mother, sometimes fathers pushing their babies onto the train. Some of them even had babies strapped to the front of their bodies. Any one of these parents could have been me. Would be me so soon, in less time it than took for a season to change.

When I got home, I took macaroni off the shelf and poured it into a pot of boiling water on the stove. I decided to call Ma, tell her she'd be a new millennium modern-day midwife. I hoped that she would take the news graciously. Ma picked up the phone on the first ring.

"Hey, Ma. I just got back from the doctor."

"Kel, is everything all right? You still going in to have the baby next month? You want to come and stay with me?" she asked, all in one breath.

"Now, settle down, Ma. I'm doing fine and so is the baby. Yeah, I'm going in next month. Dr. Valesco said that you can come to the hospital to give me emotional support."

"That's what I'm going to do anyway. Be by your side."

"See, Ma, it'll work out. It'll work out just fine."

"It better work out, because if it doesn't I'm going to be all over that doctor's ass like white on rice!"

"Anyway, where you and that boy going to get married at? Y'all going up to Reno to one of those little old chapels with the red crushed velvet pews?"

"We're getting married right here at home. Ma, I want you to be at my wedding."

"Honey, hush. That's fabulous. You don't even have to tell me twice."

"I know, Ma. I've sent you an invitation. I'll talk to you later," I said, hanging up the phone.

When Chad got in later in the evening, we sat down to dinner. We had the pasta with baked chicken breasts, butter beans, and sourdough bread. I had to coach Chad into eating a mouthful or two of banana pudding that I'd been having a craving for. After we got done eating, I went into the living room and flipped on the cable to his favorite channel E!. Chad came in moments later and flipped it off. He took me by the hand. We started up the stairs to the bedroom. We got naked and Chad ran a bubble bath. I got in the warm water, and Chad slipped in with me. I felt like I was sitting in a Jacuzzi. I looked at his face.

"Chad?"

"Yeah, Head."

"I'm going to have a gazebo built in the yard. It should be up by Saturday. I want to marry you standing inside of the gazebo."

"Good idea, Juicy Head."

"Great, so it will be done."

"On earth."

"As it is."

"In heaven."

Chapter 27

It was Sunday. The week had shot by. Everybody sent RSVPs to our invitations. Chad and I were standing in front of the floor-to-ceiling mirror in the bedroom. We both were wearing black tuxedos with red bow ties. Chad looked deliciously handsome. I kept my mind on my wedding vows that I'd burned into my memory like an old song. I ignored my swelling member between my legs that wanted to burst clean through my slacks like a gangbuster. After Chad adjusted my bow tie I returned the favor. I walked over to the window and looked at Mt. Tam. The mountain seemed to have grown bigger overnight. Or was it me feeling that I'd grown bigger since last night? The tuxedo slacks felt a little awkward because the tailor let the waistband out to five times the size of my previous slacks. I looked at the orange gazebo that was put up quick and easy just yesterday by a company I found online. Down on the patio, Chad had set up a tripod with a camcorder aimed in at us to videotape our wedding. I had set a broom in the grass that we were going to step over to seal our vows in the old African-American tradition of marriage when blacks weren't allowed to wed during slavery. I found it ironic that gays had now picked up where African Americans left off. Today it is gay Americans who have to pay taxes but can't marry legally in most states. So stepping over the broom as a black gay man took on doubly symbolic meaning for me.

Ernest was the first to arrive. I went over the plans once again with him. He refused to accept payment for his services. He told me again that it was an honor just to be presiding over our wedding.

Within an hour, the dining room table was set with so much food that I knew I'd have to give some of it away to the soup kitchen over on the corner of Macdonald and Twenty-Third Street. I decided to make Naomi my best woman. Scott was going to be my best man. Ma acted as a matron of honor. I asked Randall to be Chad's best man. To my surprise, Randall agreed. I've got to confess I still had fantasies about being wrapped in the arms of both of those men. It was a mischievous thought but tantalizing just the same. Naomi looked ravishing. She was wearing a red Valentino satin evening gown that draped her body perfectly and a white diamond necklace. She looked like a princess! Ma was snazzy. She was wearing a chiffon knee-length silver skirt and blouse. Draped across her shoulder was the mink stole I'd bought for her sixty-fifth birthday. Shuntria was the cutest little flower girl I'd ever seen in my life. All of the men wore basic black tuxes. Scott and Ricky looked good enough to eat. Mary and Cerrita were sitting in their favorite chair gazing into each other's eyes like they only met each other a few minutes ago. It was the second time I'd seen Mitch in a month. He was sober and collected. Mitch had brought a date, a tall licorice-complexioned man with dreads and bedroom eyes. Nina and Andrea were smiling like they were at their second high school reunion.

"Oh, Brotha! I'm so happy for you. Well, looks like you done beat me to the punch!" Naomi said. Her long legs, folded, reminded me of those belonging to a high-fashion model on a Paris runway.

"Not to worry, Sista. You'll be next. You just wait and see," I assured her.

All of the rooms were filling with the sound of jazz. The soft voices and laughter put me in a tranquil mood. I'd been nervous about the wedding, but having all of my friends there to celebrate a blessed event gave me the courage I needed to meet Chad at our own private altar on the patio in my backyard. I looked out on the patio. All of the dozen or more seats in front of the gazebo were filled. I watched Ernest walk across the patio to the gazebo. I looked at my watch. I motioned to Scott and told Naomi it was time for the ceremonies to begin. I nodded to Chad and Randall. I locked arms with Naomi and Scott as we walked out on the patio. Chad and Randall were behind me.

Chad and I stood face to face in the gazebo. The sky was a deep blue. The sunshine was warm and seemed to me to be winking at us in its brightness. Chad had brought the stereo out on the patio. Ricky put on Luther Vandross's song "Here and Now." I looked into Chad's chestnut eyes. Ernest said a few words about love and commitment. I gave Chad my vows.

"Baby, standing here under the blue heavens I pledge to you a life-long commitment. A love and brotherhood so new only you can bring. So real until it's older than tradition. This world we were both born into is not something that we have to catch up to. It has to catch up to us. As long as God gives me the air to breath, I vow to honor and keep you forever and always like a memory in a tiny place in my heart to call upon when I'm sick. A memory to call upon when I'm well. A memory to wrap around my heart just as the sun shining above us right now is wrapping us up in its warm rays. I want to re-create black history with you. With this ring, I pledge my love, respect, and honor to you, baby. Not just for today but until time is no more."

I took Chad's old friendship ring off his right ring finger and put it in my pocket. I put a new wedding band on his left ring finger. Chad delivered his vows.

"Head, I pledge my devotion to you, the most tender, loving man I've ever met in my life. As I gaze in your eyes, I'm reminded of the spring of my youth, the warmth of the sun, the magic of a whole new day dawning. I pledge to stand by your side through thick and thin when the world becomes too heavy to carry upon your shoulders. I pledge to be there when you need someone to reassure you that a life lived is a life worth living. I pledge to smooth out the wrinkles in your brow when you realize the errors of the ways of this world. I pledge to try to make every day, if not new, then something that we may be able to look back on with wonder. Head, you and I can conquer the world with our love. We can wrap ourselves up in the finest of clothes, yet they may as well be rags if they can't give us the warmth of love that is a blessing from God."

Chad took his old friendship ring off my right hand. He put a gold wedding band on my left hand.

We kissed and held each other for a few moments. We went down the short wooden steps of the gazebo and hopped over a broom. We whooped and laughed with joy. Our guests roared with congratulations, hugging and patting us on the back. I looked at Ma and Naomi, who both were crying. We were married, Chad and I. Boom! Like that! Shuntria walked up to me. She handed me one solitary red rose. I threw it toward our guests. Naomi caught it. I looked at her and smiled. A cheer went up in the yard. Chad and I went over to a table in the yard that had a huge wedding cake. At the very top of the cake were two black men wearing tuxes and hugging. Chad took a knife and cut the cake. He put a piece of it in my mouth. I returned the favor. Again, everybody broke into applause and cheered. After the reception, Shorty, Naomi, and Ma were the last ones to leave.

"I'll say. What a lovely wedding," Ma said, still teary eyed.

"Don't cry, Ma. You're going to mess up all that wonderful make-up."

"All right, honey. Ma's so happy for you. Always remember that. I'm going to go home. These pumps kicking my behind." She smiled. Chad and I kissed her on the cheek. I watched her disappear out the door.

"Brotha, you and Chad know how to throw a wedding. Good Lord," Naomi said.

"Yeah, dude, it was dope," Shorty added.

"Glad you guys had a good time," Chad said.

"Brotha, call me later, all right?"

"I will, Sista. I will."

My estate documents were lying in a legal-sized envelope on the bench in the gazebo. I decided to let Chad take possession of my will now that we were married. I'd finished the necessary paperwork and put him on the deed to my home as co-owner. The Jeep was paid off, which was put in his name as co-owner. He was made the beneficiary of my life insurance policies. Ma was kept as the beneficiary on my common stock portfolio. Apart from the baby, I'd given just about everything away that was worth anything to me. Was I making my peace? Or tying up loose ends? As the day to give birth to my baby drew nearer, I couldn't shake the feeling that I'd better put my house seriously in order this time. I was confident but practical. I knew that nothing could be left to chance. When I got seriously ill last year I was caught off guard. I had not made provisions to pass along what little I had to my survivors. The state would have taken over all of my possessions, left Chad and Ma with nothing more than a memory and a sore heart. This time I was ready. I had summoned up in me courage and bravery found in the slave past of my ancestors. I wondered if the eyes of my ancestors were watching me, egging me on, pushing me forward, onward, toward a new life.

Chad and I sat out on the patio as if we'd just returned home from our honeymoon. Yet when he came over and rubbed my pregnant belly and lay his head in my lap, I knew my ancestors were watching, smiling down on me from the heavens. The October sun streamed down in a fan of rays shaped like the folds of a great wedding gown. That was when I first realized that it was the sun that gave me a signal that Chad and I were married.

Chapter 28

The month of November brought with it cold winds and rains. I was going into the hospital to have the caesarean the next day. Thanksgiving Day was less than a week away. Two red poinsettias sat atop the dining room table like bookends next to a bowl of apples, oranges, bananas, tangerines, pecans, and walnuts. The fireplace gleamed and the room was aglow, casting the shadow of my pregnant body larger than life against the snow-white walls. Over the past two weeks, Chad had taken over as grocery shopper and household cook. He had dished up a baked turkey, smoked ham, dressing, sweet peas, potato salad, yams, dinner rolls, corn muffins, cranberry sauce, hot apple cider, and homemade vanilla ice cream. The intoxicating smell of food wafted through the house. I was snuggled underneath a quilt Ma made for me when I was a small child. I was eating a large bowl of ice cream topped with peaches. A little over a week before, I had several little scares when pains shot down across my lower stomach. I began sweating and Chad rushed me to Mercy Hospital. I was told that it was false labor. I was surprised how nonchalant the hospital staff was toward me. It wasn't as if I really was expecting anyone to have a red carpet spread out for me. The attitude they had toward me was just that I was like anyone else who was pregnant who had a false alarm. They assured that going into false labor was no big deal. It happened all the time. Each time I was examined I was told by the triage doctor to go back home to relax and get some rest. After the second time, I couldn't help but get a little apprehensive. Every time my baby kicked hard these days, it made me think that it was time.

Chad had returned to watching his old favorite channel, E!. He came and sat down on the sofa next to me.

"Head, you all right?"

"I'm doing good. I'm just a little tired and sleepy though."

"It's late, Head. Let's scoot upstairs."

"All right, baby."

By the time I got underneath the covers, I began to have sharp pains between my legs and lower back. I felt like calling Dr. Valesco every name but the child of God! I had told Dr. Valesco that it was time for me to go in and have my baby. Why did Dr. Valesco wait up to the last minute to schedule my surgery?

"I've got to get to the hospital, Chad. Fast! I'm having some serious pain in my back and between my legs. I'm ready, Chad!" I said, grabbing my back. I wondered if I could stand up.

"Let's go! Head, put this on!" Chad said. He found some fresh clothes for me. Within minutes, we were off to Mercy Hospital.

I protested about having to sit in a wheelchair in the waiting room so they moved me to the delivery room. I watched Chad punch some numbers on his cell phone.

"I'm calling Dr. Valesco and Sister Woman."

"Ahhhhhh! Chad! It hurts soooo baddddd! Oh baby! See! You didn't want me to have this baby from the get-go! Are you trying to kill me!" I yelled as the pain rode down my thighs and centered on my lower back.

"I'll be right back, Head. My cell phone isn't working. I've got to get to a phone."

"Chad, don't leave me!" I begged. I watched Chad disappear through the door. I felt as though he was leaving me never to return. I was desperate to find some way to equal the pain of childbirth with some of the other pain I'd felt in my life. If not equal to, then certainly to bring it as close as possible to the other pain and suffering that I'd never thought I would get through. I had to do this. Otherwise, I was as good as dead. It came to me—the fifty spinal taps with the injection of amphotericin B for the treatment of my misdiagnosed valley fever. After getting injected, for hours my body would go into convulsions. My teeth rattled and clacked against each other. I'd come close to biting my tongue off. I had to lay prostrate after the injections like Jesus nailed to the cross.

I took the memory of that pain and set it against the pain of childbirth. This made me relax a little and allowed me to think that this pain too shall pass. I had to concentrate by thinking that I'd feel great once the pain stopped. I told myself that this was temporary. I told myself that I was suffering to bring my baby to life outside of me. I told myself to be brave, that it didn't matter what the world thought about me. I told myself to keep it real. I told myself that Jesus wept, he bled, died on the cross so that we could live. I told myself that I wasn't going to let what Ma told me about childbirth, "It could cut a man in two," work on me like a self-fulfilling prophecy. I told myself that I was the kind of man that would not let any kind of pain and suffering cut me in two. I told myself that as long as I could feel myself breathing, hear myself thinking, then I knew I'd live through my labors. I told myself that Cayleen's baby didn't die after Sugar smacked her down. I told myself that Cookie aborted my child but I got through it.

I told myself that it didn't matter that I had to sleep on my side for the rest of my life after being circumcised when I was twelve years old. I told myself that I was only living because I stopped taking ten tiny pink pills every day like clockwork for a disease that I never really had. I told myself that Mary the mother of Jesus gave birth through the Immaculate Conception. I told myself that if Atlas were alive, he would be proud to see me with my child in my strong arms. I told myself that if Chad should leave me then I'd raise my baby on my own. After all, didn't Ma raise me on her own?

I told myself that I would out-father the straight fathers of the world. I told myself that I would not baby my son but would raise him to be a man, teach him to be independent of mind, of thought. I told myself that I'd give him room to grow, to explore life's possibilities. I told myself that I'd let my son be the kind of man he wanted to be. I told myself that I would teach my son that he doesn't have to accept the world that he was born into that was not of his own making, that he can change it if he wants to. I told myself that I'd teach my son that true manhood doesn't mean that we must become fathers of children born in every state, city, town, and hamlet the world over without rhyme or reason. That a man, gay, straight, black, white, old, young, saint, or sinner must have the courage to be willing to sacrifice everything to see a child through in this world. That being a father means not walking away from one's responsibility to care for a child the best way one knows how. I told myself that I would share my love of God, my baby, my Chad, then leave love in a tiny corner of my heart so that I'd always have some to hold onto for me. I told myself that I was a survivor of a mysterious illness, homophobia, racism, and sexual addiction. I told myself that I was going to have my baby. I told myself that this pain, this suffering, would pass through me.

The last five faces I looked into before I went into a deep sleep were those of Dr. Valesco, Chad, Naomi, Reverend Edwards, and Ma.

When I fell asleep, I remember walking through a cold, long, dark tunnel that had a bright, nearly blinding light at the end of it. The farther down the tunnel I got, the more I felt like I'd left behind my sexual addiction, heartache over the lost of my firstborn, and near-death experience last year. I had rid myself of a subconscious worry about how the world would look at and treat me as a man having a baby. I was traveling light. I was being transformed into something wonderful and new. My mind was clear; my heartbeat was normal and steady. When I finally came to the end of the tunnel, all of the pain was gone and my burdens were no more.

I woke up.

My body felt so small! I was transformed! I was my newborn baby! I had little hands, feet, arms, and legs that were tiny versions of me. I blinked. I found myself wrapped in a blue and white receiving blanket I bought from Sears. I'd been given another chance to live, not only through the eyes of my child, but also through my own. It was as though I now had double vision. Chad was holding me in his arms.

My spirit had merged with the young spirit, the soul of my child. We were now one body with two souls, two spirits, and two visions. I was the father and the son. I felt strong. I'd been reborn into a man-child. I listened to the child's voice inside my mind that told me, *I know you because I've lived you.* Dr. Valesco, Ma, Naomi, and Reverend Edwards stood around Chad and me.

Dr. Valesco looked in my face.

"We should all be proud of Kel. He went through a lot. Yet he took the risks and made the appropriate sacrifices. Gave up his life in the name of medical science. He'll be missed but a model for male pregnancy for generations to come. He was a kind, thoughtful, and coura-geous man," Dr. Valesco cried.

Reverend Edwards' head was lowered to his chest. I could hear snif-fles coming from him.

"Look, Sista Woman! Oh, he's so cute. A doll baby," Chad sobbed.

"Lord, he sure is. Look like Kel when he was born. With all that thick black hair and them long eyelashes. Child, what you going to name him?" Ma wept. Tears streamed down her face.

"I'm going to name him Kel Smith Junior. But I'm going to call him Baby Head," Chad said as he wiped the tears from his face with the back of his hand. He gently stroked my dimpled cheeks.

Chad handed me to Ma. Ma rocked me some and kissed my tiny face. I felt her body shake from grief. She passed me along to Naomi.

Naomi was trembling. She was the last one who cried. One of her tears fell in my mouth. It tasted salty.

"Oh, Kel! I wish you were here. Give us a sign, baby. Please give us a sign, let us know that you are all right." Naomi wept.

I thought of what Cerrita told me the night of my birthday party, that fairy tales can come true if you only believe. I summoned up the great belief of my ancestors, knowing that one day they would be free. I did what I had to do.

"Sista, you're holding me in your arms. See, your brotha hasn't left you alone," I said in a child's voice. Naomi startled, nearly dropped me. Then she held me tighter.

A collective gasp engulfed the room.

"Brotha, I was feeling you. I knew it." Naomi seemed to weep this time from joy.

Reverend Edwards drew the sign of the cross over himself.

"For the love of Jesus!" he bellowed.

"My baby! He's back! Thank you, Jesus! Kel, is that you, honey?" Ma asked. She seemed to be regaining her composure.

"It's me. I'm back, Ma! Look at me, Naomi, Chad, and Dr. Valesco," I said, as if they weren't paying attention.

Dr. Valesco had a look on his face of a man who was watching someone walk on water.

"Never before in the annals of medicine have I witnessed anything so spectacular!" he said, rubbing the day-old gray stubble of his beard. He seemed to be confounded. Ma looked in my face.

"And you know this! Kel, your old dead body may be in the morgue down the hall, but look at you now. Your living spirit can't die! I knew you would still be with us here in the flesh and soul," Ma said and pointed at me. "Naomi, girl, you are holding his very life in your hands."

Ma was right on the money. Naomi held me right in the palms of her hands.

ABOUT THE AUTHOR

Durrell Owens is a California native and lifelong resident. Born in Martinez, he grew up in Richmond, a mid-sized coastal city about ten miles outside San Francisco. He was educated at California State University in Sacramento. He currently makes his home in the Bay Area.

THE SONG OF A MANCHILD

_____in softbound at $14.96 (regularly $19.95) (ISBN: 1-56023-480-6)

Or order online and use special offer code HEC25 in the shopping cart.

COST OF BOOKS_____

OUTSIDE US/CANADA/
MEXICO: ADD 20%_____

POSTAGE & HANDLING_____
(US: $5.00 for first book & $2.00
for each additional book)
(Outside US: $6.00 for first book
& $2.00 for each additional book)

SUBTOTAL_____

IN CANADA: ADD 7% GST_____

STATE TAX_____
(NY, OH, MN, CA, IN, & SD residents,
add appropriate local sales tax)

FINAL TOTAL_____
(If paying in Canadian funds,
convert using the current
exchange rate, UNESCO
coupons welcome.)

☐ **BILL ME LATER:** ($5 service charge will be added)
(Bill-me option is good on US/Canada/Mexico orders only;
not good to jobbers, wholesalers, or subscription agencies.)

☐ Check here if billing address is different from
shipping address and attach purchase order and
billing address information.

Signature_____

☐ **PAYMENT ENCLOSED: $_____ . _____**

☐ **PLEASE CHARGE TO MY CREDIT CARD.**

☐ Visa ☐ MasterCard ☐ AmEx ☐ Discover
☐ Diner's Club ☐ Eurocard ☐ JCB

Account # _____

Exp. Date_____

Signature_____

Prices in US dollars and subject to change without notice.

NAME_____

INSTITUTION_____

ADDRESS_____

CITY_____

STATE/ZIP_____

COUNTRY_____ COUNTY (NY residents only)_____

TEL_____ FAX_____

E-MAIL_____

May we use your e-mail address for confirmations and other types of information? ☐ Yes ☐ No
We appreciate receiving your e-mail address and fax number. Haworth would like to e-mail or fax special
discount offers to you, as a preferred customer. **We will never share, rent, or exchange your e-mail address
or fax number.** We regard such actions as an invasion of your privacy.

Order From Your Local Bookstore or Directly From
The Haworth Press, Inc.
10 Alice Street, Binghamton, New York 13904-1580 • USA
TELEPHONE: 1-800-HAWORTH (1-800-429-6784) / Outside US/Canada: (607) 722-5857
FAX: 1-800-895-0582 / Outside US/Canada: (607) 771-0012
E-mailto: orders@haworthpress.com
PLEASE PHOTOCOPY THIS FORM FOR YOUR PERSONAL USE.
http://www.HaworthPress.com   BOF03